ACCLAIM FOR JOHN ED BRADLEY'S

# MY *J*ULIET

"This is one of those Southern gothics in which everyone turns out to have a deep dark secret . . . Bradley captures the shabby grandeur of New Orleans and paints a convincing portrait of life in its lower depths."
—*The Washington Post*

"*My Juliet* is lowdown Cajun-flavored James M. Cain—drenched with plenty of doomed sex, besotted men, murder, money, and of course that all-American pastime, betrayal."
—Elwood Reid, author of *Midnight Sun* and *What Salmon Know*

"[A] steamy blend of Southern gothic and noir thriller [and] a psychologically astute study of obsessive love overlaid with the powerful mythic allure of the femme fatale."
—*Booklist*

"Bradley is so enticing in his storytelling that you begin to sympathize with Sonny's desire for Juliet, even though you know nothing good can come of the liaison. You know in your bones that *My Juliet* is a train wreck about to happen, but you cannot avert your eyes."
—*St. Petersburg Times*

"The steamy ambience of suburban New Orleans tartly flavors this latest of Bradley's wistfully comic portrayals of likable losers and the hardhearted women who rev up, then clog their engines. . . . Bradley's best yet."
—*Kirkus Reviews*

"John Ed Bradley is one of the finest writers of his generation, and *My Juliet* is his funniest, most fascinating novel yet."
—Mark Childress, author of *Gone for Good* and *Crazy in Alabama*

JOHN ED BRADLEY

MY *J*ULIET

John Ed Bradley has been a staff writer at
*The Washington Post*, is a regular contributor to
*Sports Illustrated*, and has written for *GQ*,
*Esquire*, and many other publications.
He lives in New Orleans.

ALSO BY JOHN ED BRADLEY

TUPELO NIGHTS

THE BEST THERE EVER WAS

LOVE & OBITS

SMOKE

# MY JULIET

ANCHOR BOOKS

A DIVISION OF RANDOM HOUSE, INC.

NEW YORK

JOHN ED

BRADLEY

MY JULIET

FIRST ANCHOR BOOKS EDITION, AUGUST 2001

*Copyright © 2000 by John Ed Bradley*

All rights reserved under International and Pan-American Copyright
Conventions. Published in the United States by Anchor Books,
a division of Random House, Inc., New York, and simultaneously in
Canada by Random House of Canada Limited, Toronto. Originally
published in hardcover in the United States by Doubleday,
a division of Random House, Inc., New York, in 2000.

Anchor Books and colophon are registered trademarks
of Random House, Inc.

The Library of Congress has cataloged
the Doubleday edition as follows:
Bradley, John Ed.
My Juliet/John Ed Bradley.—1st ed.
p.  cm.
ISBN 0-385-49803-9
1. Man-woman relationships—Fiction.
2. New Orleans (La.)—Fiction.  I. Title.
PS3552.R2275  M9  2000
813'.54—dc21
99-089051

**Anchor ISBN: 0-385-49804-7**

*Author photograph © Jerry Ward*
*Book design by Dana Leigh Treglia*

www.anchorbooks.com

Printed in the United States of America
10  9  8  7  6  5  4  3  2  1

FOR CONNIE DORSEY

# MY JULIET

"HOW'S ABOUT I END WITH A QUES-
tion, Mother? Do you remember those shoes you and
Daddy bought me that Easter at D. H. Holmes on
Canal Street when I was little? We played like
tourists and toured the French Quarter in a sightseeing buggy and later had lunch at Galatoire's. I bet you
remember.

"This is how sharp my memory is: you had trout
meunière but you sent it back because you said the sauce
was too runny. The sauce looked fine to Daddy and me
but you always were the type to send your food back. Even
after the chef put some starch in it you wouldn't eat. I guess
in your mind that proved something. I guess that proved
you were better than me and Daddy and everybody else in
the place. For somebody without an ounce of culture you
sure were snotty. You had that nose up in the air. You
thought you were too good for food.

"Daddy: Marcelle, dear, please eat.

"You: Johnny, please don't embarrass me.

"Daddy: Are you trying to make a point? I'm not sure I understand.

"You (voice loud enough to attract stares from diners nearby): I think I said don't embarrass me. I think I even said please don't embarrass me. Juliet, did I just say please don't embarrass me to your father?

"I didn't answer. I was too young and unformed yet to calculate a sufficient reply. Well, now that I'm grown I've come up with something. Let me give it a try.

"Me: Shut the fuck up and eat your fish!

"When we got home I put my shoes on and Daddy said don't run in the grass, baby, I'd stain them. So, me, I took to the sidewalk. I loved them things. I loved the soft white calfskin and the shine and I loved the silk bows and the maker's stamp on the leather bottoms. Daddy watched from his chair on the gallery and I could hear him laughing and yelling and rooting me on. I actually ran staring down at my feet to see my shoes they were so pretty. Back and forth I went on the sidewalk, dizzy from looking down, wild with joy. Was I innocent once or what? Goddamn right I was innocent.

"I ran maybe fifty yards like that, and then when I rammed into the lamppost on the corner and nearly knocked myself out I could hear Daddy screaming and hurrying to help and the maid close behind but where were you, white girl? (My guess is you were hiding in the kitchen, eating cold trout out of a doggie bag.)

"Daddy put me to bed and I lay there with a knot on my head crying under the covers while you chased him down the stairs with a hairbrush and blamed and cursed him and called him ninny and queer when all along you knew it was the shoes. What kind of wife were you, anyway? What kind of mama? Didn't you realize my door was open? Didn't you understand I had ears?

"Mother, at this moment I see your nightgown pulled up to your waist, your dimply thighs and nest of unruly gray pubes. How quiet you are for a change. Did it hurt when he lifted the club high and whacked your big, fat noggin? What about his hands on your neck? How did that feel?

"I see blood at your lips and your nose leaking some too. Your eyes being open I can't help but wonder what they see. Surely not that crystal chandelier you seem to be staring at. Maybe it's a light shining bright at the end of a tunnel. Maybe the angels are welcoming you home.

"Well, I guess I've provided enough proof for now. I'd stuff this thing down your throat but I'd rather not get my hands dirty. Along with the blood, I'm seeing something else suddenly. What is that, by the way? Meunière sauce?

"Oh, and one last thing: If you bump into Daddy please tell him his little girl is some kind of lonesome."

## 1

LAST OF THE WHISKEY CONSUMED, the butt of his cheap Honduran cigar smoldering in a glass tray, Louis Fortunato staggers to his feet finally and slips the unlabeled videocassette into the VCR. It's what he came for, after all. And Sonny, if not yet drunk, is having a hard time staying awake.

"You sure you want to see this?" Louis says, punching buttons on the machine. "Hey, Sonny? I need to know, man. You sure you want to see this?"

Sonny LaMott, slow to open his eyes, sits up tall on the little Naugahyde sofa by the window. "It's not that I want to," he says. "I need to, brother. We both do."

The audio is poor and she makes more noise than either of them remembers but it's Juliet all right: the great head of hair, the hungry mouth, the breasts capped with nipples no different in color than the too-pale flesh around them. She's sitting on a corduroy love seat with panties looped around one ankle, a thin gold chain around the other. Her legs are spread open. A mound of expertly trimmed pubic hair, the same golden shade as the hair on her head, holds the middle of the screen.

"Jesus," Louis says with a whistle, then abruptly breaks it off.

A man has entered the picture. He is tall and narrowly constructed, with a mole on his lower belly. It looks like a mole, anyway, although as easily it could be a botched tattoo. When after some encouragement from Juliet the man's penis comes up, Sonny lowers his head and looks away. He has to swallow, and this is difficult. Where on earth do they find guys like that? he wonders.

Juliet is happy and energetic, loud when expressing her pleasure, all too eager to please. Give her partner credit, he doesn't pander. He goes at it, working with concentration so high in his face that he could be trying to solve a math problem.

"This way . . ."

*"Everything."*

"Like that?"

"Come on, you. Give it to me. . . ."

Even louder than in the old days, if that is possible. To end it, Juliet uncorks a cry that sounds like an animal being tortured.

Sonny is about to say something when Louis, leaning close to the screen, snaps his head back and lets go a low gurgle of laughter. "God, man, can you believe the dick on this guy?"

The screen dissolves to bands of crackling white on a black field. The whole room, they're in Sonny's house, buzzes in the sudden silence.

Louis puts a fresh cigar in his mouth and lights it leaning into a burner on the kitchen stove.

Sonny, able to control himself no longer, retreats to the bathroom and weeps at the sink, scooping hands of water to his face.

He isn't there long when the sound of the movie comes again, the sound of Juliet like that.

"Hey, Sonny, does she still have her mannerisms?" Louis says to the empty space, his words mangled for the stogie in his mouth.

When Sonny returns to the living room Louis is crouched in front of the TV, pressing buttons and making the tape squeal in the box. "You

4

want me to leave this with you?" he says. "Or you want me to take it? Better I take it, huh?"

"Leave it," Sonny says. "Leave it so I can put it out with the trash in the morning."

He throws the curtains open, a cloud of sun-bright dust spiraling around him. The effects of the whiskey have dissipated and all that remains is a taste of aluminum in his mouth. Sonny stands looking out past Chartres Street in the direction of the river, eyes drawn to a squint, lips bunched up close. Past the top of the levee and the Pauline Street Wharf the spires and funnels of a freighter move by.

Maybe it was the camera angle that made the guy look like that. What in school when he was a kid they called an optical illusion.

Now Sonny wonders if he ever satisfied her at all.

"Didn't I tell you she went crazy? I believe it now, brother, your girl went nuts."

"Just get out of my house, Louis."

"You remember Adelaide Valentine, right? Well, blame Adelaide for this. Don't blame me. She came in the restaurant the other night and she'd just found out about it herself—"

"Louis, did you hear what I said?"

"Your Juliet grew up to be a head case, brother. In and out of those drug clinics where nobody ever gets fixed. Arrested so many times for possession they named a wing after her in the county jail. Sonny, you have any questions call Adelaide."

"What will it take to make you go home?"

"Sometimes you act like you're the only guy who ever had it bad for a girl. You think you're special that way? Jesus Christ, man, have another look. Look at the little sweetheart you've been pining away for."

"Get out, you sonofabitch. I mean it."

Louis leaves the tape in the machine and limps to the door, his nub sucking and squeaking where it meets the leather sleeve of his prosthesis. It's a noise Sonny has never been able to get used to, even after all these years. At the door Louis turns back around. "Remember I only did this for your own good."

"Yeah? Well, thanks. Do I seem all better now?"

After he's gone Sonny cleans up the room then falls asleep on the sofa and sleeps so hard that when he wakes a couple of hours later he isn't sure where he is. He's a kid again. His father's outside on the lawn with a can of beer watching purple martins cut circles in the air above the birdhouse. His mother isn't dead years now but in the kitchen making supper. If he were to pick up the phone he could dial the Beauvais and hear the voice of Juliet, telling him their plans for the evening: *"I was thinking we could start in the Quarter. I have an envie for oysters. Ever have an envie for something, Sonny? Ever get where you have to have it and if you don't have it you feel like you could just die? Do you love me like that, Sonny? Tell me how much you love me, Sonny. Tell me you love me so much that if you don't have me you'll just die. Tell me you have an envie for Julie, baby . . ."*

Sonny sits up and lets the world reach him. The noise of ships unloading at the wharf, the stink from the seafood plant down the street. It takes him a minute to understand that he's alone in the Bywater, that he's Sonny at the surprising age of thirty-two: no wife, no kids, no family but what passes as his father in an Arabi nursing home. No birds outside, no food to eat. No nothing, really, but that tape in the VCR.

He watches it again, revisiting the part with Juliet half a dozen times, his face less than a foot from the screen. "Everything," she says. "Give it to me . . ."

Sonny recalls the line from the days when they were together. "What do you dream for us?" he asked her. "I know what I want," he said. "I want everything. Don't you want everything, Julie?"

"Yes," she said. "Oh, yes, Sonny. Everything. Give it to me. . . . Yes . . ."

Now when Sonny cries he doesn't care how loud he is or who hears.

₩

She comes home finally. It is April 1986, nearly fifteen years since she last saw the place, now as her plane descends a mossy green pod surrounded by fields of black water, still spooky as shit. "Oh, you," she whispers sadly to the view from her oval window.

She comes home wearing a light summer dress and big, blocky clogs with three-inch soles. Her Walkman plays a compendium of dance tracks from the decade before: the Bee Gees, Donna Summer, K. C. & the Sunshine Band. She doesn't look like a girl who once

6

acted in dirty movies but rather like one who's just finished exams at college and who's coming home for semester break. Sleep past noon, catch a tan by the pool, eat a plate of red beans at Mother's then sip a few at Pat O's. That's Juliet. She carries a dog-eared paperback on self-actualization that a fellow traveler left on the seat next to hers, and she reads half a page before encountering a trash can in the main concourse and throwing it away.

As Juliet strides through New Orleans International, her shoes clopping on the dull, gum-pocked tiles, people look at her in a way that she considers unkind if not outright rude. If they know about her time in front of the camera, however, nobody says anything. She would like to tell them all to go fuck themselves. Never does it occur to Juliet that they're staring because she is beautiful. Some people have a natural aversion to anyone who has sex, she has decided, and it doesn't matter with whom that person is having it — whether a marriage partner or, as in her recent case, professionals.

Every now and then, feeling exhausted by things, Juliet has an urge to walk up to a stranger and say, "Wanna do it?" And today is one of those times.

Cutting through Baggage Return, she focuses on an elderly man sitting by himself with a sports magazine and a packet of trail mix. Juliet strides to within a few feet of the man but the words that leave her mouth are not the ones she'd intended to deliver.

"It's not the heat so much as the humidity," she says.

"No, it isn't," the man answers, smiling a mouthful of nuts and yogurt-covered raisins. "But that's Nawlins for you."

She comes home with ten dollars in her pocket and one good credit card. With the cash she buys a cheese sandwich, a mound of fries, a family-size jug of Coke and a copy of the *New Orleans Times-Picayune*. With the card she rents a yellow Ford Mustang convertible at the Hertz counter. "Where will you be staying during your visit to New Orleans?" asks the clerk at the desk.

"I'm a Beauvais. Wanna take a guess?"

Confusion colors the young woman's face. In the end she says, "I wouldn't know where to begin. You look like a French Quarter B-and-B."

"Try the Beauvais Mansion on Esplanade," Juliet says. "You aren't originally from here, are you?"

It is oppressively, stupidly hot this early afternoon, and Juliet drives in heavy traffic through suburban Kenner and Metairie before entering New Orleans proper. A warm Gulf storm is sweeping over the area, lashing rain against her windshield with a force that makes Juliet wonder if she should pull over on the shoulder and wait it out. She almost forgot how shitty the weather can be in southern Louisiana. By the time she pulls in front of the mansion the sky has cleared and the sun is shining. And it comes to her that this is yet another item her memory has obscured: one minute you can be in a giant toilet bowl getting sloshed around and the next in a natural paradise too glorious for words.

Juliet comes home happy. Just the day before, the family maid phoned her in California with news that her mother was eaten up with cancer and close to death, and so she comes home believing that a large inheritance will soon be hers.

She is thinking about this fortune when she steps out of the rental car. And she thinks about it as she walks up the macadam path to the front door and lets herself in with a key she's kept all these years.

Money is on her mind, in fact, all the way until she sees her mother come charging down the hall.

Her mother isn't dying. Her mother is the picture of health. Nobody who moves like that has cancer or any other disease. The damned cleaning woman has tricked her. The tearful story on the phone was nothing but a ruse to get her to come home.

"Why aren't you dying?" Juliet says.

"I'm too much a woman to die," her mother replies.

Juliet's eyes seek out the maid on the other side of the room. "Anna Huey, you lied to me."

"Oh, sugar, we're all dying."

᭾

The house is haunted, or so Juliet often told Sonny. Some time in the 1920s it appeared on a widely circulated picture postcard depicting New Orleans as an exotic, unexpected paradise, and in the image one seemed able to make out the silhouette of a man hanging by a rope in a window upstairs, the noose tight on his neck. In all likelihood the silhouette was just a part in the curtains, but Juliet, who first showed Sonny the postcard, claimed that one of her ancestors had lynched a rival there. "What kind of rival?" Sonny said. "And how'd he get in the house?"

"What do you mean, what kind of rival?" She obviously was stalling for time.

"Why were they rivals, Julie? What were they at odds about?"

He knew she was having fun at his expense; he could see the mischief in her eyes as she tried to come up with a response. "How serious you are," she said. "That's very appealing, you know? When you're serious your temples throb and your eyebrows bunch together. They're like a caterpillar, those eyebrows, and just as fuzzy. Do you believe everything I tell you, Sonny?"

"I just want to know about this rival."

"Oh, you. Shut up and kiss me."

During the Civil War the house served as a hospital for Union soldiers wounded in battle, and this was how Juliet explained the many apparitions that allegedly resided there. They were Yankee boys who died on the grounds and whose spirits had not returned home. They showed up suddenly in doorways, then as suddenly vanished. At night they cried in empty rooms, and their wanderings were loud on the wood floors and stairway. One night Juliet woke to find a being in her room. (That, Sonny recalled, was how she referred to the ghosts, as "beings.") His uniform was stained with blood and his saber dragged the floor as he moved toward her in the bed. He didn't want sex, she explained. He was pleading to be set free.

"Free from what? Free from you?"

She didn't answer and Sonny said, "You're trying to tell me that you dream about other boys."

"Oh, but he wasn't that kind of ghost," she protested. When she raised her mouth up to his face he could see past the top of her blouse and her breasts loosely bound in a thin white brassiere.

"I don't believe in ghosts anyway," he murmured, staring.

"Tell me that when I'm gone and return to haunt you," she whispered, then kissed him so softly that it was a long time before he was able to open his eyes again.

Haunted or not, the house by any measure is a mansion, and Sonny has always heard it referred to as such. The Beauvais, people call it, pronouncing the word "Boo-vay" as the family likes to. Once a showplace in an affluent area, and the finest example of French Colonial plantation architecture in the southern United States, the house today backs up to a corridor where illegal drugs are sold and murder is commonplace. And yet Juliet's mother has continued to live there as if the neighborhood doesn't recommend burglar bars on every window and a team of Dobermans in the yard.

"Miss Marcelle, you think you'll ever move out to the suburbs?" Sonny asks her today. "Get yourself a town house maybe with all the modern conveniences?"

She stares at him, as if waiting for the punch line. "Not unless Anna Huey makes me," she answers at last in all apparent seriousness, then allows a dark trickle of laughter.

Sonny knows Miss Marcelle to be a hermit, as one too tired and dispirited to have much to do with the world, and as one too smart to trust a stranger. For years he has made a point of visiting her on those days when he's on a painting expedition in the neighborhood or out shooting reference photos for later use. He and Miss Marcelle sit in the parlor and, careful as to the scope of their conversation, talk for hours about subjects that hold little interest for either of them.

"Ever try Funyons, ma'am?"

"No, Sonny, I haven't. What are Funyons?"

"They're this food, somewhere between potato chips and Styrofoam. Don't be put off by their appearance. They're actually pretty good. You should try them."

Today instead of tea Anna Huey has served a substitute, a fruit brandy with a high alcohol content, and inside of an hour Miss Marcelle and Sonny are working on a second bottle.

"My favorite is still barbecue corn chips," he continues. "I like a bag at lunch with my ham and cheese sandwich. Sometimes I eat two ham and cheese sandwiches."

"Corn chips were popular even in my time, if you can believe."

"What time was that, Miss Marcelle?"

She looks at him as if he's just asked the most personal question a man can ask a woman. "When I speak of my time I mean the days when I first met Juliet's father, when I was young and in love. A person's time is always the time when he or she was happiest."

"Would you please tell me about Juliet's father, Miss Marcelle? I didn't get to know him too well."

"I met Johnny Beauvais in 1953 when he came to Opelousas to

judge the Miss Yambilee beauty pageant, in which I was a contestant. Apparently he was a last-minute selection; the first choice, a radio personality for KSLO, our hometown station, took sick with gout and his doctor confined him to bed. Johnny happened to be visiting Saint Landry Parish with one of his fraternity brothers from Tulane. How he was recruited to judge us beauties I never really knew, but there suddenly he stood at the foot of the stage in the old World War Two Quonset hut where the event was being held. Girls swooned for him, and not a few boys. He selected me Miss Yambilee. Toward the end, when we fought, he still called me that."

"Miss Yambilee?"

"Yes. And Miss Sweet Potato Pie. He thought he was so funny."

"What else can you tell me?"

"He never really cared for me. In the beginning he responded to my looks, my naïveté. But that didn't last long. Johnny was searching for someone to bear his children. He didn't want a wife." She hesitates, the brandy at her lips. "Johnny was a Beauvais to the very last, Sonny. I could tell you more, but that would still be the best description I could come up with."

"He used to wear white suits."

"Yes. And white bucks with them. Even his socks were white."

"He drowned in Lake Pontchartrain. Fell out of a boat."

"*Fell*, did you say?"

"Yes, fell and drowned."

"Fell and drowned," repeats Miss Marcelle, in a way to suggest that she herself isn't quite sure about the facts connected to the incident.

Sonny admires Miss Marcelle's carefully made-up face and hairdo, and how she always seems to dress even though she has no plan to leave the house. She is lovely for a woman her age, which Sonny puts at about sixty-five. When he lets himself, as he does now, he can see past the paint and the wrinkles and find the face of Juliet. And he understands that this, and not companionship, is the real reason why he continues to visit the mansion.

"Miss Marcelle?" he seems to hear himself ask this day. "Miss Marcelle, do you think Julie loved me? If she loved me," and he still can't believe he's hearing it, "how could she leave like she did? How could she do it, Miss Marcelle?"

Sonny has barely spoken when he realizes that, looped or not, he's made a terrible mistake. Miss Marcelle shifts in her chair. "Sonny, you've had too much to drink."

"Please, Miss Marcelle, I'm tired of the mystery."

"But not tired enough, obviously, to let it go. For your own good you need to do that."

"I can't. I've tried and it's no use. She told me she would come back and haunt me. She's doing it. She might still be alive somewhere but I'm living with the ghost."

"Your ghost is not well. Juliet today is a deeply troubled girl. At the risk of disillusioning you more let me just say that she's not the person you keep in your heart. Sonny, you're a fine young man and you need to forget about Juliet. Meet someone who shares your values and wants what you want and raise a family together. Start a life, in other words."

"I've got a life. I'm an artist and I date plenty and I even got engaged once. That's having a life."

Sonny reaches for the bottle but, finding it empty, settles on a cookie. He finishes it before saying anything more. "You like Oreos after they've been in the freezer, Miss Marcelle?"

"Yes, they're good frozen."

"I think I'll freeze some Funyons and try them that way."

"Sonny, I think I'll have Anna Huey drive you home now. You can come for your truck later." Sonny stands. As he starts to leave the room Miss Marcelle says, "Don't come back again, Sonny. Don't ever come back. You won't find what you need in this house."

♆♆♆

Her mother runs off screaming, and Juliet picks up one of the many greeting cards displayed in the parlor. It shows her name and so, too, does the next one she inspects. *Juliet*, they both say in a clean, composed script, not at all similar to her copperplate.

All told there must be a hundred such cards in the room, most of them standard-issue Hallmark with sentimental inscriptions and pictures of flowers, birds and unicorns.

"Anna Huey, what are these cards?"

Anna Huey, who for some reason has always gone by her full married name, places a hand on Juliet's shoulder and attempts to guide her out of the room. "Sugar, why don't you surprise us all and be a dear for a change. If you can't be a dear at least lower your voice."

"I'll show you a dear," Juliet shouts.

"Sugar, I don't want your mother any more riled than she already is."

Juliet swings her arm and knocks Anna Huey's hand away. "What are these cards, I said. And why is my name in them?"

"Sweetie? Please don't get—"

"I demand to know who sent them. Tell me."

"Anthony," comes the whispered reply.

Disgust darkens Juliet's expression as she flashes to Anthony Arceneaux, Anna Huey's kid brother. She sees the boy at her father's funeral, approaching the coffin in an ill-fitting, hand-me-down suit that smells rudely of mothballs, the rose boutonniere at his lapel wilting in the heat. Anthony speaking gibberish to her father's corpse, his voice lifting above all others in the great parlor at the Jacob Schoen & Son Funeral Home, then the wild cries from the mourners as Anthony presses his mouth against Johnny Beauvais's mouth. "Anthony," Juliet said to him later, "kiss my daddy again and I kill you."

"Sweetie, I send Anthony a little money each month and in exchange he sends the cards. I tell him it's his job, along with some other things. Anthony lives in California, too. I guess you know that. He tells me it's more expensive out there than New Orleans and he's always looking for anything extra to get by. Did you know he was still in Los Angeles, sugar? I always hoped the two of you would run into each other and sit down and talk. Anthony could really use that. And I always thought you could too."

*"Anthony, run downstairs and answer the door, son. I'm going to time you. Run, now, Anthony . . ." And turning to Juliet, his pocket watch in hand: "Oh, you. Oh, darling. What's wrong? Why the long face? You're not . . . ? My heavens, Juliet. Anthony? Juliet, Anthony's thirteen years old. Please, darling . . ."*

"Your mother believed them at first," Anna Huey says. "She actually thought it was you writing. She knew the time when the mailman made his delivery and she waited by the door to open it as soon as he came up the steps. Does a mother who doesn't love her daughter do this?"

"Goddamn Anthony," Juliet says.

"Don't be mad at Anthony. Anthony was just a boy then, Juliet. A baby."

Juliet starts up the stairs to the second floor, one hand on the banister, the other extended way out to touch the red felt wallpaper crowded with portraits of her Beauvais forebears. When she reaches the painting of Johnny Beauvais she can barely hold his eyes with her own and she feels all the old shame and sadness and the steps are harder to climb.

She makes it to her bedroom and nudges the door open, and here is a piece of time cut free of the present. The collection of Louisiana plantation furniture is just as she remembered it: the four-poster bed and armoire and commodes, the secretary with its panes of wavy glass, its shelves crowded with Newcomb and Shearwater pottery. Offering a weird juxtaposition to the antiques are posters of rock and TV stars, souvenirs from Sacred Heart socials and Mardi Gras balls, and a plastic book unit overcrowded with mementos. Even the bedspread is as she remembers it: a net of spidery lace stained with thin, roiling clouds.

Have fifteen years passed everywhere on earth but in this room? Juliet stands at the window gazing out at Esplanade Avenue, the old tree-lined boulevard that stretches southeast to the Mississippi River and northwest to Bayou Saint John and City Park. Children in school uniforms play hopscotch on the sidewalk, just as she did long ago. Once after a night out together—it was her spring formal, she recalls now; they were dressed in evening clothes—Juliet and a boyfriend played the game on a diagram left in magenta chalk on the cement. High above, a full moon shone and from the river came a breeze. The boy held her with his back against the fence and they kissed in a stubborn, determined way as a passing police car slowed and stopped by the curb and splashed them with light. A man emerged from the car. "I'm a Beauvais," Juliet yelled, pointing to the house. "Imagine that," he said, then left without another word.

"What's it like to be you?" she recalls the boy asking.

"Tonight it feels slippery. I've had too much champagne."

The boy's name was Sonny LaMott, and he watched as she hopped from square to square and back again. "That's not what I mean, Julie, and you know it. I want to know how it *feels.*"

"It feels dangerous and it feels dreamy. It feels like it feels for any girl who's seventeen and in love with a boy."

Her shoes dangled from the fence's iron pickets, framing his handsome face. She loved his face, its perfectly carved features and pale, unblemished skin; she even loved its regrettable tendency to pout.

She also loved how at the dance earlier Adelaide Valentine, who herself could date practically any boy she wanted, pulled her aside and said, "I am *so* jealous."

She loved as well how this boy kept his hands in the pockets of his rented tuxedo trousers, puffing them out, in a futile attempt to hide his excitement.

"What I mean is," he was saying now, "I wonder how it must feel when you're alone in your room late at night and your room is in a mansion and the mansion has the same name as your name and all you have to do is say that name and people know the place and know you? 'I'm a Beauvais,' and the cop gets in his car and drives away."

She couldn't tell if he honestly expected an answer. Did Dickie Boudreau, when they were a couple, ask what it felt like to be who she was? Of course he didn't. Dickie lived in a giant wedding cake of a house on Saint Charles Avenue. Dickie drove a Jaguar. Dickie was going to be a Deke at Tulane, then a partner in his father's oil exploration business. The only thing Dickie Boudreau ever seemed to ask was whether she was on her period. That and if she wanted to get a room somewhere.

Juliet was barely listening when Sonny said, "My family's all of three people, Julie—Mom and Dad and me. I never even knew my grandparents—both sides, they were dead before I was born. Family, Julie—it's everything around here. Let me ask you a question: In New Orleans when you run into somebody you haven't seen for a while what's the first thing they ask?"

"The first thing?" She paused, standing on one leg, and glanced at him. "The first thing, after tonight, will be why did you break up with your beautiful boyfriend? That will be the first thing."

" 'How's your mama and them?' " Sonny says. "It never fails. It's not 'How are you doing?' Or 'How's life?' Or 'How's work?' Or 'What do you think of the weather we're having?' It's none of those. 'How's your mama and them?' *History*, Julie, where you come from—that's all that matters. . . ."

Down on the street the children scatter as rain begins to fall, and Juliet moves away from the window. From a pocket she removes a slip of notebook paper containing a list which she started on the flight in and titled "The Proof." Now she adds to it, using a ballpoint at the secretary. *"How's your mama? Well, let me answer that question. My mama ain't so good. My mama has bionic ears. My mama hears spiders on the window screen and thinks it's somebody trying to break in. My mama screams and wakes the whole house up and Daddy is in a bad mood in the morning because he didn't get his eight hours. Is this your fantasy, woman? Do you honestly expect to satisfy the natural sexual desires of your assailant any better than you satisfied those of your husband? Scream all you want, see what I care. One day it won't be spiders. It just might be me."*

This is entry number forty-two, and it requires the last of the space on the back of the page.

"I don't appreciate being duped," Juliet tells Anna Huey as she trudges back down the stairs.

Juliet has lighted a cigarette and she makes a point now of depositing clouds of smoke in both the foyer and the parlor. (Her mother, after all, claims to be allergic to tobacco.)

"It was for a purpose I asked you back," Anna Huey says, stumbling out onto the gallery in pursuit. "For one thing your mother's scared, sweetie—she's scared for your health and for your life. We found out all about California, sugar—your friends and bad habits, the visits to the emergency room, even the time in that club they gave you mouth-to-mouth. Juliet, have you been taking your medicine?"

Juliet smiles. "Oh sure."

"You're gonna catch yourself something you don't want, Juliet. I've seen it happen. Juliet, we're gonna lose you at too young an age."

And this from a cleaning woman.

Out in the street now, in the rain, Juliet opens the car door and turns to face the house, pale and gray in the watery sunlight, a battleship. "The Beauvais was stolen by the enemy before. Anna Huey, do you remember your history lessons from school? The Yankees had it almost three years before we got it back."

"The way you talk. Nobody ever studied about this old house in school."

"How's your mama and them?" Juliet says, not sure herself where it came from.

"God, baby. Them drugs really have fried your mind."

Juliet flicks her cigarette in the direction of the house, halfway wishing it would catch the grass on fire and burn everything down, people and all.

✠✠✠

The blue hour of twilight, the hot, narrow streets, tourists filing past. Sonny LaMott, his step uncertain after too many highballs, leaves a top-less/bottomless called Lulu's and walks to the corner of Chartres and Saint Louis streets and the fabulous Napoleon House.

Louis Fortunato greets Sonny at the door and escorts him to a table with a view of the street.

Sonny stares out at pedestrians and passing traffic, but what he sees are women in G-strings and high-heel shoes bumping and grinding against firehouse poles and sashaying along runways pulsing with col-ored lights. In the restaurant Pavarotti's voice soars from hidden speak-ers, and yet Sonny hears the points of stilettos making contact with parquet.

"It's Frank," Louis says when half a minute has passed and Sonny still hasn't said anything.

"It's Frank? Frank who?"

"Frank my Siamese."

"Oh, yeah. All right. Frank."

Louis nods and only now does Sonny acknowledge what an absolute ruin he is. Louis's eyes are shot red, his hair is an oily nest, and his stubble is several days in the making.

He removes a slip of paper from his shirt pocket and places it on the table. "I took him to the vet—a guy named Coulon over on Esplanade? He's been taking care of Frank a few years now. I took him there to get spaded. Well, Coulon, the bastard, he spaded my Frank, all right. Spaded him but good."

"It's *spayed*, bubba. You spay it."

"I don't think I ever told you Frank was a female. He was Frankie to start. Anyway, the vet says it's no big thing. A day at most he'll need to keep him. Forty-five dollars with tax, simple procedure, piece of cake. That morning I take Frank in and kiss him good-bye. I wave as I'm leaving the room, give him one of these." Louis makes a windshield wiper of his arm, moving it left to right.

Sonny studies the bill as Louis continues talking. A list of unintelligible items traces down the middle of the page, accompanied on the right by an equally unintelligible list of figures. The total is clear, though. It has a box scribbled around it and the dollar sign needs no less than four slashes.

"Later that afternoon the phone rings on the wall here and it's the clinic. 'Mr. Fortunato,' comes a voice, 'I'm afraid there's bad news.' 'Bad news?' I'm not even imagining.

"What happened, the vet cuts him open and Frank's hot as can be. You'd think the man, a doctor, would be smart enough to know you don't operate on a cat in heat. Everybody knows that—shit, I know that and who the hell am I?"

Louis seems to expect an answer. Sonny folds the paper and slides it across the table.

"Murdering bastard," and he looks outside now. "What I oughta do . . . what I . . ."

"Relax," Sonny says.

Louis folds his hands in front of him. "So a couple of days go by, and I get this bill in the mail for three hundred bucks, I get this thing. I call the vet but the vet can't come to the phone. What I have is this secretary telling me about kennel fees, about the doctor having to suture Frank again after the first sutures burst, about this, about that. I'm thinking, I'd like to do to that vet what he did to my Frank."

"I'd want to whack him, too," Sonny says.

"Whack!" Louis says, clapping his hands together. "Just like that I'd like to whack him." He shakes his head with black, murderous resolve and it isn't hard for Sonny to imagine what he's thinking. Louis is seeing the vet on his knees pleading for mercy. He's seeing a stick or a club or some other weapon going up and coming down with a force powerful enough to crush a human skull.

"Whack!" Louis says, then claps his hands again.

"Be quiet for five seconds and go get me my Crown," Sonny tells him.

Louis obeys. He returns and puts the drink on a paper coaster. Sonny could never understand why the place uses coasters when the tables are so badly scarred anyway. He takes a sip and Louis puts his hands on the top of Sonny's chair and brings his mouth to within an inch of Sonny's ear. "You think you could help me with the vet? You think you might consider that?"

"No."

"But I thought we were brothers, Sonny. Ninth Ward boys."

"We are, Louis. I'm not whacking the vet."

"And I thought we've known each other since first grade. What about you and me serving as altar boys at Saint Cecilia until we outgrew the priest and had to quit? What about carpooling to Holy Cross every single day of high school and me having to drive most of the damned time because your daddy needed his pickup? What about our birthdays being two days apart and always celebrating with a bottle of Veuve Clicquot on the one in between? What about the times I lighted votive candles and said novenas for you when you were sweating out the draft and me saying maybe there really is a God after all and you saying, "Yes. Yes, there is. And he listens to Louis Fortunato'?"

"Louis, you're giving me a headache."

"It's just that I thought we had a commitment here. And I thought you were a man of loyalty, of blinding, stupid, unwavering loyalty. Your family, your church, your city. Even your lunatic girlfriend who's been missing in action for fifteen years. Everything and everyone but Louis, huh, brother?"

"You can't whack him yourself? I'd think you'd want the satisfaction."

"Yeah, I could whack him. Sure I could whack him."

"Then whack him. It wasn't my cat that got killed."

"Coulon will recognize me. That's the problem. I guess I could wear a disguise or something. But he'd figure it out. There ain't many people in this city dragging around a fake leg." Louis brings his hand down hard against his prosthesis, producing a deep, hollow sound that turns several heads in the room. "If you love me, Sonny. If you love me, brother . . ."

And all Sonny wanted was a drink, a view of the street, some opera on the stereo. "Okay, Louis," he says. "All right. If you promise it'll make you feel better."

"Yeah," Louis says. "It will. It'll make me feel just fine." But there is no conviction in his voice, and no hint of gratification either.

Louis staggers away making as much noise on the leg as possible, and Sonny drinks the rest of his Crown vainly trying to recall the girls at Lulu's topless/bottomless.

✧✧✧

She isn't sure where she stands in terms of a credit line, but nevertheless she hands her credit card to the man at the desk. He says he needs it to make an impression on her registration form, and she figures her luck has turned when he gives it back along with a passkey to a room.

"You look familiar," he says.

"Yeah? We all do, I guess. To someone."

"No, I mean it. I've seen you before."

"You ever watch soap operas? I was in one once. They had me as a waitress in a café that really was just this set in Burbank. I didn't get to talk."

He studies her face, his own expression revealing nothing. "Maybe that's where."

Juliet knows better than to count on her mother and Anna Huey to reimburse her expenses, so she's decided to try to scrape a few dollars together, if she means to eat. The one-way airline ticket cost her nearly four hundred dollars. Or cost her card. The distance between the gutter and her rear end, she often says to herself, is the width of that Visa.

"Have a nice stay," says the man at Check-in.

"I did some adult films, too," she says. "Maybe it was there you saw me."

"I'd have to think about that."

"*Spanish Fly Reunion, Sindy's Gotta Eat, Days of Wine and Hormones.* Any of them ring a bell?"

"I'm a married man, Miss—" he checks the registration form— "Beauvais."

In the room she looks up Boudreau Exploration in the business section of the White Pages. The listing includes nineteen different numbers; Juliet counts them. She chooses the one set off in bold type. "Boudreau Oil and Gas," a female voice answers.

"Juliet Beauvais for Dickie Boudreau, please."

"Let me see if Mr. Boudreau is available, Ms. Beauvais. Hold, please."

But Juliet doesn't get Dickie Boudreau. She doesn't even get the one who answered the phone. "Ms. Beauvais," comes a voice, "this is Mr. Boudreau's secretary. May I help you?"

"I haven't talked to Dickie in years. I'm in town and wanted to say hello and see how he's doing."

"He's fine, thank you," the secretary says. "But he's tied up at the moment. However, I will make sure to tell him you asked after his well-being. Now is there anything else I can help you with, Ms. Beauvais?"

Juliet puts the phone down. She gets the picture. Dickie Boudreau, who once vomited at her feet while on the dance floor at the F&M Patio Bar, doesn't want to speak to her.

She hasn't dialed her mother's number in years and yet she finds herself doing so now. Anna Huey answers after a few rings and Juliet listens to her say "Hello" half a dozen times.

Catching on finally, Anna Huey says, "That you, sugar?"

Juliet says, "Your husband dies and you move in my house and now you act like you own the place. When was the last time you actually cleaned anything?"

"Do you want to speak to your mother, Juliet?"

"Not necessarily. Just tell her she owes me my money."

"And what money is that?"

"Money for my flight, money for my car, money for my room, money for the food I'll have to eat. You know what money!" Juliet hangs up.

They seemed such an odd pair: her mother in her Joan Crawford makeup, Kmart housedress and rubber flip-flops, Anna Huey in her Hazel-the-maid uniform and white hose that whistled when she walked. "Must be turning over in your grave," Juliet says out loud. "And you," she adds, "an actual Beauvais."

Juliet opens the door to the balcony and lets the noise from Bourbon Street spill in. Across the way she sees Houlihan's Restaurant and a run of bars and souvenir shops. Juliet smells the aroma of boiled Lucky Dogs, along with the equally nauseating odors of urine and throw-up.

She hears the little black boys dancing for tourists, zydeco music way far off, the insectlike buzz of neon lights burning even in the daytime. She's home, all right.

In the room she picks up the phone and dials the Beauvais again. This time her mother picks up.

"You're a Lavergne," Juliet says. "Your father grew sweet potatoes on a thirty-seven-acre farm in Opelousas. Your mother sat on the porch all day shelling peas in her dirty bare feet."

"Is this you?" her mother shouts.

"Yes, it's me. The one that blew cigarette smoke in your house. The one you owe five thousand dollars to. Where's my money, woman?"

Miss Marcelle stammers to speak, and Juliet says, "I want you out of my house and I want you out now," then slams the phone down.

❦❦❦

Every morning they're forced to listen to Sonny's pickup as it comes plowing through Bywater and Faubourg Marigny at a speed twice the posted limit. In the Vieux Carré they hear him even before he's crossed the neutral ground on Esplanade Avenue. It's a muffler problem, but it's also an attitude problem: Sonny's.

Up on the galleries of the old town houses, and in adjoining courtyards where for most of the day the only sound is that of water trickling in great stone fountains, they lower their morning newspapers and demitasse cups and squeeze their eyes shut against the wretched intrusion. Oh, for the poetic clip-clop of horses on the macadam! Oh, for the fruit and waffle and Roman candy vendors in mule-drawn lorries!

Oh, for any time but this one and for anything but that truck!

"How'd that rusted-out piece of crap ever get a brake tag, anyway?" Sonny likes to imagine them saying.

Even at high speeds he drives with headlights on, as if to inform other drivers that, lead foot notwithstanding, he is cautious and self-protective, a person to trust. But the headlights, like his smiles and waves and shouted hellos, are artifice. For months now Sonny has been wondering if the day will come when, unable to resist the impulse any longer, he steers straight into a tree or a wall of stalled traffic and ends his life at once and forever.

Sonny is an artist. Or perhaps more accurately he's a former hotel bartender posing as an artist. In any case, he owns a mayoral permit licensing him to ply his trade in the French Quarter, and there he reports each day and displays his paintings on the tall iron fence that surrounds Jackson Square. In earlier days Sonny had dreams that involved wealth and fame beyond measure—dreams that found him hanging for sale in the city's best galleries, a Sonny LaMott right alongside other desirables with exorbitant price tags. But it's been more than five years now since Sonny, sure to be an immortal, left his job as a bartender at the Pontchartrain Hotel, and he's succeeded in selling only a handful of his more ambitious creations. Tourists want portraits of themselves and the occasional rendering of Elvis before he was fat.

"Would you have a look at my stuff?" Sonny says to the gallery owners.

"Sorry," they tell him, "we're not taking anyone new at the moment."

When Sonny isn't stationed at the fence, he drives around the city looking for things to paint. He carries with him a tablet of cheap paper and a box of charcoals and he likes to perch on the tailgate of his pickup and sketch whatever his eye travels to. Other times he sets up an easel and paints on location, hours given to applying oils and acrylics to canvas, Masonite, odd shapes of tin, corkboard, newsboard and crude lengths of burlap fitted onto homemade stretchers. Sonny's choice of subject matter tends to be images too often conferred on the city, and ones that he himself once regarded as hackneyed.

"This city," he said to Louis, "it really is different from all others, isn't it?"

"It's New Orleans, Sonny. You need to find a better word than *different*."

Sonny paints the jazz halls and monuments, the Carnival balls and parades, the funeral marches and the food and music festivals. He paints fruit vendors selling Sugartown watermelons and Creole tomatoes from the backs of dilapidated pickups, and shotgun shanties all in a row, each a different color. He paints cemeteries and historic buildings and parks and oak trees and river bridges and bayous and swamps and ships and schools and warehouses and petrochemical plants.

Said Louis, "You actually expect someone to hang a picture of a refinery in their living room?"

"Sure," Sonny replied. "People like pictures of cows, why wouldn't they like pictures of refineries?"

Rather than an original talent to be reckoned with, Sonny has become perhaps the biggest cliché going: a man in filthy, paint-stained clothing and a fuzzy beret, whose stomach growls from hunger as he tries to hustle pictures that nobody wants.

Today he has dared to present himself to an elderly gentleman named Royce Michaud, who's wearing a tan crepe suit with food droppings on the sleeves, and around his neck a tie decorated with Tabasco peppers. Michaud's gallery is in the Warehouse District, one of several in the upstart arts enclave on Julia Street. Sonny and Royce Michaud stand together in a poorly lighted storage room, unrolling canvases and sheets of paper, carelessly spreading them on a table. "You want advice, Mr. LaMott? I'll give it to you straight."

Sonny nods.

"Well, to begin, your scale is off."

"My scale?"

"Yes. But your palette is rich and bold, I'll grant you that. I see talent here, Mr. LaMott, I do, but, sadly, and this is difficult for me to say . . . I don't see enough to take you past the fence. Your work is uninspired, Mr. LaMott. It lacks passion, and what is a painting but an expression of individual passion? It's as if you paint in your sleep. Wake up, you somnambulist, you listless man. Wake up and show thyself!"

Royce Michaud is holding an eight-by-ten watercolor depicting a Mardi Gras parade on Saint Charles Avenue. "Take this one as a case in point," he says, studying the scene so closely that Sonny feels himself growing warm and uncomfortable. "Your perspective here, Mr. LaMott . . ."

Sonny nods.

"The Carnival is moving away from the viewer. See that? The people on the street, those on the floats, the ones on the balconies here, even the animals on the sidewalk . . . everyone is turned away, there isn't a single face to make out. Where is the emotion? An artist must emote, Mr. LaMott."

"Yes. Yes, he must, Mr. Michaud."

"Has the world passed you by, Mr. LaMott? Is that what you're saying?"

"The world? *What* world?"

"I ask you, do you feel like an outsider, separate and apart from everyone else?"

"Sometimes."

"All the time, more like. Of course you do. You are totally disengaged. That is what you're telling me with your work. That is the statement you're making to the world. 'I could give a fuck.' You're standing there at the epicenter of one of this country's most popular tourist destinations and you're saying, 'Hello, my name is Sonny LaMott, and I could give a fuck!' "

"I could give a fuck," Sonny repeats.

Royce Michaud stuffs the parade painting in Sonny's open rucksack and removes another, this one a portrait of Juliet. "Now now *now*," he says, thrusting the small canvas under the green glass shade of a pharmacy lamp. "At last I see it."

"Did I get the scale right?"

"No, Mr. LaMott. *Passion!* I see it. And, oh, how delighted I am. You are not a somnambulist, after all. You are not dead on your feet. Oh, how nice."

Sonny clears his throat. "That's Juliet."

"It's more than any one girl," says the dealer. "It's love. It's sex. It's longing and desperation. It's also very beautiful. Now this is *art*, Mr. LaMott. Perhaps you do give a fuck."

"Juliet," Sonny says quietly. "Sometimes I think that if not for her I might've been a real artist, and a successful one. She's made every other painting unimportant."

"Nonsense," says Royce Michaud. "Who taught you to talk like that?"

"That woman ran me over like a dog in the road."

The dealer continues to study the image, his fingers delicately following the lines of Juliet's voluptuous form. "Yes, but of course she ran you over. This is clear now. And that is precisely why you will never be able to place this painting. More bad news, Mr. LaMott."

"Just say it."

"Nudes are a hard sell to begin with, and one such as this, though compelling, is particularly difficult. It's your best work, far superior to anything else you've shown me, but every woman who encounters this picture will find herself lacking in comparison to your Juliet. She'll sense her own inadequacies, and I don't mean simply tits and ass, Mr. LaMott. She'll feel as if she doesn't measure up. She'll know only frustration at never having experienced the obsession of a man equal to

25

that which is so evident here. You've made your love a prison, my friend. No"—Royce Michaud puts the piece away—"I'm afraid I have but one suggestion."

Sonny waits, his Adam's apple throbbing in his neck.

"Now, now, Mr. LaMott, it isn't easy for me to say this. But don't give up your day job."

♆♆♆

She knows she's good. Her stomach is flat, her hips and thighs devoid of cellulite, her boobs as fat and pointy as when she was fifteen. She likes the sassy Veronica Lake haircut her friend Wade gave her back in LA (whoever Veronica Lake is). She likes her feet. She likes her eyes, nose and ears. When she was young, a little thing yet, friends often teased her about the size of her lips. "Inner tubes," they called them. And as much as she hated them then, Juliet likes her lips now. These days big lips are in; they're all the rage. Models on magazine covers have big lips, and people pay good money for collagen injections. Ask anybody: a big mouth beats out a skinny one any day.

Once at a place off Ventura Boulevard a man paid her five hundred dollars to run her tongue over her lips while he sat in a chair and played with himself.

An hour later she was at an electronics store on Sepulveda buying a VCR.

They don't need dancers at the first two clubs she tries. They do need waitresses, however. Does she have any experience waiting tables? This she figures is a polite way of saying she doesn't look good enough to dance, that her look is too old or too hard, too something. The third place is too sleazy, the fourth too dead. They seem to like her at the fifth place. A woman called Lulu runs it.

She and Juliet sit at the bar and drink diet ginger ales.

"You say you're originally from here?"

"Ever hear of the Beauvais over on Esplanade? I grew up in that house. That's my family it's named after."

"You're one of them Beauvais, are you?"

"My people go back to the earliest Creoles who settled in the city. You know what a Creole is, don't you, Lulu?"

"A high yellow?"

"Well, it could be a high yellow. But your earliest Creoles were foreign people—Europeans—who came from France and settled in New Orleans. Some of the wealthier and more distinguished ones built big houses along Esplanade. How your mulattoes came to be Creoles is the white Creole men had light-skinned African women as concubines on the side and they had babies together and your babies grew up and learned who their daddies were and they started telling everybody they were Creoles, too. It used to be a very special thing to be a Creole. In Louisiana at one time it was like being royalty."

"Everybody's got to be something," says Lulu, who couldn't seem less impressed.

"The Beauvais will be mine any day now. My mother's sick, riddled from head to toe with inoperable cancer. I'm her only heir—and the last of my particular branch of the Beauvais—so I'll get the place and everything else that's been handed down from one generation to the next for going on two hundred years now."

"I had an uncle left me an old Buick once. I sold it for scrap for forty-five dollars."

Juliet, not sure how to respond, sips her beverage.

"You know how at them retarded schools they teach those kids shop?" says Lulu. "Well, at this one school over in Chalmette they make barbecue pits out of barrels and I went there with that car money and I bought myself one. I still got it. It cooks some beautiful meats."

"Let's make a deal, Lulu," Juliet says. "Let me dance here at your club and once Mama dies I'll make sure to invite you and the girls over to the house for an afternoon tea party?"

"Sorry, dear, but I'm afraid I'll have to pass."

Juliet lets on a look of disappointment and the woman says, "It's on account I have this phobia about old houses. Them and antiques. Stand me by an antique chair, for instance, and I like to faint."

Lulu lets her start that same day, and after Juliet has danced a few songs she sits with a man in a business suit who identifies himself as a schoolteacher from nearby Saint Bernard Parish. Like a lot of men his age, which is about forty, the schoolteacher's wife doesn't understand his needs. Juliet is tempted to ask what those needs are, but she's not sure she wants to hear them. They're about all talked out when the schoolteacher leans in close and says, "I think it would be neat to get some lady to pee on me. You ever think you might like to urinate on an individual?"

"I only do that in the normal place," Juliet answers.

This seems to be devastating news for the schoolteacher, who sits in silence hanging his head and picking at the label on his bottle of near beer.

"Well," she says, "I did squat and do it behind trees before. Do trees count?"

"I know now where I've seen you before."

She smiles in a disinterested way, not wishing to share her filmography with another one.

"Ever been to the Napoleon House?" he says. "It's that place across from the back of that hotel, the Royal Orleans; I forget the street. I think they got your picture hanging on the wall."

"What kind of picture?"

"Some painting. Ever pose for a painting?"

"Long time ago I did." She laughs. "Boy was always doing me naked."

The schoolteacher says, "Breasts and everything."

Juliet uses her straw to push her lime wedge down under her ice. "This famous movie producer in California paid me five hundred dollars once to run my tongue around like this." And now she demonstrates.

"You got yourself some monster lips, all right."

"They're just like some others in my family. I inherited them from the Beauvais, I guess. Kiss them too long and you know what happens?"

"I'd like to find out," says the schoolteacher.

"They turn a color too pretty for words. Us of my stripe don't even need lipstick."

✝✝✝

Sonny has painted other women, not a few of them nude. But the funny thing is—funny to him, anyway—most of his models end up looking like Juliet, and those who by some fluke actually come out resembling themselves never fail to own at least one of her features: the smart eyes, the puffy lips, the thick yellow hair. Sometimes, when unsatisfied with a picture, he's even substituted her large breasts and generous snarl of pubic hair.

"She's not me," a model told him once, "but I think I know this person."

They were at his home on the back porch, and the girl, whom he'd managed to have his way with a few hours earlier, was standing with a paint-stained sheet held close to her chest. Her own body was small and angular, while the nude in Sonny's painting was fleshy enough to draw comparisons to Marilyn Monroe.

"Okay, I know now," the girl said. "It's Juliet Beauvais. We went to the Academy together. Oh my God, Sonny! You've gone and made me a slut!"

Over the years Sonny's enjoyed his share of girlfriends—a few easily as pretty as Juliet, and all of them more kind, more generous—but somehow none has been able to keep him. These women simply were not meant for him, he decided, after casting them aside. The hours on the telephone, letters written and letters received, weekend dates to movies and coffeehouses. It all died away finally. His relationship with Polly Bienvenue, for example, reached the point where they were shopping for antique wedding bands in the French Quarter before he realized that he could never marry a woman with such stubby hands. "She was really quite lovely," he explained to Louis after crushing the woman, "but the one thing I could never get past were her hands."

"She's not missing any fingers, is she?"

"No. They're all there."

"What's wrong with them, then?"

"Besides their being stubby, you mean?" Sonny thought about it for a while. "Nothing, I guess, short of the fact that they're not Juliet's."

In his mawkish hours with strangers in Decatur Street bars, Sonny has confessed to looking for Juliet in every mouth he ever kissed, and the same went for her sex. The more he experimented with other women the more he became convinced that only she could make him happy. At night when he went to bed he imagined the two of them holding vivid conversations, Sonny employing a gift of gab that he in fact did not possess, while Juliet nodded admiringly and listened for a change.

"Sounds like she put some powerful voodoo on your ass," a fellow beer drinker told him once.

"That could be it."

"It also sounds like you need some counseling."

"Why do you think I'm talking to you?" Sonny answered with a laugh.

Sonny dreams about the perfect children they might've produced together. And he envisions the one who, had they chosen to let the pregnancy run its course, would be a teenager now. When he imagines this person Sonny sees either a son in his image or a daughter in Juliet's, and he sees his own life as he was meant to live it. As a family man he'd have discovered a happiness that is nowhere near him now, and his days, given to others, would have a greater meaning, a higher purpose. Every aspect of his existence, both large and small, would be improved. Collectors would covet his paintings; he would not have to paint Young Elvis and tourist portraits. Roaring through the French Quarter on his way to the square, his presence would elicit excitement. *"Ah, yes, here he comes. The great man!"*

"I was wrong about something," Juliet told him. "Remember how you said it only takes one drop and I said there was nothing to worry about?"

"Oh, Julie."

Had he only been more brave. Had he then said, "Okay, now, let's think about this," or, better yet, "No, we're keeping it," the whole world would be different today. To begin, Sonny would not be such a broken-down thing. His mother would be alive, his father well and prospering. Sonny might even be driving a car, a new one, instead of his father's twenty-three-year-old pickup truck. He would have a house in a neighborhood with trees, central air instead of window units, a lawn without weeds.

It also occurs to Sonny that, had he not agreed to the procedure (Sonny still can't call the abortion by its name), he would be nowhere near the situation in which he finds himself tonight.

No way would Sonny be waiting for an old cat doctor to leave his office and make his way across the Esplanade Avenue neutral ground.

"On the one hand you seem like such a normal, well-adjusted guy," Sonny is saying to Louis Fortunato. "You give good, smart advice and you're trustworthy and you can make more sense than anyone I know. Then on the other hand you think it's okay to whack a vet for allegedly killing your Frank. Please help me with this picture, Louis."

"Blame it on my leg. Everyone else does."

"Your leg is what made you a weirdo?"

"That's what they tell me."

It is almost 8:00 P.M. before the vet emerges from the building. Small and humped over, he's wearing a baggy seersucker suit with a black bow tie drooping at the neck. He is much older than Sonny imagined he would be; in fact, he is so old that his hair and mustache are bleached white.

"Bloody, murderous bastard," Louis says, sipping from a bottle of whiskey.

"I pictured him different," Sonny says. "He looks about a hundred. Poor old geezer."

"Sorry, bubba. But being a hundred don't make him immune from being a cold-blooded killer."

Sonny has come to this event "dressed for success," as he himself described his outfit earlier. He is all in black save for the surgical gloves covering his hands, which are white.

"I dream a thousand pictures," Louis says. "Frank on the windowsill at home watching cars go by, Frank batting a ball of yarn across the kitchen floor, Frank on his birthday eating a platter of fried chicken livers I bought him at Popeye's."

"Do you dream one of Frank squatting in his litter box?"

"Frank was a saint," Louis says. "And saints can speak directly to God. They have the power. As long as you have Frank in your corner there's nothing to worry about."

"You think if I pray to Frank people will start buying my paintings?"

"I'm not sure Frank can perform miracles," Louis says, "but it wouldn't hurt."

Sonny stares out at the wide boulevard, its trees and footpaths and solitary lamps. He's heard stories about the neighborhood, some of them hard to believe to look at the area now. In the years before the Civil War New Orleans had more millionaires per capita than any other city in America, and here in the district populated by French Creoles there lived some of the wealthiest, Juliet's people among them. One of the first families, true pioneers, the Beauvais helped settle three miles of rich farmland from the Mississippi River up to Bayou Saint John, building the magnificent homes that still stand today. In 1872 and 1873 French Impressionist painter Edgar Degas lived for five months with relatives in a nearby Greek Revival. Many of the original Creole houses on Esplanade, like the one that belonged to Degas's family, later became blighted property. Plywood covers the windows; graffiti marks the ancient façades. Still others, inhabited until only recently, have been abandoned as the criminal element digs in. And who is this criminal element?

Sad sacks like Sonny LaMott and Louis Fortunato, as it turns out.

"I guess it's time," Louis says.

"Guess so." Sonny takes in a deep breath. "If nothing else today proves that we're the two most pathetic sonsabitches in the entire city of New Orleans."

"And that we lead the emptiest lives, don't forget that."

Louis hands Sonny the club he spent the better part of the day putting together. It's a piece of PVC, about two inches in diameter and two feet long, and he's filled it with something dense and heavy. Both ends are capped, and one is wrapped with electrical tape. The handle, Sonny presumes.

"That's sand in there in case you were wondering," Louis says. "I tried kitty litter but the sand proved more effective. It felt harder in the pipe than the kitty litter did. This'll really hurt but it's not likely to kill him. Hit him in the shins, Sonny. Make him feel it."

"Feel what?"

"The *pain*, brother. Make him feel the *pain.*"

It's hot to be wearing black clothes, let alone gloves and a mask, but Sonny figures that half an hour from now he'll be back home in shorts and a T-shirt, lounging under the little window unit in his bedroom, absorbed again in a life without a whole lot to do.

He gets out of the truck and looks around to make sure no one is watching.

"Dr. Coulon?" he calls, striding toward the old man. "Dr. Coulon, I'm here on behalf of Frank."

The vet wheels around and looks at Sonny with as much resignation as terror. Maybe it's the clothes Sonny's wearing, or maybe he's kept abreast of the city's crime statistics, because in either case he doesn't seem altogether unprepared for this moment.

"There isn't much," he says, reaching for his wallet.

"You killed Frank," Sonny tells him.

"I killed *who?*"

"Drop to the ground after I pretend to hit you," Sonny demands. He takes a step closer. "Come on, you old fart, fall to the ground."

"Hey, look. I'm an animal doctor. I didn't kill anyone."

"Tell that to Frank," Sonny says, raising the club. "Now I'm going to act like I'm hitting you and I want you to act like it hurts. Come on. Fall down, you bastard."

Sonny levels the club against the vet's shin, barely bumping him. "Fall!" Sonny says, taking another phony swing. "Come on, old man. Fall!" And down the vet goes, really hamming it up now. He screams and writhes in the grass, his arms stretched out over his head.

"Grab your leg," Sonny says. "Come on, old-timer. Grab it."

The vet does as he's told and Sonny pretends to whack him a few more times. He lifts the club high and brings it down, each time stopping just short of making contact.

"That's for Frank," Sonny says.

The old man shrieks.

"For Frank from the one who loves him. You cat-killing bastard. You murderer. You . . ."

By the time Sonny returns to the truck Louis has already started the engine. Louis, pounding both hands on the dashboard, is all nerves; even his eyes seem to wobble in their sockets.

"You killed him!" he calls as Sonny makes a U-turn and roars away. *"You killed my Frank!"*

From beneath the trees the vet yells again, louder than before.

They drive a few blocks before Sonny pulls over and removes the gloves and ski mask and stuffs them under the seat. He says nothing until they reach the painted lady on Prytania where Louis rents a small apartment. Originally built as a single-family residence, the grand but tumbledown Victorian now houses a dozen small units. Sonny stops beside a collection of overflowing trash cans standing in the rear alley.

"Now that is one old guy who'll think twice before neutering another cat," Sonny says.

Louis gets out of the truck and staggers to within a few feet of the cans before, skidding to a halt, he throws up violently at his feet.

Through his open window Sonny says, "Listen, you lunatic, if you call that man or go by his office again we'll both end up in jail. I'm not serving time for you, buddy. I'm not."

Louis, bent over, rests his hands on his fake leg, a rope of saliva hanging from his mouth.

"So don't be gloating about this tomorrow," Sonny says, "and don't you ever mention it again. Do you hear what I'm saying?"

Louis cleans his mouth with his shirttail and gives a nod. "I owe you," he says.

"No, you don't. You don't owe me anything."

"I owe you," Louis says again.

❦

*"You color-coded our lives. Daddy was blue, I was red, you were green. My piggy bank was a glass bottle with a red lid. My dinner plate was red plastic. My glass was red glass. You gave me that sweater that Christmas and guess what color? I told you I wanted yellow but goddamn if you didn't go and make it red.*

*"Daddy: I'm tired of my blue plate. Can we use the china?*

*"You: No, the china is for special occasions only.*

*"Daddy: It's Sunday and I just bought a bucket of chicken. That's special enough. I'm using the china, Marcelle. Juliet, do you want to use the china?*

*"Me: Yes!*

*"You (pretending to be pleased): Great! Fine! Wonderful! Okay, everybody, let's use the china!"*

❦

For a prime spot on the fence you have to arrive early and stake your claim or else settle for a location that puts you closer to tarot card readers dressed like genies than to customers with money to spend. The best spots are near trees and restaurants on the upriver and downriver sides of the square. The trees provide shade and keep people from squinting in the sun, and the restaurants have bathrooms. The worst spots are those situated in the middle of a row of painters, away from the shade. There the competition for tourist dollars, intensified by the heat, is so fierce that fistfights have been known to break out. During his first week on the job Sonny watched in amazement as two of his more genial colleagues went to blows on the flagstones. The brawl, Sonny later learned, started when one man's beach umbrella, aided by a sudden gust of wind, brushed up against the other's.

Sonny's favorite spot is under the magnolia tree across from the French bakery on the corner of Saint Ann and Chartres streets. The spot, however, is everybody's favorite. And in order to claim it you have two options, neither pleasant: hire a drunk to leave his midnight bottle and reserve the space or get up before dawn and secure it on your own.

Having no funds to waste and little faith in bums, Sonny sets his alarm clock for 4:00 A.M. and endures the agony.

He's at the fence today when a couple of charter buses lurch to a stop on Decatur Street and deposit loads of Japanese tourists in front of Jackson Brewery. After brief experiments with beignets and café au lait, the tourists drift into the park and tour the pedestrian mall.

"My forehead is too big," complains the subject of Sonny's latest portrait.

Sonny almost forgot she was there. "What's that?"

"My nose too small, too pointed. My eyes are not blue, and my hair is yellow? When is my hair yellow?"

The woman glares at the image Sonny has just finished painting on a perfectly nice sheet of Saint Armand's Sabretooth. It looks nothing like her, but as far as his interpretations of Juliet Beauvais go, Sonny has never been more on his game.

"Look," he says, scumbling chestnut into the hair. "I'm fixing it. All gone. Hair brown. Hair black."

Suddenly a crowd has gathered around them, and Sonny does his best to look as if everything is under control. It is rare to hear a complaint, and the worst possible luck to get one now. He's already done three pastel portraits at forty-five dollars a pop, all of them featuring Japanese from the buses. And he hoped to paint six or seven more.

Sonny can oblige those who want their pictures matted and framed with the supplies he keeps in his cart. Add to that the likelihood of gratuities . . . *Jesus, what has he done?*

And now the woman begins to cry.

"You're absolutely right to be upset," Sonny says, trying to sound sensible. "Here, darling. Picture free. Take. No charge. You handsome woman. Very handsome."

She's sobbing now with such intensity that people begin leaving the shops of the Pontalba Building to investigate the commotion.

"Lovely brown hair," he continues. "Most lovely brown hair . . . picture free . . . here . . . picture . . ."

Sonny LaMott is a jingoistic ass, he's proven that finally. Dreaming about a woman he hasn't seen in years, he's turned a nice-looking Asian into an American Barbie doll, and now he's further humiliated her by trying to imitate a foreigner with little command of the English language.

She doesn't talk like that!

The woman's husband removes a wad of cash from his pocket and throws a fifty on the flagstones at Sonny's feet.

"You want me to frame it?" Sonny keeps on. "Don't you . . . ? Wouldn't you . . . ? *Please!"*

The couple is helped away finally. And along with them goes the crowd. "Way to go, LaMott," mutters the painter next to Sonny. "You scared them all away."

Out in the street the buses cough and roar, their front and rear doors cocked open. And from the fence come the calls of other artists:

"Thanks a lot, Sonny!"

"Three cheers for you!"

"Nice work, buddy boy!"

Even Roberts the caricaturist offers a few rough words, Roberts who is never rough on anyone. It is almost enough to make Sonny wish he were still mixing cocktails at the Bayou Bar in the Pontchartrain Hotel. At least then no one complained when he botched a drink, using Beefeater's instead of Tanqueray, green instead of red cherries.

"Sorry," Sonny calls to his compatriots on the mall, only to hear them shout him down again in response.

The buses with the visiting Japanese storm away, and Sonny wishes he'd brought a blanket along. His cart, painted fire-engine red, displays his name in big block letters: SONNY LAMOTT: WORLD-RENOWNED FRENCH QUARTER ARTIST. With a blanket he could cover the cart. Or cover his head.

Roberts shambles over and points a finger. "Stop hanging your lip."

"Sorry, old man," Sonny says.

"It's a little late for sorry. And don't call me old."

Roberts stands barely five feet tall but he carries himself with the swagger of an NBA basketball star. Though born and raised in the Mississippi Delta, the son of a black sharecropper, he speaks with an accent more Continental than American, and he's rarely seen without a crisply starched white dress shirt and conservative necktie—the clothes, he once told Sonny, "of a professional at the office." No artist gives Roberts any grief because his tenure at the fence dates back forty years and nearly doubles the next most senior in line, and because Roberts holds a status in the French Quarter equal to few but the truly legendary. There's entertainer Chris Owens. There's trumpeter Al Hirt. There's Banjo Annie and Ruthie the Duck Girl. And then there's Roberts, who now is wagging a finger in Sonny's face.

"Listen to me, LaMott. LaMott, are you listening to me?"

Sonny nods.

"People come to this fence and hand themselves to you. They give you a face to paint, but in actual fact they're asking you a question. 'Am I worth it?' they ask every time they sit down in your chair. *'Am I worth it?'* And you sit or stand there, boy, with your blank paper and tray of Cray-Pas chubbies and try to find that which makes them most themselves, too often having to correct a bent nose, a chin rolling with flesh, teeth all gone to ruin. Yours is a great responsibility. Do you understand what I'm saying?"

"I won't let it happen again," Sonny says.

"Am I worth it?" Roberts repeats, nearly shouting. "Am I worth it?"

Things quiet down and Sonny returns to work. Tired of portraits, he doesn't bother to try to recruit another tourist to paint. Instead he turns to his sketchbook and traces pastel sticks over a blank sheet of paper, and as if by magic an image appears. It's the Beauvais, a picture he's made so many times before that he doesn't need reference photos. Sonny shows the columns and the rows of green-shuttered windows and the upper and lower galleries crowded with wicker furniture. He shows the iron fence with the gate open, and above it the legend BEAUVAIS in a rusty crescent barely visible past clumps of morning glory.

Sweat trickles down his face and dampens his shirt and he feels the rush that comes with being lost in the work and unfettered to the world around him. "Keep her out of it," he says to himself. "She doesn't have to be there. Just the house, for once. Come on, goddammit . . ."

It wasn't until May 1971, months into his love affair with Juliet, that Sonny saw the house for the first time as the artist he dreamed of becoming. Parked by the curb in his father's pickup, he studied the mansion past the fence and crape myrtles and wondered at the fortune of one born to a destiny that included a home such as the Beauvais. A thin sliver of moon hung up past the slate rooftop, and he saw it as a yellow blip against the heavy impasto of a cobalt sky. The stars burned like Van Gogh's, each a pinwheel. He saw the wind in the movement of the chimes dangling from the eaves of the rear carriage house and the leaves skittering in waves across the lawn. "The birdbath in the lilacs," Sonny said out loud, providing details to the image as he would reproduce it. "Plantation chairs as pale as ghosts. Shutters shut on every window but yours."

Short of living there himself, Sonny would paint the mansion and that way make it his own.

Juliet appeared finally on the upper gallery and began her descent using drainpipes and a trellis bound with bougainvillea. She moved fluidly and quickly, and despite the height seemed sure of herself.

In the light from the street Sonny could see the white of her buttocks, the dark fist between her legs. Her summer dress hung up on the vines, fifteen feet up.

"The garden path," he said out loud, providing even more details for his painting. "The magnolias and the privet pink against the lanterns by the door."

She made a last short jump to the lawn and ran to meet him. He heard the gate creak open then clank closed and that would do it, watch if Miss Marcelle didn't come out now.

As she crossed in front of the pickup Sonny pulled the knob for the headlamps, throwing light. This was his favorite part, Juliet did it every time: yanked her skirt up and flashed him. But tonight she failed to include the gesture. Eyes cast down, she entered the truck without a word.

"Julie? Julie, what's wrong, baby? Are you okay?"

They brought their mouths together and he felt the dampness on her face and the back of her neck. "Oh, Sonny," she said, then lunged at him and forced her body close to his.

Only now did Sonny register the swelling around her eyes and her mouth cracked and raw.

"What's wrong? Darling, what's wrong?"

"Nothing. Can we just go?"

"Sit by me," he said. "Come sit by me. Tell me what's wrong."

She shook her head and began to cry and he asked her again to talk to him. "I can't take their fighting anymore," she said. "I can't. She calls him names. Queer and pervert and ninny and reprobate—think of the ugliest things imaginable and she says them. She called one of his friends on the telephone and shouted at him and told him to leave Daddy alone."

"His friend?"

"Yes. And this is a married man from one of the finest old families in town."

Sonny started the engine and pulled into the street. As they were crossing the intersection at North Rampart Juliet said, "What she doesn't tell him, Sonny. What she doesn't say."

They drove on in silence. By the time they reached their place by the river Juliet had settled down and become quiet. She reached for his hand and brought it to her mouth. "Sometimes I think I'd go crazy if you weren't here to help me."

"I'll always be here, Julie. Always."

"I know," she said, tears bright in her eyes.

Hours later when they returned to Esplanade Sonny sat parked at the curb watching as she moved under the trees along the path to the house. It was both the loveliest and the loneliest image he'd ever seen and he felt an overwhelming desire to paint it so that others might see what he saw, the beauty and the sadness. He would place her there in the moonlit garden beneath the Van Gogh stars. Upstairs lace curtains fled her open window and flapped one next to the other like flags of surrender, and he would show this and the viewer would feel the wind and find it repeated in the chimes and the leaves and her summer dress. From the avenue came horns bleating and the calliope of a passing ice cream truck and Sonny felt an ache of regret that seemed to intensify the moment she turned and sent him off with a wave.

Sonny finishes the painting and signs his name in the lower left corner. He uses a black Othello pencil and includes looping flourishes to show his satisfaction. Lastly he adds the date to inform future generations exactly when the work came into being. He sprays the picture with a fixative and fits it in a gilded, prefab frame and hangs it on the fence with all the others.

Sonny sits in his chair and watches his compatriots at the fence, each absorbed in his work. Half an hour goes by and he wonders at his weakness and his inability to forget what obviously meant nothing to her. "You shouldn't have put the girl in the picture," he says out loud.

Certain now that no one is looking, he takes an oil stick and blots out both his name and the date, leaving in their place a black rectangle the size of a postcard.

᷁ ᷁ ᷁

She doesn't recognize the waiter who shows her to a table by the window. He's gimp-legged and she doesn't know any gimps. He hands her a menu and stands waiting to take her order. The place is empty and she can't figure why he'd want to rush her.

"I'm not hungry," she says. "How about a beer?"

"You still like ponies, Juliet? Those little baby Pearls used to be so popular?"

She drops back in her chair and examines him more closely, and his name flashes in her head at the same moment it comes to her lips: "Louis."

He smiles in his old familiar way. And she feels a flood of dread wash through her. "All right. Make it a pony, then."

"I would but if they still make them, we don't stock them."

She really isn't hungry, but she gives some time to the menu, tracing a finger down the list of sandwiches, then up to one of the house specialties. "I'm sorry to see you lost your limb there," she says, her eyes on the soups and salads now.

Louis's loud snort of laughter lets her know she never should've come here, picture or no picture.

"I didn't actually lose it, to tell you the truth. After that little Dodge hit me on Tchoupitoulas the doctors just took it without permission. It was more stolen than lost."

"Could you be a waiter for a minute and go get me my beer?"

"Last thing I remember is me and Sonny having a night at the F&M Patio Bar. This was right after you skipped town, and we went out to drown the sorrows, know what I mean? Sonny insisted on paying the tab, and while he did I ran out into Tchoupitoulas Street for some reason. People always ask me why I'd go and do such a dumb-ass thing and I never answer them. But now I can say it, since you're the one who needs to hear it. I ran out in the road because I was happy. I was happy that you were finally gone from his life. I was happy because I believed Sonny was free of you forever."

"I order a beer and get a lecture. Jesus."

"I blame you, Juliet. You took my leg. You and you alone are responsible."

"Fine. Now use that other leg and hop over there and get me my drink."

Behind the bar Louis pops the top on a Dixie and places the bottle on a tray. At her table he pours the beer cold and icy in a glass and the head swells up more than she usually likes. She doesn't complain. Some people have to blame everybody else for their troubles. Even the beer foam would be something she did years ago. If he has earwax you can bet that's her fault, too.

"I was told they got my picture hanging in this place."

"We put it over the toilet in the men's room."

"Did Sonny remember to put a couple of horns growing from the top of my head?"

He gives another noisy laugh and levels his face with hers. "Juliet, let me tell you something you might not want to hear. Sonny LaMott was never right in the head when it came to you. And he still isn't."

"Okay."

"Sonny's got this big old sappy heart pounding away down deep in his chest. Still goes to church, still gets on his knees to say his prayers at night. The boy is pure, now. And it's this pure thing in him that I want to make sure to protect." Louis lowers a hand to his fake leg and gives it a tap. "I lost a lot on account of you and it's in your power to have Sonny lose even more. I'm asking you, Juliet, and I'm asking nice—stay away from that boy."

She sits picking at the corner of the menu where the plastic is peeling. "I hate to disappoint you, Louis, especially after that deeply moving testimonial, but I didn't come here today to catch up on the news about Sonny LaMott. Somebody told me last night that one of his paintings, presumably of me, is hanging here in the restaurant and I wanted to see it."

He glares at her for half a minute longer, then takes a step back as if to let her through. "The door with the frosty glass, then to your right."

"Anybody in there?"

"Not at the moment, if that matters."

She walks to the bathroom and turns the light on and locks the door behind her. She wishes she had a missing leg to blame her life on. It sure would simplify everything in a hurry.

"*What got you to liking cocaine so much, Juliet?*"

"*My leg.*"

"*What made you turn to adult cinema, Juliet?*"

"*Leg.*"

The picture is where he said it would be, and she is unprepared for how beautiful it is. Or how beautiful Sonny made her. "Why, look at you," she mutters to the face in the image.

He did give her a lot of pubic hair, though, and this is her only complaint. But then she remembers that those were the days before you could find a decent wax job. Maybe she really did look like that—a regular ligustrum hedge.

She brings her face closer to the canvas and finds Sonny's autograph in the corner. "Sonny" is all it says, a name as plain as he was.

Under that he's scribbled something else, but the writing is so small she has a hard time making it out. The room's poor lighting doesn't help either. At first she thinks it's a date, signifying when Sonny finished the thing, but her eyes adjust and she figures it out.

*My Juliet*, it says.

By the time she returns to the dining room he's already cleared her table. The menu is gone, the flatware put away.

"Oh, I'm sorry," he says. "I thought you'd left."

"You know what I think, Louis? I think you were a cripple long before you ever lost that leg."

He doesn't seem to be listening. "Leave him be, Juliet. That's all I ask."

"Cripple," she repeats in a small voice.

"I'll tear your heart out if you hurt him again. I'll lay it hot and bleeding between some French bread and make me a Juliet poboy. Don't think I'm playing, either."

"I'm just now remembering something," she says. "Maybe this was just a rumor spreading around—it reached me way out in California, anyway—but that leg wasn't all you lost, was it? You left something else in the road, didn't you?"

"You got a lot of nerve bringing that up," he says.

"Too bad. Because even before, you were a little sawed off in that department, weren't you?"

On the banquette outside she stands at the window watching as he moves to the bar and pretends to eat a Juliet poboy. She sticks her tongue out and presses it against the glass, but he keeps munching on the imaginary sandwich.

She shoots him the bird and still he eats.

"*How come you peed on the schoolteacher, Juliet?*"

"*Penis.*"

"*How come you killed your mama like that, Juliet?*"

"*Penis.*"

In the end she walks off dragging her right leg just as he dragged his, the echo of her laughter bouncing off the old buildings pressing in on her along the street.

※

When Sonny parks the truck in front of the Maison Orleans Nursing Home Mr. LaMott is already waiting outside with a nurse's aide. The woman holds her arms crossed at her massive chest, rather like a schoolyard bully without an ounce of mercy left. She seems less likely to greet him with a hello than to punch him in the mouth.

"You know I'm always on time, Agnes. Won't you forgive me this once?"

"I don't like being out the air condition."

"Yes, and I feel terrible about it."

The woman helps Mr. LaMott into the truck and Sonny thanks her with a pat on the back and he and his father start on their way to the Rigolets. The old man is wearing what he always wears when they go fishing: rubber boots, khaki pants, a golf hat decorated with antique lures, and a navy polo shirt with the name *Paul Piazza & Son* scripted in gold thread across the breast. Until a few years ago when he was diagnosed with Alzheimer's, Mr. LaMott was the top salesman for Piazza, a wholesale shrimp distributor with headquarters near the cemeteries just north of the French Quarter. The last time Sonny asked his father about Piazza, Mr. LaMott said he liked his with anchovies and extra cheese.

Earlier this morning Sonny strapped the rods, tackle box and ice chest to an anchor in the truck bed, and every few miles he throws a glance back to make sure everything's riding okay. "Looks good," he says, nodding at his father.

"Looks good," comes Mr. LaMott's enthusiastic reply.

Today the weather is nice and balmy and Sonny and Mr. LaMott drive with the windows down. Music plays on the radio, show tunes from long ago. Sonny tries to coax Mr. LaMott into singing along but the old man is too busy opening and closing the window vent.

"You know this one, Daddy? Let me hear it."

Mr. LaMott doesn't do so much as hum.

On the Chef Menteur Highway they pass a settlement populated with Vietnamese immigrants and Sonny remarks as to how hard these people work shrimping the Gulf but Mr. LaMott seems as clueless about shrimping as he is about Vietnamese. Besides, he has that vent to fool with.

"I think I've been here before," Mr. LaMott says as Sonny turns into the parking lot at a waterfront restaurant/lounge called Captain Bruce's.

"Daddy, we were here last week," Sonny says, glad to hear his father speak again at last. "You don't remember we came fishing here last week?"

Mr. LaMott seems to be trying to remember if he remembers.

"It's okay if you don't," Sonny says. He steps out onto the lot covered with crushed oyster shells. "The only bites we got were from mosquitoes, anyway."

The building is uneven sheets of tin and plywood inexpertly applied to a skeleton of two-by-fours. It rests on cement standards maybe fifty feet from some of the best fishing in the southern United States. A sign on the door advertises a 1-800 number for alcoholics and inside fishermen crowd the bar running from the front to the rear of the room. Everybody seems to be drinking the same brand of beer and picking from identical platters of boiled shrimp and new potatoes. Up high near the ceiling a muted TV set shows a home shopping channel and the deal of the day: a ladies' curling iron slashed to more than half the manufacturer's suggested retail price. "I need me one of them," Sonny hears one of the drunks mutter from the middle of the bar.

"You ain't got no hair to curl," shouts another.

"Yeah, but at least I can get it up," says the first man, confounding Sonny but drawing a great riot of laughter from everyone else.

Captain Bruce drifts over and Sonny gives him a five-dollar bill, the fee for fishing rights off the pier behind the building. The captain wears

Wrangler jeans a size too small and his shirtsleeves cover tattoos of fight roosters raining feathers. Today the captain has little to say except for how the Saints did themselves no favors in yesterday's draft of college football talent. "Eleven picks and every one a colored," he says. "You'd think they could find one white boy that can play."

"Mark my words, they inheriting themselves some serious behavioral problems," says the man who wanted the curling iron.

Sonny puts another bill on the bar and asks for beer and ice and bait shrimp. No surprise, Captain Bruce gives him a six-pack of the same cheap stuff everyone else is drinking, Old Milwaukee in the can.

"Your daddy don't even know who you are, does he, LaMott?" the captain says as Sonny is heading back outside.

"You're wrong there, Captain," Sonny says after deciding the man means no harm.

"He's senile and retarded, both. Got it coming and going."

"He suffers from Alzheimer's. It's a disease that mainly afflicts senior citizens."

Captain Bruce seems to be sizing Sonny up. "Yeah, well, that's what you say. But he's too young for no Alzheimer's."

"He's sixty-four."

"I'm sixty-two and how come I don't have it?"

"I guess the good Lord has given you a pass on that one, Captain"

The captain shakes his head. "That man, your daddy? I want you to leave him at home next time, LaMott. He's got no bidness coming out here. My insurance finds out I got somebody like that fishing off my pier they raise my premium overnight."

Sonny stares for a long time. "Thank you for the beer, Captain."

Sonny loads the ice and beer into his Igloo, his father watching through the back window. Then he lugs the cooler and the rest of the gear to the end of the pier. Lastly he helps Mr. LaMott from the truck, offering encouragement as his father tests his footing and gets his bearings. "Okay, Daddy. Take it slow now. Take it slow. I'm here."

When they reach the pier, Sonny ties a length of rope around the old man's waist then loops the other end around his own. The distance between them runs about ten feet, but if Mr. LaMott suddenly were to decide to go for a swim Sonny would be able to fish him out. You can never be too safe with people sick like his father. In the news they are constantly drifting off, heading for the woods or the interstate, too lost to know they're lost. By the time the bloodhounds find them it's too late but for the undertaker.

"Hey, Daddy. What say we go catch us some fish?"

After a few hours the lake breeze dies and the air starts to heat up and Sonny and Mr. LaMott drink the beers and suck on chunks of ice as the sun broils their arms and necks. As usual the fish aren't biting so Sonny crowds the time with stories about when he was a kid and his mother was alive and Mr. LaMott was the top shrimp salesman for Paul Piazza & Son. The more Sonny talks the more he is able to recall. He describes the Ninth Ward as it was twenty years ago before most of the old families moved to the suburbs and you stopped feeling safe to walk the streets at night. He names the neighbors, the Irish and the Italians who worked the riverfront, the blacks who played music and staffed the kitchens in the bars and restaurants of the Vieux Carré. He names the coaches who coached him in summer-league baseball at the Saint Roch playground. He talks about Otto's Pharmacy, now a grocery store, and about the year it snowed and how school closed and everybody ran in the streets biting at the flakes in the cold air. He names the meals his mother used to cook: crawfish étouffée, shrimp surprise, ground meat casserole, round steak with rice and gravy, stuffed bell peppers, mirliton dressing, bread pudding made with fruit cocktail, raisins and whiskey or "hard" sauce. Sonny talks about waking up before dawn and walking with his mother to Saint Cecilia and Father Michael saying Mass in Latin and Sonny, an altar boy then, ringing the bells whenever Father Michael lifted the blood or the body of Christ. He talks about how sometimes afterward he and Mrs. LaMott took a bus to the French Quarter for beignets and café au lait and the water trucks washing down the streets and on Mondays the smell of red beans cooking and how his mother would still be in her church veil and carrying a missal. Sonny talks and it comes back and he feels a deep, swimming sadness for all that will never be again.

"Where is Mama?" Mr. LaMott says when Sonny seems to have finished.

"Mama died in 1982, Daddy. She had that stroke, remember?"

Mr. LaMott seems to take this as a surprise. He reels in his line and sits for a long time staring at his artificial lure.

"I been meaning to tell you something, Daddy," Sonny says, "and I hope you can grab ahold of this." Mr. LaMott doesn't respond, and

Sonny continues, "I been wanting to tell you you were right about most everything you ever said to me. You were a real good father to me."

Mr. LaMott just stares—not at Sonny, but at his lure.

"After high school when the government didn't draft me I should've been a man about it and enlisted and gone on to Vietnam or else enrolled at LSU like you wanted me to. You were right about me being just a so-so bartender and an even worse painter. I'm sure that wasn't easy for you to say, and I'm sorry I didn't listen. Because I realize it now, I realize all you said was meant to help me. Sometimes I think that that war, crazy as it was, might've helped me. Korea helped you, right?" Sonny reaches over and takes the lure from his father's hands. "I wish you'd said something about Juliet, though. That time I brought her to the house for dinner? You should've talked to me about her then—you and Mama, both. Not that I'd have listened, understand? But at least now you could be saying 'I told you so.' "

"I told you so," says Mr. LaMott.

"No, you didn't. That's the point I'm trying to make. You didn't tell me anything."

It had been his mother's idea, to meet Sonny's girlfriend and have her over for dinner. After she'd finished cooking Mrs. LaMott went down the hall to her bedroom and changed into an outfit heretofore reserved for weddings and holy days of obligation. As for Mr. LaMott, he wore his lone sport coat, the tweed one with elbow patches, even though it was a muggy spring evening. Sonny can still remember the meal his mother prepared: smothered pork chops, white beans and rice, wop salad crowded with black olives and artichoke hearts, French bread lathered with garlic butter and toasted to a crispy brown in the broiler, and sliced Creole tomatoes still warm from the sun. Juliet contributed the dessert, a pineapple upside-down cake studded with maraschino cherries. "You made that?" Mr. LaMott asked.

"Yes sir. Well, me and Anna Huey did. She's the lady who works for us."

"It's beautiful."

"It's made from scratch. I didn't even use a mixer to mix the batter."

"You mean you did all that by hand?"

"Yes sir."

"Now isn't that something," and he seemed truly amazed.

Sonny was too nervous to say or eat much. How Juliet, a fancy girl from a fancy family, would take to his humble Bywater family had put his stomach in knots. He remembers little of what was said at the table, but afterward he and Juliet went for a drive in the Vieux Carré. They stopped for beer at the A&P on Royal Street and Sonny kept a bottle between his legs as he held the wheel with one hand and rested the other on her shoulder. "What did you think?" he said, anxious to know if he had passed muster.

She looked at him with a dreamy expression and leaned over and softly kissed the side of his face. "Now I know why you're so beautiful."

He was back home before 10:00 P.M., and his mother, having cleaned the kitchen, had already gone to bed. Mr. LaMott, however, was sitting in his chair under a lamp reading a day-old copy of the *Times-Picayune*. He had his pajamas on. "What did you think?" Sonny said. He had become hungry again, and in the dark kitchen he pulled the refrigerator door open and stood bathed in cold yellow light.

"What do I think about what?" his father asked casually.

"You know about what. About Juliet."

Mr. LaMott turned the page. "Oh, Juliet. Yes. Seems like a fine girl."

"Did Mom like her?"

"Yes, she did," Mr. LaMott answered. "Your mother did like her. In particular she seemed to enjoy something Juliet said when the two of us were out of earshot."

"Oh, yeah? What was that?"

"Well," and his father still seemed to be reading, "they were picking up in the kitchen before dessert, and your mother asked Juliet if she was ready for pineapple upside-down cake. Juliet—and even I was surprised to hear this—Juliet put her hand down around her midsection here and said, 'If I eat another bite I think I'll vomit.' "

Sonny almost dropped his bottle of milk. "She said she'd vomit?"

His father put the paper down and removed his glasses. Then suddenly, unable to maintain the guise any longer, he erupted with a bright roar of laughter. "Just pulling your leg, boy. Relax."

How had a girl who ate his mother's smothered pork chops become an actor in dirty movies? It made even less sense then Mr. LaMott's decline from the best and funniest guy Sonny knew to the halfwit sitting before him now. Sonny leans forward bringing his face up to search for something that hasn't been in his father's eyes for years. He's looking for life.

"Daddy, why didn't you tell me Juliet would go bad like that?"

Mr. LaMott, his cheeks growing red with blood, pushes past Sonny as he comes to his feet. Sonny anticipates a weighty declaration, something to hang on to forever. But his father unzips his pants and pokes his hand in the opening. "Hey, look, mind if I pee in your water?"

It is dark when they start back for the city. Sonny, who's run out of memories to share, drinks the last of the beer as his father sleeps on the bench seat beside him. No one is waiting when they pull up at the Maison Orleans. Sonny reties the tether between them and none of the staff says anything when they pad through the front door and enter the building.

Sonny helps Mr. LaMott all the way down the hall to his room, the rope dragging the high-polished floor. "I think I've been here before," Mr. LaMott says in a quiet voice as Sonny takes his clothes off and puts him to bed.

❧❧❧

He stops her as she's crossing the lobby headed for the elevators. "May I have a moment of your time, Miss Beauvais?"

"A moment? Sure, you can have a moment."

There are two important matters they need to discuss, he explains. First is the condition of the bed in her room. Did a child sleep over last night? The mattress was so saturated with urine that it had to be changed.

He advises her to call Housekeeping and request a plastic sheet to safeguard against future accidents.

Next is her credit card account, which has rejected more charges. Will she please follow him to the desk and make other arrangements to pay her bill?

"Not now," Juliet says.

"Yes now," says the man.

"Suppose I don't feel like it?"

"Then I'm afraid I have no choice but to ask you to vacate the premises."

She gives him most of what she earned from the schoolteacher. But

49

that only covers the balance and room charges for tonight and tomorrow. Was it her idea to fly to New Orleans and stay in an expensive hotel and rent a car and eat by herself in restaurants? Schoolteachers don't make any money!

Blood rising in her face, Juliet returns to her room and phones the mansion. "Anna Huey, it's me and I want my money and I want it now."

"Yes," says the maid, "yes, of course."

"Don't you yes-of-course me," Juliet shouts into the mouthpiece. "I want my money."

"And you'll get it. Or get some. How much do you want?"

Juliet, figuring, is slow to answer. "Five thousand should do."

"We think two's enough. But you'll have to come get it . . . come here to the house."

Anna Huey is silent, and Juliet can hear a clock ticking in the background. The Beauvais grandfather clock in the parlor. *Her* clock, goddammit.

"Your poor mama," Anna Huey says. "She's upstairs now, crying her precious eyeballs out."

Juliet makes a sound that could be another laugh. "She should be in her room crying. The guilt alone must be awful." She waits a few seconds, then adds, "Mother killed him, after all."

It feels good to have said it finally, even if it is just the maid on the other end. Juliet has wanted to say those words ever since the truth about her father's demise popped in her head as she was working on "The Proof" during the flight in.

"Juliet, you can come get your money whenever you're ready to sit and act like a normal person. Your mother has something to talk to you about. Until you can do that, let me advise you to keep the lid closed on your sick, deranged mind. Do you understand what I'm saying?"

"Hey, look, first of all you're a maid—"

But Anna Huey has already terminated the connection.

Juliet walks out on the balcony and stands leaning against the railing with the bustle and roar of the Vieux Carré below. She hates that piss-and-wiener smell, hates the tap-tap noise of the dancing boys, hates the neon burning at all hours. They can romanticize New Orleans all they want but in her mind it will always be a lousy excuse for pretty.

"You're a maid!" she yells down to the crowd on Bourbon Street.

A clutch of tourists looks up, squinting for the sun.

"A maid!" she says again, then stalks back inside.

Juliet soaks in the tub without using soap or a washcloth. She enjoys the water's powerful healing effects. In fact, its powerful healing effects almost put her to sleep. When the water grows tepid she drains some then adds more hot. She lights a joint and it isn't long before a memory of her father's death, invented now for her viewing pleasure, plays out in her mind in the blurry Technicolor tones of a 1970s caper flick. Her mother with her precious crying eyeballs has perpetrated the crime of the century!

Now comes another memory, to counterbalance the previous one. Whether it's real or imagined Juliet can't decide, but clearly she sees her father at home in the library, standing before the fireplace with his hands in the pockets of a pale linen suit. His shirt is open at the collar, and tasseled loafers cover his small, bare feet. Her father bears a strong physical resemblance to the young Cary Grant ("Yes, they're both men," Miss Marcelle said when Juliet told her this). And her father talks like the actor. "Darling," he says, "you seem so sad today. Is something wrong?"

"No. Well, yes, Daddy. It's Leonard Barbier. They were saying things at school, some girls were."

"Leonard's a fine young man from a fine old New Orleans family. Can't your father have friends?" Then before she can answer: "Now what else is troubling you? If there's a first thing there's bound to be a second."

She can't bring herself to say it. She sits staring at her hands.

"Oh, you," pleads her father. "I'm your *daddy*."

Juliet gets out of the tub and towels off and walks naked into the room. She lies in bed sucking hard on what remains of the doob, wet hair fanned out on the spread. Wouldn't her father just die to know a colored woman is answering his phone, handling his money, condescending to an actual Beauvais?

"Juliet, I'm here for you, sweetheart."

"Daddy, I heard what Mama told you when you got home last night."

"Your mother says a lot of things, especially when I've been out in the Quarter. We know that by now, don't we?"

It hurts too much to look at him. And in his presence she is unable to repeat her mother's words.

51

"I'm sorry you had to hear those things. None is true, of course. Will you let them go, darling?"

"I can't, Daddy. I try to but I can't."

He leaves the room and when he returns he is holding a small shaving mirror. "Come with me," and he signals for her to rise. He takes her by the hand and leads her through pocket doors and halfway up the mahogany stairway crowded with family portraits. "I have something to show you," he says. "It's something my father showed me when I was a boy. One day when you're older and have a child of your own I'm sure you'll want to continue the tradition." He points to a face in one of the portraits. "Have a good look at your great-grandfather there," he says. "Now have a look at yourself."

As he holds the mirror she studies her features: the chapped and peeling lips, eyes swollen from crying. "His name was Etienne Beauvais," her father says.

Somehow she manages a laugh.

"They're your eyes, aren't they? They're not your mother's eyes. Now look at that painting farther up the stairs. That's Etienne's father, Jean-Jacques. Notice the mouth?"

Juliet brings a hand to her lips and touches them with her fingertips.

"Now where have I seen that mouth before? Oh," and her father places the mirror closer to her face, "here we are. My heavens, you have that man's mouth. Where did you get that man's mouth?"

"I stole it."

"You stole it!"

They embrace and Juliet laughs and cries both at once as her father holds her head against his chest and traces a hand through her hair. He smells so much like himself, so uniquely like himself, that she feels strengthened and renewed simply by her proximity to this smell. "She was just being mean, wasn't she?"

"Right," he answers. "Just being mean. But I suppose she can't help it. Consider her limited experience and education. If I came from a yam farm in an outpost as spare and bucolic as Opelousas I suppose I would be intimidated, too. I'm not so easy to live with either, you know?"

"You're great," Juliet says.

"You're the last of us, darling. Promise your daddy there'll be more. Sons and daughters. There aren't any portraits on the other side of this stairway. You've noticed that, I'm sure?"

"I love you, Daddy," Juliet says. And now in the hotel bathroom she is startled to hear a voice, and doubly so to discover that it is her own.

Juliet is standing at the mirror, her face inches from the surface. The mirror, still damp with steam, reflects an image only vaguely similar to the one she saw earlier in her father's glass.

At this moment Etienne and Jean-Jacques Beauvais are not visible in her features, and neither, come to think of it, is Johnny Beauvais. Juliet hates to contradict the man she loves most in the world but her mouth today is just a mouth. And the same goes for her eyes. Everybody has them. Now as she looks more closely the reflection excites in her a sudden feeling of horror, for it is her mother who is staring back, her face gripped with the same contempt she once held for Johnny Beauvais.

Juliet lets out a yell and flees the room, stumbles into the hallway. Where did they put the goddamned elevator? There are more yells as she propels herself down the hall to the nearest stairway exit.

"Yes, I was hoping somebody might help me find my friend Leonard Barbier," Juliet says to the concierge in the lobby.

"Miss Beauvais, you're down here in a robe."

"He's a musician. Leonard Barbier?"

"Leonard Barbier," the man says, as if by repeating the name she'll be mollified.

"Yes, that's the one. He plays saxophone in a jazz band. Or used to, anyway."

"Miss Beauvais? Miss Beauvais, you should go back to your room and put some clothes on."

"Big 'fro, gold in his teeth, chains."

Only now does it occur to Juliet that the concierge himself is black.

"Leonard Barbier," he says again. "Let me make a few calls and see if I can't locate him. But please, Miss Beauvais, go back to your room."

Twenty minutes later the phone rings. "Good news," the concierge begins, then tells her that after some determined sleuthing he was able to locate her friend Leonard. "His band performs three nights a week at a club in the Marigny," the man says, referring to Faubourg Marigny, the neighborhood on the downriver side of Esplanade Avenue from the Vieux Carré.

The concierge says he took the liberty of calling the club himself and, this is wonderful, the woman on the other end gave him Leonard's address. It's a place, a weekly/monthly, down on North Rampart Street.

Juliet couldn't be less interested in the man's detective work, but she lets the militant bastard have his say. He probably thinks the more he talks the more she'll be obliged to tip him.

"So I call and speak to Mr. Barbier," the man says.

"You talked to Leonard?"

"As it happened, I caught him as he was walking out the door. I told him to expect an old friend at his show tonight. He kept asking for a name, he seemed excited, but I wouldn't tell him."

"Tell me where he lives, and what was that club again?"

The man provides names and addresses. She writes them down.

"Are we done yet?" Juliet says when the concierge seems to have stopped.

Silence at last. She can hardly believe it.

ϟϟϟ

Daylight fades, the last of it gold on the buildings of the French Quarter. The old streets teem with pedestrians heading to nightclubs and to supper. In the windows of the oyster bars shuckers in black rubber gloves pry shells open and lay them twelve to a serving on platters covered with shaved ice. In the strip joints women dance on lighted platforms, their soft bellies scarred from cesarians and appendectomies, their beauty lost to all but the sailors in from sea and the fraternity boys on holiday. Here and there a preacher waves a book. Here and there a transvestite tries gamely to navigate in heels.

Sonny sits by the fence facing the square, the park in front of him closed and padlocked for the night. In front of the cathedral a lone futurist flips tarot cards and mutters at the horror of things to come. From the Presbytere come the haunting riffs of a clarinet. Sonny watches the wind stir the oaks and magnolias. Past the boughs he can see a faint sprinkling of stars.

Whenever a fellow painter dies, Roberts told him once, those who survive him plant a tree in Jackson Square as a living memorial. The square is crowded with trees, Roberts said, and this is proof that nobody, not even someone as important as an artist, leaves this earth alive.

"See that beautiful crape myrtle? Why, that's Clarence Millet. The banana tree next to it? Miss Alberta Kinsey."

Sonny always liked that story. Tonight it makes him feel a part of something, not just a solitary sort with no one but an Alzheimer's patient for a father and a mentally unstable waiter for a friend.

Feet planted on the fence, he tilts slightly backward in his chair and studies the blue forms of the trees, the oleander and camphor and mimosa, wondering which of them belong to the memories of dead artists. Surely these people suffered rejection, too. Surely they gave blue eyes to Japanese women, and white-blond hair when the color called for was black.

"The live oak there, the big one, that's Drysdale," Roberts said. "Who else, Sonny, but Drysdale? He painted so many, some ten thousand in his lifetime, we all just knew he'd come back as one."

Sonny has yet to witness the ceremony where artists turn out to plant a sapling, and now that he considers them none of the trees looks to be very young. Maybe Roberts's story is something he made up to help make Sonny feel better. Maybe the truth is nobody really cares about artists anymore.

Forget the trees, Sonny says to himself.

From his chair he watches through the windows of the bakery as chefs empty display cases of breads and pastries. It is a picture he thinks he should make one day. The brown loaves, the fruit tarts, the men in stovepipe hats, the women in hairnets. It will be yet another record of the time when Sonny LaMott was alive, and that alone is reason enough to paint it.

I like you, Sonny, Sonny tells himself. I like you even when you're leading your own cheers.

♔

"Where y'at, my brother," Juliet says as Leonard Barbier (or the one the bartender identified as Leonard Barbier) comes bounding off the stage and joins her between sets.

"Juliet? Good God, Juliet, is that you, baby?"

She stands and gives him the right side of her face to kiss, and his mouth sounds fat and wet smacking against her ear. "You look nice, Leonard."

"Yeah, well, thanks. You too, sweetie. You too."

Leonard has lost his big bowl of hair and slim physique, but it's clear

55

he's still holding fast to his program of self-improvement. Though born to local aristocracy, Leonard never wanted to be an Uptown blueblood, nor for that matter did he want to be white. "I realize we all have to be something," he once said to Juliet, "but why did I have to be so *pasty?*" As a teenager he rejected all invitations to Carnival balls and debutante parties and instead hung out in the blues clubs of the Seventh Ward where the only other white patrons were occasional air-conditioning repairmen on emergency call. Under his school uniform Leonard was known to wear bikini briefs with red, green and black stripes, the colors of the African nation. Even his diet was black. If a menu failed to offer fried chicken, black-eyed peas and collard greens, Leonard wasn't likely to frequent the restaurant. "Racism sometimes comes disguised as nouvelle cuisine," was how he saw it. Juliet always said he was the best black friend she ever had. Careful not to rile him, she knew better than to admit he was the only one.

"Hey, Leonard, let me ask you something."

"What you got?" *Wha-choo-gah?*

"You ever run into Sonny?"

"Sonny?"

"Sonny LaMott."

On the table, compliments of the house, a glass of whiskey materializes. Leonard takes a swallow and licks his mouth.

"You see Sonny, right? You see him around."

"Well, yeah. Everybody sees Sonny around. Is that why you're here, to ask me about Sonny LaMott?" Leonard laughs and whiskey leaks from the side of his mouth. "Sonny's got himself a cart at Jackson Square—'Sonny LaMott,' it says, 'world-famous artist,' or some shit like that. But let me let you in on a secret. Sonny LaMott is world famous in no world but his own."

Juliet smiles at her friend, her ridiculous friend.

"I used to see him behind the counter at the Bayou Bar at the Pontchartrain Hotel," Leonard says. "He waited on me a few times. He had on his red coat, his black pants, his black bow tie, his shirt with all them ruffles in front. He looked like an ass. Now when you see him he's wearing a little beret and dirty clothes and jackboots colored from where he dripped paint. He could be one of them beatniks you drive by waving a thumb on the side of the road."

Juliet feigns disinterest, her expression suggesting a particular attitude: *Like who got the nappy-headed motherfucker started on Sonny LaMott?* "Can you keep a secret?" she says.

"Me?" As if that is answer enough.

"My mother's being investigated for the death of my father. I thought you should know, since you and him were so close."

Leonard nods. He seems uncertain what else to do. "I appreciate you letting me in on that. I was very fond of your father. I had what they call a deep, abiding affection for the man. And I admit I always found his death suspicious. He was an interesting person, always in his white suits and all. A little conflicted in certain areas but not the type who would go jump off a boat and drown hisself."

"My plan is to call a press conference and make a statement when the task force completes its investigation and local authorities get their indictment."

"God, they're going to indict her, too? Jesus." He shakes his head. Sips again. "What do you mean by that, Juliet? What do you mean they're going to indict her?"

"They're going to officially charge her with first-degree murder. She's going to face a trial and she's going to go to jail and the dyke guards there are going to rape her ass."

"Wow."

"Ever have an epiphany, Leonard? I had one the other day when I was on the plane flying in. I saw how Mother did it. My eyes were open, I was looking straight ahead, but instead of seeing stewardesses and passengers I saw my mother killing my father."

"Okay."

"This is how she did it. They were sailing on Lake Pontchartrain and she got him in the water somehow and she beat him over the head with an oar."

Juliet seems to have lost him somewhere along the way. "Tell me that word again."

"Oar?"

"No, that *epipha* word, however you called it."

Juliet buys him another drink, and when he returns to the stage she has the waitress bring him a few more. The band might rank as the all-time worst she's ever heard. To start, the singer is unable to remember most of the lyrics and subsequently she hums a lot. Juliet finds it funny at first, then tedious beyond measure. Between sets, she decides to get to the point with Leonard.

"While we're on the subject of epiphanies," she says, "I thought I'd mention the one I just had."

"You had another one?"

"You were up there playing, and I closed my eyes and I saw somebody, Leonard, I saw him hitting my mother with an oar."

"You saw somebody hit your mother? Why would they do that?"

Juliet leans closer until their mouths are almost touching. "They did it because, like me, they wanted what is right. They did it to avenge what she did to your friend, Leonard, and to my father. They did it because the indictment and jail and bull dykes aren't enough. Why else would they do it?"

Leonard takes on a puzzled expression, his face squeezing into a fist. Juliet understands that she's lost him. "I better get back on stage," he says.

"Epiphanies," she says again.

"I'll have to remember that," Leonard replies. "But you better make it something different than an oar. I don't swim, for one. You won't never catch me in no boat."

❦

Sonny nods off after a time. It isn't a deep sleep because he can hear things: the mournful clarinet, pigeons murmuring in the eaves of the Pontalba Building, transit buses on Decatur.

He also hears footsteps on the flagstones, coming toward him.

The beat of the steps mesmerizes, and eventually Sonny hears nothing else. Slightly in advance of the steps comes a smell, and the smell is familiar. Maybe he's dreaming. Sonny hopes he's dreaming. But at last a voice fills the darkness.

"This old plantation house I know," she says. "Come to think of it, I grew up there."

For half a minute Sonny doesn't move.

"You forgot to put the dead guy in the window, the one hanging from the rope? That's my only criticism."

He sits up and opens his eyes and there she stands. She's studying his painting of the Beauvais with a hand delicately placed against her chin, in the thoughtful manner of a seasoned art observer. She's wearing a short skirt and a pair of blocky shoes that look big on her feet. Her peekaboo hair catches the moonlight and shines a new bottled yellow, pretty if you go for that.

Sonny lifts himself out of the chair. He can feel his heart hammering in his chest, and the sudden swelling of the veins in his neck, and a hollow ache down deep in his gut.

"Well if it ain't Juliet Beauvais," he says.

She curtsies and holds a hand out, which he accepts with too limp a shake.

"Sonny," she says, edging closer, "I was afraid you'd gone and forgotten me after all these years, especially now that you're world famous and all."

The line sounds rehearsed, and it's poorly delivered. But Sonny forgives her that when she comes to her toes and presses her mouth flush against his. He doesn't want to respond, doesn't want to like it. But that was always his problem when it came to Juliet. It never really mattered what he wanted.

## 2

THEY WALK TO DECATUR STREET AND
sit at a table in the fan-blown shade of Café du
Monde. Juliet orders beignets and café au lait and
Sonny a black coffee.

Sonny can't seem to make himself speak. A
fist has seized his larynx and holds it tight. His
brain has gone to mush.

The silence, at first uncomfortable, quickly
gains a more complex dimension, that of suffocating embarrassment.

"This is hard," she tells him.

"You're right."

"Harder than I ever dreamed it would be."

"Yeah? For me too."

Unable to bear looking at her any longer,
Sonny seeks comfort in the familiarity of their
surroundings: the old neon sign at Tujague's
Restaurant, a fire-eater on the sidewalk, sight-

seeing mules wearing straw hats crowned with plastic flowers. Lifting a hand, he attracts the attention of a busboy. "Ice water, please."

"You gonna be all right?" asks Juliet.

"I guess I'm hot."

He wishes he were still at the fence, alone in the dark, watching the trees blow in the sky. It's too hard loving anyone. Too hard having to look at them again.

"You know what just came to me?" Juliet says. "Give us each a puka shell necklace and put us in platform shoes and polyester and it'd be like old times."

"Was that 1971? I thought those things came later."

She inhales cigarette smoke, then noisily blows it out. "Yeah, maybe you're right."

Their order arrives and Juliet folds one of the beignets and dunks it in the coffee and eats with her head tilted close to the marble-top table, her hair dragging the surface and picking up traces of confectioners' sugar. "I'd nearly forgotten," she says with a satisfied groan.

"Not bad, huh?"

She holds up the beignet, what remains of it. "This little piece of fried dough is the most incredible thing I've ever put in my mouth."

Against his will a smile comes to Sonny's face. He knows exactly what she's getting at. "I can place another order," he says.

Juliet shakes her head, her mouth still white with sugar, cheeks fat and lumpy. "No. I'd better save room for the oysters."

"Oh? Are you having oysters too?"

"We both are," she says. "Oysters at Acme then a Lucky Dog on Bourbon Street then hurricanes in the courtyard at Pat O'Brien's. After that we'll stop by the little Takee Outee stand for egg rolls and beef-on-a-stick."

"I'm not sure the Takee Outee is even there anymore, Julie. You might want to consider something else."

"Fine. Then I'll just have you."

A surge of heat inflames Sonny's face. He resists an urge to jump to his feet and topple the table over and storm away. "You're being a little presumptuous, aren't you? Forgive me for bringing up anything unpleasant, Julie, but you must take me for a fool. I saw one of your movies. Is that what you call them, by the way? Are they movies?"

Juliet puts the half-eaten beignet back down on her plate. "You're going to hurt my feelings, aren't you? Yes, I think you are."

"You've got some explaining to do, Julie. You can't just waltz back home and pick me up for beignets and not expect to answer questions about where you've been for the last fifteen years."

"There's a picture in my head, Sonny. A picture of Mama sticking a cassette in the VCR, returning to her chair and punching the Play button on her remote control. Does that explain it?"

Sonny stares into her eyes but he can't tell whether she means it. "That's pretty damned sick. I hope to God you're not serious."

She wets the tip of her finger and dunks it in the drifts of sugar on her plate. When she brings the finger up to her mouth it leaves a mark on her upper lip. "There weren't but a handful of movies," she says, "all of them for the same production company. It was such a bush-league outfit I never really thought anyone would see them. Before agreeing to appear on camera, I signed a contract saying that I work with one actor only, and that was my boyfriend—now my ex-boyfriend, of course." Juliet nods to emphasize how important this is. How Sonny should pay attention. "Believe it or not, I did it because I wanted to eat, and because I had rent to pay, and because I was stupid. It was the worst mistake I ever made in all my life. I don't think you'd want to be judged by every mistake you made in the past. The difference between your mistakes and my mistakes is that mine are on videotape. It was a long time ago anyway. I can't believe we're talking about it now."

Sonny can feel himself cooling off. And it seems he's breathing better. He can hold her eyes with his eyes without much effort. "Exactly how long ago was it?" he says.

"Oh, a year, year and a half." From the way she sounds it could be a lifetime.

※

They finish and walk parallel with the river on Decatur, passing cafés and souvenir and praline shops, squeezing past tourists who, mesmerized by competing jazz combos stationed every few hundred feet, crowd the sidewalks and make the going slow.

In time they come to the French Market, an area that Juliet has always identified with home even though it now seems less designed to serve the shopping needs of neighborhood residents than to satisfy the whims of tourists looking for an authentic Creole experience. At this hour the place is nearly deserted, as most of the vendors have gone home for the evening. Juliet stops to observe garlands of garlic hanging from the rafters, too far to reach, and no doubt placed there to ward off evil spirits. On the tables balsa-wood crates for produce stand empty.

Where, she wonders, are the salesmen in porkpie hats popping open paper bags and dickering loudly over prices with customers? Where are the ancient French Quarter dowagers determined to cook fresh or not at all?

Juliet pouts to show her disappointment.

"If ever I lose my Beauvais family legacy this is where I hope to end up," she says. "Selling okra and acorn squash and lima beans and homemade fig preserves."

"Remember years ago how crazy the market used to get every spring when the first batch of Creole tomatoes came in from Plaquemines Parish? I remember the fistfights, people practically killing each other to get to them."

"Yes," she says. "And that's how they'll be for my squash and okra."

As they stroll from one end of the cool, dark pavilion to the other, Juliet describes how it felt to be in the Beauvais earlier today, to see the rooms and smell the smells. All the same old ghosts were hiding in the shadows, and she wonders if Sonny noticed them on his visits there. Her father and her father's father. The father of her father's father. They whispered to her when she went upstairs to her bedroom. They begged her to return and bring the house back to its former glory. Put simply, they didn't want a Lavergne and a cleaning woman living among them any longer.

"You're joking, right?"

She shakes her head.

"You'd think ghosts would have better things to do than haunt a house," Sonny says. "And then to concern themselves with nice people like your mother and Anna Huey. . . ."

"Maybe they know something you don't."

"Think so? Like what?"

"I could give you a list, Sonny. Show you the proof. Would that help?" Before he can answer she says, "My feet are tired. Listen, why don't we go back to my room and lie down."

They start on their way again, silent now as they head uptown. Juliet takes his hand in hers and studies each of his fingers. Blips of oil paint stain the skin and his nails are cracked and dirty, palms padded with calluses.

"I was going to be a writer," she says. "Remember that?"

"You were always scribbling something."

"And you were going to illustrate the dust jackets for my books."

"That was a long time ago, Julie."

She brings his fingertips to her mouth and presses them against her lips. "Only half a lifetime," she says, a wash of tears coming to her eyes.

They enter the hotel at Bourbon Street and cross the lobby and Juliet feels a bump of fear anticipating another visit from management. To her relief, however, the coast is clear but for the usual guests studying maps and arguing about which is the greater priority, taking a cemetery tour or a riverboat cruise. Juliet and Sonny board an elevator and she turns to face his reflection in the great brass doors. "I never stopped thinking about you," she says. "Some nights I'd wake up and want to call and ask you to come get me and take me home but I never could. I was too ashamed." She looks away from the doors and he is staring at her. She reaches for his hand again. "I'm not asking you to forgive me. That would be wrong. You should never forgive what I've done."

"I do anyway, Julie."

"You can't."

"Yes, I can. And I do. I forgive you, Julie."

She begins to cry and Sonny offers a handkerchief from his pocket, as colorful with paint stains as the rest of him.

What feels like terror grips him the moment they enter the room. Hoping to shake it off, Sonny walks out on the balcony and takes in the sights from the street below. When that doesn't settle him, he goes back inside and turns on the TV and flips through the channels. In the bathroom he flushes the toilet and tests a blanket of facial tissue. To complete his inspection, he holds the phone to his ear and listens for a dial tone, then he punches the keypad for the front desk. "Just checking," he says when a voice answers.

He puts the phone down. "Everything seems to be in working order," he says to Juliet.

"You forgot my Bible," she says, pointing to the dresser. "Don't you want to check and see if they got all the words spelled right?"

Sonny opens a drawer and finds the Gideon's. "Looks good to me," he says, riffling pages.

Juliet is leaning against the wall, arms crossed at her chest. She seems to be trying to make sense of something. "Sonny, you're scared of me."

"I'm not scared."

"You're scared, Sonny."

He sits on the edge of the bed and lowers his face into his hands. "Yeah," he says. "I guess I am."

Sonny is praying now, the words loud in his head: "Lord, send somebody up that elevator to save me. Send me a disaster to fix. A Louis run over in the street. The murder of a cat to avenge. Lord, send somebody. Send something." Then it comes to him: if not the voice of God, an inspired answer, a way out. "My cart!" he says. "Jesus, Julie, I left my cart down at the square! I forgot all about it. Listen, this is bad. I mean, the few artists that are still working this late—my friends—they'll watch it for as long as they're down there, but I really do need to lock it away for the night. Before everybody goes home."

Juliet nods and rests the back of her head against the wall. "Sonny, I'm coming over there. Want me or not, I'm coming, do you hear?" And this is what she does. She comes over and crowds the narrow space between his legs.

"Go get your cart, if that's what you need to do."

She places her hands on his shoulders and Sonny feels his face moving to find her, feels it pressing against the warmth of her belly.

She grabs her skirt and hikes it up, and his hands trail after the fabric, climbing from the backs of her thighs. She holds the skirt at her waist and leans her head forward looking down at her pubic hair waxed to a narrow strip. "Do you remember me without panties?"

He doesn't answer and she says, "I wasn't like this then, all shaved down there."

"It was still you."

"I'm halfway ashamed to think how I was. The world has changed so much. The world didn't even have VCRs back then. Can you believe that? It's 1986, Sonny. Can you believe we're thirty-two years old? Why, when I was a girl at Sacred Heart thirty-two was ancient. It's how old old people were. And now it's young, it's almost babyfied to me."

"When it comes to age we're all going in the same direction together, Julie. Everybody is."

"Speaking of babies, our little boy would be fourteen years old now, a teenager."

Juliet can feel his shoulders tense in her hands. He jerks his head back.

"I'm certain it was a boy. I knew instinctively. We were going to have a son."

"Do we really have to talk about that now, Julie?"

He presses his face against her again and takes her in his mouth and when he looks up she's still watching with the skirt in her hands. "Tell me you love me, Sonny LaMott." He is silent and she says, "Tell me. Tell me you love me."

"I love you," he says.

"Tell me again."

"I love you."

"Again."

"I love you."

A minute passes and she steps back and starts pulling at his clothes and it seems a long time before he can get out of his pants. She looks at him and her face brightens with mock surprise. "Oh, Sonny. Oh, no. Not with that big thing you're not."

They come together and together make their noise and they could be seventeen again with the levee beneath them and the sky bright with stars. When it's over, Sonny begins to weep and Juliet holds him tight in her arms and rocks him and tries to console him. "Oysters," she says. "Big and juicy plump ones. Oysters so cold and briny they make your teeth hurt. Then a Lucky Dog and then hurricanes in the courtyard at Pat O's with the fountain shooting flames and someone asking if you want your picture made and the palm fronds rattling and the waiters in green jackets doing their tragic massuh routine thinking you'll tip them better."

"Yes," Sonny says. "All that."

Sonny pushes the cart to Chartres Street and the parking garage at the rear entrance of the Royal Orleans Hotel where he rents a space in a thicket of VIP slots on the ground floor. Juliet follows a few steps behind as he moves along the crowded streets, guiding the cart through cars stuck in traffic, bumping people who stand in the way. "Coming through," he calls. "Make way! Artist coming through!" She enjoys watching him. The effort brings a dark expression to his face and his arms tighten with knots and sinew.

Even in the old days Juliet wished she were as humble as he, and not so easily bored and distracted, not so hungry to consume all that she could of life, the good and the bad. She recalls a night when Sonny invited her over for dinner at his parents' house. By force of will alone she had kept from barking out an appreciative laugh in the middle of the meal, so tickled was she by the simple, thoughtful beauty of the affair. Mrs. LaMott was a large person who dressed as if for church, and whose many chins jiggled even when she was sitting still. Her appearance was almost as folksy as that of Juliet's mom, and yet her generosity was beyond compare. Sonny's father, likewise, was quick to please; in particular Juliet was moved by his eagerness to share his knowledge of the purple martin, a type of bird she'd never heard of until that night. "They're great fliers," she remembers him saying. "Sometimes they almost seem to be performing, like at an air show. Also, they eat bugs." Mr. LaMott, wearing an autumn jacket in a house cooled by wheezing air-conditioning units, sweated so much that stains bloomed on his shirtfront even as Juliet watched. The LaMotts were nothing like Dickie Boudreau's parents, who employed their own cook, and who talked about the meaning behind the massive abstract expressionist art on their walls with such passion and intelligence that it left Juliet feeling slightly intoxicated. But their sweetness—the same sweetness that first attracted her to Sonny, and that provides a burp of pleasure now as he muscles his cart down the street—made up for their lack of sophistication. "What do you think?" she recalls Sonny asking her at evening's end. In response she leaned over and kissed him, knowing that to answer candidly meant admitting that what she liked best about them was how perfectly they fit her image of the Bywater working class.

"You're a manly damn man, Sonny LaMott," Juliet yells to him now.

"You'd be too if you had to do this every day twice a day."

"It's a miracle you don't get hit by passing traffic."

"Or beat up. People don't seem to appreciate being run over by me and my cart."

They leave the garage and visit the places and do the things she listed in the room, then they occupy a bench on the Moonwalk overlooking the river and watch the brightly lighted boats passing by, the party rigs and the paddlewheelers. They kiss as tourists tramp past them on the wooden boards, and she touches him and his warm, beautiful hardness climbs all the way over to the knot of change in his pocket and beats in time with the beating of his heart. In the moonlight the leaves of the birches flash silver and the water moves and from behind them comes the musical clopping of buggies on the old black streets, the mules snuffling, drivers barking.

"Can we do it here one night?" she says.

"We can do it wherever you want."

"On this bench?"

"Here," he says, placing a hand on the spot.

They return to the room and Sonny performs with less fear and anxiety than before and without the crying jag. The curtains are open and so is the door leading to the balcony. From the street she hears police sirens competing with the wolf calls of drunkards. Juliet has always enjoyed sex in hotel rooms. "Which one tonight?" Dickie Boudreau used to say, flashing a credit card.

Juliet sits up in bed and looks at the restaurant across the way and the diners at the windows along the street.

"Sweetie, do me from the back," she says to Sonny.

She rests on her knees and leans forward with her chest and chin resting on a pillow. Her rear is sticking up. Sonny, slow to respond, stands behind her and rests his hands on her hips. "Actually," she says, reaching back and showing him the place, "I meant the other back."

Half a minute goes by and he doesn't do anything. "I've never done this before," he says.

"Neither have I."

"Are you sure about this?"

"Just do it, Sonny. Let's see what happens."

At first the pressure is great and it seems she will tear in half but after he finds a rhythm she starts to relax and he probes deeper. She keeps her face turned toward Houlihan's and the noises she makes are different from the ones she was making just a few minutes before. "Look, Sonny," she whispers, then points outside.

He glances over at the street and the restaurant where a woman, huge and frowning, sits with a fork poised at her mouth. The fork is coiled with spaghetti, and the woman's mouth is open wide to accept it. Her eyes, however, are trained on them; she seems shocked into paralysis.

When Sonny begins to withdraw, Juliet reaches back and slaps him on the leg.

*"Whuh . . . ?"*

"Come on, goddammit. Finish."

Juliet rests her face on the bed and clutches the sheets and slowly rocks against him. It feels better with the audience down below and Juliet's cries grow louder and she curses and praises him, both at once, all the while waiting for a knock on the door, a voice ordering them to stop.

"We'll get arrested," Sonny says.

"Everything . . . Give it to me . . . *Yes!*"

"The cops'll come. They'll come, Julie!"

"It's New Orleans, Sonny. *New Orleans!* Come on, baby. It's what you do! *It's . . . what . . . you . . . do. . . .*" She slaps him on the leg again.

Even after Sonny finishes and falls over on the bed Juliet stays as she is, pleasuring herself with one hand and teasing her nipples with the other. "I like it when people watch," she says. "I think it makes me come harder."

Sonny pulls a sheet off the bed and wraps it around his middle.

"You aren't embarrassed, are you?"

"To be honest I don't know what I feel."

"God, Sonny, you're so beautiful, you're so perfect. If I had a cock like yours I'd want everyone to see it. Know what else I'd do?" He doesn't answer and she says, "I'd play with it all the time."

Juliet props herself on an elbow and looks out at the restaurant. There are fewer diners at the windows than before, but those who remain are real troupers. Every last one is watching.

A man raises a hand and Juliet waves back.

"I think we've just given new meaning to the term *dinner theater,*" she says.

Minutes later someone arrives at the door and raps the knocker and shouts to be let in. Sonny wrestles the sheet closer, but Juliet can't seem to find anything to cover herself with. She considers getting dressed, but whoever is in the hall seems eager.

Naked, she pulls the door open.

"You can kick us out," she says to the befuddled figure in the hallway, "but I'll need a refund in cash for both tonight and last night. If you can't do that, I'm afraid I'll have to sue."

"It'll be at the registration desk," comes the reply. "You've got half an hour." The man raises a finger as if to wag it, but something in Juliet's expression stops him.

While Sonny is in the bathroom, Juliet sits naked on the balcony and adds to "The Proof."

*"The birds and the bees were different from how you said, Mama. They were better. Me, I love to fuck even when it hurts."*

✙✙✙

Sonny lives in the same house where he grew up, a two-story double owing in appearance to no single architectural period but rather to that amorphous claptrap style that once existed in his father's brain. Mr. LaMott built the house himself when he returned from Korea, and budget constraints forced him to exclude all extravagances except for screened-in porches, a stone barbecue, and the carport that Hurricane Betsy flattened in 1965.

The other side of the building, originally conceived as a source of easy income, for thirty years has housed one alcoholic malcontent after another, the latest a wife beater with a habit of urinating on the banana plants from his second-floor bedroom window.

Chartres Street and the levee are all that stand between the house and the Mississippi River, an uncomfortable intimacy for many Bywater residents, but for Sonny one that informed his childhood with dreams of floating away on a raft and never returning. After years of living in cheap Uptown efficiencies he moved back to the house when his mother died and his father volunteered to check into a nursing home, and he plans to remain only as long as he has to. That is to say, only until he can attract buyers for his paintings or until he finds a girlfriend/wife with better digs—prospects that appeared unlikely until a few hours ago.

As much as Sonny likes the prospect of being alone with Juliet, he is uncertain about letting her stay over. Not that the house has changed much since she last saw it, but he still can't get past the fact that she grew up in one of the city's most important homes and, as he explains now, "this is more a glorified camp than anything."

She's parked her rental car on the street, and this is another concern. In New Orleans, and in this neighborhood in particular, the incidences of auto theft are so many that off-street parking often seems the very key to happiness. If his house isn't embarrassment enough, how about having her car ripped off fewer than a hundred feet from his front door?

"I hope you don't mind roughing it," Sonny says, leading her up an outdoor stairway to the entrance on the second floor.

She shakes her head. "I just want to be with you, I don't care where."

It's well past midnight and Sonny needs sleep. He totes Juliet's bag into the living room and places it on the sofa, then he showers, brushes his teeth, rolls deodorant under his arms, sifts talcum powder on his groin and splashes cologne on his neck and chest. When he finishes, his body gives off a riot of scents that negates any possibility that she'll take him seriously, and this recognition brings him to wonder if he should just start over and shower again.

"Sad sack," he says to the image staring back at him in the lavatory mirror.

Sonny lies in bed under the covers wearing briefs and a T-shirt and he watches as Juliet strips naked and rubs lotion on her hands and legs and removes her makeup with cotton balls soaked in witch hazel. All these years apart and suddenly they're an old married couple, executing their routines in silence before calling it a night. "You make me happy," he says in a sleepy mumble. "You've always made me happy."

"You make me happy, too."

The last image he registers is that of Juliet dragging a brush through her hair, as she stands naked before the mirror on his closet door.

Toward dawn Sonny awakens to an empty bed and a river breeze from the window. A digital clock on the nightstand says 5:14 A.M., too early for him to get up, too late for her to still be awake. Across the room French doors leading to the porch are open a crack, allowing a tendril of smoke to drift in. Sonny shifts his weight to an elbow then reaches out and runs a hand over the other side of the bed. It's cool enough to suggest she hasn't been there for a while.

"Julie, what're you doing? Come back to bed."

He finds her on the porch sitting on a metal patio chair and gazing off at a sky stripped of stars and black with distant thunderheads. Her hair hangs in a yellow sheet and her skin radiates a color as weird and vivid as that of bones. Sonny recognizes the scent of marijuana smoke in the air, and this brings him stalking heavily across the wood floor.

"Julie, time for bed. Let's go back inside."

She is slow to respond, slow even to look at him. "Give me a minute. Let me finish this first."

"Finish later. Come on, baby."

"I'll finish when I goddamn want to finish. Jesus, Sonny." The remark is so dark and hostile, and so unexpected, that even she seems surprised by it. "Go back inside," she says. "I'll be there in a minute. I've got some things to sort out in my head."

He sits at the foot of the bed and watches through the open doors as she comes to her feet and takes another long drag before dunking the joint in a plastic cup. She's facing in the opposite direction now, out toward the city, and Sonny can see her breasts hanging full and thick by her rib cage, and down in the space between her legs an untamed tuft of hair illumined by a neighbor's security light. It is immortal, this picture, and he vows to paint it one day. The light and the hair and the girl and his heart madly beating in his chest.

He will not be able to show the heart without confusing the image, but if he gets Juliet right you will see the heart anyway.

When she comes back inside she elbows the door closed and everything is dark and quiet and he watches her, afraid to talk for the risk of upsetting her again.

He lies on his back with his head in the palms of his hands, his lean, well-muscled body dark against his underclothes.

"I wish it were true," Juliet says, standing at the foot of the bed. Her voice is as small and pitiful as a little girl's. "I wish all of it were true."

"You wish what was true?"

He waits but she gives no answer. Instead she crawls toward him on the bed, her breasts dragging across one leg and then the other as she weaves left and right. Sonny feels his breath go thin, then the burn when all the air seems to have left his lungs.

She pauses and lies flat against his cock and the dense, bound-up weight of her breasts momentarily pins him there. She settles beside him at last, and when he turns and presses his mouth against hers he tastes a salty wetness on her face.

Juliet lets out a sob and grabs him hard, digging her nails in his back. "What Anna Huey said to get me here," she says. "I wish it were true. I wish she'd just die, Sonny."

He doesn't respond but to pull her closer. He wonders if any words can help a misery as big as hers, and he wonders if any act short of seeing Miss Marcelle slipped in a tomb will mediate a peace in Juliet's mind. He's just a fence artist, and before that he tended bar. Who is he to fix anything?

"She killed him, Sonny. She killed my father."

"Your father drowned, Julie. He drowned in Lake Pontchartrain. We were dating at the time and I went with you to the funeral. For weeks after, it was the biggest story in all New Orleans. I clipped the stories out of the *Picayune.*"

"Sonny, I'd get everything if she died. I'm her only heir and that's the law in this state. Help me, Sonny. I'd get the house."

"I'm not sure I'm hearing you right, Julie. At least I hope I'm not hearing you right."

"We could live there. It would be ours and I'd never need to leave again. I'm just so tired of running when all along I know where I should be, and that's living on Esplanade. You don't want me to go away again, do you, Sonny?"

A long time passes and neither of them says anything and Sonny watches as daylight shows in the cracks of the curtains and colors the walls.

"Tell me how it is Miss Marcelle is supposed to have killed him."

"How? You mean the details how?"

"Yeah. How'd she do it?"

"You remember how Daddy's big thing was the yacht club? Sure, you remember. He kept his boat at the marina. Well, one day he and Mother were out on the lake. It was a Sunday afternoon and they were sailing and they were arguing like they always did. My father was having an affair, and I share this with you now because I want you to understand why she did it. He was involved with a much younger person, and he was in love, and when he told her as much she flew into a jealous rage and hit him with something, an oar probably. He fell overboard, into that horrible water, and when he tried to get back in she hit him again."

"With an oar?"

"I think that's what it was. I keep seeing one, anyway."

Sonny shakes his head. He knows this story. "You're talking about a movie. Julie, I saw that one. It had Elizabeth Taylor."

"I can't believe you'd bring Elizabeth Taylor into this conversation. And here I am trying to explain to you the most important thing in my entire life."

It also had Montgomery Clift and that horrible Winters woman, Shirley or Shelley, *Sh——* something. Nowadays it often aired on Sunday-morning TV between church programs and cooking shows. The name of the film escapes him, however.

"Let's look at it another way," Sonny says. "The New Orleans Police Department must not've thought Miss Marcelle killed him. She'd be counting the hours on death row in the state penitentiary for women right now."

Juliet gets out of bed and walks to the closet and stands watching him in the mirror. Knots the size of bottle caps throb in either side of her jaw and her eyes are narrow slits. It's just a reflection, but that doesn't make looking at her any easier.

"You know what?" she says. "Sometimes you piss me off you're so naïve. Sonny, the police in this city . . . anybody can buy the stupid police. You're such an innocent, you know that?"

"All right, I'm an innocent. But I still don't think your mother killed anyone, let alone your father. She's a lady, and a nice one."

"You little ninny. You little Ninth Ward ninny. When are you ever going to grow up?"

"Me grow up? Why don't you grow up? You're the one who ran off to California and showed what you're all about by making those *movies.*"

She wheels back around and faces him and her lips quiver and angry tears drain from her eyes. Why couldn't she have just come to bed like a normal person? Does a normal person smoke a joint at five in the morning then accuse her mother of murdering her father?

She starts putting on her clothes, fighting each article as if it were to blame. "When they found him in Bucktown Harbor—*God, you're dumb!* When they found him his head was all bashed in. You tell me, where are the rocks in Bucktown Harbor?"

"Juliet, you're crazy."

"There are no rocks, motherfucker. Maybe if they'd found him along Breakwater Drive, somewhere down by the Point, say, I could see it. You have a rocky shoreline there. But, Sonny, his body never came ashore. They had to fish him out. And with his skull like that."

Sonny is leaning against the headboard, his eyes lowered in concentration. "Maybe a boat hit him. Maybe something in the water got to him—I don't know, Julie, a lot can happen to a body out in that lake, especially a drowned one. And not only rocks."

She's got everything on but her shoes now. "Let me tell you one other thing before I go," she says. "And let me say it loud and clear. Dickie Boudreau puts you to shame."

"Dickie Boudreau? What does he have to do with anything?"

"Let me share something else with you, you goddamn creep—"

"Dickie's a happily married man. He's got a family and a home and his wife—let me share this with *you*. Dickie Boudreau's wife never made any movies having sex with her boyfriend. Dickie Boudreau's wife's got class. She goes to Mass, she goes to her kids' ball games. She doesn't need to perform in front of people in a restaurant just to get off—"

"How do you know what she needs or doesn't need to get off?"

"Oh, shut up. Just shut the fuck up."

"One more thing . . ." And now, tears wiped away, she seems perfectly calm; his violent response was what she was angling for. "When I was looking at your pictures on the fence last night? Well, my first impression was that you're an amateur. And I wonder why they even let you hang them there. I mean, there oughta be a law! That beautiful fence, and then all your weak shit cluttering it up. I'll be honest with you, Sonny, I've never seen an artist as lame as you. Not ever. Not in my whole, entire life."

"No?"

"More than no. More like *fuck* no. You're pathetic."

Juliet is no less kind to the screen door on her way out, nor to the stairs as she descends them.

He hears the door of her rental car slam shut, then her tires laying rubber, then the engine roaring as she puts a distance between herself and his shack in Bywater.

Every sound she makes has a concussive effect, but Sonny feels none of them as much as the silence when he stands at the window and looks toward the road and realizes she's gone.

❦

It isn't easy to find a legal parking spot near Leonard's weekly/monthly on North Rampart Street. Juliet navigates the blocks of the upper Vieux Carré a few times before stopping in a tow-away zone marked with metallic reflector stripes. She puts on the car's caution lights and locks the doors, then files past a clutch of winos lounging by the entrance.

The Garden District and the Barbier family estate are only a few miles away, and yet Leonard lives in the kind of fleabag where heroin-addicted jazzmen go to die. The hotel, if it really is one, is named for its street address, which this morning is nowhere to be found on the building's distressed façade. Hanging from the rafters of the second-floor gallery is a shingle, once white. "Rooms," it says, "with Stove-&-Ref. WEEKLY-Monthly."

Long considered an offbeat destination friendly to Bohemian types, the French Quarter today is home to scores of trust-fund babies who choose to slum it for a few years before resigning to their preordained lives of wealth and privilege. It isn't uncommon to find children of the country's most important families living there in pseudo-poverty, nor in other of the city's dangerous neighborhoods. But it is strange to find a local boy living in such a place. Local boys tend to travel elsewhere, far away from Mom and Dad and old school chums keen to their pose, to prove that being a millionaire at eighteen doesn't preclude them from being hip.

"Yoo hoo," Juliet calls as she enters the building.

Past the door rotting carpet of an indeterminable color leads to a tiny office where a man is dozing with his head on a desk. He seems more comatose than asleep, no doubt owing to the near-empty jug of vodka at his feet. She has to nudge him awake to get Leonard's room number.

"Leonard Barbier is a homosexual," he says, slapping a hand on the desk and producing a hollow bang.

"I ain't Leonard," Juliet replies.

He seems to be trying to determine if this indeed is a fact or mere speculation. "A homosexual," he says again, louder than before. "What would he want with a *girl?*"

"Shut up you old motherfucker and go back to sleep."

Leonard's room is on the second floor, the first to the right of the stairway. She knocks hard and calls his name, then adds after it seems he has taken too long, *"C'est moi."*

He pulls the door open muttering under his breath and rubbing the crusty rim of whiskers on his face. He is shirtless and in the greasy half-dark his large, erect nipples resemble plum tomatoes way past ready to be picked.

"Hey, sweetie, you want to go out for beignets at du Monde? My treat." She pushes past him and enters the room. "For some reason I got an envie for beignets."

"Can we eat later? I'm sleeping."

"Sure, Leonard. Sleep. Sleep all you want. Sleep so much you miss my whole, entire trip."

He shakes his head and looks down at his bare feet, white like the rest of him. "Listen, I been up at the club all night. I hope you understand."

"Yeah, sure. I understand. I understand you don't care about me worth a good goddamn, that's what I understand."

He is quiet. "Juliet, I'm sorry but I've got to get back to sleep."

"Look, I need a place to hide for a day or two. You don't mind if I crash here, do you?"

"Juliet, you're my friend and everything but one of the guys in the band just busted with his wife and he's staying over. We got only my one bed and it ain't even a queen."

She manufactures a look of unutterable disappointment, and Leonard, shaking his head, says, "Ah, shit. Come on, then. I don't mind the floor."

She can see somebody under the covers. A male white, as they call his kind. The male white's skin is so white that Juliet, even in the gloaming, can make out his tattoo: a single strand of barbed wire forming a loop around his upper right arm.

"I didn't know where else to go," she says, removing her clothes and letting them drop to the floor. "I can't afford a hotel. I can't stay with my mother."

"This the mother that killed Johnny Beauvais?" Leonard asks.

"No," she answers, rolling her eyes. "My other mother."

The male white is lying in a trough in the middle of the mattress, covered by a sheet with curious stains that may or may not be something to worry about. He looks like a little kid, Juliet thinks, too young to break with his first girlfriend let alone a wife.

She slips in beside him and brings her face up against his back. He smells like an old wet dog, but Juliet has always liked old wet dogs, even when they're as young and dry as this one. More than that, she finds his purple tattoo strangely beautiful against his pale skin, the pink bedding.

"I guess we all can fit in here," Leonard says with high optimism.

He climbs in on the other side and faces the opposite direction.

"What instrument does he play?" asks Juliet.

"Drums."

She thinks about this for a while. "He smells like a drummer, and a good one."

It isn't but a few minutes before all three of them are asleep, Juliet lost in a world of dreams that doesn't make a bit of sense, that never did.

*⁂*

It is late afternoon when Sonny leaves the Bywater. The night before he had only stale French bread and a can of beans to eat. Now he makes Tujague's his first stop.

He sits alone at a table by the street and orders a green salad, sliced garlic potatoes and an off-the-menu item called *bonne femme* chicken. He has a Crown-and-water and he reads the *Times-Picayune* in the splash of light falling through the picture window.

It is nice in the restaurant with the fans slowly rotating and the view of Decatur Street and Café du Monde where waiters on break cluster by the curb smoking cigarettes and watching tourists walk by. Most of the waiters are Vietnamese-Americans. They wear paper hats shaped like canoes and aprons splotched brown from coffee spills. Using his index finger, Sonny makes a sketch of the scene on the linen cloth covering his table. When he finishes, he signs his name, but instead of "Sonny" he writes it this way: "Cecil LaMott, Jr."

The world, if you can believe the newspaper, is going on as usual. Even in New Orleans people are robbing banks, surviving car crashes, getting married, delivering babies. They have exercise equipment and used furniture to sell. They are interested in what the weather is going to do.

The waiter brings the check and Sonny pays with cash, a sum large enough to cover a week's supply of groceries, but one he doesn't mind paying under the circumstances. He needs this: the white tablecloth, the fans, the smell of newsprint and roasted garlic. He needs the waiter clearing away the plates and raking up the crumbs and helping Sonny from his chair and saying what a pleasure it was to serve him.

Sonny, standing now, says to himself: *See there, big man? You did all that and you didn't think about her once.*

But, in praising himself for not thinking about her, of course Sonny has thought about her. And what he allows himself to recall now as he leaves Tujague's are those weeks immediately after her father died. They were a nightmare for Juliet, but Sonny remembers them as the most intimate they shared together. She seemed to surrender to him at last; her grief left her too weak to resist. The two of them sat up late when she needed to talk. And when she needed silence they took long drives in his father's truck with the windows rolled down and the radio dial dark. Their lovemaking, whether at their secret place by the river or at the Beauvais in the parlor after Miss Marcelle had gone to bed, gained an intensity and confidence that had not existed before. And always afterward there was the quiet sobbing, the hot tears against his chest. He was foolish enough to believe that he could absorb her pain simply by placing his body next to hers and holding her when the inevitable spasms came. "Don't leave me," she told him.

"I won't. I won't ever leave you."

His fate was sealed then. For after all it wasn't the sex that kept him. Nor had it been the house past the trees or the name in iron above the gate. What kept him was the feeling that his love was big enough, that he alone could save her. "Promise me," she said.

"I promise you. I promise you, Julie. I promise you."

It is almost dark now. Sonny walks to the parking garage and retrieves his cart and he pushes it along the street to the square and sets up across from a gift shop that has already closed for the day. He hangs

80

his pictures on the fence and he tries to ignore the stares of his colleagues along the row. But everyone seems to be looking at him, looking as if for an explanation.

"Where the hell have you been?" Roberts calls from a few spots away.

"Nowhere," Sonny answers. But then after a moment he says, "Everywhere."

Roberts has a customer, and in caricature her nose has become an alpine slope with snow skiers tumbling down, mouths open wide, equipment flying everywhere.

"How do you expect to sell paintings if they're locked away in a parking garage?" Roberts asks as he continues to work.

"Good point," Sonny says with a nod.

"Everybody's got to take care of business, even an artist."

"That's true," Sonny answers.

When half an hour passes and nobody comes for a portrait, Sonny walks over to Café du Monde and fills his Thermos with black coffee.

"Y'all make a lot on tips?" Sonny asks the woman at the register.

"Okay, I guess."

"What do you have to do to get a job here?"

"Go talk to man in charge. He no here now. Sorry."

By the time he returns to his kiosk all the artists have gone, Roberts included. Glad to have the place to himself, Sonny leans back in his chair and watches the last of the day bleed out of the sky. So as not to think any more about Juliet, he thinks about dead painters and their trees. He recalls their names as he does those of lost family members. Charles Reinike, Clarence Millet, Colette Pope Heldner, Knute Heldner. At the end of his life Knute, a transplanted Swede and former WPA easel painter, was trading his paintings for booze—pieces that a few decades later would bring thousands at auction.

They gave Knute a mimosa that miraculously blooms all but three months of the year, its blossoms fat and pink and forever weeping.

By nine o'clock the mimes and futurists abandon the square and the pigeons roost in the eaves of the buildings and the benches stand empty under the ancient lampposts. Sonny lights a citronella candle to keep the mosquitoes away and he chews on the stem of a tobacco pipe. He sips coffee from the cap of his Thermos and he wonders if Johnny

Beauvais even bothered to keep an oar in his boat. It was a sailboat, after all. Sonny knows nothing about sailing, but he can't imagine a boat such as the Beauvais's needing oars. A mast or two, maybe. But oars?

"Come on," he says out loud. "Who do you think you're dealing with here?"

An occasional tourist strolls by, hardly giving him a glance.

"Would you like a picture?" he asks a woman.

She has been straining to see his work by the dim, broken light of the Pontalba Building.

"That picture," Sonny says. "Would you like it?"

Her face registers surprise. "I don't have any money."

Sonny removes one of Lulu's cabaret on Bourbon Street. "It's yours."

She holds the picture at arm's length and studies it for a while. "It's lovely, but I can't just—"

"Take it."

"May I have one, too?" comes a voice. It belongs to a man Sonny has seen before. He runs a jewelry store over on Royal Street. "That one depicting Preservation Hall. May I have it, please?"

Sonny and the man look at each other, neither speaking. Sonny nods finally and the man removes the painting from the fence and hurries off, only once throwing a glance back.

"What about me?" asks another fellow.

Sonny gives him a streetcar.

"And me?"

The Saenger Theatre on Canal Street.

"May I have one, too, please?"

Flambeau carriers leading a Carnival parade.

*"Mister! Mister!"*

Giant elephant ears in an Uptown garden.

Sonny gets rid of them all—all, anyway, but the ones of Juliet. A few people try to put money in his hands, but he refuses it.

Short of tearing the paintings into tortilla-shaped pieces and eating them with salsa, he wants his collectors to hang their Sonnies over their Barcaloungers and waterbeds. He wants them to study their Sonnies the way art students study the old masters, always with an eye for some highfalutin unmeant meaning. "Here is my Sonny," he wants them to say to those who visit their homes.

A teenage girl drifts over. "Just the other day I had people lining up from here to Esplanade," Sonny tells her, "some willing to pay any price."

"I should pay, too," says the girl. She has accepted Sonny's offer of the old Falstaff Brewery, with its famous weather ball brightly shining against a hurricane sky. "Look, mister, I feel kind of bad about this. Is there something I can give you?"

"Something like what?"

In seconds the girl turns on a heel and runs away, too, apparently having seen more in Sonny's expression than he intended to show.

Sonny feels better now that his paintings are gone. He can start over and do something else with his life.

ʬ

The little young one wakes up not long after Juliet does. To leave the bed he has a choice to make: climb over Leonard or climb over this Marilyn Monroe–looking person he's never met before. He chooses the Marilyn Monroe, just as Juliet figured he would.

She doesn't watch him on his way to the bathroom, but her eyes do snap open at the sound of his violent pissing. God, he makes such a racket as to rouse the dead. At first he seems to be hitting more bowl than water, then more floor than bowl.

Juliet sits up on her elbows and takes in the bathroom. The door is open a crack and inside a bare bulb shines over a sink. The boy is standing at the toilet, bird chest sticking out, penis a different color than the rest of him. His tattoo is badly done, more crooked than straight, and she makes it for a jailhouse job.

It comes to her that the color of his penis is almost identical to that of his tattoo.

When he returns to bed Juliet pretends to be just now waking. She stretches her arms up over her head and lets out a yawn. "You should shake it better next time," she says.

He seems surprised to hear a voice, surprised to see from whom it originated. "Maybe there won't be a next time," he says.

"How do you plan to relieve yourself then?"

"I got my ways."

She turns her head only enough to see his face. Except for the

83

pockmarks he looks no more than eighteen. "I'm sorry, I was just trying to be helpful," she says. Her smile is as friendly as she can make it.
"You peed everywhere but where you were aiming."

"It's over with, at least."

"They should teach little boys in first grade how to pee at the same
time they're teaching them the alphabet. Train them young and spare a
lifetime of accidents."

"Peeing ain't something you teach, lady. It's something you do."

"Not peeing straight it isn't." This inspires a laugh, but not from the
boy. When he looks at her again she says, "I don't know why but I like
hearing a man. Something about it arouses me."

"My ex-wife was like that, too," he says.

She's staring at him now. "Since when are you old enough to have
an ex-wife?"

"Since yesterday when I left her. Before that I just had a wife."

She reaches under the sheets and places a hand on his monster
prick, all the while holding his eyes with hers. In seconds he comes up
as thick and firm as her forearm. "What is the meaning behind this
tattoo?" she says.

"Lady, that ain't a tattoo."

"I mean that wire. You supposed to be an inmate or something?"

His breathing is slow and heavy. His eyelids flutter. "I really wanted
it around my heart," he says, swallowing, "but the tattoo artist couldn't
get inside my chest."

It shocks her past speaking to hear him talk like that, to hear
such poetry. Most musicians she's ever met could barely string a sen-
tence together, let alone spin words into something pretty. She wonders about the ex-wife: how old she is, how pretty, what happened
between them. Juliet pushes up closer. She likes this little young person, this drummer boy with a loud case of BO. He has one of those
mouths that are more teeth than lip, and thus not so good to kiss.
But she presses her mouth to his, anyway. Then without bothering
to ask permission she crawls up on top and reaches back and puts
him in.

She holds on as if afraid to let go, like someone on a trapeze with
a great distance to fall.

She leans forward and dumps her breasts on his chest. "One time in
LA," she whispers in a sexy way, "this famous movie producer paid me

84

five hundred dollars just to do this." And she runs her tongue over her lips, trying to be true to the memory.

"Endlessly fascinating, I'm sure," the boy says, shaking his head.

"What?"

"I said you got a big mouth."

"Thank you. I got myself some inner tubes. You aren't the first to accuse me of that."

Juliet can't believe she can take someone like that. It feels like it's way up in her belly, and for some reason it makes her want to cough. "If I had a tattoo like yours chewing at my arm," she says, "I don't think I could ever get to sleep at night."

The boy, in the dark, is watching himself going in. "My wife has a man mowing the grass."

"Who?"

"She shaves a strip of her pubic hair at a diagonal, 'bout a quarter-inch wide." For all the activity it isn't easy for him to talk. After every few words he lets go with a grunt. "At the top of the shaved part she has a tattoo of this little yardman pushing a lawn mower. You can see clips of grass coming out from where the blade is—there's tattoos of that, too."

"Can we finish?"

"Don't let me stop you. I'm just trying to make conversation."

When it's over, Juliet gets out of bed and stands at the window. It feels as if someone fucked her with a fence post.

To her surprise it's nighttime and pouring rain outside. How long did they sleep? She has no good sense of the world outside the room, outside the pulse loudly beating in the space between her legs. She gazes out in the direction of Congo Square, the old park where back in the 1700s slaves used to gather on Sundays to sing and dance. Forbidden to congregate anywhere else, the slaves came together independent of their owners and practiced voodoo and tribal rites, and now Juliet imagines herself among them, the lone white chick, raising hell with the sisters by a big roaring bonfire.

Would Dickie Boudreau's wife go to a voodoo ceremony? Of course she wouldn't. Dickie Boudreau's wife is too busy going to Mass and to her children's ball games.

The weather pounds against the window, rattles the glass. New Orleans manages to attract storms such as this one so frequently that locals take them as a matter of course, while in any other American city a disturbance of similar magnitude would close schools and public buildings and have the governor ordering the National Guard to start filling sandbags.

"What's it doing out there?" the boy says.

"Making almost as much noise as you did in the bathroom."

"Show me that mouth of yours again."

But Juliet is somewhere else, her head is, and he was rude, anyway.

It was coming down just as hard that day when she and Sonny went to the abortionist on Gravier Street. Sonny borrowed his father's truck and as they were headed uptown on Basin Street the windshield wipers suddenly stopped working. "Must be a short in the wiring," he said. "Or maybe a fuse." Intending to wait it out they stopped in front of Saint Louis Cemetery Number 1 and parked by the curb, but the weather only intensified. Finally, with the appointment minutes away, they had no choice but to head back into the storm. Juliet remembers the drive past the Iberville housing development, and how black kids, naked to the waist, played in mud puddles under the trees, oblivious to the lightning crashing overhead. Along the sides of the Saenger Theatre and Krauss Department Store people stood with their backs to the wall, a few under wind-lashed umbrellas, but most without any covering at all. Desperate to see the road better, Sonny stuck his arm out the window and tried to make it function as a wiper. Back and forth the arm went. Now the rain came in through the window, blinding him and soaking his shirt, some of it reaching Juliet in the form of swirling mist that stuck to her hair and shone in the tangles like glass beads. She licked her mouth and tasted oil from the street. "If we die in a wreck then we just die in a wreck," she said. "At least I won't have to go through with this."

"Let's turn back. It's not too late."

"No way."

"Please, Julie."

She just shook her head.

Juliet remembers the old office tower with its torn and faded canopy in front, the ride in a hot elevator that strained to reach their designated floor, a long hallway with exposed fluorescent tubes over-head dripping water from open housings. It was after-hours and the place was deserted, although she got the feeling it was always deserted.

When they found the right door Sonny put his hand on the knob and hesitated before turning it. "I don't think I can go through with this."

"You're not going through with it, I am." She pushed past him and stuck her head inside.

A solitary floor lamp, its shade denuded but for a couple of linen strips, shone in the middle of the room, and beneath it a young man lounged on a ripped leatherette sofa reading a magazine. He looked hardly older than she and Sonny were. He wore Chuck Taylor basketball sneakers, a plaid button-down shirt and khakis with a rip in the knee. Although his hair was well groomed, his stubble, especially around his mouth, looked stiff enough to pop a balloon.

He stood and turned off the light. "Adelaide's friend?"

"That's right. I'm Juliet and this here is Sonny."

"Nice to meet you both. If it's all the same to you I'm not going to tell you my name. I'm sure you understand my reasons."

"Should we just call you Doctor?" Sonny said in apparent seriousness.

"I'm not a doctor, but you can call me that if it helps."

Sonny was looking at Juliet when he said, "I thought we were coming to see a doctor."

"Fly to London if you want a doctor, Sonny. No doctor here will help you—at least none but those willing to sacrifice their medical licenses and ruin their careers."

While Sonny seemed reluctant to walk more than a few feet from the door, Juliet hurriedly crossed the room and placed her overnight bag on the sofa, then she removed her raincoat and lay it out on the floor to dry. "If you're not a doctor then what are you?" she said, trying to sound as if she weren't at all concerned.

"Sorry. But telling you that wouldn't be wise, either." The young man (she didn't think of him as her abortionist yet) had a high-pitched voice that seemed to emanate from the top of his head rather than from his mouth. "Let's suppose I were to tell you that I was a third-year medical student at one of the local universities and something were to go wrong today. Nothing is going to go wrong, but let's just say something did, for the sake of argument. Well, you could go to the police and they in turn would go to the dean's office and find out my identity and bring criminal charges against me. This is the scenario I want to avoid. What we're doing here is against the law, after all."

Sonny stepped away from the door. His shirt was still wet from the windshield wiper episode. "Have you done many of these things?"

"Yes, quite a few."

"Any problems?"

"No."

"None? None at all?"

"Well, once there was an unusual amount of bleeding. But the girl was never in danger."

Rain hammered the windows. Juliet looked up at the ceiling and the tiles stained brown from leaks. The sofa and several plastic waiting room chairs, hooked together, were the only furniture in the room. "What is this place?" she said.

"Once upon a time it belonged to a dentist. Through a source I was able to secure a key to this suite, but it's only for the time being. Should you decide to contact the authorities you won't find me here again after tonight."

"We won't be calling any authorities," Juliet said, "so stop it."

"Good," and now the abortionist clapped his hands together. "Did you bring the cash?"

By the time it was over the rain had stopped. Juliet, who somehow endured the ordeal without passing out, never knew such pain in all her life. It was the kind of pain that makes you cry and makes you vomit, both of which she did. She'd never sweated as much, either. Even the nylon straps of her brassiere, which the abortionist had permitted her to keep on, were soaked through. Lying supine on plastic sheeting thrown over a table, she kept her eyes on the windows, the streaks and beads of water that brought to mind the paintings at Dickie Boudreau's house. In all probability the baby had been his, resulting from a single meeting in his backyard swimming pool when Sonny was off fishing with his father. "Chlorine kills everything," Dickie had said as he lured her to the steps at the shallow end. Determining paternity had been an easy calculation, as had Juliet's decision to come here today. "I feel so suffocated sometimes," she said to Adelaide Valentine. "He calls me Julie. No one else does that."

"My mother's sister left her second husband because she couldn't stand looking at his nostrils. The guy was a multimillionaire, but he had these big, hairy nostrils. They drove her crazy."

"It's going to kill him, he's so sweet. But I can't live that life."

"God, Juliet, the boy's only seventeen. He'll get over it."

The abortionist removed his gloves and stuffed them in one of the Schwegmann bags he was using for trash. The gloves were canary yellow Playtex, the type for washing dishes. His speculum and curette—instruments he'd insisted on identifying, presumably to put her at ease about his experience—lay streaked with blood on the lining of an old valise, which he closed now with a snap.

"You might be done," she said, "but I can still feel you scraping and poking."

"The pain won't last. The pain won't last but the beauty will endure. Somebody said that."

Just at that moment she thought she was going to vomit again. When the feeling passed, she said, "Will somebody please tell me where's the beauty in all this?"

"The beauty is in being able to make choices. You've made an important one today, and whether you realize it or not it'll probably shape the rest of your life. I hope for the better. I also hope that when you remember me you do so without regret."

Her eyes were still on the window when she said, "I won't remember you at all."

He helped her into a diaper layered along the bottom with feminine napkins, then into her jogging pants. Sonny, silent but for his weeping, held her hand as they took the elevator down. It was almost midnight and up above the city stars hung close in the sky. From a block away she heard a streetcar go by. Sonny helped her in the truck and on with the seat belt. Then when he turned the ignition to start the engine the windshield wipers came on. He was too preoccupied, and too upset, to notice the phenomenon, and he drove Juliet all the way home without turning them off, blades squealing and painting streaks against the dry glass.

That was 1971, the year when everything changed forever. Less than a week later Juliet left New Orleans in another storm. This time she took a cab to the airport. "Where you headed?" the driver said, meeting her eyes with his in the rearview mirror.

"LA," she answered.

"What's that they say? 'Go west, young man'? Something like that?"

"Today the young man stays home. It's me who's going."

So this is what the rain does. It makes you remember something you'd meant to forget. It brings back your first abortionist and the taste of oil from the street and the look in Sonny LaMott's eyes when he put his arms around you for the last time.

Now in the weekly/monthly it's Leonard's turn to take a leak. He makes less noise then the boy did. But like the boy he leaves the door open. "Must be all that rain," he says in a loud voice, apparently in explanation for his prodigious output.

"Wanna do it?" she's tempted to say to the little young one in bed, then hop on top of him again. But down on the street she notices metallic bars burning against black pavement, right where her rental car was formerly parked.

"Motherfuckers took it," she says, more resigned than defiant.

"Took what?"

"Motherfuckers towed it."

Juliet sees winos standing against the side of a laundromat, heedless of the fact that the rain has stopped. They look like people condemned to a firing squad, stunned to paralysis, and here at last is the moment for the bullets.

"Some people must not know who they're fooling with," Juliet says, talking not so much about the cops who towed her rental car, but about her mother and the cleaning woman who live in the house that bears her family name.

The boy stirs in bed. He seems to look at her for the first time. "Are you that girl that Leonard said her mother killed his lover?"

Juliet thinks she understands, but rather than answer she runs her tongue over her mouth again.

# 3

SONNY'S BANK STATEMENT IS THE only piece of mail in the morning delivery. He has but three hundred dollars left in his account, almost half of that recent deposits. Take away the tourist portraits and the Young Elvises and he's broke, studying the want ads for a job, making novenas to whichever saint handles employment.

Sonny rarely entertains dreams of packing up and leaving New Orleans, but today he wonders how it would feel to live in a place where the smell of the rain didn't revive a memory of Juliet's smell, and where certain music didn't recall wild times at the F&M Patio Bar, and where when you woke in the night you didn't automatically reach for somebody who'd never really been there.

"I'm thinking about giving up the fence," he says to Louis Fortunato in a telephone call.

Louis, who'd been asleep, mumbles incoherently, then says, "Do you need a lift?"

"A lift? A lift to a new life, do you mean?"

But Louis has already hung up.

Sonny visits a barber in the French Quarter for his shortest haircut in years, then he drives uptown to the Pontchartrain Hotel, his former employer. After warm greetings from staff Sonny is ushered into the manager's office situated in the suite of rooms directly behind the registration desk. Though oblivious to the irony, he sits in the same chair where, only a few years before, he announced his intention to resign his position as bartender and to pursue full-time his dream of becoming an artist.

The manager, a chunky, red-faced man named Royce Griffin, makes a great fuss over seeing Sonny again, and shakes his hand with such tenderness that Sonny has no doubts as to his sincerity. "And what brings you back to our neck of the woods?" Griffin says.

As Sonny describes his decision to return to "a real job," Griffin regards him with equal measures of pity and discomfort, his complexion growing even more inflamed. Drumming a pencil against his desk, Griffin lets Sonny ramble to a finish before saying, "It breaks my heart to have to tell you this, my friend, but we don't have anything at the moment. However, if something in the bar does come up, I promise you'll be one of the first people we call."

This satisfies Sonny until he gets outside and considers Griffin's remark more closely. How belittling to be called "my friend" by a man before whom he knelt for mercy! And what did "one of the first people" mean exactly? How many other "first people" were queued up in the hotel's breadline, desperate for charity?

And what is this "we" baloney? Will more than one be calling him?

Sonny considers removing Louis's club from under the seat and whacking Royce Griffin with it. *"Hey, fat boy, do you feel it? Do you feel the pain?"*

He sits in the truck listening to the radio until his anger passes, then he returns to the Vieux Carré and stops in at Café du Monde. An attractive young black woman, who seems to be the highest-ranking employee in the restaurant today, gives him an application to fill out, and Sonny sits at a table not far from the one where he and Juliet were reunited only days before. This afternoon a group of tourists occupies his and Juliet's table, and the sight of them wolfing down beignets and slurping coffee is disagreeable enough to lighten the weight of Sonny's memory. Concentrating on the questionnaire, he manages to avoid seeing Juliet every time he looks up.

And then who but Roberts shows up. The old man, toting a Thermos and brown paper bag, engages the cashier in noisy conversation. Sonny lowers his head. How will he explain the close-cropped hair let alone the lengthy employment form detailing the history of his life in the American workforce? The café is swarming with diners, but too few apparently for Sonny to keep from being noticed. Roberts wheels around suddenly as if to address the source of a voice whispered in his ear, and his eyes cut through the crush of people and travel directly to Sonny, or that slim piece of Sonny visible from the front of the room.

"I thought that was you," he says, working his way through the crowd.

"It's me, all right. Sonny LaMott, world-famous French Quarter artist."

"Jesus, look at you. You're all cleaned up." Roberts glances down at the application and his face registers first confusion then disgust. He might've tasted something sour.

"I guess I should've told you," Sonny says. "I'm going back to work. To regular work, I should say. It's time I stop the dreaming."

Roberts places the Thermos and paper bag on the table. "Back to work?"

Sonny is trying to come up with something to say, when Roberts takes a seat. "I've got a sack lunch here. It's a sandwich, a big one. We could split it and talk and maybe you could help me understand what's wrong with dreaming."

In the bag Roberts has a muffuletta-to-go from Central Grocery and he spreads it out between them. The sandwich, as big around as a Frisbee, has already been cut into quarters. But Roberts, using a small pocketknife, saws it into even smaller sections and he and Sonny eat in silence, oil from the olive salad forming clownish rings around their lips and dripping down their hands and arms and staining the cuffs of their shirts. To help ingest the heavy Italian bread they gulp down steaming coffee from Roberts's Thermos.

"Only you would get to bring a muffuletta from Central Grocery in this place," says Sonny.

"Yes. I suppose that's what one gets for being a legend in the Vieux Carré."

"My point exactly."

It is a pleasure to eat and drink in the open air with the music of tinkling silverware and murmured conversations, and Sonny's black, boiling sadness begins to dissipate.

When they're finished, Roberts lifts a hand and points. "Hear that horn?"

Sonny settles back in his chair and listens. Nothing.

"It's a Greek ship, probably passing under the bridge just now. Oh, it's a Greek, all right. I know my horns. They'll dock for a few days and give the clap to half the whores in town. The whores, then, will infect the locals. Then the locals their wives. Then the wives the milkmen. Then the milkmen the milk. Or the cows that produce the milk. Soon we'll all be sick. And this, Sonny, explains why I'm a Communist.

"Below the waist," Roberts adds, "we are all of us connected, no one superior to the next."

Sonny considers telling Roberts about his recent troubles with Juliet. Roberts with his wide experience and gift of gab might be able to help. But Sonny lacks language for how he's feeling, as well as the willingness to hear it spoken.

Roberts, nevertheless, seems to intuit what's troubling him. "If it's any comfort," he says, "I'm just now recovering from my Mary. Only lately has it gotten that I can rest nights, and she's been gone fifteen years now." He picks at his scalp. "Left with a neighbor with whom she'd been consorting, a man I despised."

Sonny looks around to make sure no one is eavesdropping. For some reason he finds it important that only he hears Roberts's confession.

"After she left," the old man continues, "I couldn't sleep for the dreams. I imagined the two of them in bed together, madly humping— his lovemaking infinitely more satisfying than mine had ever been. But eventually this picture began to fade and she left me alone—the bright memory, in any event, became a shadowy one. I knew I'd recovered when she stopped being the first thing I thought about when I woke in the morning. But now, invoking her name again, I admit to feeling a certain heat, and if I let myself I could cry. Does what's happened to you make you feel like that?"

Sonny nods his head.

"Your heart in your throat, eh?"

"Everywhere," he says, "but where it should be."

"Love is a torture and women the whip. Remember that."

"I will," says Sonny. "Because I do feel whipped."

Roberts leans forward and places a hand on Sonny's forearm. "We're dealing with some weighty self-esteem issues here, am I correct?"

Sonny lets out a laugh. "I don't think I'm worth a shit if that's what you mean."

They stay at the table half an hour longer, quiet except for their eating. Sonny listens but still can't hear any evidence of a ship on the river, a Greek one or otherwise. Finally Roberts slaps a hand against his leg. "Well, shall we head back to the salt mine?"

Sonny doesn't get up. He picks at the remains of his sandwich. "You go ahead," he says. "I'm through." He pauses to chew on a crust of bread. "The truth is I don't see the point anymore."

Roberts is a long time before speaking. "Just for my enlightenment, what point is that?"

"The point of hanging pictures on a fence and waiting for people to come and claim them. Why do we bother, Roberts?"

"Why do we bother?" The old man smiles. "I don't know, Sonny, why do we bother breathing?"

"Nobody wants them, let's be honest. I used to think that if I didn't quit—if I just kept at it, you know—I'd eventually be discovered. Somebody would recognize what I was doing as smart and original and maybe even good, and he would introduce it to somebody else who in turn would show it to another. I'd find my audience this way. But lately when I turn and face that fence when I see them there, all huddled together like that—it's terrible, old man, but I wonder if I've wasted my life." Sonny looks over to make sure his friend is still with him. "Roberts, have I wasted my life?"

The old man rises to his feet and shuffles around the table, finally coming to stand a few inches away from Sonny. "If I weren't so old and worn out I'd hand you the worst beating of your life. How many years have you given to that fence, boy? *How many?*" He sucks in a breath of air. "Show me the place where Sonny LaMott's blood stains the flagstones. *Show me!*"

Sonny doesn't speak—he doesn't dare to.

"Stand up, you little shit. Come on. On your feet."

Roberts has attracted an audience. Diners watch as if trying to decide whether to be alarmed or amused. "What is it you want, anyway?" he continues. "Do you want to be an artist who sells paintings or do you want to be one who paints them?"

Roberts starts to shadowbox in place, then he yanks his shirttail free of his trousers, exposing his gut. Sonny looks at the old man's body with a mix of horror and fascination. Roberts is so thin a tight net of bones shows at either side of his rib cage.

"Hit me," Roberts says. "Rare back and hit me. Okay, boy. Okay." Roberts has braced himself. He's ready. "Let me have it. Hit me with all you've got. Come on."

"Forget about it," Sonny says, waving him off.

"I said *hit* me. Hit me, boy." Roberts seems to mean it, and the crowd, or most of it, is laughing now, including the waiters who stand nearby hugging trays.

"Pretend I'm your Juliet. Pretend I'm the world that hasn't found you. Wallop me, boy. Be done with it."

"No way," Sonny says.

"You're a yellow coward. I'm telling you to hit me, coward."

And so Sonny hits him. Still seated in the chair, he raises a fist and drives it into the old man's midsection.

"Harder," says Roberts, clenching his jaw. *"Harder . . ."*

Sonny stands and hits him again, hard enough this time to push Roberts back a step, but not hard enough to hurt him. A gasp comes from the crowd and a wash of tears fills Roberts's eyes and there is a spot on his belly equal in size to Sonny's fist.

"Happy now?"

"Happy," replies Roberts, struggling to breathe. "Goddamned right I'm happy. Sonny, if you're not improved by morning I'll have you hit me again."

"Can I hit you in the face next time?"

"Hit me wherever you like."

"I'll hit you in the face."

"Shit, no, you're not hitting me in my face."

To dull applause, which Sonny refuses to acknowledge but which Roberts recognizes with a bow, the two men leave the café and shamble across the street to the square. Roberts carries himself as if fully aware that he alone created all that is good in the world. You should've punched him harder, Sonny says to himself.

As they near Roberts's kiosk Sonny realizes that the painters at the fence are staring at him, and he begins to feel uncomfortable in his clean clothes and neatly coifed hair.

He wishes he hadn't been so easily seduced by Roberts's dramatics.

"Just remember your Juliets," the old man says. "So what if she's broken your heart, she's also given you a gift. She's helped make you an artist. Nobody else here paints the human form with such feeling as you, boy. Can you give that up?" He shakes his head. "You can't."

Sonny doesn't respond. To do so would invite more, and he wants only to disappear.

"Thanks for the sandwich, old man. I need to be going."

It isn't Roberts's fault Sonny has made all the wrong choices. It isn't his fault Sonny is a pathetic loser who can't give up what hasn't been his in fifteen long years.

"I love you, boy," Roberts says.

"Yeah? Well, I love you, too, Roberts. Now leave me alone."

✷✷✷

As the boy sleeps, Juliet, standing by the bed, rests a finger on his tattoo. It doesn't bite, but its teeth look almost as sharp as the barbed wire that her mother, in the weeks after her father died, wrapped around the drainpipes to keep Juliet from slipping out at night.

"The Proof" is now in her shoe, folded flat against the leather insole. She removes it and finds a pencil on the dresser. Sitting on the edge of the bed with the moist, crumpled piece of paper leveled against her thigh, Juliet writes: *"You claimed the wire was to encourage the path of your bougainvillea when all along we both knew it was meant to thwart my efforts at escape. Liar! I still have scars on my hands and legs. You could have bled me to death up there, Mama, killed me like you killed your husband and my father, Johnny Beauvais. Maybe that was the plan."*

Juliet seems to have finished, but then adds: *"They use barbed wire to train animals to keep within their bounds. I will die bleeding on drainpipe before you train me."*

She puts the list back in her shoe and, still barefoot, walks to the bathroom on the balls of her feet to minimize the risk of contamination. The floor is gummier than slick, the odor not so bad that she has to cover her nose. Determined to avoid contact with the toilet seat, she squats over the bowl and misses the mark just as badly as the boy and Leonard did. Urine bounces off the rim and splashes against her bare thighs and ticks against her calves. In a reflexive response she squats lower and rings her bottom, which makes her pee more, and splash more.

"Is this my life?" Juliet shouts, but no answer is forthcoming from the bedroom.

She cleans herself with a towel thin enough to see through, then places it back on its hook over the lavatory—readily available to her roommates when they brush their teeth later on.

In the mirror over the sink, its surface spotted brown and spidering with age, Juliet stares at a stranger. The features are hers, but the face belongs to someone else. Where is the girl who once stood on a stairway and compared her eyes to those of Etienne Beauvais? And where is she who so inspired an artist that he hardly is able to paint anyone else? "Wanna do it?" Juliet says sadly to the face, and no sooner has she spoken than the face shoots back a reply: "Not with you."

Piece by piece she picks her clothes off the floor and puts them on. Although she makes plenty of noise, Leonard and the boy are too dead to the world to hear. On the dresser there's a ceramic plate holding Leonard's wallet. Leonard seems to collect credit cards the way some losers collect souvenir baseball cards. She fishes out a collection of bills and receipts and counts sixty-eight dollars cash. In the pockets of the boy's jeans all he has worth stealing are a half-smoked joint and several pills whose color vaguely resembles that of her long-expired prescription for Stelazine.

She swallows the pills and saves the doob for later.

"Thank you both for making me feel even worse about myself than I already did," Juliet says on her way out the door.

The city lot for impounded vehicles is about twenty minutes away by foot. Surrounded by a towering chain-link fence, it occupies a narrow patch of ground under the elevated I-10 at North Claiborne Avenue, and borders a pocket of housing projects, abandoned shotgun shanties and blacks-only bars and pool halls. Juliet would invest in a cab ride if not for her financial situation, which, now that she considers it, is really the fault of one person only, a person other than herself.

As she makes her way along the neutral ground dividing the street, the thunder of traffic beating down from the elevated roadway, Juliet encounters plenty of people to worry about. But everybody's cool. Juliet is cool too, striding along with the unlighted stick of marijuana in her mouth, the boy's pills beginning to make her heart flop around like a big, excited fish in her chest.

Despite the danger posed by the neighborhood, she stops and contributes another notation to "The Proof." Although it is her longest entry yet, Juliet needs only seconds to write it, as the markings she applies to the page owe less to the English language than to a language she alone understands. *"You were soft once, Mama, way back in the beginning. I'm charitable enough to admit that. But time made you hard. Time set loose the softness and the hard took hold."*

An ancient black man pushing a shopping cart loaded with cans clatters by in a miasma of dust and BO. He stops to observe the white girl sitting in the weeds. "What are you doing, mama?"

Juliet looks up. "Giving proof for when I kill her. What are you doing?"

"Doing what I do," the man says, then continues on.

*"Shall I remind you, Mother, you once were the kind of woman who warmed baby oil and poured it in your daughter's ear when she complained after swimming practice? Or that you were the kind who fed your child chicken soup and saltines in bed when she had the flu? Mama, your little daughter loved you soft. She loved it when you put your hand on her forehead and checked for fever. She would've stayed sick forever to keep you soft. As soon as you left the room, she put a pillowcase over the lamp to warm it then she put the pillowcase on her face to warm her face. 'Come check my temperature,' your daughter said. When you saw where the lamp had burned the pillowcase and left a brown spot— when you realized the trick your daughter had played—you didn't even beat her. Tears ran from your eyes and you leaned forward and kissed your dear, precious child right smack on the mouth. The child tasted those tears and tastes them today.*

*"Now, Mama, your baby has a question and here goes: Where the fuck is my goddamned check?"*

To recover the Mustang she pays with Leonard's money in the tin shed that serves as an office. The car is dirtier than when she left it in front of the weekly/monthly, its hood smudged with oily handprints from the tow-truck driver. She flirts with the notion of returning it to the rental agency and demanding a refund for its quirky steering and/or sticky accelerator. But doubtful that she can prove these nonexistent problems, and afraid that Hertz double-checks her ability to pay, Juliet decides to count her blessings and accept the car as is/where is.

Blowing pea gravel in a wide arc, zydeco on the radio blistering the big, water-soaked night, Juliet wheels onto North Claiborne Avenue and drives to the Beauvais.

"Where is it?" she shouts after letting herself in at the front door.

Her mother and Anna Huey, sitting in the parlor just past the doors to the right of the foyer, jump to their feet as if for battle.

"Hello, girls, y'all got my money ready?"

Miss Marcelle, wearing nightclothes and slippers, and holding a paperback novel of the Harlequin variety, ventures to within a few feet of Juliet. "Sweetheart, give me the house key. I'll have Anna Huey write you a check."

"If I stuck my hand in your face and said give me my mansion back do you think I could expect to get it? Forget the key, Mother."

From the hallway comes the ticking of a clock, and from the street the irregular rush of traffic headed to the French Quarter. Juliet hears them past a constant echo whose origin she cannot determine. Did the boy's pills come with sound effects?

"Something's been bothering me and I'd appreciate an answer," she says, moving past her mother deeper into the room. "How'd you find me and get my telephone number?" She glances at Anna Huey. "Did you pay Anthony for that, too?"

"We hired a detective agency that specializes in missing persons," her mother answers. "They filed a complete and comprehensive report."

"Since when was I missing?"

"Please, darling. Don't shout." Her mother's hands are already shaking and Juliet hasn't slapped anybody yet. "We were concerned for your well-being and quite frankly we were at a loss as to how to find you."

"Maybe I was missing to you," Juliet says, "but I wasn't missing to me. Believe it or not, I knew where I was the whole time."

"Juliet, why don't you relax and have a seat?" Anna Huey pats the back of one of the chairs. "I'll run to the kitchen and get you something cold to drink."

"Why don't you run to the bank and get me some cash?"

"Please sit for a few minutes," her mother says. "Juliet, there's something we need to talk about. Please, darling. Sit."

The echo sounds louder than before, its reverberations no longer isolated to the space behind her eyeballs. She feels it bouncing around her upper torso as well, and distracting her almost as much as the just-caught fish that is her heart. She figures the boy's tablets weren't antipsychotics, after all. Speed, maybe. Amphetamines. Why else would she feel like this? "I'll talk to you, Mother," she says, "but first you have to answer a question."

Miss Marcelle answers with a nod and Juliet says, "Why aren't you dying?"

"Now, Juliet—"

"Mother, Anna Huey lied to me. She promised me, she promised you were dying."

"Juliet, I'm going to have to ask you to lower your voice."

"All the time I've been out there," Juliet says, "all that time I kept thinking something cataclysmic would happen to tell me which way to go with my life. An earthquake or a fire, and I'd come out stronger than before. Don't you hate survivors, Mother? Mother, of all the disappointments I've endured none has been greater than walking through that door and seeing you ain't sick."

"That might be the meanest thing you've ever said to me," Miss Marcelle says.

"I know you think I'm crazy. I can tell by how you look at me. You think I'm sick, don't you? You think I'm like he was."

"Juliet, I don't think anything."

"Oh, yes, you do."

"Juliet, I needed to talk to you, darling. That's why we conspired to bring you home. If it means anything I apologize. Feel better? Juliet, I'm sorry. I'm sorry and I regret the subterfuge."

She regrets the subterfuge. Juliet tells herself to add that to "The Proof" when she has a minute. To sit down and write: *You and your big words. Whenever Daddy had enough and took off and wouldn't come home you were always practicing them on me. Carrying your dictionary around. Wanting to sound smarter than you are. Hey, lady, a big heads-up: Daddy's gone for good and you and your subterfuge can go fuck each other.*

Juliet drifts over to a rosewood console standing against the wall. A lamp with a stained-glass shade stands in the middle of the table. She rests a hand on its heavy brass base. "I'm going to count to three," she says, "and if I don't have my check something here takes a tumble."

Miss Marcelle lifts the paperback to her face and begins to read in a powerful voice. The book describes a conversation in which two lovers are expressing how they feel about each other.

How Juliet feels is telling her mother to shut the subterfuge up.

"One . . . *two* . . ."

"Juliet, are you holding that lamp hostage?" Anna Huey says with a laugh.

Now in the book the man and the woman have stopped talking and moved to a bedroom. Juliet likes the way the man's expression remains serious, revealing nothing, even as his beautiful seductress undresses in front of him.

"Know what happened to me once?" she says. "I meet this guy in LA and he pays me five hundred dollars to do this."

"Go get her the money," her mother says to Anna Huey.

But Juliet, who's really begun to enjoy herself, has already given the lamp a push. She steps back as it falls to the floor, the glass shade exploding on impact. Somehow the lightbulbs are spared and keep burning as bright as when the lamp was on the table.

"Look at what you went and made me do," she says. "I'm breaking lamps, all because you owe me five thousand dollars."

"We agreed it was two," says Anna Huey, showing the appropriate number of fingers as she starts toward the back of the house.

"Mother, I know what you did that day on Lake Pontchartrain," Juliet says.

"Darling, I'm going to have to ask you to leave now."

"Beat him with an oar. Beat him and then sat there and watched him die."

"Miss Marcelle," Anna Huey says, "I'm sorry but I'm calling Nine-one-one."

For a place with a maid, the Beauvais isn't very clean. This comes to Juliet as she's searching for something else to destroy. Particles of dust float in the light of a chandelier, and mildew is the predominant odor. A solitary ring is visible on the surface of the console where the lamp stood. In the dust Juliet writes: "Clean me, please!"

"The police are coming," Anna Huey calls from the kitchen.

Tired of its ticking, Juliet spins around and kicks the tall case clock, striking its delicately carved door and sending more glass to the floor.

Miss Marcelle walks over and places her hands on Juliet's shoulders. "Darling, won't you let your mother help you?" she says quietly. "I know you can't feel good about yourself right now. Please, darling, let Mama help you."

Juliet knocks her mother's hands away and tries to push the clock over. It's heavier than she anticipated and doesn't easily budge, so she uses her foot for ballast and pulls at the crown. "Now that's the trick," she says in the moment before the clock crashes to the ground.

Out on the gallery, as she leaves without the check, Juliet can still hear her mother's voice from inside the house. Past that mysterious echo, and past the still-distant siren, it is stuck on but two words, and these don't come from any book.

"Why, Juliet?" she is screaming, over and over.

Louis Fortunato, dressed in a collection of khaki safari clothing that only the day before hung on racks at a Canal Street sporting goods store, has joined Sonny and Mr. LaMott on their weekly fishing trip to the Rigolets. Munching pork rinds and sipping from a can of Dixie beer, he sits in the middle of the cab seat and tries unsuccessfully to jog the old man's memory about people and events that even Sonny has difficulty recalling.

"Think back, Mr. Cecil. Think way back. Don't you remember how you and my dad—this is Santo Fortunato, Mr. Cecil, remember your good friend Santo . . . ? How you and Santo played hooky from school and went down to the recruiter's office and enlisted together?"

Mr. LaMott is fooling with the window vent.

"Y'all signed up and did boot camp together then got sent in different directions before meeting up again in some muddy trench out in Korea?"

Now it's the glove compartment.

"You're wearing him out with all those questions," Sonny says.

"He doesn't look worn out to me."

"Daddy, is Louis wearing you out?"

Mr. LaMott doesn't say anything and Sonny says, "See? He's too tired to talk."

At Captain Bruce's Sonny and his father lounge on lawn chairs at the end of the pier with the rope hanging lax between them. Louis's clothes, unwashed yet, excite his proclivity to sweat a lot. Bad leg used as a prop for his fishing rod, he sits on top of the Igloo until the lid starts to bend and Sonny orders him to move his big butt elsewhere. No one catches a fish but for most of the afternoon no one tries to. By evening empty beer cans lay scattered across the warped gray boards and all the chips and sandwiches have been consumed. On the water lights from fishing rigs look like small fires burning and up in the heavens contrails from passing aircraft spiral toward the stars. A steady breeze keeps the men cool. Mosquito dope, two whole bottles of it, keeps the bugs away.

"Ever wonder what it must be like to forget practically everything you ever knew?" Sonny says to Louis, then nods in his father's direction.

"No," Louis answers. "To be honest, brother, I never have wondered that."

"Neither have I," Sonny says, then pulls hard on his line, pretending to have a bite.

Toward the end of the night Sonny starts talking with the same moronic emphasis on the past that Louis did earlier in the truck. In particular he gets stuck on the year 1965 and the weeks after Hurricane Betsy ravaged the city, when Mr. LaMott, working alone, rebuilt their carport and raised a birdhouse in the yard. The birdhouse, fixed atop a platform on a twenty-foot iron pole, was a replica of a Louisiana plantation home called Uncle Sam that had been razed in 1940 to accommodate the Mississippi River levee. Each year purple martins returned to Mr. LaMott's house and nested in the dark space past the portholes cut between small white columns. Mr. LaMott gave names to the birds and seemed to know each one personally. "I liked the one you called Little Billy," Sonny says to his father. "Do you remember Little Billy?"

"Little Billy?"

"That bird you called Little Billy?"

"Who is Little Billy?"

Mr. LaMott's joy, as Sonny recalls, was to sit in the yard late in the afternoon after work with his necktie thrown over a shoulder and his brogans off, feet in the grass. Some days he dozed off with his face turned to the sky and the birds cutting circles above him. With darkness Mrs. LaMott sent Sonny out to get him. "Supper's ready," Sonny routinely called as he bounded down the stairs outside, taking two at a time. "Hey, old man, Mama says supper's ready."

This was how they did it, a piece of the day they could always count on.

"I'm hungry too," his father says now, sitting up in his chair.

"Do you remember what you'd say whenever I said 'Supper's ready'?"

"Let's eat," says Mr. LaMott, lowering his rod to the weathered boards.

Sonny shakes his head. His father would rise to his feet and slip his shoes on and straighten his tie. "Sonny, I wish I was a bird," he always said. Then he'd flap his arms more like the wings of a chicken than those of a purple martin as he and Sonny raced to the house and up the stairs to the kitchen where his mother waited with dinner on the table and her face lit up in a smile and years and years to go before the stroke that would take her life.

"I wish I was a bird," Sonny says now. "Daddy, you don't remember that?"

His father is sipping from the empty beer cans, lifting one after another.

"There was Speedo. He was faster than the rest. Speedo, Mr. Jones, Blue Boy, Pencilneck, Popeye. They used to fly around eating all the bugs."

Mr. LaMott throws each can in the water when he's certain he's sucked out every drop.

"The termites finally got to Uncle Sam like they get to everything else in New Orleans. They must've been hungry to climb all the way up that pole, huh, Daddy?"

"Jackpot," says Mr. LaMott, finally finding a can with more than a few drops left.

"Was there a Jackpot?" asks Louis.

"No," Sonny says. "There wasn't even a Jack."

Sonny reels in his line. He takes his time doing it, driving the plastic cork down into the water before letting it bob back to the surface and forcing it down again. "What about my name, Daddy? Do you remember my name?" Sonny puts the rod down and squats in front of the old man. "What is it? Come on and tell me. What's my name?"

"Little Billy," says Mr. LaMott.

"I'm Little Billy? You think I'm Little Billy?" Sonny's voice is shaky. He brings his face closer to his father's. "Look at me. You still think I'm Little Billy? Do I look like a bird, Daddy?"

His father stares without recognition.

"Sonny," Sonny says. "It's Sonny, Daddy. Well, Sonny's not my real name. My real name is Cecil, Cecil Junior. You and Mama named me after you. Don't you remember?"

Mr. LaMott gently places a hand on Sonny's face. "I wish I was a bird."

They are only a few miles from the Maison Orleans when Louis, whom Sonny had thought was asleep, clears his throat and announces in a soft voice, "I'll whack her for you."

"No," Sonny answers. "Whack me instead."

♦♦♦

*"I break the tall clock but I don't stop time. Saw, Mama, how the light stayed on even after the lamp crashed to the floor? Likewise there is a thing in me that will never die. And don't think I mean spirit, either. What I'm talking about is deeper than that.*

*"Daddy used to say it's the thing that colored my eyes. He'd say we were going to write to the Crayola crayon people and tell them there's a new color to include in their box. It was aqua and royal and navy and powder and turquoise all mixed together. It was the prettiest color there was. Kids would want to use nothing else once that one got in the box.*

*" 'We'll call it Beauvais,' he said.*

*"You may have spirit but, bitch, I got soul."*

♦♦♦

For two days after the fishing trip Sonny doesn't leave his house. He takes the phone off the hook and he runs a box fan in the living room. He plays the radio louder than usual to keep his mind from unwanted ruminations and he sleeps for long periods without caring whether it's day or night. He eats canned tuna and beans, bananas whose skins have turned brown, and French bread so stale that it turns to dust when he attempts to slice it. He takes one shower after another until his skin begins to shrivel and there isn't a dry towel left in the house.

At last he puts the phone back on the hook and gets dressed, determined to go out for a hot meal and conversation, for anything. But down in the street his pickup won't start. Hoping to fire the engine, Sonny pushes the old heap a ways down Chartres, then jumps inside and pops the clutch. He succeeds only in wearing himself out.

Panting for breath, his shirt and trousers wringing with sweat, Sonny goes to his neighbors' apartment and bangs a fist on the door. It slowly opens a crack and Florence Bonaventure, her face muddy with bruises, hair a mess, appears in the narrow space. Discovering that it is only Sonny, son of the landlord, she turns and walks away without inviting him in.

Moments later her husband appears wearing a sleeveless T-shirt and boxer shorts. On his bare arms and shoulders stand bunches of wiry hair and a mélange of coin-shaped moles.

"Can't get my truck to start," Sonny says.

"Saw that from the bathroom."

"Did I make a fool of myself?"

"You just look like a person needs some help."

"Right. Me and my truck both."

They head down to the street and Curly Bonaventure drives his station wagon up to the pickup and juices Sonny's battery. The truck comes to life and over the roar of the engines Curly says, "You sick, Sonny? I notice you been home a lot."

"A case of the quiets, Curly. Nothing serious."

"And how's Mr. LaMott getting along?"

"About as well as that thing he's got will let him be, I suppose."

Curly removes the cables but leaves his motor running. "Not that it's any of my business," he says, "but you don't answer your door. I notice that."

"How much I owe you for the jump?"

"Oh," Curly Bonaventure glances at the cables in his hands as if hoping they will give him a number, "you don't owe me nothing."

Sonny figures he likes his neighbor about as much as you can like a man who regularly beats the living crap out of his wife.

"You knock again, Curly, I'll make certain to answer."

"Oh, no, Sonny, that wasn't me that knocked." Curly shuffles from foot to foot, eyes cast down. "She came yesterday and spoke to me out in the yard. Said if I saw you to leave a message." Curly looks at him. "The Lé Dale on Saint Charles Avenue. Said you could find her there."

Sonny doesn't understand until Curly says, "Real pretty thing with titties out to here." He drops the cables and shows Sonny how far.

Sonny knows the hotel. It's a flophouse downtown just a block away from the Hummingbird Grill, the greasy spoon where he and Juliet often dined together in the old days. It never closes, does the Hummingbird, and it owes its considerable reputation to the diversity of its clientele and to the breakfast it serves around the clock. Sonny and Juliet liked to go there on weekends after movies and walking tours of the French Quarter, and to sit at the counter chugging black coffee and gorging on chunks of sweet Virginia ham and homemade biscuits stuffed with pats of oleo. It was always exciting to be among the odd mix of pimps and politicos, homeless drifters and Uptown frat boys, hookers and debutantes, and even more so to survive such a night without getting robbed at gunpoint outside on the street.

"One day when we're rich and married and too tired to drive home we'll be able to walk over to the Lé Dale and get a room," Sonny said once to Juliet. "The Hummingbird rents rooms, too. I guess we could just go upstairs. But I always liked the Lé Dale."

"What is it you like so much?"

"The name. I like the name, Lé Dale. I like any hotel that would call itself that."

"You're a classy guy, Sonny LaMott."

"Durn right I am."

They generally stayed until around 11:30 P.M., when Sonny, faced with midnight curfew, announced that it was time to be getting home. "Mama says nothing any good happens after twelve o'clock," Sonny routinely told her.

To which Juliet routinely replied, "Mine says the same. But for different reasons."

Today Sonny chooses to take Juliet's staying at the Lé Dale as a nod to the past, as a gesture with as much promise as a blown kiss.

Without bothering to go back upstairs and change clothes, Sonny leaves Curly Bonaventure standing on the lawn with his jumper cables and heads downtown.

"Juliet Beauvais, please," he says to the clerk at the front desk.

The man, a greasy sort with a face eternally damaged by an adolescent siege of acne and ingrown hair follicles, doesn't seem to appreciate being inconvenienced. He's busy eating a box of candy, after all. "What's your name?"

"Sonny LaMott."

The man, gnashing red hots, picks up the phone and dials a number. "Yeah. You have Sonny somebody down here in the lobby. You want me to send him up?" The man nods and puts a hand over the mouthpiece. "She ain't dressed. She says to wait." The man nods again. "I'll tell him." After he puts the phone down he says, "She says she'll call me soon as she's decent."

Sonny feels like telling the man he finds it odd that he has to wait for Juliet to be decent after all they've experienced together lately, particularly at the Royal Sonesta. But the man doesn't look like the type you complain to. He looks more like the type who makes others complain.

Sonny sits on a couch with yellow sponge poking through tears in the fabric. On the wall behind him hang a crucifix, a pay phone and a small, hand-lettered sign that reads YOU ARE TO BE FULLY DRESSED WHILE IN THE LOBBY. Three different fans churn at high speed, all failing to dent the heat. Nearly twenty minutes go by before the phone rings at the desk and the clerk gives Sonny the room number and tells him he can go on up. As Sonny climbs the stairs, he passes a boy who is coming down them, and who seems to speak Sonny's name under his breath as he walks by.

"Did you say something?" Sonny is standing in the middle of the dark stairway.

"I didn't hear nothing."

Sonny starts to climb again, and the boy says, "What would I say? Do I know you?"

Sonny looks at him. The pale, stringy hair, whiskers not nearly as plentiful as pimples. The whites of the boy's eyes are shot red, while the irises are so clear as to seem diluted of color. He is wearing jeans and a sleeveless T-shirt similar to the one Curly Bonaventure had on earlier. A tattoo, made to resemble a strand of barbed wire, encircles an upper arm.

Sonny says, "I thought I heard you say my name."

"How could I say your name? I don't even know you." The boy laughs and pulls at his nose. "You think I guessed it—I just picked your name out of all the names in the English language and all the other languages—out of Japanese, Russian, French, Spanish, Italian, Portuguese. There's a lot of fuckin' languages, man. And, holy moly, think of all the names."

"You're right," Sonny says.

"Todd, Tim, Bill, Brent, Jeff, Tarzan, Tonto, Coco, Mojo, Bobo, Toto. That would make me a mind reader, to come up with your name."

Sonny has the impression the boy would name names all day if he let him. "Look, I'm sorry. I must've been mistaken." But as he starts back up the stairs, and the boy starts down, Sonny hears him say it again. "Sonny," he hears him say, louder now than before.

Bath towel in hand, Juliet is waiting for him on the second floor, the door open to her room. "Where on earth have you been?" she says. "I went by the square, I went by your house."

They embrace and she kisses him. Despite the stage prop, it is plain that she hasn't taken a shower. Her skin is hot and damp with sweat, and her hair needs to be washed. Her clothes smell of smoke and grease, the cloying stink of a hash house like the Hummingbird. Neither does her makeup look right. It appears to have been hastily applied—there's just enough color to mask whatever needs to be hidden, but not enough to fool whoever might be looking for it.

"There was a boy on the stairs who said my name," Sonny says.

She looks at him expectantly, as if waiting for the rest.

"I thought maybe he was coming from your room."

"A boy was coming from my room? What boy would that be, Sonny?"

"He had a tattoo on his arm."

"What kind of tattoo?"

"Barbed wire, looked like."

"Oh, no, that one wouldn't have been coming from my room. The guy coming from my room had a tattoo of a big, red heart with his mother's name plastered across it."

Sonny steps past her. The room, though far from elegant, isn't the pit that Sonny imagined. The bed doesn't take coins and vibrate, in any case. And the hotel has provided a TV set. A black-and-white model, but a TV no less. "Look," Juliet says, throwing a door open, "I even have a bathroom."

"I'm impressed."

"It's cozy," she says. "Fifteen bucks a night, you can't beat it."

"Not for fifteen you can't," Sonny says. "But think of what sixteen will get you."

His attempt at sarcasm doesn't seem to register. "Sonny, I was just watching this episode of *The Andy Griffith Show* that reminds me of us. Do you like Andy?"

"Andy's all right."

"Andy has his high school reunion coming up, and his old girlfriend is going to be there. She's gone off and made a big life for herself in Raleigh or someplace. Well, they get together at the reunion dance, and everything is like before. They're happy as can be, and Andy's wondering what broke them apart. They go outside and sit on a bench under the stars and they get to talking. And before you know it they're arguing over some little nothing. She's upset and so is he, and Andy's screaming and she is screaming. Then all of a sudden it comes to them why they didn't make it together way back when."

Sonny has never seen that particular show, but his recollection of events that broke Juliet and him apart differs dramatically from those she just described. "Why didn't they make it?"

"They were different people. Different people like that never last. One wants Mayberry, the other Raleigh. If not for their differences they wouldn't have anything."

Sonny walks over to the window and looks down on the avenue. Streetcar rails lie in silver ribbons against the blacktop. "Did that girlfriend of Andy's ever ask him to kill her mother?" he says.

"What did you say?"

He doesn't answer and she makes a noise meant to imitate a buzzer going off; it takes Sonny a few seconds to understand that this is the sound of a game show contestant giving the wrong response to a question. "Sonny, listen to me, sweetheart. I'm going to say something now and say it once and that's it; you won't hear it again. Sonny, the other night in the wild heat of an argument I said some terrible things— things I didn't mean of course and would gladly take back if only you let me. First and foremost were my comments about your work. Just for the record—and you must know this; you have to . . . Sonny, I think you're a genius, an absolute genius."

"Thank you."

"Your paintings smack of immortality. I mean this."

"Yes. They smack, all right."

"What's the point of my being nice if you can't take a compliment?"

"They smack butt, that's all they smack. Forget about my work, Julie. It's what you said about your mother that I can't stop thinking about."

"Sonny, what I said about my mother isn't true. Happy now?" When he doesn't answer, she says, "Happy? I need to know you're happy. If you're happy, I'm happy."

"I'm happy," Sonny says.

"Good. Now let's get out of here."

He follows her into the hallway then down the stairs. He wonders about Andy pining away for the same girl for so many years, and whether his love was anything like Sonny's. Did Andy ever bump into a boy leaving her hotel room? If so, how did Andy feel about it? Did he feel like throwing up? Did he feel like taking his fist and slamming it into the wall?

"Can we go riding in your truck? I could use the air."

"Sure, Julie."

"Riding like we used to ride."

"However you want."

"Remember the levee? We always went there, didn't we?"

"Yes, we did go there."

"Remember that blanket you used to keep behind the seat? God, whatever happened to that thing? It belongs in the Smithsonian."

"That's funny, Julie. That's very funny."

Sonny also wonders what Andy did after the reunion dance, when it was clear he'd wasted so many years of his life on dumb, empty longing. Did Andy mute his telephone and run a box fan in his living room and play the radio too loud and take his meals from the can? Did he sit in the dark and the quiet of his porch and weep into big, open hands? Or did Andy take a more assertive approach and plot ways to win his girlfriend back, to prove that he was worth another try? Andy never seemed the type of guy to quit on anything. Why quit on the only girl he ever loved just because they had a small disagreement after a dance?

Juliet stops at the door to the lobby. "Bye, Leroy," she says to the clerk at the desk.

"Bye, sweet thing," he replies, smiling a mouth gone red from candy.

"Bye, Leroy," Sonny tells the clerk.

But the man doesn't answer.

♈♈♈

They circumnavigate Lee Circle in another loud silence, Sonny following the troughs of the streetcar tracks, the tires of his pickup popping against the iron rails. After half a dozen turns he veers onto Saint Charles Avenue and the road straightens. New Orleans is Sonny's home, the only one he's ever known, but it occurs to Juliet that half the time he seems lost and in need of directions, worse off than a tourist.

"Where are we going?" he says.

She slides over and waits until he looks at her. "Sonny, are you upset with me?"

"I just want to know where we're going."

"Be honest with me, baby. Is it over Mother and Daddy and Lake Pontchartrain or is it the boy you met on the stairs? Sonny, don't be mad."

"You want someplace in particular," he says, "or someplace in general? If you want someplace in particular you'd better speak up."

"Particular or general," she replies, falling back against the door. "Today it looks like one is as bad as the other."

And so they go everywhere and nowhere, both at once. They drive along Magazine Street passing block after block of Victorian and Greek Revival buildings that now house secondhand and antique stores, then head to Prytania Street and the Garden District where leafy mansions and luxury apartment buildings rush by one after another. After doubling back and driving several blocks to the north they tour a blighted but historically significant area called Central City, where urban renewal has been kicked hard in the crotch by urban decay and it seems the old, mistreated homes stand but for the grace of Formosan termites.

"Sometimes I can't decide if New Orleans is the most beautiful city I've ever seen or the ugliest," Juliet says.

They explore Canal Street up to the cemeteries then take City Park Avenue to Moss Street and Bayou Saint John for a long loop and finally they're driving down Esplanade Avenue headed to the Mississippi River and the Beauvais.

"I want to take back some of what I took back earlier," Juliet says, watching the great house approach through a dense blur of trees. "That business about Mama killing Daddy? I wasn't making it up. Sonny, I meant every word."

She doesn't think she can take more of his whining, but some things need to be said. That is just one. Now comes another: "Stop the truck, Sonny. Stop it now."

He pulls over and parks directly across the street from the house. His hands are gripping the steering wheel, arms extended, elbows locked.

"Sonny, I have a favor to ask. It isn't a big one but it's important."

"What is it, Julie?"

"Sonny, my mother owes me some money. I'd go to the house and get the check myself but she and I had a terrible argument the other day and I just refuse to let her treat me that way again. Sonny, the favor I need to ask—"

"You want me to get it."

"That's right. I do, I do want you to get it. If it's not too big an imposition, of course. I hope you understand, Sonny, I'm trying to avoid another argument."

"Walk up to the door, Julie. You don't have to go in. Just walk up and have Mrs. Huey—"

"Trust me, Sonny. Mother will be there, and we'll only fight again."

"It's too embarrassing," he says. "I won't do it."

"Please, Sonny. Help me with this. Is it really so big a deal?"

"You honestly expect me to walk up there and tell your mother I came for your check?"

"I honestly do."

"Jesus," then, no real surprise to Juliet, he gets his act together and steps outside.

The eternal path through the crape myrtles, the columns as big around as he is, the Boston ferns pinwheeling in the breeze. As always, Sonny runs a hand through his hair to make sure he's proper. Then he uses the knocker.

"Well, I'll be," says Anna Huey, pulling the door open wide to let him in. "I thought they'd gone and kidnapped you. Where've you been hiding, sugar?"

Sonny steps inside but doesn't go past the foyer, which for some reason is the limit he's posted in his head. What's not right about the hallway? What has been changed? At last he discovers it: the grandfather clock is missing. Now in its place there is a plant stand holding a ceramic jardiniere.

"Why don't you come in and have a seat, Sonny. I can run and get Miss Marcelle."

"Thanks, Mrs. Huey. But I don't have time. Juliet's waiting out in the truck."

"Don't tell me. You came for her check." Anna Huey studies him over her reading glasses with a tired, dissatisfied expression. "Sonny, don't you want to say hello to Miss Marcelle first?"

"I can't now, Mrs. Huey." After a moment he adds, "You know how Juliet is."

She starts for the rear of the house but then thinks better of it and turns back around. "Listen, sugar, I know you mean well. But why don't you let Juliet come for the money herself? While she's here she can talk to Miss Marcelle. Miss Marcelle has something to tell her."

"Mrs. Huey, obviously this is none of my business but can't Miss Marcelle talk to Juliet later? Juliet's been staying downtown at the Lé Dale Hotel. You can have Miss Marcelle call her there."

"Sugar, I can't believe this."

"I can't either," he says. "It's ridiculous."

Anna Huey looks past him in the direction of the avenue. "Sonny, I may be overstepping my bounds by saying this but I really think you need to be careful running around with that girl."

"I haven't exactly been running around with her," he says.

"Sonny, you should know what Juliet's all about by now."

"Probably better than anyone. And that's why I'm here today, Mrs. Huey. I'm only trying to prevent another fight between her and her mother."

"That girl thrives on chaos. She's dangerous, sugar."

Now it's his turn to look back at the truck. "Are you going to get the check, Mrs. Huey?"

"No, I'm not." Anna Huey's look of fatigue gives way to one of warmth and she reaches out and places a hand on Sonny's cheek. "Sonny, be careful."

Sonny is walking back to the truck when Juliet appears on the path up ahead, striding toward him with her arms swinging wildly, a look of mad determination on her face. She bumps past him without a word.

"Juliet, where the hell are you going? *Juliet!* Juliet, don't do this . . ."

"Anna Huey! Anna Huey, why don't you make yourself useful for a change and go get my goddamn money." She's standing at the open door now, hands wrapped around her mouth. "It's the Beauvais Mansion, Mother. The *Beauvais*, do you hear?"

Sonny grabs her by the arm and tries to pull her away but Juliet gives him a shove and breaks free. "I'm tired of being intimidated by these people," she says.

"I think you've got that turned around, Julie."

From the rear of the house Miss Marcelle comes stalking toward them, moving with such urgency that the color has drained from her face.

"You're a Lavergne," Juliet says in a plain voice. "Admit to me you're a Lavergne."

"That I'm a Lavergne?"

"Say to me you're a Lavergne. Say it, Mother."

"I'm a Lavergne," answers Miss Marcelle. "But you need to remember something, darling: you're a Lavergne, too. Or half of one."

"I'm no Lavergne," Juliet says.

"You're equal parts Lavergne and Beauvais. And I'm equal parts Lavergne and Doucet. My people weren't fancy, I admit this. But some Lavergnes are. The de la Vergnes in town like to think of themselves as important. I guess that little *de* in the front of their name is what does it. Wish I'd have grown up with that. Give me that *de* and my only child might halfway respect me. Might love me, even." Miss Marcelle steps up closer, moving past Anna Huey to within a few feet of Juliet. "Hello, Sonny. And how are you, baby?"

"Hello, Miss Marcelle. I'm fine, thank you. But I have to tell you,

I'm really sorry about this. I feel like it's partly my fault. We shouldn't be here."

"Sonny, what are you?"

"Ma'am?"

"What is LaMott? That's a French name, isn't it?"

Sonny has to think about it. "I'm almost certain it's French. But to be honest I never got around to finding out for sure. I think *la* means *the*, but it's anybody's guess what a *mott* is."

"And you!" Juliet is talking to her mother. "Shall I tell everyone who you are?"

"Please do," answers Miss Marcelle, seeming truly interested.

"Only two months into her marriage," Juliet begins, "some of Mother's people were threatening to leave their tractors in the fields and hitchhike to the big city for Carnival. Mother pulled my father aside and asked him—and *pleaded* with him, I should say—not to say anything about being a Creole, as Daddy was known to be quite proud. When he asked why, she said she was afraid they'd think she'd married a Negro."

"Now, Juliet, that isn't how it—"

"Don't even try to deny it, Mother. Daddy told me the whole story. You didn't even know what a Creole was."

Miss Marcelle brings a finger to her chin, as if trying to come up with a definition.

"How could you have told him that?"

"All right, Julie," Sonny says. "Enough."

Miss Marcelle seems to be trying to understand something. "Where I come from," she says, "the Creoles were colored people. I'm sorry if that sounds racist to you, but they were all like Anna Huey here. They were light-skinned blacks and they had French names. Huey is a French name, isn't it, Anna Huey?"

"Yes, it is, Miss Marcelle. So is Arceneaux, my maiden name. They're both French—as French as Beauvais, as a matter of fact."

"Not that French," Juliet says.

"In 1953 when Johnny and I were married," Miss Marcelle continues, "people tolerated race-mixing far less than they do today. I loved the man, and I didn't care if he was a white Creole, a black Creole or a polka-dot Creole. I just didn't want my family asking questions that might offend him. I was trying to spare *him* that, not myself."

117

"Spare him that," Juliet repeats. "Spare him that just like you spared him that drowning in Lake Pontchartrain, right, Mother?"

"What did you say?" Miss Marcelle steps out onto the welcome mat.

"What do you think I'm saying? You killed him—you killed my daddy!"

From Anna Huey comes a rough gasp, and Sonny adds another as he steps up and grabs Juliet by the arm. But Miss Marcelle hardly seems bothered. She shakes her head and waits until Juliet looks at her. "You're mistaken, darling. That isn't how it happened at all."

"You killed him, Mother."

"Juliet, your father drowned. You know this."

"*Killed* him."

"Sonny?" It is Anna Huey. "Sonny, you two need to be going."

"Come on, Julie," he says. "Let's go."

He places his hands on her shoulders and guides her to the street. She tries to push him away again but without success. Sonny is holding on so tightly now that his fingers turn white from the effort. "Let me go, you bastard."

"Settle down, Julie."

He lets her in on the driver's side but not before she's hurled a final invective in the direction of the house: "You want the proof, Mother? I've got the proof!"

Sonny drives toward the French Quarter, pushing the truck harder than he has in years. After hurtling through the intersection at North Rampart Street he finally glances over at Juliet, expecting to confront a tearful face, lips pale and quivering. He sees neither.

"Still didn't get my check," she says, now the picture of composure.

※

Somewhere on Dauphine Street Juliet removes her shoe and "The Proof" from under the insole. She unfolds the slip of paper and lays it on the seat between them.

"Sonny, you got something to write with?"

He checks his shirt pocket. "Look in the glove compartment."

Under old receipts and tubes of paint she finds a ballpoint. She tries to write but pokes a hole in the paper. She gathers together a couple of road maps and places them on the seat, then she puts "The Proof" on top and tries again. *"And to complete the picture you have bad hair. I don't know which is worse: having to look at that rat's nest or smell your coffee breath. Pee-you!"*

"Julie, what are you doing?"

"Giving proof why I'm in my rights to hate her."

Sonny takes the paper and holds it flat against the steering wheel. He glances down at the list, then up at the road ahead, then down at the list again. Something that might be a smile comes to his face. "Is it writing? What is this?"

"Proof for when they try to pin it on me."

He's squinting, his face filled with disbelief. "It doesn't make sense. You can't read it, the writing's just a bunch of squiggles. Is it a code? If that is writing, Julie . . ."

She shakes her head. "I know what it says."

"You can read this?" He seems frightened by it. Or maybe it's Juliet who scares him. "Better put it away," he says, then drops the paper on the seat. "And don't let anybody else see it. Shit, Julie, they'll really think you're crazy."

She folds the paper and puts it back in her shoe, then she slumps in the seat, lifts her feet up and spreads them wide apart on the dashboard. She's wearing a short skirt and the air from the open windows gives some relief. "Sonny, it feels like my pussy's on fire."

He looks at her the same way he did when he tried to read "The Proof." "Juliet, is there anything you won't say or do? Is there anything?"

"I'm on my period. And my pussy burns today for some reason."

"You want me to stop and get you something?"

She closes her eyes and slips farther down in the seat. "Why can't men say a word like Kotex or tampon without being embarrassed? It's men who started calling them feminine napkins, you know?" When he doesn't respond, she says, "Say Kotex for me. Say the word."

"I won't."

"Kotex. Come on, Sonny. Let me hear it."

"Look, I'm trying to drive, all right?"

"Since when can't you drive and talk at the same time? Say tampon, baby. If you say tampon I'll give you a blow job." She claps her hands together. "Let me hear it."

"Juliet, what the hell is wrong with you?"

"Ever wonder how they thought up that word? To my ears it sounds almost Chinese. I bet they stayed up all night thinking up that one. Bunch of guys in a room with their sleeves rolled up. You still won't say it, will you?"

"Tampon," he says suddenly, then faces her with a smile.

"Bunch of guys with their sleeves rolled up." And she nods, certain now that this is how it happened. "Cigar smoke everywhere. Big bellies wanting to pop their shirts open. Sansabelt slacks all thin where their thighs have rubbed together. Can't you see it, Sonny?"

"I see something."

"Grease stains on their shirts . . ."

She doesn't burn as much downstairs, although now that general area does seem to have its own private pulse. She wishes she were soaking in a tub of hot water, enjoying its powerful healing effects. She fiddles with the radio knobs and finds a jazz station, someone playing a mournful piano.

"They've had Chinese delivered," she continues. "Egg rolls, Kung Pao chicken, moo goo gai pan, fried wontons. They're so tired they can't think straight. Guy with rolled-up sleeves says, 'Pass me the tampons.' He's so exhausted, you see, he's got the names of the dishes mixed up. Everybody's eyes pop open. *Yes!* "

Sonny keeps driving. He's smiling the whole time, shaking his head, rubbing his jaw. "Tampon," he says again.

She reaches down to the floor at her feet and comes up with Louis's club. "What is this?"

"That?"

She grips the handle and acts as if she's going to hit him. "It's a club, isn't it? What in heavens are you doing with this club in your truck, Sonny LaMott?"

"I used it one day to whack an old man on the neutral ground."

"You did that?"

"Actually I pretended to do it. I wasn't really hitting him. I did it to satisfy a debt I owed a friend of mine who was watching nearby."

"What kind of debt?"

"The old man killed my friend's cat."

"Well, of course he did."

For blocks cars idle in a long, unmoving procession, and now in theirs—a 1963 GMC pickup truck with running boards and a collage of faded stickers on the back bumper—Juliet Beauvais scuttles over in the seat, unzips Sonny LaMott's jeans and lowers her head to investigate.

To their left stands the palatial Monteleone Hotel with crowds of visitors loitering near the gilded entrance, and to their right the Hurwitz Mintz furniture store, which today has drawn hordes of its own to its magnificent show windows.

"You missed this, didn't you?" she says.

"I missed you."

"Tell me you missed this."

"I missed this."

"Say you missed having your girlfriend suck your big, beautiful dick."

"I missed having you do that."

"You didn't say it right. Say it how I told you to say it."

"I missed having my girlfriend suck my big, beautiful dick."

"Again. Say it again. Say it until I tell you to stop saying it."

Sonny finishes as the bottleneck clears and traffic starts to move. A liquid sound comes from the back of his throat and he bucks forward in the seat and punches the horn with his chest. Soon other drivers are blowing horns, the whole area seeming to trumpet Juliet's daring indiscretion.

All done now, she sits up and examines her face in the rearview mirror. Her cheeks are dark and swimming with blood and her lips seem twice their normal size. She opens her mouth and studies the stalactites inside. It's always amazed her to see how little actually comes out. No more than a teaspoon and men lose everything over this.

She leans over to kiss him and when their mouths meet she passes it on, the oyster thick and warm in her mouth, now thick and warm in his.

♕♕♕

They sleep for a few hours and when he wakes the light is gone and a stormy darkness fills the room. Outside a breeze stirs the palms and banana trees and a shutter slaps against the house. Occasional rain flicks against the windowpanes. "What time is it?" he says.

"Nine, ten. I'm not sure."

She is sitting by the window, looking out at the weather. What remains of the boy's doob juts out from her mouth, its tip flaring when she takes a last sip before putting it out. "White girl thinks by keeping my check she's keeping me. Bitch forgets I still have a key."

It isn't immediately clear to Sonny what she's talking about.

"You'll just have to go back and get it," Juliet says. "That's all there is to it."

He rolls over and hugs a pillow. The rain has begun to fall in hard gusts, in sheets that look white against the streetlights. Lightning splinters and reveals the sky, the endless banks of clouds meeting the black expanse of the river.

"Wait right there while I go pee," she says.

In the dark of the bathroom she sits on the toilet without closing the door. Sonny can see her when the lightning flashes. She keeps her head down and her hair hangs between her knees. He wonders if they taught her that in California, too.

She finishes and wipes herself and looks at the wad of paper. They know how to do it in California. Sonny has to give them that much. They know the tricks.

He turns his head away so as not to think about it.

"Bad weather—that ozone smell?—reminds me of when I was a little girl," Juliet says from the bathroom. "Nights like this, when there's thunder and lightning and rain, I can hear Daddy pacing the floor downstairs in the library in the dark. I used to think it was the most miserable sound in the whole, entire world. Mainly because he was so miserable."

"I remember," Sonny says.

"We talked about that?"

"A long time ago we did, after the funeral. You told me everything."

"Yes," she says. "I suppose I did tell you a lot."

Sonny sits back against the headboard, wondering what more there could be to know. He likes the rain but he isn't sure what it reminds him of, not that the past even matters at this moment. Sonny keeps hearing the sound of Juliet's water meeting the water in the bowl, keeps seeing her expression when she brought the wad of tissue up from between her legs.

"Just let yourself in," she says. "Just go upstairs and get her out of bed. She sees you up there she'll know we're not playing."

"I'm sorry, Julie, but I'm not going to do that."

She is laughing as she leaves the bathroom. "I'm going back to the Lé Dale then."

Sonny, his penis stiff, angling up past his navel, gets out of bed pulling the sheet around him and shuffles across the room. He wants to show her something, a postcard depicting the Beauvais Mansion that he's kept on the dresser for years now. It's stuck in the mirror between photos of his father sitting outside on the lawn with his eyes on the sky and one of his mother as a girl standing on Annunciation Street in the Irish Channel. "Remember this?" he says.

Juliet moves to the bed and rolls over on her back, holding the card close to her face. "Oh, my gosh. Where'd you find it?"

"Bookshop on Magazine."

"Bookshop?"

"George Herget's. The guy's so nice, he offers you a can of Coke as soon as you walk in the door."

"You don't even have to buy any books?"

"Nope, but you want to, mainly on account of that Coke."

Juliet places a finger on the small block of text, the delicate print. "The Beauvais Mansion," she reads out loud. "Built by Creoles in the years before the Civil War, this gracious example of French Colonial architecture has been in the same New Orleans family for more than a century." She waits a moment before finishing. "An exotic, unexpected paradise."

Now she examines the other side, the photo in grainy sepia. "Look how little the trees were," she says, laughing but in a sad way. "They were babies, all of them babies."

Tears pool in her eyes and slip down her face, and Sonny takes a corner of the bedsheet and wipes them away. "We should have had our own babies," he says. "It makes me sick sometimes, Julie, I actually get sick. I can't believe we did what we did. It was the biggest mistake of my life and I will go to my grave regretting it. Who did we think we were, Julie?"

Juliet doesn't answer for a long time. "The Beauvais Mansion," she whispers, still studying the card. "It says so right here."

⚜

Juliet sits at the kitchen table and draws a diagram on the back of Sonny's bank statement. Anna Huey occupies the first room to the right at the top of the stairs, her mother's room comes next, then after that is Juliet's. Or what once was Juliet's. All the rooms to the left of the hallway are either empty or used for storage.

"Don't let her trick you," she says, scribbling with such purpose that the tip of her tongue pokes out of her mouth.

"Julie, listen, I don't think I can do this."

"Don't let her go without signing the check or putting the date. A check is worthless without that and she might pull a fast one. She's capable of anything."

"No, Julie."

"At a bank the thing they look for on a check is not the numerical amount in the little box on the right-hand side. It's what's written out on the long line under the line that names the payee. So you want to make sure that the numerical number in the box is the same as the amount she writes out. This is another way she might trick us."

"Julie?"

"Yes, my baby?"

She turns and faces him and it is a long moment before he speaks: "Does the Beauvais have an alarm system?"

She shakes her head, careful not to push any harder. "While you're inside," she says, "will you do something for me?"

She walks over to where he's standing by the sink and offers him the envelope. He hesitates before taking it, and when he does she sidles up close to him, her breasts grazing his chest. "Go in my bedroom and get me some clothes, please."

"Will those old clothes still fit?"

"They'll fit." She lightly touches him with her breasts again. "You know my body better than anybody. Do you think it's changed any in the last fifteen years?"

"No," his breath beginning to shallow. "But don't you think the style of clothes hanging in your closet might be a little dated?"

"Sonny, you need to remember something, sweetie." Now she presses up close, her chest flat against his. "When you look like I do everything you put on is in style."

The earliest painting, an imposing neoclassical oil on canvas signed by antebellum portraitist Jean Joseph Vaudechamp, hangs on the wall at the bottom of the stairs, ambient light from the foyer making it possible to observe its nattily dressed subject, a Creole gentleman wearing eye-glasses that rest low on his nose. Just to the right of the Vaudechamp is one by Jacques Guillaume Lucien Amans, and directly above that an Ellsworth Woodward, legendary founding instructor of the art depart-ment at the city's Newcomb College. Even without reading the signa-tures Sonny is able to identify the paintings' creators: they easily are among the most important to work in New Orleans in the last two centuries.

Pausing at the first step, Sonny runs his fingers over the thinly painted surface of the Vaudechamp. He sniffs the Amans. When he passes the John Genin showing Etienne Beauvais (as the small plaque on the frame identifies the sitter), Sonny blows against the canvas and inhales the master's celestial dust.

As he ascends the carpeted stairway each step groans louder than the one before. Or so it seems to Sonny, now more than halfway up. He takes his time not only to admire the artwork but also to consider the best way to announce himself. Does he simply nudge Miss Marcelle awake and tell her what he's come for? *Just dropped by for Julie's check, ma'am. Will you get up and write it, please?* Or does he show good man-ners and begin with an apology? *"I know this shows poor judgment on my part, madam, and I want to say at the outset that I'm as disappointed in myself as you are. But at the same time your daughter does need her money."*

Higher up the modern era of portraiture as practiced in the south-ern United States is represented by the likes of Arnold E. Turtle and Henry Casselli, who painted the masterwork at the top of the stairs, depicting Johnny Beauvais. Here Juliet's father is shown wearing the uniform of the prototypical southern gentleman: white silk suit, panama hat, polka-dot bow tie, wing tips with laces as thin as fishing line. Casselli somehow managed to get Johnny Beauvais just right, down to the downy texture of his yellow hair and the carefully trimmed fingernails coated with clear polish.

Sonny leans back against the balustrade and trains his eyes on those of the vividly painted man, who seems to stare back as if curious to learn Sonny's reason for being here tonight. "Couldn't tell you myself," Sonny whispers under his breath.

Sonny dated Juliet for seven months before Johnny Beauvais's death at Lake Pontchartrain, and though the man was generally cordial (he was always good for a hello, in any case), only once did he and Sonny have what might qualify as a conversation.

"Excuse me, but is your truck the noisy one that woke me from my nap?"

"Sir?"

"I was sleeping."

"It might've been. Forgive me."

"I'd rather have my rest than your apology, young man. What is wrong with you?"

"My lord, are we cross today?" Juliet said to her father.

"Darling, have you seen Anthony?"

"No, Daddy. Daddy, you were rude to Sonny."

"Was I? I didn't mean to be. Sonny, was I rude?"

"No, you weren't, Mr. Beauvais."

"By the way, why do they call you Sonny? It's a curse, isn't it? Having to go through life as Sonny? It's rather like being called Junior."

"I don't mind it," Sonny said.

"My name is really Jean-Jacques. I'm named for my paternal great-grandfather. As a boy I couldn't stand being called that, thus the name Johnny. Now I wish I could go back to the original. Sonny, what were you originally?"

"Cecil, Mr. Beauvais."

"Wise choice, then, going with Sonny. Who would name their child Cecil? It's cruel. Juliet, if you see Anthony send him up, please. I have a chore for the boy."

"Another one?"

"Nice visiting with you, Sonny."

"Same here, Mr. Beauvais. And I promise to do something about that muffler."

Not until Sonny reaches the mansion's second floor does he understand precisely where Juliet has taken him, and this knowledge stuns him to momentary paralysis, every part of him stilled. He looks around as if for a familiar landmark, something to spare him this reality and to safely place him elsewhere. What in God's name has she made you do now?

Sonny moves past an antique étagère and a marble pedestal holding a vase of freshly cut Louisiana irises, the purple at the head of the stalks glowing in the semidarkness. The hallway is wide enough to accommodate an entire army of intruders, and yet Sonny feels the walls pressing in. Checking the map, he passes two doors and approaches a third. Juliet's room.

As he swings the door open and steps inside he hears something altogether unexpected. There are voices and music, TV sounds, as well as the rumble of a window air conditioner. Sonny scans the room and finds Anna Huey lying in bed. Her crown of dreadlocks lies black against white bedding. A light summer throw covers her body.

He exits as quietly as he entered, but this is little comfort.

Why is Anna Huey sleeping in Juliet's room?

Sonny stands without moving, his back against the wall, his breath coming in stinging gasps, bowels beginning to feel fluid.

From his pocket he removes the envelope with Juliet's directions and studies the diagram by the glow of a night-light shining at his feet.

"Lou," she's written in her peculiar scribble, the word trailing an arrow that points between the first and second doors. Who is Lou? Sonny wonders.

Could Lou be *loo*, as in bathroom?

He moves on to the next room and slowly opens the door. A flood of relief washes through him as he discovers it empty and steps inside. Images from another time crowd the walls. Hendrix playing guitar, Joplin flashing the peace sign. "Chicken Little Was Right," says a poster showing an atomic bomb explosion. "The Sky *IS* Falling."

A corkboard holds a jumble of photographs depicting Juliet and friends celebrating at high school graduation parties, dancing at now-defunct French Quarter nightclubs, posing in cap-and-gown. Sonny recognizes many of the faces: Adelaide Valentine, Terri Edelstein, Brook McCaffety, Dickie Boudreau. Dickie looks even drunker than he usually did, an arm draped over Juliet's shoulder as she holds him with an adoring gaze.

Then Sonny spots himself in one of the pictures, a thin, sad-faced boy with too much hair. "I remember you," he mutters out loud.

Next to the corkboard stands a white plastic book unit and it, too, contains items from Juliet's days at Sacred Heart. There, for instance, is the small hourglass that Sonny gave her the night of her eighteenth birthday. No more than four inches tall, the brass timepiece includes a metal plate on its base with an inscription that reads *Forever*.

Sonny traces a finger over the lettering, the word both too large and too small for him to comprehend at the moment.

Juliet, he decides suddenly, will have to come for the clothes later. He can't do this and furthermore he won't do it; let her pout and treat him badly again. The two of them can always go to Canal Street in the morning, can't they? Once there Sonny will buy her whatever she wants, just as long as it's less than three hundred dollars, which is all he's worth. A new pair of jeans and a shirt, a dress from the discount rack. Leave the hippie duds in the dark of the closet where they belong.

*Get out of the house. Forget the check. Go.*

Sonny starts back down the hallway, moving more quickly than before, pressed by a sudden urgency to be anywhere but here. The portraits are in sight, the face of the dead father who knew Sonny only as the insensitive boy who disrupted his nap. But as Sonny is passing the door nearest the stairway a voice, too loud to ignore, stops him in his tracks. "Juliet? Darling, is that you?"

It is Miss Marcelle, and she seems to be waiting for an answer. Sonny must say something, but what? Against his will he reaches out and places a hand on the knob. Miss Marcelle is a friend. She'll understand if he walks in and presents himself. *"Oh, hi. Great to see you again!"* Just that simple, and without any suggestion that his uninvited presence is at all out of the ordinary.

"Juliet, darling, will you ever forgive me? Not only for the way I acted this afternoon, but for the other day when you first came home? I'm sorry, I haven't been myself lately."

Sonny doesn't speak, and Miss Marcelle says, "I can't bear how we are any longer. Juliet, in the morning, darling . . . in the morning can we please start anew. Let's be friends and forget everything. Can we do that? Is it really too late? Darling . . . oh, sweetie, I want so badly to be your mother again. I do, Juliet, I do . . ."

Sonny's brain screams in the silence. He glances at the stairway and the odd, boyish face of Johnny Beauvais. If Sonny doesn't say something Miss Marcelle will walk out and confront him. She needs an answer. Show yourself, he tells himself. Who better than Miss Marcelle to understand the might of her daughter's will? But presently the old woman's voice, weary with resignation, cuts through the darkness. "Go to bed, dear. Go to bed now. I do have something to tell you, but there's no reason to trouble you with it tonight. Let's talk in the morning. First thing."

Sonny leaves the hallway and starts down the stairs, his hand on the banister. He is nearing the foyer when a sound stops him. He strains to hear, and there it comes again. Someone is pacing the floor of the library, his step slow and deliberate as if to suggest a contemplative state of mind.

Frightened now beyond caring, Sonny doubles his fists and gulps huge drafts of air. He bounds down the final few stairs and throws the doors open.

The chairs and sofas are empty, the fireplace a black hole behind a black screen. Tall windows reflect the rain.

Sonny closes his eyes and listens for the steps again. And this time when he hears them he has no trouble locating their source.

The ghost of Johnny Beauvais isn't walking the floor after all, and neither are the long-dead Yankees of Juliet's imagination unable to return home.

Of all the things, Sonny was hearing the sound of his own heart.

ψψψ

"You need to work on your directions," he tells her in a rough tone.

"Don't tell me you got lost. Why doesn't that surprise me?" Juliet shakes her head and glances at the ceiling, the water stains that look oddly beautiful on the tiles, and that remind her of something, either a place or a time, that she can't quite grasp at the moment.

The room is dark. She's been waiting by the window.

Sonny shuffles into the bathroom and closes the door. He stays there for perhaps ten minutes and when he comes out he's wearing a fresh change of clothes and carrying the other ones bundled in a towel. He walks to the kitchen and, just past it, to the laundry room. He loads the washing machine, turns it on. "Weird time to wash, isn't it?" she says when he returns to the bedroom.

He doesn't answer and she says, "Do you have my clothes? What about my check? At least you'd better have that."

He sits on the edge of the bed and winds an alarm clock. "Juliet, you said your room was the third door off the stairs. It was the fourth."

"The fourth if you count the loo."

"Since when do you call it a loo? Is that a California word?"

He's jumpy and he seems to be having a hard time catching hi

129

breath. She stares at him, then says, "Yes it is, as a matter of fact. As soon as you get off the plane at LAX there's a group of volunteers who come up and teach you the right words from the wrong ones. 'We don't call it bathroom here in California,' they tell you."

He keeps winding the clock, hardly paying attention. "I opened the third door," he says, "and Mrs. Huey was snoring away on a little bed by the window."

Juliet finishes her drink and puts the cigarette in her mouth, squinting as smoke climbs past her face. "I guess that means Mama moved back to her original room. When I was in high school she stayed in the one next to mine because she could hear through the wall if I brought anyone there." She picks at a fleck of tobacco on her tongue. "Goddamn spy."

Sonny tests the alarm. It gives Juliet a jolt and brings her hopping to her feet. She can't make sense of his behavior. Maybe it's for the best she didn't give up the room at the Lé Dale, despite the expense. She takes a cassette tape out of her travel bag and slips it into the boom box on the table by the bed. She presses the Play button and a sax plays a lonely tune. It's Leonard Barbier, accompanied by his band. She finds herself listening for the drums, trying to extract the beat from the rest of the music. The boy who gave her the tape the day before.

"Sonny, did Anna Huey see you when you went in her room?"

"I don't think so. She had the TV on."

He walks over and turns down the music. "I still have your house key. I'll put it over here in your bag."

She nods. "Thank you."

"And I still have the map you drew on that envelope. I can show you where everybody is now, if you want."

"Sonny, what's wrong with you? What's wrong with you, Sonny?" She dunks the cigarette in her coffee cup with all the others. It's starting to fill up, the cup. She tries to count the stubs but is unable to focus for long. "Forget the key and forget the map and forget the clothes. If she wrote me my check, Sonny, that's all I want."

Half a minute goes by before he moves over to the dresser for his wallet. He fiddles around with his cash and removes a slip of blue-green paper and hands it to her.

The check is from a local bank. It is signed in the elaborate hand of Mrs. Marcelle L. Beauvais, and it has been issued to Juliet Beauvais 'n the amount of five thousand dollars.

# 4

JULIET LIES BACK ON THE PILLOWS
with her arms thrown over her head and her eyes
open. She lets out a low growl of pleasure. Does
she surrender to another orgasm? Does she fake
one? She's starting to feel a little punch-drunk
and a little detached from the moment, while
Sonny, his eyes closed, no less, seems to be performing as much for her benefit as for his own.
Anything for Julie.

She taps him on the shoulder and offers a
defeated smile. "It's starting to feel like the towering inferno down there."

"What?"

"Sonny, my period doesn't bother you?"

He rolls over with a sigh, and in the darkness
Juliet can see the muddy cloak covering his penis.

"Do you want me to help you finish?" she
says.

His head moves left to right on the pillow.

In the bathroom she closes the door and checks the medicine cabinet. A bottle of aspirin, a tube of ointment to treat poison ivy and a second one for muscle soreness. What else did she expect?

"I'm going to take a bath," she calls out.

She fills the tub and squats in cool water until her bottom stops throbbing. A cloud of blood swims to the surface, shining and iridescent in the soap bubbles. Juliet has always wondered at the sense of God who'd make something, a woman, with a hole like that, a portal without a latch for a lock, conveniently open to whoever and whatever you please.

"Sonny, that was wonderful, sweetie. I'm sorry I pooped out on you."

He comes in and sits on the floor by the tub, watching with a look of wonder as she soaps her breasts with a washcloth. "Did you clean all that stuff off?" she says.

"At the sink in the kitchen. I used paper towels."

"Your mother would die."

Sonny laughs but without much feeling. "If she hadn't gone and done that already, huh?"

"Sonny, why are you always so serious, baby. Can't you ever relax?"

"I can't let go of anything, can I?"

"No. Now do your girlfriend a favor and grab her a towel, please."

Juliet gets out of the tub and he lowers the toilet lid and instructs her to sit there. Clearly he's trying to redeem himself. He dries between her toes, dries each finger, dries her armpits, behind her knees, between her legs. His face is filled with stubborn intensity; he could be outside washing a car. Sonny grows aroused by the intimacy and he leans forward so that his cock, still streaked in places with blood, bumps and bobs against her. "Endlessly fascinating, I'm sure," she tells him.

"How's that?"

"Your penis. It's endlessly fascinating. It's also quite large."

He shakes his head but doesn't say anything.

"You don't think you're big, Sonny?"

"I think I'm average."

"Oh, if only that were so, sweetheart. If this is average there'd be many more happy ladies in the world. You men would give us nothing to complain about."

Juliet puts on his father's robe and although it's one o'clock in the morning and she could sleep food is the greater priority. She can't recall the last time she ate. A day ago? Two days ago? She and Sonny move to the kitchen and scavenge the cupboards. They find only noodles in a Tupperware container dating back to when Mrs. LaMott was alive. Hidden behind a forest of aerosol cans, the noodles are no less than five years old, but Juliet has Sonny cook them anyway. After they've finished boiling he splashes olive oil and sprinkles salt and crushed black pepper on them then adds half a stick of butter.

"This is the best pasta I've ever eaten in my whole, entire life," Juliet says, although in actual fact she's able to get little down.

Sonny says, "This is the same table where we sat that night you came for supper."

"Yes. I liked my yellow plate then and I like it now."

"I'm sorry there isn't more to eat. I need to make groceries soon."

"Only in New Orleans do people make groceries. Everywhere else they buy them. When I first got to LA I told this neighbor in my apartment complex that I needed to go make groceries and she thought I was asking for directions to the bathroom."

"Julie, do you think we'll ever get married?"

"I don't just think we will, baby, I know we will."

"I'd like children."

"Mmm . . ." As if the noodles are really that wonderful.

After the meal they clean the kitchen and retire to the bedroom and huddle against the headboard watching an old black-and-white movie on TV. The movie features Ronald Colman as an artist who loses his sight and is unable to paint anymore. Ronald Colman with his skinny mustache, dapper clothing and fine, gentrified manner looks and acts nothing like any artist Sonny ever knew, and Sonny determines to change his approach if ever he returns to the fence. This is what he says to Juliet, in any case.

Maybe with a different style he'll have more success selling his work. Maybe if he sounds less like the Ninth Ward and more Uptown. Maybe maybe maybe.

The movie ends and Juliet looks at him, eyes draining tears, a trickle at her nose. "Sonny, don't ever go blind."

"Not me, Julie."

They stay up until almost 3:00 A.M. The rain slacks off then stops altogether and a dense, eerie quiet settles in. Sonny opens a bedroom window and the cool, wet breeze cuts the fecund odor of fucking. "Don't ever go blind," Juliet says a second time, somehow loving and hating him both.

But by now Sonny is asleep, too far gone to answer.

Five hours later, at a little after eight o'clock, a hard knocking at the front door awakens Sonny to an empty bed, sheets wrapped around his legs.

Sonny comes to with a fat headache that only gets fatter when he realizes Juliet isn't there.

He throws on a robe and pulls the door open. Standing on the landing at the top of the stairs are two men in black plastic raincoats, both of them dripping water.

Sonny knows they're cops before they identify themselves.

The older and more physically substantial of the two gives his name as Lieutenant Peroux. "Me and Sergeant Lentini here are NOPD, Criminal Investigation Division."

Peroux looks to Sonny like one of those black Creoles Juliet lectured her mother about, his small, sharp features and fair complexion betraying more French than African blood. His hair, too, is straight and fine with comb lines sweeping from left to right. He's so wet from the rain that even his mustache shines with glass beads.

Lentini, in contrast, is small and fat and sports just enough stubble to look stylish. He wears horn-rimmed glasses and a weatherproof golf hat. Sonny can't decide whether he looks more like a fifties beatnik or an electronics technician on call for cable TV.

Neither he nor Peroux bothers to show credentials.

"Is Juliet Beauvais here?" Peroux begins. He has a Yat accent (as in the local colloquialism *"Where y'at?"*) and one almost as hard and flat as Sonny's.

Talking carefully, tightening the sash on his robe: "Ah, no. I'm sorry, Lieutenant. Juliet's already left."

"Did she say where she was going?"

"No. No, she didn't."

Sonny's head is pounding and he can barely speak for the dense, cottony weight on his tongue. "Would you like to come in?" He opens the door wider but Peroux stays outside, fingering a page in a reporter's notebook.

Lentini, on the other hand, brushes past Sonny without a word, glaring from behind too-thick lenses.

"Any idea where she might of run off to?" Peroux asks.

Sonny needs a moment to answer. "She had a room at a hotel downtown."

"What hotel was that?"

"The Lé Dale on Saint Charles. Just down the street from the Hummingbird." Once again Sonny tries to swallow but can't get anything down. "Lieutenant, can you tell me what's the problem?"

Peroux lowers his gaze and quickly brings it back up, his muddy brown eyes exploring Sonny's face as if for an answer to a question he isn't prepared to ask.

Then from inside Lentini speaks with a tone so low and unaffected he might be describing the room's thrift-store furnishings. "Somebody got in her mama's house last night." He waits until Sonny looks at him. "They killed her."

Sonny leaves the doorway and crosses the room and sits on the sofa by the window. Nearly a minute goes by before he starts to cry, then it comes with an intensity that racks his body. The cops watch him without saying anything. Finally when Sonny seems to finish, Peroux knocks on the door as if they just got there. "Hate to interrupt, but can we have a look around?"

It is hard for Sonny to answer, hard for him to say anything at all.

"In the room back there . . . mind if we look? You don't want us to look, just say don't look."

"You can look."

But Peroux stays where he is. And it's Lentini who looks. Sonny hears him opening closet doors, pulling back the shower curtain, rifling drawers.

"Are you sure it was Juliet's mother?"

"Positive, Sonny." The detective smiles and points a finger. "You are Sonny, right, podna?"

Lentini returns and flashes a pair of open palms.

Peroux takes a business card from his wallet and hands it to Sonny. SAMUEL PEROUX, JR., it says, and includes the phone number and South Broad Street address for police headquarters.

"We'll be needing to talk again," he says. "So don't be going nowheres."

Sonny keeps his eyes on the card.

"You see Miss Beauvais you have her call that number, you hear?" Sonny doesn't answer and Peroux says, "Hey, podna, I'm talking to you."

"I'll tell her."

As soon as they've gone, Sonny puts the police chain on the door. In the bathroom he forces a finger down his throat but nothing comes up. He kneels on the floor next to the tub and runs the water and tries a second time. Still nothing.

He can't stop shaking and can't seem to get warm and he lies on the rubber bathmat and holds his legs with his arms. He stays on the floor for nearly an hour then he remembers something and he gets dressed and walks downstairs to the street.

In the truck he starts with the passenger's side. Finding nothing, he moves down to the driver's side and feels under the seat. A Coke can. Paper candy wrappers and empty corn chip bags. Digging deeper, he finds the gloves and ski mask wadded together against the seat frame. He finds a tire jack and an empty can of oil. But the club is gone.

Sonny is careful not to slam the door.

He looks back at the house to make sure Florence and Curly Bonaventure aren't watching.

It's no big thing to find a ride, even at this time of night. The old Pontiac rattles to a stop and the passenger door squeaks open. Juliet, standing in a wash of red from the brake lights, flicks her cigarette in the weeds and steps forward trailing smoke. She doesn't think she can stand being kidnapped and raped just now, but her feet hurt. She bends in the door and spies a brother and his woman, their faces green in the glow from the dash. "Need a ride?"

"Did you see my thumb?" Juliet says to the man, then gives a loud, dishonest laugh. "Last I checked your thumb needs to do something."

"I don't play by them rules," he says. "If you're coming, get in. Otherwise, good night."

The woman shoves over and Juliet sits on the torn rubber seat. The window is down and she sticks her elbow out. "I'm going up the street here 'bout half a mile."

"On our way, then," says the woman, as the car thumps over train tracks. "You starting the day or you ending it?"

Juliet likes the woman's face, her smile. Also, she smells nice. Sweet, like cane syrup warmed with butter. "My days don't start or end, sweetie. They just go on and on and on."

"I hear you," says the man, cackling with laughter.

Juliet wants to ask about their day, but here they are in Faubourg Marigny already. She gets out and bumps the car with a fist as it drives away. The brake lights flash in recognition, then the blinkers, both sides. It is always nice to make new friends, even at three-thirty in the morning when it is a brother and his woman and she wouldn't be caught dead talking to them in the sensible light of day.

Her vagina's sore, but nevertheless Juliet feels deep affection for all mankind.

She walks a block and arrives at Leonard's club. Except for the handful of kids hanging out in front the place seems to have packed it in for the night. Inside a couple of boys are stacking chairs and folding tables. At the bar a woman is counting money. And over on the bandstand Leonard is coiling electrical cords.

Juliet walks up to the foot of the stage. "I've got an envie for crawfish étouffée," she declares in a happy voice.

"Huh?"

"You ever get like that? Like your body craves a certain type of food."

He nods and returns to his work. "Me, it's barbecue."

"When I get my inheritance I'm going to open a restaurant on the first floor."

"I hope you sell barbecue."

"You don't like étouffée?"

"Too rich," Leonard replies, dropping the cables long enough to pat his belly. "Pardon my French, but it gives me the runs."

Juliet shrugs. "I'll sacrifice the runs if it's étouffée."

The little young one has already left, as have the vocalist and the two others in the band. Leonard allows as to how he's hanging around here only until they get paid for the night, which is always an iffy proposition with the club's current management. "They didn't appreciate my man Bird when he was alive, either," Leonard says.

"That that white guy plays for the Celtics?"

"No, that's that black dude played the sax. Charlie 'Bird' Parker. He used to do gigs and they wouldn't want to pay him, neither. That's what you get for being an artist these days."

Juliet's about had it up to her eyeballs with artists, and she'd say as much if she didn't need Leonard's help. She wants him to drive her to the Beauvais then later to the Lé Dale.

They tramp out of the club ten minutes later, Leonard counting his money. It doesn't seem to occur to him to ask why she's shown up at such an hour, and this is a trait of his that she both admires and despises: Leonard Barbier might be as thick in the head as they come, but he doesn't meddle. He doesn't even ask about her encounter with the drummer, not that she holds the subject as sacred. They are strolling under the streetlights when Juliet says, "Ever see one purple like that?"

"Not on a white person I haven't."

"It looks like it got dipped in an inkwell, don't it?"

"You call that color eggplant. People nowadays are using it for home decorating. It's all the rage."

They move on a few paces before she thinks of something else to ask about. "What was my daddy like?" Trying to sound as casual as possible.

"What do you mean, what was he like?"

"Did it have a color?"

"Everything has a color. Even water has a color."

"You think he was a bona fide homosexual or do you think he liked it with girls, too?"

"I don't know, I never got around to asking him. But I'd assume he was content to go either way, considering he had a daughter to his credit. You don't grow fruit without planting seed, as they say."

"When you're young you don't understand about human sexuality, do you?"

"No, you don't—human or any other kind."

"When you're in high school and you hear your friends saying things about the man you love and admire most in the world, when that happens you can get really confused."

"Tell me about it. I got confused and the only thing my father ever wanted to have sex with was his money."

Leonard takes out a small glass vial with a rubber stopper. It holds cocaine and he dribs some out on the back of his hand and offers it to Juliet, who consumes it with a single inhalation. After he ingests a line of his own he puts the vial back in his pocket and starts a doob going. Leonard the medicine man. He drags for a long time before sharing with Juliet.

"We were discussing my daddy?"

"Right."

"I'm just trying to remember if my memory is correct."

"I know you are."

"Was he a good lover, Leonard?"

"I'm a little uncomfortable with this line of questioning, Counselor," Leonard replies. But after a few seconds he says, "Yeah, I suppose he was, if you really have to know."

"Did he feel guilty afterwards? I always feel guilty."

"I'd say he suffered like we all suffer, Juliet, except in his case he got on the phone and called room service. Your father was a bon vivant, I'll give him that."

"Did he ever mention me?"

"Not when we were doing it, if that's what you mean."

"I mean in general. Did he talk about me?"

"All the time. The man loved you, Juliet."

They reach his car finally. It's parked on Esplanade Avenue, not far from the Beauvais. She tells him to drive her there, and he's too busy smoking his dope to protest.

He parks by the curb and they sit awhile looking at the house past the windblown shroud of crape myrtles. She watches the window where the Yankee allegedly hanged himself but tonight it's as dark as all the other windows.

She wonders if they'd pay her another thousand if she broke another lamp.

"I always liked the Beauvais," says Leonard.

"Then let's go see it. I have a key." She shoulders the car door open.

Leonard holds up the joint. "Can I bring my little friend here?"

"Only if you promise to blow a lot of smoke."

The trees drip rainwater as she and Leonard walk up the path. At the front door she tells him to take his shoes off, and when she removes her own she remembers "The Proof" and pulls it out from under the insole and sticks it in a pocket.

They place their shoes side by side on the welcome mat, as if they belong there. When she slips the key in the knob the door swings open, sounding a rusty lament. Sonny must've forgotten to lock it after he left. Juliet and Leonard stalk in. She wishes she could talk out loud and give him a real tour. *"Now as we enter the foyer you'll note the crystal chandelier hanging from the ceiling overhead . . ."*

They move through the parlor. It was her mother who started calling it a parlor, but Juliet prefers to think of it as the Grand Ballroom. It was the Grand Ballroom to previous generations of Beauvais, back in the days when people liked to capitalize the names of their rooms.

When she gets it back it'll be the Grand Ballroom again—at least until she converts it to a restaurant.

"Oh, look, that's the couch where Daddy got caught one night," Juliet says to Leonard. "It used to be in a bedroom upstairs. They must've moved it."

Leonard smiles. "Got caught doing what?"

She pretends not to have heard. But in her head now another voice: *"Juliet? Juliet, wake up, baby. Wake up. Put some clothes on, Juliet. We're leaving, baby. We're leaving this house . . ."*

She turns away from the sofa. "Daddy ever bring you here?"

Leonard shakes his head and mouths the word: "Hotels."

They troop past the TV. That's the next thing gets broken, Juliet says to herself. She wishes she had some tape to tape "The Proof" to the screen. Give her mother something to think about when she sits down tomorrow to her *Good Morning America*.

"I can make you a sandwich," Juliet says as they tramp through the kitchen.

"My mind's stuck on barbecue," Leonard replies.

"What about some Neapolitan ice cream? Mama always did keep a half-gallon handy."

"No, ma'am. Ice cream, étouffée. Anything rich like that and I got to go."

She opens the freezer door and sure enough there's the ice cream. Her mama and that cheap K&B drugstore brand comes in a paper cube. "You ever wonder why they call it Neapolitan?"

"No. Not me personally I haven't."

"It's that ice cream with chocolate, strawberry and vanilla stripes? It's good when you can't decide on any one particular flavor."

"I don't like to mix my foods," Leonard says. "I got this phobia about it. I like my peas on one side, my rice on another, then my meats over here."

They prowl through every room on the first floor and end up in her father's library, casually sitting on leather furniture. Although Leonard's doob has stopped burning, he heroically sucks on it for vestiges of life, a last sweet spin across wherever. When it gives nothing he curls up on the couch and clutches a throw pillow to his chest. "You're not gonna fall asleep on me, are you?" she says.

He looks so peaceful, though, that she can't bring herself to protest any more.

Certain that he's asleep, Juliet takes the coke vial from his pocket and empties it on an occasional table. "Is this my life?" she says to the enormous room, then snorts the powder without bothering to cut it into lines.

She leans back in the wing chair and listens to the silence, her mind tumbling in the purest of space. She suddenly feels energized, and strong. Too bad Leonard's not awake to arm wrestle. Too bad Anthony's not around to race in the yard. Her father used to time Anthony when he sent him out on chores, ticking off the seconds. "*Twenty-four . . . twenty-five . . . twenty-six . . .*" If only her father were here, she would break Anthony's records.

"*Juliet? Juliet, please, sweetie, get up.*"

"*Where are we going, Mother?*"

She's about to get up and rouse Leonard when her father, dressed in white and holding his favorite panama, appears on the other side of the room.

"Darling," he says in his beautiful way. "Darling, how splendid. You've come home."

Her throat is dry from the coke and it takes an effort to speak. "Daddy, this might sound funny but death has been good to you."

"Still look like Cary Grant, do I?"

"Yes, Daddy. You look so young."

He's facing outside, eyes trained on something in the distance. "Juliet, I heard what you said about the couch and me getting caught. I have to ask you: is that anybody's business?"

"I didn't tell him who they caught you with."

"That's private information."

"I know it is, that's why I didn't say it. Don't be mad at me, Daddy."

"Then don't give me a reason to be." He turns away from the window and confronts her at last. Yes, it's him, all right. His face is shiny and white, illumined by a source she can't immediately locate. It is a while before she understands that her father looks exactly as he does in the Casselli portrait on the stairway. Same clothes, same hair, same everything. He might've stepped right out of the canvas.

The light shining on him must come from the small lamp fixed to the frame.

"Daddy, are you real?"

"Of course I'm real, darling. Now go upstairs and kill your mother."

Juliet leaps to her feet, prepared to obey, but in that instant Johnny Beauvais disappears. He's no longer at the window, anyway. Her father who until a minute ago was entombed in a crypt in a cemetery just up the street, its pale Italian marble now sugary with age, his name crawling with lichen. Her father who by now is a skeleton or, worse, dust.

A crush of hopelessness drops Juliet back in the seat, and the sound of the chair legs meeting the yellow pine causes Leonard to stir. He props himself up and gives a yawn.

"Damn, girl, you look like you saw a ghost."

Her heart feels as if someone with large hands is squeezing it and trying to make it stop.

"Juliet?"

"It was Daddy," she says, her voice sounding jagged for the pain. "He told me something."

⚜

Through stop signs and traffic lights Sonny drives without braking, pushing the old truck harder than it seems willing to go. He stops only once: to deposit the gloves and ski mask in a Dumpster behind a Marigny soul food restaurant.

In front of the Beauvais cars stand bumper to bumper by the curb, and a second line blocks the near lane. People crowd the fence peering past the iron bars and trees.

Sonny parks about a hundred yards away on the opposite side of the boulevard and runs to the gate. It occurs to him that by running he's likely to draw attention to himself so he slows to a walk and joins the onlookers at the gate. Past the fence men and women of an official capacity huddle under the trees while others dig around under shrubbery bordering the property. Crime scene tape hugs the columns in front of the house, running from one to another and forming a loose girdle. All together Sonny counts half a dozen patrol officers, one of whom stops him as he tries to squeeze inside. "You're going to have to wait out here."

The cop grips Sonny's elbow and leads him back to the sidewalk.

Sonny lingers with the others at the fence until Anna Huey appears on the first-floor gallery, Peroux at her side. This time when Sonny tries to clear the gate the cop plugs the entrance with his body. He lifts a finger and starts to speak, it's going to be a lecture, but Peroux calls out "Let him in," and Sonny pushes inside.

He and Anna Huey embrace on the lawn and she begins to weep and Peroux lumbers off and joins the others under the trees. "It isn't true," Sonny says.

"It is, sugar. It is true. She's dead. Madam's dead." Tears run down her face and her voice is tired and weak. "Five o'clock," she says, holding up a hand spread open. "Five o'clock and I go to wake her up and I can feel it isn't right. I pull the curtains open expecting to hear a good morning. Miss Marcelle always gave me a good morning." Anna Huey shakes her head and squares her arms at her chest. "She wasn't there. The bed's been slept in, but empty. So I walk down the hallway and I see Juliet's door open and madam inside lying real quiet on the floor."

"Jesus."

"They beat her, sugar. Beat her so hard whatever it was they did it with broke and rained pieces all over the room. Little white plastic pieces and sand and dirt maybe. Madam looked peaceful, though. Take the blood away and she looked fine. Like she was sleeping."

Sonny shoots a glance at Peroux and he's dismayed to discover the detective fixed on him with a stare, his countenance dark and bothered, hair plastered close to his scalp. Like most of the cops on the scene, Peroux is wearing transparent booties over his shoes and latex gloves on his hands, the gloves barely extending past the heels of his palms.

He lifts one of those hands and gives Sonny a wave.

"That detective and another one came by my house looking for Juliet," Sonny says.

"I knew they were going to, I'm the one who told them she might be there. But the police . . . Lieutenant Peroux, anyway, he just told me they found her in a hotel downtown. She's on her way now."

Sonny sees past the mansion's open door where dieners from the coroner's office are carrying a gurney with a black body bag down the stairs. As they near the bottom one of the men bumps the Vaudechamp, exposing a lighter shade of paint underneath than that which covers the rest of the wall. The men place the gurney on the ground floor, lift its bed and wheel the body to the back of the house where, just past another open door, an ambulance is waiting.

Sonny is listening only halfway when Anna Huey says, "I blame myself. Why'd I have to call and tell that girl to come back home?" She pivots away from the house, unable to finish. "Sonny, what I told you yesterday . . . listen, sugar, I meant it, I meant every word. And I want you to know I told the detectives the same thing."

"Yeah?" He's distracted, still watching the attendants with the body bag. Still wondering why the cop keeps watching him. "You told them what, Mrs. Huey?"

"The truth."

She has his attention now. "And what is that?"

"That she's dangerous, to start. I also told them she's not right in the head and hasn't been for years. She's even worse off now than Mr. Johnny was at the end."

"Mrs. Huey, with all due respect, it's hardly your place to be talking to the police about Juliet like that."

"No? Well, with all due respect to you, Sonny, you're ignorant. And I can tell them whatever I want. Somebody's got to say it."

"Yes, ma'am."

"Sonny, a few months ago Miss Marcelle and I hired an agency to locate Juliet and file a report about her whereabouts and activities. This agency was able to get Juliet's medical papers, don't ask me how. Would you like to know what we learned?"

Sonny shakes his head. "No, ma'am, I don't."

"Good. Because I'd have to go get my dictionary. Paranoia, narcissism, delusions, histrionics. They're hard enough to say let alone to understand."

Sonny doesn't speak and Anna Huey says, "Want to guess where I reached her to tell her that story about her mama being sick?"

"No, ma'am."

"Now if this isn't sad, now if this won't break your heart. Juliet was at work, sugar. It was eleven o'clock in the morning, California time, and she had to come off the stage at a club called the Bend Over out by the airport."

"Doesn't make her a killer," Sonny says, his voice barely audible.

"Oh, Sonny, I hate to hurt you, sugar, but your Juliet is gone forever."

Sonny needs a moment to think, to absorb it all. Too stunned to cry, he offers a quiet laugh to convey his disbelief.

"Sonny, you need to get smart, baby. You've been in a trance, sugar. It's like you're hypnotized. It's like some magician put you in a spell half your life ago and he never snapped his fingers to wake you back up."

"Mrs. Huey, Juliet was at home with me in the Bywater until early this morning. There's no way she was involved in this."

She studies his face with a leery half-smile, and it's clear she'd laugh if not for a lack of energy. "Sonny, sometimes, sugar, I think you're more lost than she is."

"Mrs. Huey, Juliet was with me."

She doesn't respond and Sonny can feel her pulling away.

"She was with me," he says again.

But Anna Huey is walking toward the cops under the trees.

⚜

Leonard parks around the corner and together they enter the Hummingbird and take the lone table by a window. She likes the view of the street with the train rails lying in parallel ribbons in the bricks and asphalt, and overhead the silver-black power line that fires the streetcars running the length of the avenue. The Hummingbird isn't fancy enough for individual menus; a menu board, decorated with drawings of dancing steaks and pork chops, covers a wall in the room. "Crawfish étouffée," Juliet says, without bothering to consult the board.

The waiter points a stubby pencil at the wall. "I can give you fried shrimp. We serve étouffée only as a special."

Juliet gives her head a weary shake. "Ham and eggs, then. Coffee and toast and ice water and mixed-fruit jelly."

"The same," Leonard tells the man. "But instead of the ham and eggs and coffee and toast and mixed-fruit jelly, let me have grits and bacon and biscuits and pineapple juice."

"You want the ice water?"

"Yeah, give me the ice water."

"You ain't even funny," and Juliet draws on a cigarette. "Tell him he ain't even funny," she says to the waiter.

But the waiter, writing on his pad, seems to like it well enough.

They're almost finished with the meal when Juliet says, "I figure I owe you for tonight. You can come up to the room and sleep with me if you want."

"I'm more in my man mood these days," Leonard says, rubbing a piece of biscuit in the shallow pool of bacon grease on his plate. "But I do appreciate the invite."

"I said sleep, Leonard. I'm having my period."

"You just want me to sleep?"

"I like a warm body in the bed with me."

Leonard pays with a credit card. He has one of those old-man wallets with rows of slits on both folds. His slits are full of cards.

"Some people collect stamps," she says. "Leonard Barbier? Leonard likes plastic."

He starts counting the cards, touching each one, eighteen altogether. "Bless me, Father, for I have sinned, it's been fifteen years since my last confession."

"Speak to me, my son."

"My cards, Father? They belong to Big Leonard."

He didn't finish his pineapple juice, so she reaches for it. "You stole your father's wallet?"

"It's complicated." He takes the glass out of her hand and drains the juice, then he chews on some ice. "Can I stop calling you Father now?"

She nods and with a hand makes the sign of the cross in the air between them.

"Well, and I hate this, I just hate it, but Big Leonard's my sponsor. Or that's how I've heard him refer to our arrangement. He's my sponsor so

146

long as I, quote unquote, stay out of the paper. Big Leonard, basically, is afraid he'll pick up the *Picayune* one morning and read how Leonard Barbier III was arrested in the French Quarter and charged with crimes against nature or whatnot. That would put a serious dent in his lifestyle. He could lose a seat on one of his boards—the LSU board of supervisors, the board at the New Orleans Museum of Art. And what about his Carnival krewe? Oh, no, that just can't happen. The world would end."

"I like that name, Big Leonard. It sounds like what somebody would call their penis. 'Hi, there. Have you met Big Leonard?' "

"Yes, well, the man's a dick. You got that right."

Leonard didn't finish the bacon either. She takes it and eats it all before he can think to protest. "I could forgive Mother a lot of things if she'd given me a wallet full of credit cards," she says.

"Believe me, it's not something to be getting jealous about."

"Sure, it is. Your father's sponsoring your experience as a degenerate white Negro playing jazz and living in a weekly/monthly and taking drugs and having out-of-wedlock relations with both men and women. It isn't fair. Why won't anyone sponsor me?" She's talking with her mouth full. "The only thing Mama ever gave me was a giant case of the red ass. Just for that," and it's so much she's afraid to swallow, "from here on out I'm going to call you Little Leonard."

"No, you're not."

"Little Leonard."

"Say it again and everyone gets to hear what you did tonight."

"Little Leonard . . ."

He starts to stand on his chair but she scrambles around the table and yanks him back down.

In the room they strip to their underwear and dive under the covers and Juliet spoons with her chest pressed against his thin, unmuscled back. Although he smells of cooled sweat and grease and cigarette smoke she wouldn't call the odor offensive. She closes her eyes and tries to sleep but sleep won't come. As a girl her mother taught her to say the "Hail Mary" prayer over and over until the repetition lulled her to sleep but that doesn't work now either. The window unit rumbles and from the avenue she hears horns blowing and trucks with wailing brakes and winos arguing over a bottle. The bottle breaks and the winos fall silent. Then a couple of car doors slam. But parking on the street below is for emergency vehicles only.

Juliet knows it's the police even before she hears voices and footsteps on the stairs and a busy knocking outside.

"Five-O," she whispers to Leonard.

"Five who?" He lies on his belly and cocks his head her way.

"Fuzz, baby. They've come to get us."

Leonard scrambles out of bed. He fishes around in his pant pockets and withdraws an empty vial and what's left of a joint, then he stumbles into the bathroom and flushes them down the toilet.

Juliet answers the door in her underwear.

"Miss Beauvais?" It's a male black who in the right light could pass for a male white. "Are you Miss Juliet Beauvais?"

Juliet nods.

"Miss Beauvais, I'm NOPD, Lieutenant Peroux? This here is Sergeant Lentini." Juliet glances at the silent one and he removes his golf hat and looks at the floor. "I'm afraid we've come with bad news," says the talker. "Miss Beauvais, somebody broke into your mother's house last night and attacked her." He waits for the long beat of a heart then says, "She's dead."

"Mama?" Juliet throws a hand up to her mouth and stifles a scream. A spasm cuts through her, then a second more powerful one. "Oh, God. Mama."

Leonard, standing at the bathroom door, lets out a yelp.

"Mother's dead, sweetie," she tells him.

"Mother's dead?" Struggling to get his pants on, Leonard nearly falls to the floor as he hurries out to join her. "I mean, your mother's dead, Juliet? My God, what happened?"

"She was murdered," says Peroux. "Mrs. Huey found her early this morning."

"Who found her?" But then, oh yeah, it comes to her. "I'm just not accustomed to a cleaning woman being called like that," Juliet explains.

Peroux is staring at Leonard. "Who are you?"

"He's my boyfriend, Detective," Juliet says.

"This one's your boyfriend? I thought Sonny LaMott was your boyfriend."

Leonard stutters when he says, "I'm her friend who's a boy."

Lentini, looking up finally, seems to decide it's okay now to put his hat back on.

"You got a name, friend-who's-a-boy?" asks Peroux.

"Leonard Barbier," Leonard says.

"Who?"

"His name is Leonard Barbier. Now if you don't mind, Lieutenant, I'd like to get dressed."

"You ain't Leonard Barbier," Peroux says. "Leonard Barbier, I know Leonard Barbier. Leonard Barbier's a lawyer here in town. Got a big office in the CBD."

"I'm Leonard the Third," Leonard says.

Peroux is still glaring at him when he says, "Miss Beauvais, would it put you out terribly to have Sergeant Lentini and myself look around your room?"

"Why do you want to look around my room?"

"Are you telling me not to, Miss Beauvais?"

"Lieutenant, I don't mean to be rude but you leave me no choice. First you tell me my mother's been murdered then you want to go through my personal effects." Juliet picks her clothes off the floor and starts putting them on. "It isn't right. You're welcome to look all you want, but play by the rules and get a search warrant."

Past his whiskers Peroux's mouth turns up in a grin. "You're right, of course. How insensitive of me."

"Do you think I killed her? Is that what you think?"

"I haven't formed any opinion yet. Settle down, please, Miss Beauvais."

Leonard moves over to a window, quietly so as to avoid attention. He stands staring into a block of hazy morning light, blood drained from his face.

"Where have I seen you before?" Peroux says to Juliet.

She's sitting on the bed, fussing with a shoe. She can't believe she's being asked that again. "Ever use the men's room at the Napoleon House?"

He doesn't answer.

"They've got a picture of me naked hanging in there." After a moment she adds, "By Sonny LaMott. Have you interviewed Sonny yet, Lieutenant? Have you searched his room?"

Peroux seems to be thinking about it. But when he answers, it's to an earlier question. "No, I believe it was someplace else." From the pocket of his jacket he removes a stick of Wrigley's. He lets the wrappers fall to the floor then he folds the gum in half and sticks it deep in the back of his mouth. "You ever do any pornography, Miss Beauvais?"

149

Juliet just keeps fooling with that shoe. "When you sign the release," she says, "nobody bothers to tell you it's a death certificate. But yes, Lieutenant, I have."

Peroux finds this funny. He laughs, anyway. "Miss Beauvais, we'll need to be asking you some questions later today." Then to Leonard: "You, too, podna."

When the sound of their car doors comes again, Leonard retreats from the window and stands in the middle of the room. "Why would that man think Sonny LaMott was your boyfriend?"

"Shit if I know. And all I really wanted last night was some god-damned étouffée."

"Did you and Sonny get back together?"

"Me get back with Sonny? Come on, Leonard. Use your head."

"That's why you were asking all those questions at the club the other night, wasn't it?"

"Leonard, stop it. My mother is finally dead and the Beauvais is mine and what do you care anyway who I get back with or don't get back with? You're in your man mood these days."

"I'll show you my man mood."

Leonard has a much easier time taking his clothes off than putting them on, and the same is true of Juliet. Having no detectives at the door is the difference.

"Don't forget my period," she says.

"Just be quiet and watch for a minute."

He lies on his back and she watches him and even helps toward the end, her favorite part. She figures it's the least she can do. He finishes on her chest and she goes to the bathroom and gets a hand towel and wets it with hot water and wipes herself off.

"You think you're gonna miss your mama any?" Leonard asks through the open door.

That, as it happens, is the very same question she's been asking herself since checking to make sure her mother was dead a few hours earlier. "No," she says, "I don't."

※

"Hey, podna, you got a minute to help me out with something?" It's Lieutenant Peroux, walking over to join him at the fence.

Sonny can feel his guts rebelling at the prospect of more questions. Didn't he do his part at the house earlier? Short of his confessing, he wonders what more they could possibly need.

He and Peroux stand beneath the canopy of a giant magnolia, last night's rainwater still dripping from the blossoms and large, glossy leaves.

"LaMott?"

"Go ahead, Lieutenant."

"Now tell me if I got this right. For a long time you've been coming here to visit. You sit in the living room and you and the lady have tea or coffee or whatever?"

"I'm an artist, and sometimes when I'm in the neighborhood painting a particular house or garden or street corner I stop by to see how she's doing, that's correct."

"She was so fascinating, an old woman, you made a point to do that?"

"I've known her since 1971, my senior year in high school. And I've always liked Miss Marcelle. And her age—the fact that she was older than me—didn't matter."

"But I still don't see why you kept coming here. What did you have in common besides the daughter neither of you'd seen in fifteen years?"

"Nothing. Juliet was all we had in common."

"Nothing but Juliet. Now, Sonny, some time yesterday you stopped by and asked for money."

"Yes, I did. Well, it was a check actually. But the maid met me at the door and refused to give me one. She seemed to think it was inappropriate. Since it was Juliet's money, she thought Juliet should be the one who came and got the check."

"The maid, LaMott? Do you mean Mrs. Huey?"

Sonny nods.

"So she didn't give you the check?"

"No."

"You never got it?"

"No. Well, not from Mrs. Huey."

Peroux waits and so does Sonny.

"What do you mean? 'Not from Mrs. Huey.' Did Mrs. Beauvais give you a check later on?"

"Late last night I returned to the house a second time and she gave me one then."

"How late was this?"

"Midnight maybe. I don't know exactly. Somewhere like that."

Peroux takes his time, the activity in his mind bringing a slight wobble to his eyes. "So it's midnight—late like you say—and you come here and knock on the door or ring the bell or what?"

"I had Juliet's key."

"So you just go right straight in the house?"

"I know how bad that must sound, but it's the way it happened, Lieutenant Peroux."

"I could arrest you for that. I could take you in."

"Yes sir."

"Did you kill that woman, LaMott?"

"No, Lieutenant. I swear on my mother's grave I didn't."

A long silence. Peroux trying to decide how to proceed. He searches the grounds for Lentini, then finally: "So you just let yourself in. Let's get back to that."

"Well, as I told you, Lieutenant, I went in through the front door. First I wanted to get some clothes for Juliet from her closet—she'd asked for this—but after I went in her room I realized what a crazy thing I was doing and I started to leave. I was passing Miss Marcelle's room when she said something through the door. She thought I was Juliet."

"You remember what she said?"

"That she regretted things in the past and that she hoped the two of them could start over in the morning. She said she wanted to be Juliet's mother again."

"Go on."

"I went downstairs and at some point I decided that while I was there I'd just as well go get Juliet's check and be done with it. Obviously I wasn't thinking rationally, but I believed it would somehow keep the peace between them. So I walked back up and knocked on Miss Marcelle's door and when she answered I could see immediately her shock at finding who it was. Her face, anyway, went from an expression of absolute joy to one of surprise then to one of anger. I stood there fumbling for words and eventually managed to express my embarrassment for letting myself in without her permission. I started to leave again but she said no, to wait a minute, so I stood at the door and watched as she wrote out the check at a table by the bed. Even more than my being in the house she seemed upset that I wasn't Juliet. She kept saying they needed to talk. As I was leaving she told me I was never welcome in the Beauvais again, and never to come back. I told her I was sorry I'd compromised our friendship. And she said . . ."

The detective nods for Sonny to continue.

"She said I'd done more than that. 'You've killed it,' is how she put it."

"And the two of you had this big conversation and Mrs. Huey didn't leave her room to see what the commotion was all about?"

"There wasn't any commotion. We were just talking, Lieutenant."

Peroux seems to be trying to decide what to ask next. Once again he looks around for his partner. "That's a helluva story, son. A helluva damn story."

Sonny shrugs. "It's the truth."

The detective is smiling. Shaking his head. "And where was Juliet all this time you were prowling around uninvited in her mama's house?"

"Waiting for me back at my place."

"Okay, podna." Peroux is writing in his notebook, the effort pulling his mouth down in a frown. "LaMott, listen. I want you to come see me later this afternoon. That's police headquarters on Broad Street. Say about five o'clock."

"Down by the old Falstaff Brewery?"

"That's right, down by the brewery. Come up to the Criminal Investigation Division on the third floor and we'll find us an empty room and sit and have some coffee and go over all this again. Between now and then I want you to think about anything you might've left out."

Sonny nods. "Okay. So am I free to go?"

"Free for now, anyway," the detective says, then flashes a smile before walking away.

In the French Quarter a miracle: Juliet has found a parking spot less than a mile away from her destination, her mother's bank on Chartres Street.

She dunks a couple of coins in the meter. The bank opened less than an hour earlier and inside the floor, though pocked with gum droppings, shines from last night's mopping. Still undecided whether to take the cash in big or small denominations, Juliet joins five or six others in the queue corral and waits her turn. She's jumpy from too much coffee and too little sleep. Menstrual cramps add to her torment.

She wonders if Lentini is a mute or if with a partner like that high yellow it's impossible to get a word in edgewise.

"Give it to me in hundreds," she tells the teller when it's her turn.

The teller is wearing a tan suit identical to those worn by all the others behind the counter. A tasteful, teal-colored ascot finishes the outfit. "Do you have a current ID?"

Juliet pulls out her California driver's license and slides it across the faux marble surface. "No, why don't you make it tens and twenties. Give me a big wad."

The woman types something at her computer terminal, eyes colored with beads of amber from the screen. When she can't seem to find what she's looking for, she glances up at Juliet with a nervous smile. "Excuse me a moment, Ms. Beauvais," then she walks over to a man seated at a desk.

The man takes the check and inspects it at length and the two of them talk briefly. He looks at Juliet, then down at the check, then up at Juliet again.

"Ms. Beauvais?" the teller says upon returning. "Mr. Patout would like a word with you, please."

Something is wrong, but for Juliet to fixate on the negative would all but guarantee a lousy result. She tells herself this, anyway, and she flashes a smile intended to display an inner wealth of optimism, when all she really feels inside is hugely pissed off.

"Ms. Beauvais?" The man extends a hand for her to shake. He has a florid face shaped like a teardrop, a configuration that repeats itself in the general form of his body. "My name is Jay Patout. Please have a seat."

Juliet sits.

"Ms. Beauvais, I'm afraid this account is inactive."

"What do you mean, inactive?"

"It was closed five years ago, in May 1981."

"No, that check's good." Juliet grips the arms of her chair. "That's my mother's signature. And my mother is a wealthy woman, Mr. Patout. You know the Beauvais over on Esplanade?" Juliet nods before the banker is able to proffer a like response. "How could she live in a house like that writing bad checks? No, I'm afraid it's impossible."

Patout studies the check as if for a clue to one of the world's great mysteries. "Your mother may have made a mistake. This happens. People write checks on inactive accounts, forgetting they've moved their money to other accounts or to other banks. I'm sure there's an easy explanation."

Juliet feels nerves pushing up close to the surface of her skin. "Let's say Mama did put her money in another bank, could you tell me which one from the information on your screen there?"

"No, I couldn't. I mean, I wouldn't be able to tell. All I know is that your mother left us years ago. She had two accounts here and she closed them both."

Juliet sighs. She wants to scream, but the sigh is adequate for now. "If I find the bank she moved her money to, would they cash that check?"

"You'd have to get your mother to write a check from the bank where she now has her money. This one isn't good." Patout holds it up as if to give her one more look, then he stamps it hard and slips it in a drawer.

On her way out Juliet manages to keep her composure. She doesn't turn back around and curse the building or its occupants, and she doesn't punch or kick any of the bank's customers who seem to look at her with suspicion. She doesn't shoot a middle finger or raise a fist or spit on the floor. She displays no hitches in her stride.

Mama is having a gigantic laugh at this moment, watching from wherever the dead daughters of Opelousas yam farmers end up.

Juliet might end up in the same place one day, and that is when she'll exact her revenge. She'll whip her mother's ghostly ass. She'll pull her hair and smash a heel in her face.

Juliet reaches the Mustang, leans back against the hood and removes her shoe. She wants to add today's incident at the bank to her list, but "The Proof" is not in its usual place. And only now does she remember where she and Leonard deposited the document last night. She feels renewed suddenly. Maybe revenge won't be necessary, after all.

And now Juliet, remembering something else, is further mollified. As an heiress, and the only survivor in the family, she stands to inherit the entire Beauvais legacy. How soon that succession becomes official is a concern. But Juliet is rich.

And it strikes her, there now on the sidewalk, that her mother really is bound for the grave. Juliet's anger washes away in a single, pulsing tide. She screws her shoe back on and she begins to laugh with such feeling that her laughter takes on a musical aspect. From nearby a man clothed in rags comes shuffling toward her on the bricks. He holds out a palsied hand, as if for payment.

Juliet pushes past the hand and presses up against him.

She inhales his stench and feels his cold wine breath. He is the most hideous and repulsive thing she's ever encountered in her whole, entire life, and yet she does not yield.

Beneath her gaze the man's eyes grow small and pale, and his nostrils flare as he struggles for air. Juliet brings her mouth to the side of his face, her inner tubes brushing the mangled comb of flesh that is his ear. "Wanna do it?" she says.

The man shakes his head.

Juliet gets in her rental car and calmly starts for Esplanade.

***

In the rear garden the two detectives come back into view. They roll up their pant legs and cross the lawn splashing through puddles and join a clutch of investigators by the privet along the back fence. After a brief discussion a man in sunglasses separates himself from the group and points at something. Peroux crouches next to him to get a better look. They exchange more words, then the man in sunglasses duckwalks into the hedges and carefully picks up a shattered length of PVC. He seals it in a plastic evidence bag.

The knot of men grows tighter as each strains for a closer look. Standing alone on the shadowy lawn, Sonny experiences a jolt of fear that won't be reasoned with.

They have the club, he tells himself. Soon, bubba, they'll have you too.

A wave of nausea cuts through him, leaving him weak and dizzy. He needs to vomit again. He walks into a copse of crape myrtles by the fence, looking for a place to unburden himself, when a voice seems to speak to him. "Well well well. Look at what we have here."

It's a newsman, standing on the sidewalk. Past the iron bars, the tangle of shrubs, he wears a laminated press pass clipped to a khaki-colored fishing vest, a tortured smile confusing his otherwise relaxed demeanor. He raises a camera and starts shooting the police with their discovery. The man, rotating the instrument from the horizontal to the vertical, clicks off half a dozen frames before he speaks again. "They say she was a hermit. Came out only at certain times of the year to smell the morning glory. And only at night. She'd carry a flashlight. Can you imagine that?"

Sonny watches him.

"Old woman in a big house. Drug dealers and gangbangers thick as cockroaches in the neighborhood. They might not catch the guy but it won't be hard to figure who did this one."

Sonny is quiet. He nods to let the man know he's interested.

"I was at the scene of a homicide nearly identical to this one about a month ago in the Lower Garden District," the photographer continues. "You know that area?"

Sonny nods. "Sure."

"Only difference there, the guy rapes the old broad before clobbering her on the head."

"They ever find him?"

"Shit no. But they never find half of 'em. Not in this city." The man snaps off a few more shots. "People call it the Big Easy, but you'll never hear a homicide cop say that."

"No, you won't," Sonny says for no reason that he can make out.

"Ask one of them, the Big Pain in the Ass is more like it."

"The Big Pain in the Ass," Sonny repeats.

The man smiles and leans in closer as if to let Sonny in on a secret. "You know what I say?" And now his eyes trace back to the Beauvais. "I say it's what you get for trying to keep the past alive. Antebellum mansion, big trees dripping moss. Look over there at that little building. Nowadays real estate folks like to call that a dependency unit. I suppose it lessens the sting in certain ears. But what that is, it's a slave house. A family—black people—actually lived in that thing, and now it's where they store the lawn mower and hedge clippers. Unlike you and me, my friend, not everyone sees beauty when they look at this place. History for one person might be glorious, but for another it's chains."

Sonny leaves through the front gate. Nobody calls for him to turn around and come back. Nobody says anything.

As he's crossing the neutral ground he hears a commotion and wheels around in time to witness Juliet's arrival. She drives up in a convertible with the top down and parks behind a line of police cruisers. She doesn't see him. He's too far away by now.

She's wearing a little black fuck-me dress and the same clunky shoes that she seems never to be without. A pair of Jackie O sunglasses, black and owl-like, hides her eyes.

Patrolmen hold the crowd back, and photographers form a loose escort around her. She could be arriving for a movie premiere or an awards show, and not to visit the place where her mother was slain only hours before.

It would be no great surprise to Sonny to see her spin around and blow kisses, to wave in the obnoxious, high-handed fashion that Hollywood stars do.

Sonny glances at Lieutenant Peroux and Anna Huey, curious to observe their reaction. They're standing under the blossoms, his expression as ripe with loathing as hers. They make no move to greet Juliet, and Juliet makes none to them.

She travels along the path as far as she's able before encountering crime scene tape and the street cop who ushers her off to the side.

Alone now on the lawn, Juliet stands with both hands covering her mouth, sobs racking her body. The wind blows dust from the crape myrtles and it sticks to her hair and clothing. Sonny finds himself framing the image with his hands, envisioning it on canvas. "The dress a size too small," he mumbles out loud. "The yellow and the pink. Detectives in their booties."

He is watching as the ambulance starts for the rear drive gate, leaving parallel troughs in the grass. Juliet pushes past the cops and begins running along the side of the house. Past the garden statuary, sprinting now. Past the fountain covered with leaves. Past the outbuildings and the stone barbecue. "Mama! Mama, don't go! Oh, Mama! Mama!"

Juliet collapses as the ambulance disappears around the brick wall. A splash of rainwater comes up as her body meets a puddle.

On his way down Esplanade Sonny glances back once more, just in time to see Lieutenant Samuel Peroux lifting her in his arms.

❦

They cover her shoulders with a grass-green army-issue blanket and lead her to the front door. "Can we go in the study there?" Lentini says

158

past yellow tape. He's leaning to see through the open door. "Hey, listen, I got the lady's daughter here . . ." At last he waves her inside.

The house is crowded with people but not a one familiar. Juliet sits in the library in the same place where she sat the night before. Her teeth chatter and her hair drips water.

"I bet if you check the closet in my old bedroom Mother still has it full of clothes," Juliet says to a female police officer.

"Ask Jerry to reach in there and get her something," Lentini says.

"And also a towel, please," Juliet says.

Minutes later the policewoman returns carrying clothes that smell of mothballs. She brings hip-hugger jeans, a cowboy shirt with snap buttons and leather piping, gray athletic socks and shoes that look as if they've never been worn. The woman drops the bundle on the couch.

"Much obliged," Peroux tells the officer, then nods toward the door.

Juliet removes her wet things. The cops in the room, dedicated to the pretense that only the case involves them, feign indifference. Slipping off her brassiere, Juliet glances in Peroux's direction but he's standing at a window, facing outside in a contemplative pose.

She doesn't remember the pants or the shoes. But the shirt's familiar. She was never the cowgirl type, but she did wear it once, as she recalls, to a Sadie Hawkins dance her junior year. Her date that night was Dickie Boudreau. He wore a length of rope through his belt loops and boots with steel toes. Incredible how an old shirt can get her mind on Dickie when something as serious as a police interrogation is moments away. And now another flash: *"Sonny thinks it's his."*

*"Good."*

*"You don't want your own baby?"*

She finishes dressing and pats the water out of her hair with the towel. Peroux, turning from the window, levels his gaze on the other cops in the room, and suddenly everyone but Lentini seems to understand that it's time to leave.

"How come you like this old house so much, Miss Beauvais?" the detective begins, standing now in the middle of the floor halfway across the room. "I been looking it over and it could use a lot of work."

"All cosmetic," she says quietly. "Nothing that a little TLC won't fix."

"I always heard it was cheaper to build yourself a new house than to renovate an old one. You might be smart to tear this thing down and start over. Build yourself something with fiberglass insulation instead of horsehair and with lower ceilings so you don't have to climb a ladder every time you need to get at a cobweb."

"I'll be sure to take that under advisement, Lieutenant."

"Look at all this cypress millwork. That medallion up on the ceiling where the chandelier meets the plaster. What's the point of that anyway? Who looks at a ceiling? Some people are always showing off, aren't they, Miss Beauvais? Some people can't abide the simple life."

"I agree with you one hundred percent."

He's taking in every piece of furniture, every framed photograph, every title of every book. Everything but Juliet. Once he seems to have seen enough, he says, "You like this old barn so much you went and killed your mother for it, didn't you?"

"Don't be bashful, Lieutenant. We're all adults here."

"How's that?"

"If you have an opinion about recent events please feel free to share it."

Now he's looking at himself in the mirror over the fireplace. "Recent events. Is that what happened here last night? A recent event?"

Juliet doesn't respond. She pulls her shoes off and glances at Lentini, who's standing by the door. "Officer, would you do me a favor? These shoes are too small. Would you mind going upstairs and getting me a different pair? And bring some eights this time."

"You must think you have the shoe department," Lentini says. "In case someone forgot to tell you, lady, we're the police department."

"Miss Beauvais, look at me." Peroux is facing her now in the mirror. "Miss Beauvais, you know what just occurred to me? Your mother got along fine in this house without any trouble for years and years. Then one day you come home to visit and all of a sudden she's dead on the floor upstairs. That's quite a coincidence, isn't it?"

"I admit it's a pretty big one, yes."

"You sent Sonny LaMott here last night to do what you couldn't do yourself, didn't you?"

"Sorry, Lieutenant. But you must have me confused with somebody else."

"So you didn't send him here last night?"

"I sent him here for a check. But I didn't send him here to kill my mother."

"Why'd you hate her so much? What did that old lady ever do to you?"

"What did she do?" But Juliet stops herself and glances back over her shoulder. In her ear the voice of Dickie Boudreau just said *"Good."*

"Miss Beauvais? Miss Beauvais, tell me about your mother. Help me to understand."

"You know those icicles you put on Christmas trees, Lieutenant? They're not real icicles, of course. They're little metallic things—shiny pieces of paper or something."

"I know them."

"Then you know they cost only about nineteen cents a pack. But even at that price Mama insisted on reusing them every year. Instead of throwing them out with the tree, she'd make me take each one off and put it in a freezer bag. If I left any on the tree, she'd throw a fit. Would you resent your mother if she did that to you?"

The detective, still staring, doesn't say anything.

"Here's another one for you. When I was about four or five she caught me in the bathtub touching myself in a manner that she found unacceptable. In actual fact, I was just washing my . . . well, my genitalia, using a rag and soap. Anyway, Mother yanks me out of the tub and spanks my naked bottom, then she showers rice on the kitchen floor and makes me kneel on it and pray to a crucifix up over the door. I'm still naked, understand? I spend hours on that rice and I suppose I'd still be kneeling there today had Daddy not come home and saved me. Tell you about my mother, Lieutenant? Have a seat, sir."

The detectives exchange glances.

"Does that help any?"

"Yes, it does. The picture is starting to clear up."

"I could make a list," she says, "all this proof why I had every reason to kill her."

"Yes," says the lieutenant, removing his notebook and starting to write. "Yes, we could make a list. Let's start one now, if that's okay with you."

"Fine. Let's start at the beginning, when I wasn't breast-fed."

"Oh?"

"Yes. And you'll have a list but nothing else. No evidence, anyway. No *proof*. You think those icicles made me kill her? Or was it the bathtub incident? Which one threw me over the edge?"

161

Peroux puts the notebook back in his hip pocket. "Miss Beauvais, are you using drugs?"

"None that's illegal, unless the state of Louisiana's got a law against Midol."

From the pocket of his jacket Peroux removes a neatly folded sheet of computer paper. "In June of 1984, then again in August of that year, you were charged with unlawful possession of marijuana. In January 1985 it got a little more serious: criminal possession of a controlled substance. You violated probation and subsequently spent thirty days in jail."

"Yes, that's true."

"You also had an arrest for shoplifting."

"I had to eat."

"You stole food?"

"No. I stole a watch from a pawnshop then sold it to some people I knew and used the proceeds to put food on the table. Lieutenant, is there anything on your list about parking tickets? I got a bunch of those." Juliet drops the towel on top of the wet clothes piled on the floor. "You should've read me my Miranda rights, by the way."

"We're conducting an interview, Miss Beauvais."

She points at his notebook and gestures for him to write. "Then leave California alone, please, and ask me about last night?"

"Okay, Miss Beauvais. Tell me about last night."

"Last night Sonny and I shared what I thought was a very romantic, very gratifying evening together. At around midnight he left me at his place in Bywater to run an errand. My mother owed me some money, and Sonny generously offered to get it from her. Long story short, it was two thousand dollars, the amount I spent to fly here from Los Angeles, rent a car and hotel rooms, and feed myself."

"Go on."

"Sonny was gone for little more than an hour and when he came back he immediately went into the bathroom and changed his clothes and took a shower. Immediately after that he walked back to the laundry room and put his clothes in the wash. Believe me, nobody was more surprised than I when he came into the bedroom and presented me with that check."

"Why's that? It's what you sent him here for."

"Mother, Mother's why. I'd tried everything to get her to pay me and time and again she'd refused. Just the other day, for example, I stopped by and politely asked her for the money. She pretended I wasn't there and read aloud from a book as I tried to reason with her. I threatened to break one of her lamps if she didn't pay me. I told her the same about a clock. Mother was so determined that I ended up destroying both the lamp and the clock and she still wouldn't give me the money." Juliet tosses the shoes out toward him in the middle of the room. "Lieutenant, I'll answer your questions but only if one of you goes upstairs and gets me some shoes that fit."

"You still have that check?"

"I returned it to the bank this morning. I knew it wasn't any good. Mother had closed her accounts there years ago. She'd duped Sonny. As a further insult she wrote the check out for five thousand dollars—three more than I told Sonny I needed. I don't know how he got her to do that. Or maybe she did it without his asking. Whatever the case, Mother had the last laugh. When Sonny gave me that check—" She stops, suddenly overcome.

"When Sonny gave you the check?"

"Forgive me, Lieutenant Peroux. When Sonny gave me the check I said, 'Sweetie, what did you have to do to get this? Beat her over the head with a pipe?' "

"Sergeant? Please go upstairs and get Miss Beauvais some shoes."

"Make sure they're eights," Juliet calls after him.

Sonny finds him sitting on the back stoop of his apartment house, reading the *Times-Picayune* sports section and sipping coffee. He's wearing a Tulane sweatshirt and sweatpants without shoes or socks, and Sonny can see the foot and ankle of his prosthesis—some parts wood, some plastic, all of it hard for him to look at.

"I told her about the club," Sonny says as he climbs the rusty metal stairs.

"Huh?"

"Then I told her about whacking the vet. I didn't name you, but I did say I was with a friend. Which friend won't be hard for the police to figure, since you and Roberts are the only ones I have."

Louis lowers the paper and brings the coffee to his lips. He seems to be trying to decide whether to drink it or to throw it at Sonny. "Bubba, what's wrong with you?"

Sonny stands only a few feet away, one hand firm on the railing leading up the steps, the other pulled in a loose fist. "She set me up. She's trying to make it look like I did it."

Louis is quiet, waiting. "Bubba, what's wrong?" he says again.

Sonny's nose has begun to run and he wipes it against the sleeve of his shirt. His gaze travels from Louis's face to his prosthesis then off to a sky dull with scudding clouds. "Somebody went in the Beauvais last night and beat Miss Marcelle with that club you made."

"Is she all right?"

"No, man, they killed her."

"Don't fuck with me, Sonny. I got a bad hangover."

"Now get this, Louis: the cops are acting like I did it."

It seems Louis wants to speak but is unable to. His face grows red and veins show thick and blue in his neck. He lowers the cup through the rails and throws the coffee out into the yard, a brown curtain melting in the grass. "Jesus."

"I was there a while ago when the cops found the club. Then they come down the stairs hauling her body out in a bag."

"Jesus," Louis says again. His artificial leg bangs against the rails as he struggles to stand. "Sonny, come inside. Here. Help me up."

They sit at the dinette table in the kitchen and the apartment feels as cold as a freezer after the hot, moist air outside. Louis pours Sonny a cup of coffee and Sonny sips it while quietly examining the knots in the face of the cedar cupboard, the checkerboard pattern of the tiled floor, the lines in his hands. Tears grow large in his eyes and he tries to keep from blinking.

"Sonny, you want something to eat?"

"Huh?"

"I could fix you breakfast."

"Who can eat after what I just went through?"

But Louis cooks for him anyway. In a crockery bowl he blends half a dozen eggs with milk, sugar, cinnamon and vanilla, then he dunks pieces of stale French bread in the rich, golden-colored mixture. After letting the bread soak he moves it with a spatula to an iron skillet bubbling with grease. "The cops want to see me again this afternoon," Sonny says. "Can you believe that?"

"If you didn't do it you have nothing to worry about. Tell them everything. Well, tell them everything but what you know about the club." Louis nudges the steaming bread. "You need to see this, brother. You need to see how pretty this is coming out."

Sonny stands at the stove and looks down at the skillet and the bread cooking against the black iron. "The browns and the yellows," he says. "The hot oil."

"You should make a picture."

"It would be a good one," Sonny says as if it were his idea.

After a while he can feel himself beginning to settle down. The fear and the pain wash away and something else takes their place, a kind of quiet. Sonny stops seeing the police investigator duckwalking into the privet hedge and the Vaudechamp knocked crooked and the face of the handsome detective under the magnolia dripping water from last night's rain.

He wonders why Lieutenant Peroux, an intelligent black man in a position of authority, would choose to sound like a redneck and call people "podna." But then Sonny decides it doesn't matter what the man calls anyone. He is aware only of the smell of the bread frying and of the cold air blowing and of the taste of the chicory coffee. He is safe in the kitchen with Louis Fortunato at the stove and sunlight streaming in through the water-stained counterpane. And it comes to him that what awaits outside will never find him as long as he remains here and the air is cold and the coffee's hot and the colors in the skillet are brown and yellow.

Louis serves him a plate. He sprinkles confectioners' sugar on the fried bread then adds a generous coating of Steen's cane syrup from a can.

"*Pain perdu,*" Louis says. "That's how you call this in French."

"I didn't do it. I swear to God, Louis, I didn't kill that lady."

"And you thought I just waited tables. Look at me, Sonny. Look what I did."

Sonny eats and when he's done Louis clears the table. Sonny starts to get up to help but Louis pats him on the shoulder. "I got it."

"The doors to my truck don't lock. They're broken. She must've gone in there last night sometime after she left me."

Louis is standing at the sink with his hands in sudsy water. He looks back at Sonny and nods but he doesn't say anything.

"One other thing I keep thinking about," Sonny says. "Juliet sent me to the mansion last night to get something from her mother. She said her bedroom was the third door to the right off the stairs. I get up there and open the door and it's the maid's room. It wasn't even her room, Louis, and she knew it wasn't her room. She wanted Mrs. Huey to see me. Have her wake up and see me prowling around the house like a burglar and not say anything."

"You want some more coffee, Sonny?"

"Louis, I'm trying to tell you something."

"I'm listening."

"Why would Juliet leave me this morning the way she did?" Louis starts to answer but Sonny interrupts him. "I know why she did it," he says, "I know exactly why she did it."

Louis turns back from the sink, waiting for the answer. "I'm the one person who'd do anything for her. I'm the easiest. The reason she did it, Louis . . ."

"Yeah?"

"Because she could."

Louis dries his hands and watches Sonny with a look of great sorrow. "Hey, Sonny? Hey, listen, brother. Why don't you go in my room and take a nap? You must be exhausted. You seem like anyone but yourself. Go in there and lie down and close your peepers. I've got two hours before work. I'll wake you up when it's time to get a move on."

"I don't think I can sleep."

"Do it for me, Sonny. Sleep for old Louis." Louis walks over and stands behind Sonny and pulls his chair back. "Sleep and don't worry about a thing. If you want to stay longer than two hours, that's fine, too. Stay as long as you like. Move in, I wouldn't mind."

Louis rests his hands on Sonny's shoulders and guides him to the bedroom. He helps him out of his boots and clothes and when Sonny falls back on the bed Louis covers him with a blanket.

"She set me up," Sonny says, laughing. "She framed me."

"Okay, boy. Okay."

The small room holds two of Sonny's paintings from when he was new to the fence, efforts that display as little talent as technical proficiency. Louis was his first customer, and his first to buy anything. For fifty dollars he got pictures of the Old Brulatour Courtyard and the Saint Louis Cathedral, Vieux Carré landmarks that Sonny has since painted a thousand times, though never as badly again. Sonny's signature was large then, back when he was destined for things.

A pennant from their high school days at Holy Cross, a collection of Robert Ruark paperbacks, a mammy doll in a soiled linen dress. And this on top of the chest of drawers: a framed black-and-white photograph showing would-be track star Sonny LaMott handing a baton to Louis Fortunato. An old photograph from when Sonny ran third leg, and Louis anchor, on quite possibly the slowest mile-relay team in New Orleans history.

Sonny tries to remember whether they even finished that race. Doubtful, since they finished so few. In the picture he looks like a child, only fifteen years ago. And it occurs to him that he was involved with Juliet at the time and he felt like nothing if not a man.

Sonny lies in the dark with his eyes closed and Juliet is all he sees. She's standing at the fence with a finger at her chin studying his still-wet painting of the Beauvais. She's naked on the porch at home with her back turned to him, a wisp of pubic hair glowing in the streetlight, her breasts thick, shadowy globes hugging each side of her rib cage.

Then Sonny sees her on the dance floor at the F&M Patio Bar and the way she looked the night they met. The jukebox is playing and she's still in her uniform from school, her hair in a ponytail, long woolly socks pulled up to her knees. "Are you with anybody?" he says.

She nods and points to a group of high-born girls sitting at a table nearby. "Do they count?"

"My name is Sonny LaMott. I'm a senior at Holy Cross. If it's not too much to ask—"

"Juliet," she answers, bringing her mouth close to his ear to be heard above the music. "Do you know, by chance, the mansion on Esplanade . . . ?"

After the bar closes they walk to Napoleon Avenue past the unmanned gatehouse of a rail yard and over the tracks to the river. The port this morning is quiet. They sit on warm boards in the shade of a crudely built lean-to and watch a ship approaching on the dark water. Juliet smells of smoke and lilac shampoo and her hand, when at last she surrenders it, is small and moist in Sonny's. He tries to kiss her and kiss her deep but she clenches her lips and gently nudges him away. "I just broke up with somebody."

"You still love him?"

"I don't know, I don't want to."

"I could be your boyfriend, Juliet."

"Just be my friend first."

Now in Louis's room a suffocating heaviness bears down on Sonny's chest and for minutes it seems he is unable to breathe. He opens his eyes and gasps for air and he doesn't relax until he feels Louis's hand press deep into his own.

"I love her anyway," Sonny says.

"I know you do."

"I've always loved her, I'll always love her."

"I know it, Sonny. I know you will."

# 5

SHE HAS SOME ÉTOUFFÉE FINALLY. IT'S
at Dooky Chase's Restaurant, a black place just
across Orleans Avenue from the Lafitte housing
development, and she is disappointed when after
only a few bites she is unable to eat any more. Fifteen years of life in the California sunshine has
made her a lightweight in the cayenne pepper
department, and she feels as if she has betrayed
her Creole people. As if she should apologize to
someone: *"Look, I let you down. I let us all down.
God!"*

When the waiter returns she holds air in her
cheeks to show how fat she feels. She starts to
give an excuse for not finishing her plate but the
man nervously stops her. "They got two police
outside waiting to speak to you."

They're standing in the lot next to the Mustang, leaning against the trunk. "And I thought it

was the cayenne pepper giving me indigestion," she says as she shambles toward them.

Peroux comes to his full height and crosses his arms, as if to protect himself. "Nice to see you again, Miss Beauvais. And how was your meal today?"

"I'll tell you how it was, Lieutenant. Someone needs to franchise Dooky Chase and open fast-food restaurants all over the country. Instead of a billion hamburgers sold, I want to see signs boasting the same about stuffed jumbo shrimp and breast of chicken à la Dooky."

It seems incredible, but she's managed to make even Lentini laugh.

"You think people would give up their Quarter Pounders for Dooky?" Peroux says.

"One day this Louisiana cooking will catch on, mark my words."

"I'm glad to see your sense of humor has returned, Miss Beauvais."

"Thank you, Lieutenant Peroux. Now, tell me, how is the investigation going? Are you making progress? Is there anything I can help you with?"

Peroux glances over at the project across the street, half a dozen children watching from a piece of ground stripped clean of vegetation, rectangular-shaped buildings with graffiti on the walls and plywood covering windows. "Just one question," he says. "Miss Beauvais, before he went to the mansion last night, did you give Sonny LaMott something to give to your mother?"

She waits, closely considering the question. "Something for my mother," she says, then feigns a sudden burst of enlightenment. "Like a piece of my mind, do you mean?"

"No. Something else. Like a letter or a sheet of paper."

"You're confused again, Lieutenant. I didn't send Sonny LaMott to the Beauvais with a piece of paper. He volunteered to go there and bring me back one."

"The check?"

She nods. "What else would I want from Mother?"

⚜

Sonny follows Lentini to the small room where Peroux sits waiting at a cafeteria table cluttered with yellowing, weeks-old sections of the *Times-Picayune*. The room holds the sharp odor of Pine-Sol even though the floor looks as if it hasn't been cleaned in months. A fan with

170

blue blades churns the torpid air and riffles the dust, while failing utterly to cut the heat.

"Sonny LaMott," comes a voice, then the slap of a hand on metal. It is Peroux, shoving his chair out from under him as he rises to his feet. "Come have a seat here, podna."

The detective pulls back a folding chair directly across from where he was sitting. A service revolver, neatly tucked in a glossy leather sleeve, hugs his belt.

"You've had a rough day, haven't you, podna?"

"I've had better, Lieutenant. Thank you for asking."

Only now does Sonny notice the tape recorder on the table, a light on its face glowing red.

"Well, if it means anything, I'm glad you could make it," Peroux says, reaching over to depress the machine's Record button. "You ever get interviewed by the police before? I was telling Sergeant Lentini here how impressed I was with you earlier. You seem to have an answer for everything." Peroux leans back in his chair, as relaxed as a man in his favorite recliner at home. "Hey, Sonny, you know I'm just playing, right?" He points a finger at the recorder. "This is more for your protection than for mine. When I'm taking notes, I can't keep up too good when my interview gets a head of steam. You don't want me to screw up your statement, do you?"

"No sir."

"We're just trying to figure out who would want to hurt that old lady like that."

"They killed her, Lieutenant."

"Yeah. Yeah, they did kill her. And I bet nothing hurts more than that, huh, podna?"

Overhead banks of uncovered fluorescent tubes burble against the ceiling, several of them dripping rusty water. Something tugs at Sonny's memory and he recalls the year 1971 and a building on Gravier Street and his own voice as he and Juliet start down the long hall: *"I don't think I can go through with this . . ."*

Lentini shuffles over to a window and sits against a radiator housing, a look of such boredom on his face that his eyes flutter as he struggles to keep from nodding off.

"Sonny," Peroux says, "last night when you went to Esplanade for Juliet's check . . . ?"

"Yes sir. We already talked about that."

"It was raining pretty hard, wasn't it?"

"Yes, it was. Pretty hard. Real hard, as a matter of fact."

Peroux takes out his notebook and looks over a page. "Sonny, you said you went in the house through the front door and walked right straight up the stairs."

"Yes sir."

"And a little later Mrs. Beauvais told you something from her bedroom?"

"She thought I was Juliet."

"Right. She thought you were Juliet. Sonny, after you went down the stairs then came back up again, did you open the door to Mrs. Beauvais's room yourself or did she open it?"

"Let me think. Well, I guess we both opened it. I knocked, as I recall, and then I think I turned the knob after she said to come in. At the same time I was opening it she was opening it too, but from her side. Does that make sense?"

Peroux looks at Lentini, whose eyes are still closed. "Does that make sense?"

Lentini shrugs.

"Sonny, you open any other doors while you were up on the second floor?"

"When I was up there the first time, Juliet had said her room was the third one off the stairs to the right and so I did open that one but Mrs. Huey was sleeping inside."

"Any others?"

"Yeah. I opened the door to the bedroom between Miss Marcelle and Mrs. Huey. That was Juliet's room. Or it used to be her room. All her old things were in there."

"So you opened three doors altogether?"

"Right."

"In all your previous visits to the house, you ever go up there and open those doors before?"

"Not that I recall. I never really went up there. Me and Miss Marcelle always sat in the parlor. I did go upstairs years ago, though, back when Juliet and I were dating in school."

"In the last few weeks, to your knowledge, did you go through any of those doors up there?"

"No."

Peroux throws another look at Lentini before referring to his note-book. "Sonny, were you wearing gloves last night when you went in the house?"

Sonny folds his hands together and rests them on the table. He lets out a breath. "It's kind of hot for gloves, Lieutenant. It's seventy-some degrees out. And I was there for Juliet's clothes and check. Why would I be wearing gloves?"

"You didn't answer my question, podna."

"No, Lieutenant. I was not wearing gloves last night."

The detective leans forward until his head is almost touching the table. "Look, podna, listen. Would you go down the hall with Sergeant Lentini here and spend a minute with our friend Mrs. Townsend and let her take your prints? You think you could do that?"

"I thought I was here to answer questions."

Peroux pumps his head up and down. "And you've answered them. And we thank you. Mighty kind."

Sonny can feel the involuntary pulsing of the veins in his neck, the heat rise in his face. "Am I a suspect, Lieutenant Peroux?"

Now more head pumping. "You are a suspect, Sonny. Yes, most definitely. But right now so is Juliet Beauvais. And so is Mrs. Huey and so are the drugheads on the next block. We've got us a whole shitload of suspects, although I do admit you pretty much top the list. You're our number-one suspect. Now, Sonny, will you be so kind as to let Mrs. Townsend take your prints or do you feel like you should confer with your lawyer first?"

Lentini leads Sonny to a room nearly identical to the first. They sit on metal chairs and wait facing each other until the print analyst appears in the open doorway. She's wiping her hands on a brown paper towel, and she smiles when they rise to their feet in unison.

"Mrs. Townsend," Lentini says with a nod. "This is LaMott."

"Hello, LaMott."

She needs all of five minutes to take Sonny's prints, a process that somehow inspires in Sonny a feeling of solidarity with the woman. "I have paint on my hands," he says.

"None that's getting in my way."

"I used to be an artist in the French Quarter," Sonny says, no less surprised by the statement than both she and Lentini seem to be.

"Did it hurt?" Peroux says when Sonny returns to the first room.

Sonny holds up a hand. "It makes your fingers kind of powdery after she puts on the cream. But you really don't feel anything."

"Sonny, you know somebody name of Coulon?"

"Coulon?" He waits, figuring it necessary to give the impression that he's thinking about it. "No, I don't know a Coulon. Not personally anyway."

"You know one impersonally maybe?"

"Sure I do. I bump into people all the time I don't know but impersonally."

"Do you know any old veterinarian named Coulon you might've beat up one night with a club on the Esplanade Avenue neutral ground?"

"I've never beaten anyone with a club, Lieutenant."

Peroux is nodding his head as if he's known this all along, that of course Sonny has never beaten anyone with a club. "And I suppose since you never beat Dr. Coulon with a club, then I suppose it follows you never stuck a piece of paper up that woman's privates, huh, podna?"

Something clicks shut in Sonny's throat and it is half a minute before he is able to say anything. His face burns red and he lowers his head and thumbs his eyes closed. "Did somebody really do that, Lieutenant?"

The detective reaches over and stops the recorder, just as Sonny feels Lentini, awake now, drawing the chair out from behind him.

"One more thing," Peroux says. "Since you made such good friends with Mrs. Townsend, we were hoping you might enjoy meeting another friend, Mr. Arias. He's a polygraph expert. If you'd rather not meet him, or if you'd rather have your lawyer present when you do, it won't be no skin off my back. We can arrange to have the two of you sit together later on."

"Let's do it now," Sonny says.

When it's over, Sonny leaves the building with only a dim recollection of where he parked the truck. Outside, the humid air dumps a dense weight in his lungs and he begins to sweat so much that his clothes cling to his skin. Traffic thumps by and Sonny wonders how the state of Louisiana executes people these days, whether with the chair or an IV drip.

From behind him comes the sound of footsteps, then Peroux's voice.

"That's the first time in my twenty-some-odd years as a peace officer where a suspect didn't ask right off how he did on the lie detector."

Sonny glances at the man then turns back to the street.

"You may've impressed Mr. Arias, podna, but it still don't add up. No sir, it don't add up worth a good goddamn. Now go home, LaMott. I'm tired of looking at you."

♰♰♰

The parlor is empty but for the maid and her mother, who lies on white satin with a glass rosary in her hands. Juliet makes the sign of the cross and kneels next to the bier, her hands shaking as she brings them together in a steeple at her chest. The mortician did a good job, she has to admit. He succeeded in getting her hair and makeup right. And he's put her in a dress that appears to be from the days before her mother's wardrobe, once the envy of many a grande dame, was limited to purchases from the St. Vincent de Paul thrift store.

Miss Marcelle's face shows no evidence of the beating. If not for puffiness around her mouth she would look perfectly normal. Juliet, breaking her prayer steeple, brings a hand to her own lips. She stands and places the same hand on her mother's mouth. She is not past acknowledging the similarity in construction, and yet a voice sounds in her head: *"My heavens, you have that man's mouth? Where did you get that man's mouth?"*

Juliet recites a "Hail Mary" but for some reason today struggles to remember the prayer. She makes up words of her own to fill in where there are memory lapses. The effort calls to mind her days at Sacred Heart and the hours in chapel given to venerating a woman who had a child without ever being intimate with a man. Juliet was as mystified by the story then as she is today—Juliet who at sixteen entrusted her innocence to Dickie Boudreau, and who came away from that first experience neither pregnant with God's child nor particularly satisfied. When it was over, she cried with her face in a pillow as he snored loudly in his sleep, oblivious to her need to be stroked and spoken to. "Do you still think I'm special?" she said into the dark. Dickie answered with another noisy exhalation, his loudest yet.

Juliet moves away from the coffin and approaches Anna Huey sitting in front. "I guess now me and Mama will never have that talk," she says.

175

"Juliet, what do you have on? You should've worn a long skirt."

"Anna Huey, why are you always so mad at me?" And before she can answer, Juliet retreats to the back of the room and sits alone on the last row of chairs.

After several minutes a man enters from a side door and takes a seat near hers, and even though his face is turned away Juliet can clearly see that it's her father. She thought maybe Sonny LaMott or Leonard Barbier would attend the wake, but this is unexpected.

Johnny Beauvais removes his panama and places it on the seat next to him. "Hello, darling," he says at last, then motions her over with a finger. "This is just your father talking, but maybe you shouldn't have done that with your slip of paper."

"What paper?"

"I think we know."

Juliet shrugs and moves closer, sliding over the cold cushions. She's tempted to reach out and touch him, but something stops her. Her father is a ghost, after all; her hand would go right through him. "They won't be able to trace it back to me, will they, Daddy?"

Her father shakes his head. "Not the way you write."

"Daddy, I thought you said I had somebody named Etienne's mouth. It turns out I have Mama's mouth. It's been such a long time since I really let myself look at her that I was stunned just now to see my inner tubes on that woman's face."

Juliet suddenly is aware of a presence nearby. Anna Huey, smiling in a way that would suggest triumph, is standing in the space between the rows of chairs. "Who were you talking to?"

Juliet swivels her head to look back at her father but he's already disappeared, along with his panama. "I was saying my prayers."

"It didn't sound like praying."

"Somehow I feel like God hears me better if I say it out loud."

"You were talking about Etienne and his mouth. I heard you, Juliet. You said something about inner tubes."

Juliet touches his seat and tests for warmth. Nothing. And he was just there!

"You're still hooked on drugs, aren't you?" Anna Huey says. "You've been snorting coke. You come to your mother's wake high as a kite. Why doesn't that surprise me?"

"Oh, go swab a toilet," Juliet says, then stares until Anna Huey leaves.

Later that night at the Lé Dale Juliet can find no way to satisfy her terrible longing. Leroy, the clerk from downstairs, does what he can but it only adds to her emptiness. She feels completely hollowed out inside, and when she closes her eyes she sees the rooms of the Beauvais as if through a veil of gauze. The furnishings have been removed and the floors lie bare and dusty underfoot. Shutters slap against the side of the house, their loud arrhythmicity a torture. The voices of her parents—arguing, as usual—echo in the open space.

"Do you still think I'm special?" Juliet says.

"Better believe I do," says Leroy.

"As special as before?"

"Oh yeah."

Juliet turns over on her side and hugs herself. Maybe she and Leroy should go to the French Quarter and get loaded and recruit others to help with her loneliness. Maybe more partners are the answer. They could fuck her into forgetting. Fuck her until tonight's horror replaces all the other horrors. But her emptiness has a weight and it's too heavy to budge. Juliet can barely lift herself to a sitting position. It takes all of her strength to move to the side of the bed and put her feet on the floor.

She wishes her father would return and talk to her again. She asks him to. "You need to explain a few things," she says. "Come to think of it, you weren't so perfect, either."

"I don't remember ever hearing myself say I was perfect."

"Maybe she was from the yam fields, but she was still my mother. And she was your wife. If she was so terrible then why'd you go and marry her?"

"Hey, baby, I never even met your mother let alone married the bitch." Leroy drags a hand across her back. "I told you to go easy on that shit. God, how much did you take?"

Juliet looks at him past the sheet of hair hanging in her face. Her lips are so numb she can barely move them. "Now for the rest of your life," she says, "you'll be able to tell everyone you made it with an actual Beauvais."

"It was good," says the clerk, smiling a mouth colored red from too many candies. "But don't let it go to your head. Pussy's pussy no matter the pedigree."

They entomb Miss Marcelle beside the body of her husband in the Beauvais family mausoleum at Metairie Cemetery. Sonny shares pall-bearing duties with Louis Fortunato and four gardeners who formerly were employed to keep the yard at the mansion. Anxious to recruit strong-armed males to handle the coffin, Sonny could think of no one but Louis, who agreed to the assignment despite his disability. Then Anna Huey remembered the gardeners, each of whom accepted the detail for his standard fee of four dollars an hour.

"May I speak to you alone, please," Juliet asks Sonny when the service at the cemetery ends.

Her lips are dry and chapped, the flesh beneath her eyes dark with bruises. In one hand she holds a twisted rope of tissue, in the other the crucifix that minutes before was fixed to the top of her mother's coffin.

"I don't think I want to be alone with you, Julie."

"Please, sweetie. Just a few minutes."

"No way." He looks over at Louis waiting by his car. Louis holds up an arm and taps the face of his watch. "I'm not here for you today, Julie," Sonny says. "I'm here for your mother."

"Oh, darling, please."

"No."

"Please, Sonny."

Louis waits inside his car now, the motor running. He lowers his window as Sonny walks up and leans with his back against the top of the doorframe. "Hey, look, I think I'll stay awhile."

"Yeah?"

"She wants to talk."

Louis watches Juliet with the appropriate level of suspicion. He gives a laugh and slaps a hand against the steering wheel. "Tell me something, brother. Did I dream your visit to my apartment the other night? All that business about Juliet setting you up? Did you really say that or was that conversation something I imagined?"

"Go home, Louis."

Louis shakes his head. "No, I think I'll wait."

"Louis, go home. I'll catch up with you later."

After he's gone Sonny and Juliet start along an asphalt path meandering through the vast city of the dead. Cedar and oak trees filter the sunlight and a breeze sends freshly cut chips of grass swirling between the massive aboveground tombs. Despite ninety-degree heat it's comfortable in the shade and they stroll a few feet away from each other reading the names of the families engraved on the marble and granite façades. Here at Metairie Cemetery the rich and the powerful repose in miniature versions of the ostentatious mansions they left behind, while in other cemeteries nearby the poor, the lower classes and the ordinary have graduated from shotgun shanties to brick-and-mortar crypts with hardly more than fresh white paint to adorn them.

"This way," Sonny says.

"Huh?"

"I want to see Mama."

It is a long time before they do anything but walk. They cross under the overpass and hike down City Park Avenue to Greenwood Cemetery. They pass tombs with modest cement-cast statues, many of them angels with faces staring off in the blue distance, wings tightly tucked. They pass the figure of a cherub and Juliet stops on the path and attempts to imitate the pose.

She puffs out her cheeks to match those of the cherub, then she holds her hands at her shoulders and flutters her fingers like a pair of small dancing wings.

And only twenty, thirty minutes ago, Sonny thinks with amazement, they were sliding her mother's coffin into a vault no bigger than a broom closet tipped on its side.

When they reach the LaMott family tomb Sonny stands with his hands stuffed in the pockets of his jacket. He studies the legend carved in the cement wall, his mother's name and the dates of her birth and death. The crypt is a traditional "fours," as the city's ancestors referred to tombs designed to accommodate four bodies. "If she doesn't mind being low-rent," Sonny remembers his mother saying years ago, in a rare moment of acerbity, "and if she ever really does agree to marry the son of a shrimp salesman, maybe you and Juliet can join us when the time comes. There's room."

On the weedy floor in front of the tomb rests a wicker basket crowded with plastic flowers so faded that it's hard to tell their original color. Juliet stoops down and rearranges the blooms, and Sonny says, "Did you kill her?"

"What?"

"Your mother. Did you kill her?"

She stands clutching the stem of a washed-out chrysanthemum and brings her face close to his. "No, Sonny, I didn't kill her. Did you?"

"Why would I kill her?" he says. "Because you asked me to?" Unable to hold her gaze, he runs a hand over his face and glances back at the cemetery gates. "I don't think so, Julie."

"I do," she says. "I think so. And if I think something is so, then it is so."

Sonny can hear traffic on the interstate, the low murmur of lawn mowers. Leaves scatter between his ankles, catch in the grass. "Julie, I know about your life in California. I know about the arrests and the drug rehab. I know things about you you don't even know I know."

"Do you know about this," she asks, then licks her mouth.

Sonny takes a step back. "Look," he says, "coming here obviously was a mistake."

"What about this?" she says now, but spares him the demonstration.

"I'm leaving," he says, then starts back down the path to the cemetery gates.

He's covered about fifty yards and still she remains behind, waiting in a splash of light, the tomb at her back. He stops and turns around.

"It was you," Juliet says again, shouting now. "I know it was."

She steps off the paved surface and walks around to the rear of the tomb, and when he returns he finds her standing in weeds, arms held out to embrace him. Her face holds a look he's seen before, and Sonny recalls that Juliet, in the film he and Louis watched together, was staring at the tall blond man this way, with a desire that bordered on the comic, tongue teasing her lips to emphasize her intentions.

"Cut it out," he says. "Goddammit, Julie. Cut it out, do you hear?"

But Juliet says nothing as she removes her blouse and skirt, flips her shoes off and draws her hose down to her ankles. She isn't wearing underwear and her body shows no tan lines as the sun-darkened, hairless flesh of her pubis blends evenly with the flesh of her legs.

"You're out of your mind if you think I'm going to do that."

"Tell me you killed her. Say it."

"No."

"You hit her with that pipe—"

"Shut up."

"You hit her and when she wouldn't die you wrapped your hands around her neck and you strangled her. I know it was you. Sonny, I went to the mansion that night. I was there after you'd left and Mother was already dead upstairs on the floor."

"Goddammit, Julie."

"Admit it. You did it for me. You did it for your Julie."

She reaches a hand out and touches his face and even as he instructs himself not to Sonny can feel his body leaning to meet her. He closes his eyes and pushes her away. "No," he says. "No, Julie. That's not how it happened."

"Kiss me, Sonny. Sonny, kiss me."

"Your mother was fine when I left the house."

"Sonny? Please. Kiss me, Sonny."

"You planted that club. You wanted them to think it was me. How could you do that? I loved you. How could you do that?"

"Darling?"

"*No!*"

Sonny pushes past her and runs to the front of the cemetery. She calls again but this time he doesn't stop, doesn't look back.

Louis is waiting on the other side of the gates, his car parked against the curb nearby. Standing casually with his back against the fence, his weight propped up on his prosthesis, he might be out enjoying the sun, people watching, trying to decide how to spend his Saturday. "You knew I'd be waiting," he says. "You knew you could count on me, didn't you, bubba?"

Sonny staggers past him without a word.

In her rumpled clothes and torn hose she eats étouffée at the counter, this dish, though called the special, not nearly on par with the one she had at Dooky Chase's a few days ago. She avoids the rice and picks at the crawfish, forking up one at a time. She doesn't trust their general appearance, which is more red than brown, the color she knows they're supposed to be when prepared properly. "Take it," she says to the counterman, then gives the plate a nudge.

"Too seasoned?"

"Too red," she replies.

"Too red? Nobody never told me too red."

"Too red," she says again.

She lights a cigarette and sips a cup of coffee. It might be the worst coffee she's ever drunk in her whole, entire life, and she considers telling the counterman as much. Considers saying, "Hey, motherfucker, you make this shit with coffee beans or pinto beans?" But instead she settles on a different topic. "My poor mama. They buried her today."

"Who did?"

"We did, the ones that knew her. She died unexpectedly."

"Sorry to hear that," he says, wiping down the Formica.

"Yeah, well, it's sad all right. Somebody murdered her—beat her then strangled her to death. Stuck some kind of paper way up in her private area."

The counterman's Adam's apple moves in his long, thin neck.

"What's really weird, though," and Juliet laughs now, "what's weird is I'm sitting here trying to remember if it was me."

"If it was you what?"

"If it was me that did it."

She pays and leaves. Out on the sidewalk she looks back through the lettering on the café window. *Humming Bird*, it says. Two words instead of the regular one. It is nighttime now and electric lamps glow on every corner and a streetcar squeals as it lumbers past, tourists watching from open windows. Juliet runs after the train, figuring she'll kill time by riding uptown to the end of the line, but she's too low on energy to catch it. Finally she heads back to the Lé Dale, glad to find someone other than Leroy working the desk.

Juliet is slow climbing the stairs to her room, slow getting the key in the door. Slow to respond in the instant when she reaches for the light switch and a figure moves toward her through the darkness.

A sharp pain radiates from her throat and prevents her from shouting out, and she understands only vaguely that someone has grabbed her by the neck.

She latches onto his forearm with both hands and claws at his bare arms. As she begins to black out he lets her go. Coughing roughly, a thread of saliva hanging from her mouth, she falls against the door and watches as he steps back raising both arms high above his head. He is holding something and though she knows to avoid it he moves quickly and brings it down hard against the top of her head. She's been hit harder, and by harder things, but then a second blow buffets against her jaw and rattles her teeth.

She's digging in her mouth, assessing the damage, when the club strikes a third time and the floor comes up fast to meet her.

She rolls over on her back and stares straight up waiting for whatever is next and when he hits her again grains of sand splash against her face and momentarily blind her.

"What did I do to you?" she says as blood starts to pool in her mouth.

The club thumps against the floor. Her assailant, breathing heavily, flings the door open. When he enters the lighted hallway she can see nothing of his face for the ski mask he's wearing. Of his clothes she can tell only that his shoes don't match.

"What did I do to you?" she says again, blinking against the fire ignited by the sand in her eyes.

"You killed my Frank," he replies, then runs limping down the corridor to the stairs.

⁂

In the morning Sonny gets up early and drives to the French Quarter. He sets up at his favorite place under the magnolia across from the bakery.

A search for routine brings him here, for things whole and simple and uncomplicated.

Sonny tries to paint but the reason for it is gone and he ends up sitting with a sketchbook in his lap watching tourists move by. At noon a feeling comes over him and he understands that Miss Marcelle is dead and he lowers his head and weeps without making a sound and without tears showing on his face. As he cries, a woman sits in his chair but Sonny ignores her. After a while she stands without saying anything and moves to another of the artists along the row.

It is midday when the two detectives show up, Lentini gnashing a

183

toothpick, Peroux carrying a copy of the *Picayune* tucked under his arm. "Hey, podna, you got a minute?" The police lieutenant, wearing the contented expression of a man who just consumed too many hush puppies at lunch, sits before Sonny can answer. "I want you to be honest with me now," he says, swallowing a belch. "You wore gloves to the house that night."

Sonny lays the sketchbook on the ground under his chair. "We already talked about that."

"Maybe you heard the question wrong the first time. I'm a big believer in second chances, and I wanted to give you an opportunity to get it straight."

"I'm starting to think I might need a lawyer, Lieutenant."

"Well, we already told you you should get one, did we not?"

"You never told me that," Sonny says.

Peroux shrugs. "Look, I go back to them gloves only because our people have been unable to lift any prints of yours off any of them doors upstairs. We have you in the parlor. You're all over that goddamn parlor. But it's a mystery to me why when we climb them stairs and check them doors and them doorframes and all that furniture up there . . . why there ain't a single miserable print."

Now it's Sonny's turn to shrug. "Maybe Mrs. Huey did some cleaning afterward and wiped them away. How am I supposed to know?"

"Nobody contaminated that crime scene," Peroux says. "Don't even come with that shit."

"I don't know what to tell you, Lieutenant. I admitted I was up there. What else is there for me to say?"

"Not a single deposit," the detective says. "Not a single goddamn one."

"Okay, and what does that tell you?"

"That's an interesting question. As a matter of fact, that's the exact same question me and Sergeant Lentini been trying to answer ourselves since the print analysis came in."

Peroux springs to his feet and slaps his newspaper against Sonny's chest. He holds it there until Sonny understands that it's his to take now.

"Call your lawyer, LaMott. Ask him if it puts you in a bind to tell us you wore gloves, and while you got him on the horn ask him if he has any reservations about you standing in a lineup."

Sonny tries not to show alarm or panic, but despite the effort he can't hold the detective's gaze. He drops the paper on the seat of his chair.

"Sonny, you like cop movies? For some reason they always got a lineup in a cop movie." Sonny doesn't answer and Peroux says, "Have your lawyer call me at his earliest convenience."

"I don't need a lawyer," Sonny says.

"How's that?"

"Lieutenant, I haven't done anything. I swear to God."

"Then I tell you what. You come down to Broad Street tomorrow at twelve noon and we'll get us some more proof you haven't done anything."

"I didn't kill her," Sonny says.

"Hey, look. Just because you'll be standing in a lineup doesn't mean you did. We're working on a lead and this'll help us to understand something."

Sonny takes a long time but he answers finally with a nod.

"All right now. At ease, podna. See you tomorrow."

When they've gone Roberts hobbles over and removes a paint-stained bandanna from his pocket and wipes the sweat from Sonny's face. "Ah, Sonny. Ah, boy," he says, his hands trembling as he moves the rag over Sonny's forehead.

They want him for a lineup. But why? Sonny is unable to come up with an answer. Did somebody see him entering the Beauvais that night? What does it matter if they spotted him coming or going when Sonny's already admitted he was there?

"Let's go to du Monde and get us a drink of water."

"No. I'm fine, Roberts. Thank you."

The old man shows Sonny his sketchbook. On the top sheet he's scribbled an image of a fellow who vaguely resembles Sonny being choked into a nervous sweat by two meaty brutes. One of the strong men grips a copy of the *New Orleans Times-Picayune*, and over a two-column story on the bottom half of the page Roberts has penned a headline: ATTACKS ON ESPLANADE BAFFLE POLICE.

Only now does Sonny check out the newspaper the detective gave him.

French Quarter veterinarian Thomas P. Coulon, 75, a lifelong area resident, has intrigued police with the revelation he was attacked on the Esplanade Avenue neutral ground by a masked man wielding a club less than a month before Marcelle L. Beauvais was slain April 28th in her historic residence known as the Beauvais Mansion.

According to NOPD sources close to the investigation, the Coulon incident and the Beauvais case have several similarities, among them an assailant who targets the elderly and assaults them with a sand-filled pipe made of plastic. Coulon did not report the beating to local authorities until after learning details about the homicide from a television news program. Coulon declined to comment yesterday when reached at his office, but sources say he has provided police with the best lead yet in a murder case that horrified the city.

Mrs. Beauvais, widow of New Orleans real estate developer John Duffilo Beauvais, was the city's 45th murder victim this year. Police have made no arrests in the case, but the investigation has intensified since Coulon came forward.

"We think we can connect what happened to Dr. Coulon and what happened to Mrs. Beauvais to a single individual," said a homicide detective who asked that his name not be used in this story.

The Beauvais Mansion is listed in the National Register of Historic Places. During the Civil War it served as a hospital for Union forces. Police say the neighborhood has been the site of many robberies in recent years, but that the slaying appears unrelated to a break-in.


Sonny hands the paper to Roberts and the old man pulls nervously at his ear as he reads the account. "The reason you've been hanging your lip has suddenly come much clearer to me. If only I could offer a solution."

"They think I did it," Sonny says.

"They think you beat an old man with a pipe?" Roberts shakes his head. "Absurd."

"It's worse than that, Roberts. They think I murdered her."

Roberts lets go a roar of laughter that is both unfelt and unconvincing. "Preposterous."

"I wouldn't murder anybody, would I, Roberts?"

"No," the caricaturist says in a big voice, then throws Sonny a look that seems to belie his true feelings. "My lord, son. You're an artist!"

♆♆♆

She doesn't have health insurance, so they take her to Charity Hospital. The EMS unit travels with interior lights on, one man at the wheel, a second in the rear with Juliet. She hears the siren only faintly but its effects are obvious as cars pull over to let them pass and pedestrians rubberneck with faces creased and dark.

Juliet sits up on her elbows and watches through the windows as an old bomb station wagon jumps the curb and barely avoids a group of onlookers. "Idiot," she says. "Did you see that?"

The attendant smiles.

"I bet you see some wild shit." She glances back at the man. He's sitting on a metal stool at the foot of the bed. "I knew this paramedic in LA," she says. "One time him and his partner get this call. It's a guy with a Barbie doll stuck up his behind. My friend showed me the X rays."

The attendant is quiet. He doesn't seem impressed.

"You ever see anything like that?"

The man looks at the front of the vehicle, as if to make sure the driver isn't listening. "Only thing, we had this woman once with a lightbulb broke off in her vulva."

"Her vulva? What do you mean, her vulva?"

"Deep inside her private areas, miss."

"Okay. All right. I gotcha. I thought for a second there you'd said her Volvo."

The man looks up front again. "She bled a lot," he says. "Apparently she and her boyfriend were high on crystal meth and he wanted to see if you could see the light shining through her belly."

They drive on awhile, Juliet imagining it. The world is full of crazies. And Barbie dolls and lightbulbs are just the beginning. "Well, could they?" she says, unable to wait for the punch line any longer. "Could they see that light shining from inside her volvo?"

"I couldn't answer, miss. By the time we arrived on the scene it'd already gone out."

They wheel her into the emergency room, the gurney fixed so that she can lounge in a sitting position. A cop shows up and listens without saying anything as somebody who must be a doctor looks her over, asks questions, barely responds when she answers. He flashes a small light in her eyes. He reaches under her clothes with a stethoscope and places a cold, flat piece of metal against her back and chest. His hands, covered with rubber gloves, explore her chest and rib cage, and pinch her skin as he examines her mouth and teeth. They grab at her hair when he feels for the contusion on top of her skull.

"I'm at the auction barn," Juliet says. "I'm a heifer."

The doctor, touching and probing, doesn't seem to hear.

She gives him a loud moo, and even this fails to get his attention.

"So he just hit you?" the cop says. "Just came out of nowhere and hit you?"

"Hit me with a pipe."

"You think you could ID this person?"

"His shoes maybe. They looked worn at the heels. He must be on his feet a lot."

The cop looks at her and says, "You sure it was a pipe? Must not've been a very hard pipe. A hard pipe would've cracked you open like a watermelon."

"I think it was plastic like the kind plumbers use. It broke and I got sand all over me." She pulls at the ends of her hair. "See this? This is sand. I guess it's sand."

The cop leaves and the doctor removes his gloves. "You're a lucky young woman," he says. "I can find nothing broken. This bump here on your skull, a few cuts where you appear to have bitten yourself, but the bleeding has stopped. Cosmetically there's no evidence of trauma. No bruises or lacerations." He shakes his head and bunches his lips into the shape of a snail. "Still couldn't have been a pleasant experience. Are you in any pain?"

"I'm in a lot of pain," she says, "but to be right honest I've been hurt worse." Juliet knows she should leave it at that, but the cop has left the room and something compels her to give voice to the picture that occupies her head. "In 1971, when I was a recent honors graduate of the Academy of the Sacred Heart and mere months away from being crowned a debutante queen, I underwent an illegal abortion in an office building downtown. Now *that* hurt."

The doctor removes an instrument from her ear.

"This happened not long after my father drowned in Lake Pontchartrain in a, quote unquote, sailing accident. Long story short, my boyfriend took me to an abortionist who fixed me so that I could never have children again."

The doctor puts his instrument away. "Are you kidding me?"

Juliet gives her head a shake. "The abortionist, I learned later, was a former Tulane medical student who apparently liked raiding hospital pharmacies more than he did sawing the bones of cadavers. The school gave him the boot for this. Want to know who my boyfriend was?"

"Miss Beauvais?"

"You're a doctor, so let me ask. What do you think hurts more? Having a dirty speculum and a dirty curette rooting around in your volvo and spreading all variety of infection or sticking a Barbie doll up your rectum?"

The doctor seems to have completed the examination. He refits his eyeglasses on his face and touches his mouth with the sleeve of his lab coat. Another gurney rolls by, and he spends a long time watching after it. "Are you allergic to anything, Miss Beauvais? Any kind of medication?"

"No."

"Percodan?"

"Nope. Me and Percodan are like this." She shows two fingers entwined.

The doctor excuses himself and leaves the room. When he returns he's holding in one hand a soufflé cup half-filled with water and in the other two pale green tablets. "You have anyone to drive you home, Miss Beauvais?"

"No," extracting the pills from his palm. "An ambulance brought me here."

"I can arrange for a cab to drive you."

"I'll just catch one out in the street." As she swallows the medicine, he watches from behind the flat, opaque reflection on his glasses, watches as if trying to decide where they've met before. You look familiar, he wants to say. How do I know you?

"Ever get a girl pregnant, Doctor?"

"Well, yes. Yes, I have, as a matter of fact." He adds, after a pause, "I'm married to her. My wife and I have three children."

Juliet squeezes the cup flat and hands it back to him. "Up until I was sterilized, and even for a long while after, I dreamed about having children myself. I'm from a famous family—as a matter of fact, I'm the last of them. I'm sure you've heard of the Beauvais Mansion on Esplanade?"

The doctor's hand comes up and touches his mouth again. He

looks around to make sure no one is listening. "Miss Beauvais," he says in a dry, conspiratorial tone, "would you like for me to arrange for a private consultation with someone here?"

"You're a doctor," she says.

"I'm an emergency room physician. I'm talking about a specialist."

"You've helped plenty." She slides off the gurney and spends a moment straightening her clothes. "Thank you for listening, Doctor."

"You're welcome," the doctor says in a frail whisper that suggests exhaustion. "I have patients now." But a minute goes by before he turns and walks away.

✺

Toward dusk the jangling telephone shakes Sonny awake and brings him charging off the little sofa by the window. He bumps against a lamp and nearly knocks it to the floor, then he bangs his shin trying to hurdle the coffee table. A pain bright and screaming drops him to his knees, but closer to the source of the miserable noise.

"Wait," he mutters.

He stops the ringing and holds the mouthpiece to his chin. He grunts a rough greeting.

"Hi, sugar. It's Anna Huey."

"Mrs. Huey," he says with only a dim understanding.

"Sonny, they'll be reading the will day after tomorrow. Miss Marcelle's will?"

Where he hit the table his leg beats in time with his heart. "Okay."

"Sonny? Sonny, are you all right? You don't sound well."

"Yes, Mrs. Huey?"

"I'm sorry to wake you, sugar. But it's my duty and responsibility to call. They're reading the will, Miss Marcelle's will? You know Nathan Harvey?"

"Nathan Harvey? No. Who is Nathan Harvey?"

"Nathan Harvey is a lawyer on Poydras Street, Sonny, in that Shell Building. You know the Shell Building where they have all those offices?"

"Are you talking about One Shell Square, Mrs. Huey?"

"Right. He's the one handling madam's estate. You should be there, at his office, at three P.M. this coming Friday. You don't have to, it's not the law or anything, but you should be."

Sonny looks around for a clock. "Why me?" he says.

"Miss Marcelle put you in her will, sugar. Mr. Harvey . . . well, they call it bequeathing. Something like that. You know what they call me?"

Sonny waits.

"Executrix. Isn't that a word?" She gives an embarrassed laugh. "I like it."

Almost three hours. Past the open door to the kitchen Sonny sees the digital clock on the face of the microwave oven. He slept that long. It's past seven o'clock suddenly.

"Mrs. Huey," Sonny says, his head thick and cottony. "Mrs. Huey, those two detectives . . . ? They took my fingerprints and now they're saying I have to stand in a lineup."

She lets several seconds pass before speaking. "If you didn't do it, then you have nothing to worry about. That's how it works, right?"

The remark, though spoken plainly, isn't quite the vote of confidence Sonny was hoping to hear. "I guess so," he says.

"Listen, sugar, if it makes you feel any better they haven't been so nice to me, either. Had me answer their questions and do the lie detector and write on some paper. Had me give my fingerprints. Don't feel bad, Sonny, you ain't the only one."

"I wish I'd never gone that night for Juliet's check. None of this would've happened."

Another long pause. Too long. "How do you mean, sugar?"

"I don't know. I guess I don't know what I mean."

"Friday at three," she says. "Nathan Harvey's on Poydras."

Sonny hangs up and lies in the heat and the dark watching occasional pieces of light float across the ceiling. *"If you didn't do it, then you have nothing to worry about."* Weren't those Louis's words as well? Sonny wishes he shared such a pure and noble faith, but the picture of what awaits him isn't any good: prison and death row, a tomb nobody visits, an eternity of regret.

A breeze, smelling of river sludge, stirs the curtains and riffles the pages of his father's fishing magazines. When the next horn blows you will get up, he tells himself. But several horns blow and Sonny remains unmoving on the floor.

He seems to sleep again but after a time he understands that it isn't sleep at all but a sort of paralysis. His nervous system has shut down. His brain . . .

The next horn, he tells himself.

The microwave tells him it is eight, then nine, then ten o'clock. At ten-thirty Curly and Florence Bonaventure entertain him with a festive argument that culminates in a noisy fuck. Curly's groans, never louder, are like those of a dog at its bowl. For her part Florence alternates shouts of pleasure with ones of pain, her constant nattering laced with obscenities that Curly answers with epithets of his own. Against the common wall they share with Sonny their headboard beats a rhythmic tattoo. In the background Sonny hears a second set of voices, and these are muffled somewhat but no less agitated. Have the Bonaventures brought in another couple? Music plays, if the noise produced by an electronic synthesizer and canned drums qualifies as music.

Sonny understands finally that his neighbors are screwing to porn.

"I'm innocent," he yells at the top of his lungs. "It wasn't me! I didn't do it!"

A silence follows, then the couple, louder than before, goes at it again.

Sonny comes to his feet. Aiming to shut them out he turns on his boom box and raises the volume way past his personal comfort level. It's the tape that he and Juliet listened to the night she stayed over. A saxophone explores a haunting melody to a live audience that erupts in warm applause at song's end.

On a hunch Sonny stops the recorder and removes the tape, which isn't labeled. He and Juliet listened to the "B" side only, and now Sonny flips the tape over to the "A" side, rewinds it to the beginning, and punches the Play button.

An announcer is introducing the group. *"Messieurs et mademoiselles,"* he says, then ticks off names to a riot of shouts and whistles.

"And on alto sax," the man announces at last, providing the name that draws the loudest cheers of all.

✝✝✝

They stop her as she's clearing the hospital's automatic sliding glass doors. "Miss Beauvais," the usual one says. "Can we give you a lift home?"

"Sorry, Detective. But the Beauvais isn't officially mine yet."

She means to be clever, and they allow her this. "To your hotel, then?"

"Okay," she says. "The Lé Dale on Saint Charles. Scene of the crime."

Lentini drives. Peroux rests his arm on top of the seat and tries to engage her with a smile. "We understand he used a pipe. What do you remember about him?"

"Mainly that his shoes didn't match. His heels, his shoe heels, were really worn, but one looked to be more worn than the other."

Neither cop says anything. Maybe they knew this.

"I asked him why he was beating on me, and he said I killed his Frank. Just like that, he says, 'You killed my Frank.'"

Lentini and Peroux look at each other. She feels like saying "Bingo." Then Peroux again: "He didn't happen to mention who this Frank was?"

"I don't know any Franks that I know of."

"No Franks? What about pets? You know any pets named Frank?"

"I haven't known a pet named Frank in my whole, entire life—not when I was a child, and not now. Where I live, in my little orbit, people aren't much into pets. You know why that is?" She looks at the scenery passing by: a used car lot, a carpet remnant store, an abandoned hotel decorated with for-sale signs and sheets of warped plywood pooling off the plate glass windows. "It's because people in California can't take care of their own selves. How do you expect them to take care of a pet?"

"No Franks, then. What else do you remember?"

She thinks about it. Shakes her head. "He limps." And now of course it comes to her. The man with the club was Louis. Who else but Louis?

"Maybe you should've hired somebody to whack you with a pipe a long time ago," Peroux says. "Get the heat off that way. I got to give you credit."

"What are you talking about?"

"You get him to beat you with a pipe the way he beat your mother and that automatically eliminates you as a suspect."

"I'm sorry, Lieutenant, but I have better things to do with my time than rearrange my own face. Now why are you talking to me this way? I've been very nice to you."

They pull up in front of the Lé Dale and Juliet gets out. Peroux rolls down his window. "Tell your boyfriend who's a boy we didn't mean to hurt his feelings."

It takes her a second to understand. "You talked to Leonard?"

"Sergeant Lentini didn't appreciate his attitude. He thought he was hiding something."

Juliet glances at the other one. "What can I tell you?" he says. "I'm a terrible person."

"I don't know what it is about him and the fruits," Peroux says with a resigned attitude. "But Sergeant Lentini can smell a fruit. He claims they put out an odor." Lentini is quiet, and Peroux laughs without apparent feeling. "Hey, podna, one more thing. Do you remember a little hourglass Sonny LaMott gave you back in school?"

"Did Sonny give me an hourglass? When was that?"

"Long time ago."

"I don't remember, no . . . oh, okay, hold on a sec. Yes. Yes, Sonny did give me an hourglass. It was a birthday gift, as I remember. He gave it to me before I left for California. It was about yay big." She demonstrates with her thumb and finger held apart.

"Hard to remember that far back, is it?"

"I guess fifteen years is a long time when you're busy beating yourself with a pipe."

"When's the last time you saw it?"

"Last time I saw it? Well, the last time I saw it also happens to be the last time I thought about it." She backs away from the window. "The day he gave it to me and I put it on a shelf."

They roar off without so much as a wave and Juliet climbs the stairs to the lobby, where Leroy strays from his TV long enough to check and make sure she's still alive. "When you left it wasn't looking too good," he says.

"I don't like being victimized. I don't like a hotel with no security."

"And I don't like cops asking me questions. And I don't like whores. And I don't like worrying whether I caught something after screwing one."

"You mean a whore or a cop?"

He gets out of his chair and walks around from behind the desk. She's wondering if maybe she'll be making another trip to the hospital, but then he hands her a letter without a postmark or return address. "Colored woman brought it," he says.

Juliet tears it open and reads particulars about a meeting Friday in the law office of Nathan Harvey, Esquire. *"I called maybe ten times and you're never there,"* the note ends. *"I'm starting to wonder if you even want what your mother left you . . ."*

"It isn't Mama that left it," Juliet says.

"Huh?"

"You must have me confused with somebody else."

"No. That letter is for you."

"It's always been mine. It's just she took it for a while."

"Well," says Leroy, "she brought it back. Now get out of here."

Up in the room Juliet takes her clothes off and curls up in bed, thinking she'll have to write the gimp a thank-you note for inadvertently removing her from suspicion. She'd beat him with a pipe of her own but that would do for him what he just did for her and she isn't feeling at all charitable at the moment.

Juliet takes her medicine then lies on her back smoking. She remembers back to pets she's known and she speaks their names into the darkness.

There was a toy Chihuahua of her father's, small enough as a puppy to fit in the palm of your hand. Juliet can see the precious thing snoozing in the sun of the upper gallery and yapping whenever the mailman came. It had bug eyes and sharp toenails that clicked against the wood floors.

From outside comes the *thwumpthwump* of rubber tires on train rails, then the loud electric whoosh and squeal of the streetcar itself. That sound seems never far from her consciousness, background music of her very own. Even when she lived in California Juliet could summon the sound of the streetcars, and it kept her company the way a good friend would, without any expectation but for occasional acknowledgment. If you live forever hearing streetcars then how can you ever truly be free of New Orleans?

Juliet lights a second cigarette and uses a plastic cup for an ashtray, holding it steady in one of her armpits. Mystified as to how someone who cleans house for a living can write such clear, declarative sentences and with such a practiced hand, Juliet reads yet again Anna Huey's letter about the meeting Friday at Nathan Harvey's office.

When the house is officially hers, the first thing she'll do is hand that woman her walking papers. "You're dismissed," Juliet says out loud now, smoke issuing from her mouth along with the words. "Get your belongings and beat it."

Once she's gone Juliet will throw the doors and windows open and let some air in.

Then she'll call Salvation Army and have them send a truck for her mother's clothes and personal effects. Then she'll trip some bug bombs and fumigate the place.

Juliet is still lying in bed when her father opens the door and enters the room. He strides with that same old Cary Grant confidence and who is he holding today but the little Chihuahua whose name Juliet couldn't recall. It squirms in his arms and drives its nose against his neck and face. "I was just thinking about you," Juliet says to the dog. *"Tu aussi,"* she says to her father.

Johnny Beauvais puts his free hand on top of Juliet's head and runs it through her hair. For a ghost his hand has a powerful weight and she feels pinned to her place. "Was it Tiny?" she asks.

The dog whimpers and shoots her an unhappy look.

"Tinker?" she tries again.

"What are you talking about?" her father asks in a peculiar voice. "Come on, Juliet. Snap out of it, snap out of it!" He takes her by the shoulders and shakes her until her head snaps back. "Juliet? Juliet, what's wrong with you?"

"Tina," she says. "It was Tina. Was it Tina?"

The cup has tipped over and ashes stain the sheets. The butt of her cigarette lies cold on her neck. She looks at her father and understands that he's really Leonard Barbier. He's Leonard with his face so disfigured that it possesses a Picassoesque aspect.

Juliet shoves up to the head of the bed and leans against the wall, her naked breasts stamped with the pattern of the sheet she was lying on. She can smell the rot of her own breath. She knows now that she was sleeping. "Did you tell them anything?"

He shakes his head.

"Don't lie to me, Leonard. They told me they hurt your feelings."

"Well, they were rude, all right. They kept threatening to rat me out to Big Leonard. Like I'm afraid of Big Leonard. Then they pushed me around, but let them push me around. I'm not going to jail, Juliet. In jail . . . can you imagine what they would do to a freak like me in jail?"

She touches the contusion below his left eye, which seems fitted deeper in his skull than the right one, and inches lower. She sees where they hit his mouth, giving it a lump. And the scratch mark on his neck. And the bloody redness at his nostrils.

"Sonny LaMott is going to fry," he says. "They've got all they need now."

Juliet is trying to remember how Tina died, whether it had worms or got hit out in the road. What Leonard said takes maybe half a minute to reach her.

They come at dawn and park across the street in the weedy strip of ground at the foot of the levee. Sonny watches from the living room window where he's spent most of the night drinking coffee and listening to Juliet's tape.

Peroux and Lentini emerge from one car and a patrolman and a woman materialize from another. The woman is wearing a dress suit and her copper-colored hair hangs to her shoulders in a busy profusion of flips and whorls. She's carrying an accordion folder file and she walks well ahead of the others. She doesn't bother to look for traffic as she crosses the street.

Outfitted in the same clothes he had on yesterday, Sonny opens the door and waits inside as they climb the stairs grousing about the heat and wondering out loud who would live in such a dump. Sonny inhales a breath of air then strides out on the landing and stands with his arms casually hanging by his side. The woman seems startled to come upon him so suddenly. She pauses on the steps before deciding to proceed.

"Mr. LaMott? Mr. LaMott, my name is Patricia Kimball. I'm an assistant district attorney for Orleans Parish. And this is a warrant to search your premises."

She hands Sonny a couple of pieces of paper and nods for the others to enter the house. "When we finish here we'll also be searching your automobile. Please let me have your keys now."

Sonny removes the keys from his pocket and gives them to the woman, who then passes them along to the patrolman.

"What are you looking for?" Sonny says. "Maybe I can help."

The question seems to disarm the young prosecutor, or perhaps it's Sonny's attempt at being civil that makes her hesitate. "It's listed there in the warrant," she says, pointing. "A ski mask or a skullcap and a pair of gloves, to start with."

"I don't think you'll find any of that here."

She steps closer and holds her face level with his. Her breath smells of toothpaste and mixes badly with the fruity scent of her perfume. "There's something else we're here for," she says. "It might interest you, considering its provenance."

"Its provenance?"

For some reason she doesn't seem to appreciate the question. She stares at him. "Its history, Mr. LaMott. Where it originated and where it's been."

She waits as if in anticipation of Sonny venturing a guess but all he does is shake his head. "There was one object that Mrs. Huey was curious to discover missing, as it held little value but the sentimental kind." Her mouth turns up in a grin. "An hourglass, Mr. LaMott."

"Forever is a long time," Peroux announces from the other side of the room. It seems he wants to unload with another of his obnoxious laughs, but instead he says, "Especially when the woman has other plans."

"Maybe Juliet has it," Sonny says. "What would I want with it?"

"Miss Beauvais could barely remember the hourglass," Patricia Kimball says, obviously enjoying the opportunity to impart this information. "It didn't seem to mean anything to her."

"Actually, she couldn't have cared less," Peroux says in a loud voice.

"Mrs. Huey remembered it because Mrs. Beauvais insisted she clean the room at least once a week. Mrs. Huey said that every time she stood at the bookshelf to dust, she felt embarrassed for your sake."

"Embarrassed?"

The woman hesitates, plainly relishing the chance to share more. "To think how much you loved her," she says, "and how little she cared about you."

They spend more than an hour searching the house. Sonny sits on the couch by the window, watching for activity on the wharf. Every now and then the air seems to leave the room and something catches in his throat and he has to remind himself to breathe.

When they finish, Lentini motions him to his feet.

"Lemme check under them cushions."

Sonny moves to the middle of the floor and Lentini inspects the sofa, removing the cushions and running his hands over the batting that covers the springs.

"You drive a truck, don't you?" It's Patricia Kimball again.

Sonny answers with a nod.

"Will you take us to it?"

He walks out onto the landing and points a finger. "That one over there in the grass."

Peroux rifles the glove box and the other two men dig around under the seat. They search the headliner, the wheel wells and the bumpers. They open the hood and the patrolman climbs on top of the engine and removes the air filter cover and checks the housing. The three men consult briefly with Patricia Kimball then move to the other side of the house and begin searching the trash cans. The patrolman removes the bags one after the other and throws them on the ground for the detectives to inspect. Finally they huddle on the lawn and Patricia Kimball shakes hands with the detectives before leaving with the patrolman.

Sonny hears Peroux and his partner coming back up the stairs. This time they have no smart remarks and Peroux knocks a fist against the side of the house even though Sonny has left the door open.

"Come in," Sonny calls from inside.

Peroux is sweating so hard tiny beads of perspiration shine in his goatee and the dark outline of his chest hair shows through his shirt.

"What time do you want me for that lineup?" Sonny asks before either of them can say anything.

Peroux tosses the truck keys on the coffee table. "There isn't going to be any lineup."

"What about your witness?" Sonny says. "What about the story you planted in the paper? What about the print analysis and the polygraph? Ask me, you've gone through a lot of trouble. And just a minute ago you were digging in my trash."

"Don't fuck with me, LaMott."

"I'm not fucking with you, Lieutenant. Why would I fuck with you? You're the one who's been fucking with me."

Peroux walks to the kitchen and returns wiping the sweat from his face with a dish towel. "What do you think we're gonna do?" he says. "Line you up with a bunch of flunkies in ski masks? Let that old vet stand there playing eeny, meeny, miney, moe? No," and he's still wiping himself, "there won't be any lineup."

"Then why'd you tell me there would be one?"

The detective carefully considers the question. He balls up the towel and throws it back in the kitchen. "Sometimes things happen when people think they've reached the end. They find a memory for things they meant to lose, only can't. Now let me ask you something, podna." And he pauses now, glancing back at Lentini. He resets his feet beneath him. "What were you planning to do with all them pictures you got in your bedroom closet? You planning to sell them or keep them stored in there like that or what?"

"That a work question, Lieutenant, or a personal one?"

"Just a question. I saw the nudes. And, well . . . I mean, Jesus . . ."

For some reason Sonny finds comfort in the way Peroux is looking at him now. That one is a cop and the other a murder suspect suddenly doesn't seem to matter at all.

Sonny walks to the bedroom and removes a painting from the closet—this one, like most of the others, bearing the title *My Juliet* scrawled on the reverse.

"Back when I was at Warren Easton," Peroux says, "there was this girl in my class looked something like this. I could never get her to even notice me." Staring at the image of Juliet, the detective chuckles and shakes his head. "I had this buddy used to say if a woman could put a pencil under her breast and it didn't fall she'd never have a problem for as long as she lived."

Lentini laughs from where he's standing at the door.

Outside on the river a horn blasts, disrupting the quiet. Peroux starts for the door. "You know she's been pretty busy since she came back to town? You're not the only one. I'd tell you the names of the others we know about if I thought it would help."

"I'd rather you didn't," Sonny says.

"Mainly it's that Barbier—he's the son of this big-shot lawyer in town. He plays at a dive in the Marigny and lives in a cheap hotel on North Rampart. You might want to pay him a surprise visit sometime. He deserves whatever you got for him."

Sonny doesn't say anything.

"Mind if I tell you how I see it? How I figure it happened?"

"Please," and Sonny nods. "Enlighten me, Lieutenant."

"You go up to the Beauvais and it's crazy and you can't believe 're doing it but somehow you get that check. The old lady isn't happy and she tells you to leave and never come back and so you go. You're a good guy and you're embarrassed and you could kick yourself for letting that little bitch run you like she does. You even go all the way down to the street where you've parked. Maybe even put the key in the ignition. Maybe even *start* the engine. But then you remember something. It's that hourglass. You remember what it represents. And you say to yourself, 'Ah, what the hell. They'll never miss it.' And so you start back.

"This time, though, you're wearing a few things you didn't have on the first time. You've put your gloves on and your ski mask and you're lugging your piece of PVC, your club. Not a long time before you scared the living shit out of one old man on the neutral ground and if need be you're prepared to scare the shit out of those two old women. So you're in the room now—in Juliet's room—when who but Mrs. Beauvais walks in." Done with the story, a lopsided smile brightens the detective's face. He nods at Sonny for a response.

"Sounds possible," Sonny says. "I suppose it could've happened."

"You suppose and me and Sergeant Lentini suppose and in my book that means it's damned likely. In my book two supposes almost always equal one damned likely."

Sonny shakes his head. "But then why couldn't you find my prints on the second floor? If I wasn't wearing gloves when I went up the first time and got the check, why didn't I leave any prints then? I told you I handled three different doorknobs."

"May I?" And the detective brings a finger up to the side of his head.

"Please."

"You wiped everything down. You get the hourglass, you kill the old lady, then you do what anyone else in your situation would do. You wipe down the doors and the doorknobs and the bookshelf. You wipe down the stairway banister. Everything you might've touched you wipe down. And I'll tell you something else. I'll tell you what you used. The ski mask on your head," Peroux says. "You used the ski mask, didn't you?"

"None of that is true, Lieutenant."

"You get outside and dispose of what's left of the club in the bush out back. I bet you lost sleep over that, leaving it like that for us to and not taking it and dumping it somewhere."

"Nope."

"So you saying you didn't lose sleep over leaving it behind?"

"I'm saying none of that happened. I've lost sleep, sure. I've lost plenty lately. But not over a club in some bushes."

Peroux shrugs. He is staring at the painting in his hands. "Sometimes I want to feel sorry for you, LaMott, I really do. I think about your family situation—you coming home that day to find your mama dead in the yard, your father who's so lost he can't figure out how to wipe his own ass. I think how you chose this line of work where every day people tell you how no good you are—how they do this just by walking past your paintings without looking at them let alone asking to buy one. And I think how lonely and how shitty it must be loving a woman who's had everybody else but still won't have you. It gets to me, LaMott. It puts a lump the size of an elephant turd right here in my throat. I even get tears in my eyes. Goddamn, look at me now, would you?"

"Right," says Sonny, who in actual fact sees nothing in the detective's eyes.

"She had an illegal operation in 1971? Was that with you?"

"Sir?"

"Juliet Beauvais told someone she can't have children because she ruined herself with an abortion when it was still illegal in this country. Was that with you?"

Sonny doesn't answer.

"Nothing to worry about on that count, podna. It was a long time ago, the statute of limitations applies. Besides that, nobody could give a shit anymore."

"Right."

"Your Juliet," the detective says, glancing at his picture again. "What a dream, huh?"

"Right," Sonny says again, amazed that he's able to speak at all.

Juliet drives the Mustang to the house on Saint Charles Avenue where ꞏckie Boudreau grew up and parks in front next to a fire hydrant. In ꞏs of square footage the house nearly doubles that of the Beauvais, ꞏgh it holds far less historical significance. A wealthy American

202

built the palace as a testament to his financial and cultural superiority, and in doing so he proved not only that he was *nouveau riche* but also that he was worth nothing, or *il vaut pas rien*, as the Creoles referred to him.

Locals call the place the Wedding Cake House because the filigree on the façade resembles the icing on a wedding cake.

Juliet's been there only a few minutes when a police cruiser stops behind her and a cop walks over. "What else could you possibly want to know?" Juliet asks, lowering her window just as he's about to rap on it. "Have you been following me?"

The cop stares from behind the black pools of his aviator shades. "What did you say?"

"What have I done now?"

"You don't see that fireplug?" He points to the one on the corner then leans in close to get a look inside the car. "Are you on drugs?"

"Me? You've got to be kidding. I don't use drugs."

"Lady, move this thing before I write you up."

Juliet makes a U-turn and parks on the other side of the avenue, this time occupying a legal space, but one at such a distance from the Wedding Cake House that when a man who might be Dickie miraculously appears at the front door and walks to the driveway she can't cross the neutral ground fast enough to confirm his identity.

The back of the man's head, like the top and the sides, is completely bald. Dickie's hair, if she recalls correctly, was a bushy mop.

Another thing about the man that confuses her is his size: Dickie was short, while this person is so large that he has difficulty squeezing into a Mercedes-Benz sedan.

As she crosses the avenue Juliet dodges a streetcar and oncoming traffic and by the time she reaches the fence that surrounds the property the man has driven away. (Come to think of it, neither does he drive like Dickie, who was always peeling out.)

Juliet tries to open the front gate but it's secured with a deadbolt lock.

She yells Dickie's name but nobody comes to the door.

On her way back to the Mustang, Juliet stops between a pair of train rails and stands waiting in the path of an approaching streetcar. As the conductor draws closer he begins to clang his bell in warning, but Juliet, crying now, stays put. More bells and now the frantic shouts o onlookers. The conductor is braking; she can hear the streetcar decelerating and the squeal of its metal wheels against the rails.

It stops finally with only a foot or two to spare, and Juliet steps aside.

"Wanna do it?" she yells at the conductor, her voice broken by a sob.

As Juliet continues on her way to the Mustang the conductor and his passengers stare as if at a crazy person.

Juliet shouldn't have given the militant bastard enough room to stop. Nobody would be staring then.

*6*

IN THE MORNING JULIET FARES BADLY
on the polygraph exam. It is unintentional. Even
responses to questions with no connection to her
mother's death produce results that indicate she is
being deceptive.

Asked for a writing sample, she carefully fills
the lines with her most disciplined schoolgirl
script. If only Sister Mary Margaret, who taught
her penmanship in second grade, were here to
watch. Asked to write the numbers one through
ten, Juliet neglects to include the number seven
and her lazy nine is nearly identical to her exuber-
ant six. "Are you dyslexic?" asks the graphoanalyst.

"I am, yes." But after a pause she says, "Don't
hold me to that."

An examiner collects her fingerprints as well,
even though a set complete with a palm print
already has been culled from a secondary source.

"What I should test is your blood alcohol level and throw you in the drunk tank," Peroux tells her. "We're going to have to do this all over again."

"I'm sorry, Lieutenant."

"Tell me what's going on inside your head, Miss Beauvais. I don't understand. You think this is a game?"

"No, Lieutenant. Last night I got depressed. It was Mother. I kept flashing to Son—" She stops to collect herself, shakes her head. "I kept seeing the killer beating her with that club. I know the terror she experienced. I was beaten myself, remember? Unable to sleep, I'm afraid I overindulged. I'm a nervous wreck this morning."

The detective stares. "Go back to your hotel, Miss Beauvais."

"He won't come again for me, will he, Lieutenant?"

"Miss Beauvais? Go home. Just go home. And make sure somebody else drives."

Later that day Leonard takes her to the Vieux Carré and they walk the streets drinking twenty-four-ounce go-cups topped with frozen margarita. Shopping the windows on Royal Street, Juliet lists the things she'll soon come back to buy and Leonard blows riffs on an imaginary horn. On Bourbon Street they toss coins at black boys tap-dancing to jazz music spilling from a corner club and in Pirate's Alley they pause to pet the hot, sweating necks of police saddlebreds standing unattended near the town house where William Faulkner once lived. At Jackson Square, hot and sweating themselves now, they lounge under the trees and watch the artists stationed along the great black fence. "I'm disappointed," Juliet says, sprawled out in the grass. "The funniest thing in the world? It's Sonny LaMott and his red cart, little pictures hanging everywhere."

"He just stands there with a thumb up his ass," Leonard adds.

"Looking stupid."

"Looking *real* stupid."

"Shut up, Leonard."

She passes out finally in the ladies' room at the Old Absinthe House, and yet half an hour later, after being carried out to the street, she manages to rally and follow Leonard all the way to the entrance to Saint Louis Cemetery Number 1 on Basin Street.

Here Juliet struggles to focus on a blurry and half-seen image from ago. The picture, pulled from her own private gallery of things that went wrong, is in exceptionally poor shape today: what could be old varnish yellows the surface and soot and crazing obscure the details. She and Sonny and his father's truck and the rain lashing the windshield. They were going to Gravier Street. The smell of oil and the windshield wipers refusing to work and feeling no different really than when she wasn't pregnant. They stopped here on the side of the road, in this very spot. Right by the meter there. "Let's turn back," Sonny said then, pleading. And Juliet repeats these words now. Her voice is a whisper. *"It's not too late."*

"What?" Leonard looks at his watch. "After walking all the way over here?"

"It's not too late," she says again.

"Yes, it is, goddamnit. It is too late."

The party man shows up. He is a boy of perhaps thirteen. You can see the waistband of his boxers, small hearts impaled with arrows. His navel, also visible, looks like a maraschino cherry precisely centered in his lower belly. Clusters both of whiskers and acne mark his small, moon-shaped face and he has the wrecked voice of a three-pack-a-day smoker. When he isn't watching the street, he's watching the cemetery behind him. "Marie Laveau is in that tomb right there," the boy explains. "She comes out at night and walks around putting curses on people."

"Isn't she a skeleton yet?" Juliet says.

"Hell no. She's a voodoo queen."

"What's your name, little man?"

"What's *my* name?"

"I only ask out of a genuine interest in your personal well-being," Juliet says. "I was wondering if you might like to expand your horizons in the American workforce."

"I know what you mean. You mean like a pizza route in one of them cars with a flag on the antenna."

"This is better," Juliet assures him. "I've got this particular item and I'm recruiting an individual to take it someplace and place it some-where. You think you might be interested in a job like that?"

"No, I don't." He's watching cars pass by. He doesn't look at her.

"But you can fit this thing in the palm of your hand, it's that small. And you won't have to take it far, take you ten minutes. You take it to a parking garage in the Quarter and drop it off in this cart I'll give yo directions to. You do it late at night when no one's around."

"And it blows up because it's a bomb, right? No, ma'am, none of that shit."

"It's an hourglass. 'Bout yay big."

He thinks about it awhile. He shrugs.

"Twenty-five dollars," Leonard tells him.

The boy doesn't respond.

"Would you do it for fifty?" Juliet says. She looks at Leonard, whose money she's spending, after all. "You could do it for fifty, right?"

The boy watches Leonard with the recognition that here is one motherfucker to be concerned about. "Fifty if that's all I have to do. Drop it in a cart."

Less than twenty minutes later they consume the powder in Leonard's room with the aid of a rolled-up dollar bill and Juliet, after snorting more than is sensible, blows a gob of pink-stained mucus into the tail of a bedsheet. "Sonny was never right for me," she says, "but I did like to kiss him. His breath was always nice. He kept his teeth immaculate."

"You'll have to include that in your memoirs."

"I asked him once why he never had bad breath and he said the trick was to swallow a little mouthwash after you finished gargling in the morning. He said the taste stayed in your mouth."

"That, too."

At daybreak they turn off the television and Leonard surrenders to sleep on the shag rug while Juliet, who is naked but for a pair of pink socks, sits beside him with ocean sounds sloshing around in her head. Her hands shake and her mouth is so parched that her lips stick together. A trickle of something keeps emerging from her right nostril, while her left one merely burns. She removes the hourglass from a rumpled Schwegmann's bag and turns it over, letting the sand run.

What is the good of time, she'd like to know, if it stays perpetually stuck in 1971, visiting again and again the year when her mother killed her father and her volvo was scarred forever?

"There is no forever," Juliet says out loud to the room.

A stirring from Leonard but nothing more.

"There's yesterday, though. Shit yeah. There's always that."

She and Leonard sleep until late afternoon. When they wake he ⊃es to the bathroom and relieves himself in an erratic stream. "When ⌐land would piss it was like a horse."

"Who's Roland?"

"Who's Roland?"

And in that instant she remembers. "Oh, okay. Was that his name?" Juliet, still on the floor, rolls over and looks for something to cover herself with. "I don't think I ever went with any Rolands before. A Ronald, maybe. Maybe two or three Ronalds." All she can find is newspaper, but that is fine. "Whatever happened to that boy?"

"Went back to the wife."

"Know what I still don't get? I still don't understand how someone can be gay and straight both at the same time?"

"Yours is not to understand," Leonard answers. "It's love, baby."

He returns to the room and in the imperfect light from the window she can see what kind of old man Leonard will turn out to be. Rings of blubber around his gut, scraps of frizz for hair, long nose with bumps, no penis to speak of, a feminine chest with spark plug nipples that could use training in a brassiere. Like Anthony, Leonard was just an underage boy then, but Juliet still can't see what her father possibly could have liked about him.

Juliet stands and her brain seems to expand in her skull and the pain makes her wonder if maybe she wouldn't be better off beaten and strangled to death herself. She takes the hourglass off the table and throws it from hand to hand, tossing it higher each time. "Knowing Sonny he finds this in his cart and takes it as a message I still love him."

Leonard checks the top of the dresser for remnants of last night but there is none. A look of profound disappointment comes to his face.

"Don't pout," Juliet tells him. "It was mostly baby powder anyway."

ΨΨΨ

On the Chef Menteur Highway they make their usual stop for provisions, and today along with the shrimp bait and pork rinds Sonny buys a fifth of whiskey.

They take turns with the bottle and by the time they reach the Rigolets Sonny can barely keep the truck on the road and Mr. LaMott is sleeping with his back against the door, head lolling, neck bent like the stalk of a flower with too big a blossom. Whiskey stains the front his shirt and a rope of drool hangs from his chin. It is early after and the parking lot at Captain Bruce's holds only a couple of p a refrigerator truck and a late-model Cadillac Seville tattooed with Saints stickers on the rear bumper. Along with the beer neons, Christmas tree lights burn in the window of the building despite the fact that the holiday is more than seven months away. A cowbell clatters when Sonny pushes the door open.

"This ain't your regular time," Captain Bruce says from behind the bar.

"I had a day off. Daddy wanted to do something."

The captain is peeling boiled shrimp piled high on a platter. He laughs and shows the pink ground meat on his tongue. "Other than just sit there looking like a retard, you mean?"

"What did you say?"

"The last time your daddy wanted to do something he did it in his pants."

In the corner a kid is playing pinball, banging his groin against the machine. On one of the stools, bellied up to the counter, an old fart in a baseball cap drinks beer from a can. "Mind if we fish from your dock?" Sonny says.

Another look at the shrimp in his mouth. "Not so long as you pay me my fee."

Sonny hands over five one-dollar bills and starts back outside.

"Next time it'll be double," says the captain, then drops a heavy fist on the counter. "He scares my fish away."

The pinball player lets the machine go silent. The beer drinker, lowering his can, mutters, "Now that's some ice cold shit, Cap'n."

Sonny ties his father's waist with the rope and gives him a couple of folding chairs to carry, then he collects the fishing gear and leads the way to the pier. If not for the breeze off the lake the heat would be too much to tolerate. Sonny gives his father the bottle of whiskey and tells him to drink up but his father is unable to do so. Mr. LaMott slumps in a chair, the straw hat on his head giving a latticed effect to the shadow on his face.

"We'd better catch something," Sonny says. "This is it, our last time."

Mr. LaMott doesn't respond but to gurgle and nod and Sonny takes ▸ bottle from his hands and puts it on the warped gray boards. He tears  imp in half and baits his father's hook and casts about thirty yards  ou hear me, Daddy? This is it. Let's catch us some big ones."

He fits the rod in his father's hands but his father is sleeping.

"I never thought I'd live all that long anyway," Sonny says. "I always had a feeling." He could be talking to himself in an empty room at home. Talking to a barge on the river. Talking to a piece of raw canvas before he primes it and starts with the underpaint. "Maybe that's why I wanted to make a mark when I was still young," Sonny says. "After Juliet left I thought if I could do some nice paintings that would be enough. You think I was wrong?"

When his father doesn't answer, Sonny unties the rope around his own waist and drops it to the boards. He kneels on the edge of the pier and bends over lowering his rod into the water until the water creeps up past his elbow and chops hard against his face. He still hasn't touched bottom.

"That's at least eight feet," he says to Mr. LaMott.

Sonny takes a seat and drinks more whiskey and wonders why he never thought to paint the Rigolets. "I was good painting Juliet," he says. "Just admit that. I could really paint that woman. Everything else might not've been so great, but my Juliets had something. Know what they had?" His father doesn't respond and Sonny says, "It's called immortality. Not to brag or anything, but that's what they had. You looked at one and you knew you were seeing the big way a man can love a woman. Why am I talking like this, Daddy? These words I'm using, are you as embarrassed as I am? Jeez!" But Sonny doesn't stop. "I guess I let her do all she did to me," he says, "because I knew to let her go was to lose forever the one thing that made me any good."

Sonny removes the old man's hat and places his hand on top of his head. "Mama wouldn't want you having to live out your days in the home without me, Daddy. Hey, you. Hey, Pops. You taking any of this down?"

The shrimp boats on the water, the men made old young by the sun and the sea, the shanty camps on stilts at the end of long weed-choked dirt roads. Why didn't he paint any of it?

Mr. LaMott's rod falls to the floor and Sonny places it next to his. He doesn't bother to reel in the line. The restaurant behind them is quiet, the blinds closed. No one fishes from the piers nearby. Sonny spends a long time looking at his father, trying to recall how he was before the Alzheimer's advanced to where he stopped being recognizable to anyone who knew him.

Sonny has his father's nose and eyes. But his hair is like his mother's was. He doesn't know where his ears come from. They're smaller and better formed than Mr. LaMott's. The source of his big lantern jaw is also a mystery.

Sonny's hands begin to shake and it's hard for him to breathe for the tightening of his chest. You should be happy, he tells himself. It's the right thing to do. The *only* thing. He pulls the old man out of the chair, surprised by the weight. He kicks the fishing gear out of the way and drags him over to the end of the pier where it's deepest and lifts him to stand against a piling with his back to the water. Mr. LaMott mumbles. He seems to be coming to. His tongue is heavy in his mouth as he tries to speak. "No red pepper," he seems to say.

"No red pepper?"

"I don't want any."

The wind is coming strong and wet now and it blows Sonny's shirt flapping against his body and throws his hair back in a flutter. Mr. LaMott's hat flies off his head and lands in the water and drifts in the ripples toward the shore.

In the end it isn't necessary to give his father a push. Mr. LaMott starts to pitch forward, then he loses his balance and drops to the black water without any attempt to break his fall. There's hardly a splash. The rope screams against the boards and goes slack and Sonny can see the blurred yellow shape that is his father growing smaller as it descends. Sonny sits on the pier and takes a swallow from the bottle and when he looks again the shape resembles an angel with wings fighting for purchase against the darkness all around. Sonny drinks and he feels he has to vomit and more rope pays out. He waits then scrambles to his feet and frantically yanks at the rope until the yellow shape comes back into view.

When his father reaches the surface he comes up gasping and flailing his arms and water balloons his clothes and his hair fans out white in a single wave.

"I'm sorry," Sonny shouts in a panic. "I didn't mean it. I'm sorry."

He loops the rope around a piling and reaches down sobbing and grabs his father by the belt and pulls him up fighting to the dock. Mr. LaMott coughs roughly and he is stronger than Sonny imagined. He ˡⁱᵉˢ on his side holding his arms at his chest and Sonny lies beside him ᵃⁿᵈ puts an arm around him pulling him close. A long time passes

212

before his father's body stops shaking and quiets and he seems to sleep. "I'm sorry" Sonny says again, whispering. "I didn't mean it."

He decides to abandon the fishing supplies and the bottle. The chairs. He lifts Mr. LaMott in his arms and carries him to the truck. His father shakes as if from the cold and his scalp is pink past the ribbons of matted hair. More cars and pickups fill the lot now and a woman watches from the building, her face colored red and green by the lights in the window. "Is that a person?" she calls in a drunken voice. "Hey, what are you doing with that person?"

Sonny doesn't answer. He closes the door behind his father and walks past her and enters the lounge to the clank of the cowbell.

The same boy is playing pinball and the bar now is crowded with beer drinkers and Sonny can smell crab boil past the cigarette smoke. The captain is standing in the same place as before working on another platter of shrimp. Above him the TV shows news from the city and yet another story about an abandoned house torched by arsonists. The captain, gazing upward, absorbs it all as if with a superior understanding. "Your coloreds can't be trusted with kitchen matches," he says. He talks in the direction of the set. "They're like children that way."

"Bruce?" Sonny says.

He wishes he had the club. He wishes he had the captain alone in the room of a house in a bad neighborhood where drug dealers and gangbangers own the streets and anybody who lives there is asking for whatever they get. The story about the fire ends and one about a wreck on the Chef Highway begins. Two people were killed, one injured. The traffic delay lasted for hours while state police investigated the scene.

"Bruce?" Sonny says again, louder now. He waits and the captain slips under the shelf that serves as a door to the elevated run behind the bar. "What did you call my father when I came in here earlier? You called him something."

"I called him something?" The captain wipes his hands on a dish towel and shrimp scales fall to the floor. He laughs and his open mouth shows more of the pink ground meat and dark spaces where teeth are missing. "Oh. You mean when I said he was a retard?"

Sonny walks closer. "He's got Alzheimer's. You don't know the difference between being sick and being retarded?" And before the captain can answer Sonny lunges at him and clutches his neck in his hands. The captain is slow to react and for a moment Sonny believes he has the strength to crush him. He shoves him against the bar and some of the beer drinkers scatter and a stool topples over and meets the floor with a heavy, metallic thud. Sonny chokes him until a jolt of pain radiates up from his groin and he falls to the floor clutching himself and bellowing for the pain.

Something forces the whiskey up into Sonny's mouth and he coughs it out.

"I'll show you sick," says the captain, then spits his mouthful of shrimp at Sonny. "Jimmy, teach this boy some more about sick."

The kid who was playing pinball walks over and brings his foot hard into Sonny's ribs.

"A little more," says the captain. "He comes from town." And Sonny absorbs another one.

Somebody pours beer on his head as they're dragging him outside. As they walk away Sonny can hear them laughing but no one says anything. He crawls to where he's parked and leans back against the front bumper needing to throw up again. His chest stings and he feels where he wet his pants and where the shells dug holes in his hands. When he looks up five or six of them are watching from the window. Someone waves and he recognizes the woman who wanted to know what he was carrying earlier. He doesn't return the gesture but it crosses his mind he should show he hasn't lost his humor.

He pulls himself up and gets behind the wheel and starts the engine.

"Did we catch anything?" asks a voice.

Sonny looks over and Mr. LaMott, pushed back against the door, waits with what is either a smile or a frown, depending on your point of view.

They are a long time down the road before Sonny answers.

※※※

Nathan Harvey's bristly white mustache, stained yellow in the middle from a forty-year nicotine addiction, tarnishes the shine on his otherwise high-polished demeanor. His outfit today is a light silk weave finished with a raspberry bow tie, argyle socks and wing tips buffed to a military shine. He is older, perhaps seventy. But he carries himself with the confidence of a blue-chip athlete with miles and miles left to run.

214

His office is a suite of rooms on a top floor of One Shell Square, an imposing tower of stone and glass in the Central Business District whose majority occupant is Shell Oil, the petroleum giant. Perhaps because her mother employed him, Juliet expected Harvey to keep a less modern workplace, something of the pile-of-bricks variety, say, with flaking plaster on the walls and badly scarred wood floors protesting wherever you walked. Harvey's office commands panoramic views of the Mississippi River and the French Quarter. That it is equipped with personal computers, and not Remington Noiseless, also impresses.

"Miss Beauvais, please meet Mr. Nathan Harvey," the attorney's secretary says as the two come together. "Mr. Harvey, Miss Juliet Beauvais."

"Ah, yes, the daughter," Harvey says, giving Juliet's hand a strong, athletic shake.

Who can guess how many horror stories her mother confided to this man, most all of them casting Juliet as the villain and she the victim? Harvey, despite this secret knowledge, seems ready to pinch Juliet on the cheek and reward her with a Tootsie Pop for arriving on time.

"Maria will show you to the library," he says, "and be sure to take in the view. You can almost see the state of Mississippi—the red of their already red necks broiling in the noonday sun."

"The red of their already red . . . ?" She's playing dumb. "Oh, okay. They're rednecks!"

"Miss Beauvais?" The secretary is standing at the entrance to a hallway, waving in the fashion of a flight attendant to boarding passengers. "If you'll come with me, please."

Juliet follows her into a large, book-filled conference room where Sonny sits with Anna Huey at a long mahogany table. Although he seems loath to acknowledge her, Juliet leans over and brushes her mouth against Sonny's face. It's the sort of half-felt gesture that college sorority girls, too sophisticated for handshakes, reward each other just for being wonderful. "Hello, sweetie. How are you?"

"Julie," he allows with a note of formality.

Sonny doesn't look right. Something about his face suggests a recent trauma. He was always on the pale side, but today purple streaks mark the corners of his mouth and make his overall cast appear abnormally white. It's as if he talked too much and bruised his lips.

"Baby, are you okay? Did they beat you, too?"

"What?"

"You didn't hear about the other night? Somebody beat me with a club."

Sonny starts to speak but the cleaning woman interrupts. " 'Somebody beat me with a club.' Juliet, I can't believe you just said that. What in the world is wrong with you? Juliet, you're mocking your mother's death. You're making fun, and of all times now!"

"Hey, Julie, why don't you have a seat?" Sonny says.

Juliet stares at Anna Huey even though she still seems to be addressing Sonny. "As I was saying, somebody came to my hotel and let me have it with a pipe. I put up a fight. I kept clawing at the sonofabitch, trying to rip his eyes out. The best I could do was get some skin off his arm." Juliet, looking at Sonny finally, touches a spot on top of her head. "Come feel. It's as big as a goose egg. You believe me, don't you, sweetie?"

"Believe you? Why wouldn't I believe you, Julie? You've never lied to me."

Anna Huey, pushing her chair back, laughs as she comes to her feet and walks over to the window. The vertical blinds are open and she brings her gaze to the rooftops of the French Quarter, the neighborhoods beyond.

"Oh, okay," Juliet says. "I kept trying to figure out what was different about you today, Anna Huey, and it's the clothes. My heavens, you're actually wearing some. Hey, lady, where's the uniform?"

"I think I'm leaving," Sonny says.

"Stay where you are," Anna Huey tells him.

Nathan Harvey shuffles in carrying a stack of folders and sits at the head of the table. As he's sorting papers, Harvey's secretary passes out ink pens and yellow legal tablets. "For any notes you might want to take," he explains. "And now a surprise. Or what I hope is a surprise." Harvey waits, obviously enjoying the moment. He raises an eyebrow and screws up his face in a smile. "The great lady herself is going to be speaking to us this morning."

"The great lady?" Juliet involuntarily comes up an inch in her chair.

"Well, she won't be here in the actual flesh," Harvey says, "but your mother did elect to appear on video giving a loose reading of her will and we're going to watch that now. To avoid any confusion, I should tell ou that recorded wills such as the one you are about to see have no validity in the state of Louisiana. They've become popular since the VCR revolution in recent years and their purpose is strictly as a companion to the statutory will, which we will discuss in detail as soon as the tape is over." The lawyer glances back over his shoulder. "Maria!"

Harvey's secretary wheels a television and VCR hookup into the room. Harvey dims the lights and the screen flashes and a block of color fills Juliet's face. She shifts in her seat, and suddenly her mother appears seated in her favorite chair in the parlor at home.

"Hello everyone," the dead woman begins, fingering a thicket of index cards in her lap. "As this is my last will and testament I'll try not to ramble and veer too far off course but that won't be easy with that camera in my face. Juliet, I must say, darling, I now have a new appreciation for what you do. My heavens. And, look, I've kept my clothes on."

Only Harvey laughs. Miss Marcelle, in no hurry, pours herself a cup of coffee, and Juliet notes the antique silver service and dish of lady fingers on the butler's table. The showoff. Why didn't she use one of her regular cups? With a camera in the room, were the color-coded plastic mugs no longer good enough?

"Well," Miss Marcelle continues, "I don't plan to die any time soon, but my dying will be made less a bother by this will and that's why Nathan has advised me to do it.

"First of all, I want to leave one hundred dollars to Sonny LaMott. Sonny, this is not a gift but a commission to paint my portrait, which I'd like to hang in the parlor here at home. Anna Huey, if you can stand to look at me, I'd like it on that wall there." She points to a place in the room. "Sonny, you've been a friend and I admire anyone who aims to greatness. If I might make a suggestion, Sonny, paint me not as I am today but as I was when I married Johnny and first moved to the mansion. I was young once, too, and some say quite the lady. And you might if you look closely find a native resemblance to your Juliet, and let this inspire you, Sonny, as I know how you've always felt about her. Thank you, darling."

Miss Marcelle consults her cards again. "Anna Huey, I leave you my wardrobe. Please have your friends come by and choose from what clothes of mine you don't want yourself. The rest you can give to St. Vincent de Paul. Anna Huey, please think of me every morning when you sit down in the kitchen to your biscuit and jam. I hope you will tell Anthony how grateful I am to him for sending all those precious cards pretending they were from Juliet. I hold no grudges against the dear boy and I never have. Tell him I said so, if you would.

"Juliet, darling, I want you to have the wedding band your father gave me, as it is the most valuable item I have left in my possession." She shuffles her crib notes and uses her thumb to square them. "Also, I'd like to leave you what money I have left after Sonny gets his commission. It should amount to a few hundred dollars, but if it's less please try to understand. Money is something I've had trouble with these last years, and I'm sure when I'm done Nathan will provide you—"

"Stop the tape," Juliet says.

". . . with more details and I'll be disgraced to a degree—"

"Stop it," Juliet says again. "Stop it now."

". . . but not nearly so much as when your father . . ."

Harvey, in the dark, hurries over to the machine.

"Mr. Harvey? Mr. Harvey, what is she rambling on about?"

He punches a button and brings the show to a pause. "Miss Beauvais, I'll have to ask you to quiet down and be patient. It's coming." He turns from Juliet to the image of Miss Marcelle on the screen, then back to Juliet again. "May we continue, please?"

Harvey doesn't wait for her response. The tape starts to play again and he returns to his seat, settling in with a sigh. "Juliet," says Miss Marcelle, "I pray that you have a daughter of your own one day and I pray you're a better mother to her than I have been to you. As you well know, your father never loved me and I spent your childhood resenting you because you were the one he cared about. This is no easy admission for me to make, but there you have it. Your father and I were never meant to be together, I'm afraid, and yet we did have you . . ."

Miss Marcelle stops and clears her throat, and something in the room distracts her. It's Anna Huey, her white-stockinged thighs whistling as she carries in a glass of water. Miss Marcelle takes a sip and looks down at her cards, and the camera focuses in tighter. Her face occupies every inch of the screen. "For the record," she says, "let me say again to you, darling, that your father's death was a destiny that came at no fault of mine. I know you've blamed me but blame doesn't equal truth and the truth in this case is all I have and all I've ever had. I still dream of that sad day at Lake Pontchartrain and always I wish it were I who was lost to the water and not Johnny. I know he was your happiness."

She places the index cards on the table then takes one of the lady fingers and nibbles its edge. "Nathan," she says upon realizing that she's still being filmed, "you can turn that off now. I'm done."

✦✦✦

The overhead lights come on and Nathan Harvey reclines in his chair scratching his short yellow whiskers. Someone is crying and Sonny swivels in his chair and discovers Anna Huey racked with sobs, a hand covering her mouth.

Juliet wears a befuddled expression, but no more so than the one Sonny is wearing. Miss Marcelle did not give a complete accounting, after all.

Why did she fail to mention the fate of the mansion?

"Any questions," the lawyer says.

"Did she mean to leave everything out?" Juliet reads from her yellow tablet. "A commission for Sonny. Some hand-me-downs for the maid. An old ring and a few dollars for me. Can that be it?"

"Maria?" Harvey, snapping his head back, talks toward the door. "Oh, Maria? We're ready for you now, darling."

The secretary returns and passes out Xerox copies of a document titled with bold block lettering. Dated and signed by Marcelle L. Beauvais, Nathan Harvey and two witnesses, it is Miss Marcelle's last will and testament and it consists of two pages only. Sonny reads quickly. Finished after less than a minute, he looks up and faces Juliet.

"This is a joke," she says.

The lawyer doesn't answer.

"Mr. Harvey, the Beauvais Mansion has been in my family since the early 1800s. When it was built it was the finest house of its kind in all the South and not a few architectural historians still regard it as such. My father was the fifth generation to live there, and I the sixth."

In an instant Juliet has abandoned her sex kitten persona and adopted that of a preservationist on loan from a local historical society. Sonny, for one, couldn't be more impressed. Now she glares at the lawyer with equal parts rage and curiosity, then points to the TV set. "Am I right to assume Mother didn't include any mention of the Beauvais because it automatically goes to me?" When there is no answer, Juliet says, "I'm the last of them, in case you forgot."

219

Harvey rocks in his chair and lets a smile tug at the corners of his mouth. Sonny halfway expects him to call Maria back with more papers, with something, but in a moment the lawyer reclaims his formal deportment and makes a steeple of his hands. He takes in a breath of air and as quickly exhales it. "She didn't include the mansion in the will, Miss Beauvais, because it wasn't hers to include. Your mother didn't own it."

"She didn't own it? You're full of crap, mister."

A silence follows, and the only sound is the squealing of the video-tape rewinding in the VCR. Sonny slumps in his seat. "If not my mother," Juliet says, "then who does own it, Mr. Harvey? Tell me that. Who does own it?"

It isn't the lawyer who provides the answer.

"I do," says Anna Huey, slowly rising to her feet and returning to her spot by the window.

"I got nothing against you wearing that dress," Juliet says, "but I draw the line . . . I *do* draw the line at you claiming my house. God-damn, Mr. Harvey."

Harvey digs in his folder for another document. "If you'll allow me, Mrs. Huey?"

Anna Huey gives a nod and Harvey says, "As you either are unaware or have forgotten, Miss Beauvais, Mrs. Huey's husband, Charles, was killed a number of years ago in an accident on a drilling rig in the Gulf of Mexico—"

"Right. Charles. But what does that have to do with anything?"

"Please, dear. Let me finish." Harvey waits until Juliet is quiet, then he says, "This firm on behalf of Mrs. Huey brought a civil action against the oil company for which Charles was employed, and at trial we prevailed. Mrs. Huey's suit resulted in one of the largest jury awards in the history of the state of Louisiana." Harvey brings a hand to his mouth but too late to hide his satisfied smile. "She got twenty million."

Juliet stares straight ahead without saying anything.

"Mrs. Huey?"

"Go on, Mr. Harvey."

"If we might look back several years now, Miss Beauvais, you'll recall the extreme situation your father's business affairs were in at the time of his death. For starters, he owed everyone, having committed to assorted risky ventures that put him on the brink of bankruptcy. To protect the mansion, he logically concluded that he had no choice but to separate his and your mother's community assets. In other words, he elected to make your mother the sole owner of the family estate to keep from losing it to his creditors. Simultaneous to taking this action, your father created a trust in your name and funneled everything he had left into it, some two hundred thousand dollars. This money was to be for your college education and expenses, to be spent at your discretion. Your father died shortly after taking these steps, leaving you a generous legacy, but leaving your mother insolvent and with a vast house to keep."

"I don't know how vast it is," says Juliet.

"Pardon?"

"It isn't so vast. It's big, maybe. Maybe even real big. But I wouldn't call it vast."

Harvey seems lost for a response. "Fine. However you wish to describe it."

"Just admit to me it isn't vast."

"It isn't vast," he allows. "Now may I continue?" Harvey glances down at his notes. "Marcelle Beauvais, faced with ruin, was forced to get by on her wits. She approached area banks about obtaining a mortgage, but none was interested in making such a loan because of the condition and location of the house, and because she was without means to pay back what she hoped to borrow. Banks are not in the business of real estate, let me remind you. And a place such as that one would've been difficult to unload in the likely event Miss Marcelle defaulted on her loan."

Harvey pauses for a drink of water.

"It was a lot of things but it was never vast."

"Miss Beauvais?"

"You must have it confused with someplace else."

Harvey waits until all is quiet again. "Your mother did everything in her power to keep the mansion," he says. "In the fall of 1971, a few months after you ran away to California—" he drinks again—"she opened it up to boarders but that ended when one of her guests was mugged at the front gate. She sold off important pieces of furniture and some of the more significant works of art. NOPSI eventually cut off her power when she failed to pay her bills, and soon after both her water and gas services likewise were suspended. The house began deteriorate from neglect, and her lawn without a gardener began to resemble a jungle. She fired Mrs. Huey although in actual fact she hadn't paid her in many months. To trace back a bit now if I may, Charles Huey had died nearly four years before your father did, and at last came the trial and subsequent verdict. Mrs. Huey, through my office, hired an appraiser to assess the value of the mansion, and another—an art and antiques expert—to fix a price on its contents. These figures, added together, came to just under two million dollars. I myself considered the sum to be on the low end, but the gentleman who appraised the house, a Mr. Girault . . . he maintained that if the place were situated on Saint Charles Avenue and not in a blighted neighborhood it would be worth several times as much. 'Location, location, location,' he made a point of reminding me."

"Vast my ass."

Harvey places a hand on top of a document in front of him and slides it down the table. "This is a copy of the deed conveying the property to Mrs. Huey. You may pretend to know nothing about the sale, but I think you're familiar with the money it generated, as it's my recollection that your mother, after paying taxes and honoring your father's debts, which were many, sent the entire balance to you." Harvey smiles a cheerless smile. "It seems she thought you deserved it."

Juliet mumbles. Harvey again: "For the record, Mrs. Huey, in buying the house and its contents, elected to pay twenty percent above appraisal, acting against my better counsel. She also allowed Marcelle Beauvais to remain rent-free as a resident of the mansion, and—forgive me if I'm revealing too much, Mrs. Huey—she gave your mother a monthly allowance of five hundred dollars. In consideration she received nothing but your mother's companionship. Now, Miss Beauvais, you may choose to hire a lawyer to contest the sale's validity, but I think he or she will have a hard time prevailing, as the transfer of funds is well documented and you alone ultimately were the party enriched by the deal."

Harvey lowers his head, examines more papers. "Am I leaving anything out? Ah, yes." He brings his gaze back to Juliet and holds her with it until she looks away. "Miss Beauvais, Mrs. Huey has asked me to ask you to turn over your house key before leaving my office today." He collects his papers and puts them back in the folder. "She also would ⸱ke to tell you something in the presence of those of us here today as ⸱tnesses."

Juliet scans the room, but even Sonny pretends to be occupied with other concerns, in this instance a sketch of Nathan Harvey on his legal pad.

She swivels in her chair and faces Anna Huey.

"Juliet, get the fuck out of my house," says the maid, before quietly exiting the room

※※※

She doesn't remember leaving the law office. Was it Sonny who brought her back to the Lé Dale? She thinks they took the streetcar. She thinks she can remember sweating tourists, locals reading sections of the *Times-Picayune*, the high shine of the few empty seats as the afternoon light struck the blistered varnish. Sonny, what a hero, reaching up and pulling the cord to tell the conductor to stop.

She thinks maybe he helped her up the stairs and she thinks she remembers Sonny saying something to Leroy and Leroy looking up from his red hots and his TV. She thinks she remembers Sonny saying when he finished putting her to bed he'd come back down and write a check for what she owed and Leroy mentioning how his boss had a policy against hookers in the building and perhaps it was time Miss Beauvais take it on down the street.

But then maybe it was a dream. Maybe what she thinks she remembers she only imagined.

Juliet would like to wake up if only the sleep would let her. And then the door opens a crack and an eyeball looks in. It's who else and when he sees she's presently indisposed he quietly closes the door behind him. "Oh, please," she says. "Daddy! Daddy, don't go . . ."

She follows him out into the hall and glimpses the black form his shadow makes stretching along the length of the stairwell as he descends to the lobby. She chases after him taking two steps at a time and speaking his name and the moment she throws the door open Leroy spins around and holds a finger in her face. "What are you following me for? You're naked."

"Oh, please."

He guides her back to the stairs. "You're not bad-looking and everything but let me give you a piece of advice, lady. Always leave something to the imagination."

"You opened the door to my room. You looked inside. That's against the law."

"Call the cops. I was checking on something."

"What?"

"The maid knocked and you wouldn't answer. Your door was locked with the chain. We needed to see you wasn't dead."

"Maids," Juliet says. "Goddamn maids are about to ruin my life."

The desk clerk looks at her standing there, not even bothering to cover herself with her arms. "Ask me, baby, you seem perfectly capable of doing that yourself."

Back in the room she finds a wedding band on the bedside table. She wonders if she's in the wrong place, some other person's room, then she recognizes the ring as the one belonging to her mother. There's a note next to it and she reads by the slatted light from the streetlights pouring through the blinds. *Mr. Harvey told me to tell you he'd have your check shortly, to call his office with an address where they should send it. Anna Huey says she thinks it's three hundred dollars . . ."*

Not bothering to finish, Juliet squeezes Sonny's letter into a ball and throws it across the room. "Don't even know you're going to jail," she says, talking to the empty space.

She puts some clothes on and goes back down to the lobby.

"You remember where I parked my car?" she says to Leroy.

"You had a car?"

"I think I remember having one. A rental."

The news is on. Leroy turns down the volume. "What kind was it?"

"Yellow Ford Mustang convertible."

"I didn't know they even made those anymore. So how would I know where you parked yours? What I got to wonder," and he's nearly shouting now, "how somebody like you can pay for a rental car when this hotel's got to get your boyfriends to pay for your room. I bet you money you didn't so much rent that car as borrowed it." She doesn't respond and he says, "You know what happens when you keep a car past time and don't return it? They consider it stolen. They come and find it and charge you with felony theft."

"Is they the cops or is they the car place?"

He seems to have said all he means to, because he doesn't answer.

"Morris Barstow is my lawyer, by the way," she says. "His office was shocked to learn about my clubbing. They're doing the paperwork now. We're going to bring a lawsuit and Mr. Barstow promises me a check."

Leroy stares. "Ask me the only promise you got coming is an early grave, lady."

At last she remembers where she parked the Mustang: a metered spot on the street at One Shell Square, right at the foot of the building. But when she returns to the place, after hopping a downtown streetcar, the thing is nowhere to be found. She takes a stroll around the block but it's gone, all right. "Motherfuckers took it," she says to a business-man who seems to be waiting for a cab. "Second time since I been back they did that."

"I beg your pardon."

"Motherfuckers towed it."

She starts on foot in the direction of the French Quarter. They can have the car, they want it that bad. They took her house. What's a yel-low car compared to a house? "Vast my ass," she says out loud, momen-tarily forgetting that the meeting at Nathan Harvey's adjourned hours ago.

When she reaches the cemetery the party man is standing in the same place in the same clothes and the same puffed-out drawers. "You see what I mean by hourglass?" she tells him. "I wasn't wrong, was I?"

"When I turned it over it only ran for like a minute. But I'll call it whatever you want. Hourglass, two-hour-glass . . . shit."

"Leonard paid you your money?"

"Who?"

"The male white likes to act black."

"Yeah. Uh huh."

"So he paid you?"

"Right."

She digs in her pocket and retrieves her mother's wedding ring and only now does she notice the inscription inside the band: yet another man promising forever. "What could you give me for this?"

The boy inspects it then leads her past an iron fence into the ceme-tery and deep in the tombs washed a milky blue by the lights from the housing project nearby. He stops about halfway in and digs around under a wire flower basket and pulls out a clear plastic sandwich bag with less than half of what she and Leonard got before. "This is the best I can do," he says. "Maybe if you had some diamonds in it."

She takes the bag, halfway surprised he'd give this much. "Let me ask you something," she says in a little-girl voice. "Could you give me some more if I gave you the best, most amazing fellatio you ever had in your whole, entire life?"

The boy shakes his head. "I don't eat Mexican." He takes off in a trot through the tombs.

※※

Sonny drives to the Napoleon House for a drink and something to eat. Even as he's walking through the door he's placing an order with Louis: a tall glass of Crown, a dressed shrimp poboy, a double order of French fries and bread pudding minus the rum sauce. Sonny doesn't feel like talking, and come to think of it he doesn't really feel like eating.

Sensing his friend's desire for privacy, Louis stays away until the crowd thins and there's no one else to talk to, no one else to bug.

"Just for the record," he says in a voice too loud to ignore, "I found another Frank."

"Who?" Sonny, distracted, was watching beef gravy congeal in his plate.

"You whack an old vet on the neutral ground and don't remember?" Louis doesn't look up from his order pad. "This one ain't Siamese, though. It's calico. That means two things."

"A calico is one of those cats colored three different ways," Sonny says.

"That's one thing. Now guess the other."

"Don't make me do that," Sonny says. "I'm not in the mood."

"A calico is almost always a female. So if ever you see a strange cat with three colors you can impress whoever you're with by remarking as to how it's a female."

"You think it would impress whoever I'm with to go up to a strange cat and lift its hind leg and inspect its genitalia?"

Louis doesn't answer, doesn't laugh. He puts the check on the table and glances back at a couple of tourists who just entered the room. "You'll never guess where I found him."

"You just said all calicos are females and already you're calling her a him."

"Coulon, the vet on Esplanade. He had a sign in the window for baby kittens."

Sonny puts his fork down and pushes the plate away. "Don't fuck with me, Louis."

"I went in and Coulon's assistant has maybe five left and I pick the one I want and then Coulon walks in from the back through these saloon doors and we shake hands and he thanks me for coming in. Then guess what he says next?"

"I'm tired of guessing. All I ever do when I talk to you is guess."

"He says, 'So what are you going to call it?' And before I can think to stop myself I say the name. I look at him and I say, 'Frank.' I'm halfway out the door by now, and when I swing back around our eyes meet. It must be hell getting old. There's no way he made the connection."

"Louis," Sonny says, "tell me you're not being serious."

"I just kept walking. I left with the cat and brought him home and showed him the windowsill where the original Frank always sat. Then I went to Popeye's and got him some fried chicken livers, gave him a bowl of buttermilk and some ice cream and a peanut butter cup, showed him where the litter box was, demonstrated how to use it. Did everything possible, in other words, to make him comfortable. Are the cops going to come and arrest me? No. Am I worried about it? No. Settle down, Sonny. What's the fun of pulling off a crime if you can't go back and visit the scene?"

Sonny just now remembers something. He tugs at Louis's sleeve. "Roll it up."

"Huh?"

"I said, roll it up, roll up your sleeve."

Louis puts his pad on the table and does as he's told.

"Now roll up the other one," Sonny says.

Louis complies after hesitating a moment. He holds his arm out to Sonny, the wounds coated red with Mercurochrome, the scabs yet to form.

"Does Frank think you're one of those claw poles covered with carpet?" Sonny says.

"Yeah, well, it has been a problem. I should enroll him in obedience school. I've already tried spanking him with newspaper. They hate the noise, the sound of the paper. It's not the spanking that makes them stop." Louis rolls his sleeve back down and buttons the cuf "Look," he says, "she has no idea it was me. It happened too fast I went incognito."

Sonny pushes his plates over to the other side of the table. He finishes off the Crown and hands the empty glass to Louis. "The cops are going to come by to see you," he says.

"The cops? That's crazy."

"Did you whack Miss Marcelle, too, Louis?"

"Come on, Sonny. *Shit.*" Louis looks around to make sure no one is listening. "I can't believe you'd ask me that. What's wrong with you?"

Sonny puts twenty dollars on the table and leaves the restaurant. Outside a heavy rain has begun to fall and gullies of white water wash down from the rooftops and splash in the streets. Against the haze an occasional umbrella, colored stripes amid the gray. Sonny and Louis stand side by side on the banquette under a metal roof extending to the curb. "Dr. Coulon's going to call the detectives who've been investigating what happened to Juliet's mother," Sonny says. "I'm sure they've already interviewed Juliet. Next they're going to want to talk to you, Louis."

"This is goddamn amazing."

"They're going to arrest me. Lieutenant Peroux and his partner, Lentini. First I'm going to Parish Prison then I'm going to trial and then I'm going to Angola. Will you come and visit me, Louis? Will you promise to do that?"

"Asshole. You're an asshole, Sonny. You're an asshole for saying that. First of all, Juliet cannot identify me. There's no way she knows it was me. And, second, I bet that old man, that *vet* . . . ? I bet he's had a hundred patients named Frank. Over the years, anyway. There's no way he puts the new Frank together with the old Frank."

"When you talk to them put it all on me, Louis. Say whatever you want."

"Sonny, what the fuck is wrong with you? Why would I betray you like that?" Louis's chin trembles and his eyes begin to water. His leg has never been so quiet. "You got a cigarette, Sonny? Give me a cigarette."

"I don't have any cigarettes and you don't smoke. Go back to work, Louis."

Sonny starts across the street for the hotel parking garage where he left the truck.

"A cat scratches my arm and you make the leap you're going to ─on," Louis says.

"I'll understand whatever you tell them."

"I remember nothing," Louis says, his voice broken by sobs as he chases after Conny in the rain. "Do you hear me, bubba? I remember nothing. . ."

⁂

The top of the bag is pinched closed and Juliet pulls it open but too hard and the wind comes up and carries the powder into the night and out toward the housing project. It's hard to know whether to scream or to cry and in the end she does some of both.

She takes the sandwich bag and stuffs her face in it and inhales deeply and smells a smell that could be Clorox. She inhales a second time then tours the cemetery turning over flower baskets and concrete-cast urns and whatever else isn't bolted to the ground. She finds a couple of dirty syringes and holds them up to a streetlight. Both are empty.

"Is this my life?" she says to the small oval photograph of a woman under glass on one of the tombs. "It's not your life. Is it mine? Please just tell me if it's mine."

She waits at the gate for the better part of an hour and when at last the party man comes walking around the corner he isn't alone. His friend is himself a boy but a bigger one and when they're close enough she cups her hands around her mouth and says, "Somebody ain't very professional about how they put said items in said bag. Said customer is pissed."

"There ain't no science to loading a bag," the first boy says.

"You proved that. It all flew out when I tried to get it open."

"Find me another ring and maybe we can rectify the situation."

She's about had it with the little shithead, and the other one, mean as he looks, doesn't frighten her at all. "You ever hear of the Beauvais on Esplanade? For your information, and you should think about this . . . I'm one of them people."

The boy is quiet, confused.

"An actual Beauvais," she continues in a proud voice.

"Your name is Actual?" He glances at the other boy. "Hey, Tee, her name is Actual."

The bigger one nods as if he knows a few of those.

"I just want another bag," Juliet says. "Is that asking so much?"

She figures it must be, because they walk off and leave her there

It takes her ten minutes to reach Leonard's weekly/monthly. The old man at the desk stops her as she's starting up the stairs. "Leonard left."

"Leonard left?"

"Leonard checked out." He clears a wad of phlegm from his throat and spits in a paper cup. "Last thing he told me, he told me you came by to tell you he was sorry for everything."

Juliet comes back down the stairs and stands in the open door of his office. "How do you know it's me to tell that to?"

The man puts his spit cup on the floor and spreads his hands out in front of him. "He said tell the girl with the white hair and the big taters he was moving back home. That means his daddy's house in the Garden District. Leonard comes from money, you know?"

Juliet looks out at the street, the headlights cutting the darkness. A sightseeing buggy clatters past, its guide wearing a white tuxedo and a top hat. "Not as big as the Beauvais," she says. "Not as old, either. Don't even come with that shit."

"What was that, honey?"

When she looks back he's putting a fresh pinch of snuff in his mouth. "Why would he leave like that," she says, "so much in a hurry and all?"

"I got to believe it was them two parents that convinced him."

"*His* parents?"

"Well, the ones that drove up in the Jaguar and parked out front. I gave them his room number and they went right up. It was funny seeing a pair like that in this place. They left a smell in the building like Saturday night at the Blue Room. Anyway, I could hear them letting him have it. Everybody could. It got kind of loud." Clearly the man is relishing the chance to share this information. He rocks back in his chair and puts his feet on the desk. With both hands he holds the spit cup at his waist. "The daddy, this is Leonard's daddy, apparently he's some big lawyer, friends with the governor, the type of person they put his bust in the lobby of a building. Anyway, I can hear Leonard trying to argue, then the mother starts to cry and it's like cats screwing out on the windowsill. It's terrible. The father's yelling now. Leonard's going to come home or there's going to be an intervention. Leonard's going to Loyola, get his degree, stop this Buddy Bolden fancy. Leonard's going to be a responsible adult. Leonard's not going to embarrass them anymore. That man has plans for the boy, I'll give him that."

"Leonard," Juliet says sadly.

"They left with him in the backseat, staring out the window like he'd been sentenced to life at the state penitentiary with no possibility for parole. I never liked Leonard, he had some bad habits and some worse friends, but to see him like that like to break my heart."

Juliet knows the feeling. Her own heart seems to have stopped beating in her chest.

"Leonard," the old man says, "off on his way to be somebody."

❦❦❦

The crime scene tape has been removed, the lawn groomed, the lower gallery swept clean. But little else about the Beauvais has changed since Sonny's last visit.

He stands at the gate trying to absorb all that he can of the building's immortal façade: the windows hung with green plantation shutters, the double doors framed by open-flame gas lanterns, the giant ferns and ivies swinging in the breeze. Behind Sonny on the avenue traffic rumbles past, throwing light that streaks across the pale wicker furniture.

"Why, if it ain't Sonny LaMott!" a voice calls. And there suddenly is Anna Huey, a solitary figure in the dusk, moving toward him past the crape myrtles. "Hey, sugar. I thought that was you."

"Yes, ma'am," Sonny says.

"So nice to see you again, baby. You'll come in and visit, won't you?" She unlocks the gate and signals for him to enter, then she wraps her arms around him as he steps inside. "You want a cup of tea, sugar. How about a cup of tea?"

With her friend gone and the sad fraud exposed, Anna Huey wears the kind of casual but elegant clothing Sonny's often seen on well-to-do tourists visiting from the North, generally New Yorkers who seem to know brand names as well as they do their own family names. To add to the picture, she appears to have changed her hairstyle, which today features a loose chignon on the back of her head, about the size of a roll of socks. Her sturdy crepe-soled shoes have been replaced with smart leather pumps, and her legs, absent the white hose, no longer

231

whistle when she walks. The transformation is so striking that Sonny requires several moments to absorb it.

"You're beautiful."

"Thank you. But wasn't I before?"

Sonny follows her up the path and into the house. "I was out driving and ended up here," he explains. "Why do I always end up here, Mrs. Huey?"

"Maybe because you know you're always welcome. Come have a seat, sugar."

As she prepares the tea in the kitchen Sonny sits in his usual place in the parlor and allows the dark to press in close and hold him. Everything is as it was, everything the same, and it comes to him that this is only as it should be. The house and furnishings belonged to Anna Huey all along, after all. Even the collection of Beauvais portraits.

She returns with a tray and takes the chair next to his, and the routine, though familiar, is somehow disconcerting. Sonny can feel his heart laboring in his chest. And there seems to be an obstruction at the precise center of his throat; he coughs, twice, but it doesn't go away. "I was hoping to ask you some questions," he says.

Anna Huey nods. Pours the tea.

"They're about things that might be hard to talk about. I hope I can say them."

She finishes and sits holding the ceramic pot in one hand and his cup in the other.

"I keep thinking about what Miss Marcelle said in her will about holding no grudges against your brother Anthony."

"You want me to tell you about Anthony, Sonny?"

He brings the cup up to his mouth but doesn't drink. "I didn't understand that part."

Anna Huey returns the pot to the tray. She seems to be trying to decide whether she herself understands it either. "Anthony was only thirteen years old when he left New Orleans. That was 1971. He's never been back."

"I remember seeing him around a few times, but I never really knew him. No one ever bothered to introduce us, as I recall."

"No, sugar, you wouldn't have been introduced. He was just the maid's little brother, and that wasn't anyone, was it?" She gives an unhappy laugh and says, "Now that I reflect, Anthony really was more like a son to me than a brother. Both my parents had passed when he was a baby and me and my husband Charles took him in. We didn't have any children of our own and so we took to raising him like one. He was the caboose of the Arceneaux family—fifteen years younger than I am and seventeen years younger than my sister May."

"Didn't know May, either."

Anna Huey shakes her head. "May at the time I'm talking about was living in a place near Los Angeles called Inglewood. Ever hear of it?"

"Heard of it but never been there. I've never been west of Orange, Texas, as a matter of fact. My mother had some cousins out there. We took the Greyhound one summer when I was a kid."

She looks at him without speaking for a minute.

"I guess I'm nervous," he explains.

"I understand. I'm nervous, too."

"I'm just tired of the mystery. You have to help me, Mrs. Huey."

"I was talking about May?"

"Yes. May in Inglewood."

"Well, she and her husband had a car-detailing business out there—they've since moved on to real estate, but that's what they were doing in those days. Anyway, after what happened between Anthony and Mr. Johnny I thought it best he leave town and May volunteered to take him. It wasn't Miss Marcelle's fault he had to go, it was all Mr. Johnny's. But she blamed herself to the end. She paid for Anthony's plane ticket and opened a bank account in his name. Up until the day there wasn't any left to give she was still sending him money."

Sonny reaches out and touches Anna Huey's arm. "All of a sudden I feel like laughing," he says. "Will you understand if I have to laugh?"

"Of course. I laugh all the time about horrible things. Laugh all you want, sugar."

And so he does, Sonny laughs.

"It was a Sunday afternoon when Juliet found them together. They were upstairs in a bedroom, sprawled out on a couch apparently, and I heard a scream and a commotion on the stairs when Juliet came running down. She almost fell—she collapsed near the bottom and had to grab hold of the balustrade. She stood back up and staggered around knocking things down, a lamp and a clock and a table, some other things. I couldn't begin to imagine why she was so upset. I tried to talk to her and settle her down but it was no use, she was past hysterical and somewhere you don't go and ever expect to come back the same again. It went on like that for a while before she mumbled something about her daddy and Anthony and I ran upstairs and Mr. Johnny was standing putting on his suit like nothing had happened. 'A little less starch in the collar next time,' he told me." Anna Huey glances at Sonny. "Sonny, you still feel like laughing, sugar, go ahead."

But Sonny doesn't laugh, and he doesn't speak, and he doesn't move in his chair.

"Miss Marcelle always loved Anthony. He'd gone to her months before looking for a job and she'd let him cut grass and trim the hedges with the other men. It didn't suit him, though. Anthony was small and you might say delicate and when he complained it was too hard or too hot she brought him in the house. She bought him a suit at D. H. Holmes and he practiced being a butler for a while but somebody knocked, he wouldn't even answer the door. Most of the time he was out in the garage washing the cars with Mr. Johnny. At least that's what we thought he was doing. I remember madam used to joke that Johnny Beauvais had the cleanest cars in the state of Louisiana."

Anna Huey stares across the room at the black screen of the TV, and it's as though the piece of history she just described was being broadcast there.

"When Anthony was a little boy we used to put straightener in his hair. He always had to have a doll or a little stuffed animal. Go to church or the store, he was carrying it by a leg. Charles would say there was something not-right about him. That's the word he used too: not-right. We'd argue about it, the only fights we ever had that I can remember. I guess I was protective on account of Mama and Daddy having passed and I felt sorry for him. He was cute too. Oh, Anthony was a beautiful child."

Sonny touches her arm again. "Juliet found them together?"

"Yes."

"She never told me."

"No? Well, I'm not surprised. Think of the shame. She loved her daddy. And her daddy—did she ever tell you this . . . ? Her daddy was a Beauvais." Anna Huey falls silent, then says, "I told Juliet she had to talk to her mama and tell her what she saw, but she refused. More than hurting her mother she didn't want to hurt her father. She cursed me,

234

yelling when I told her that I would have to go and do it. I found Miss Marcelle outside watering her bougainvillea and I asked if I could speak to her a minute and we walked out under the trees. She dropped her can when I told her about Anthony. I'll never forget that . . . water splashing on her clothes, the look on that woman's face."

From the kitchen comes the sound of a ringing telephone. Anna Huey sits quietly until it stops, "A week later Mr. Johnny killed himself. In case you want to see it Miss Marcelle left a copy of his death certificate upstairs with her things. I can run and get it."

"That's okay."

"Suicide by drowning, says so in black and white."

"I believe you, Mrs. Huey."

"Miss Marcelle always told people it was an accident, and somehow she kept the *Picayune* from reporting the facts. I guess she was trying to protect Juliet. But the man did it to himself. That's what the Orleans Parish coroner ruled, and that's why in the end there wasn't any insurance for madam to collect. For doing what he did with a little boy he should've gone to prison. Instead he put his wife in one, because when he decided to die he made sure Miss Marcelle was there to see it. I guess he wanted her to have that picture, the last thing." Anna Huey lifts the teapot but seems to decide neither of them needs any more. "It wasn't just Anthony," she says. "But we didn't learn that until later."

"There were other boys?"

"The Quarter is full of children. Some will tap-dance on the bricks for a nickel. For a nickel more others will do other things. To be honest," she says, "I could never do anything but feel sorry for Juliet. Anything she ever did, I forgave her. Even today I do. That girl came into this world a sweet precious angel, her mother's joy, and the things she saw, sugar. Oh, the things she saw."

They sit without speaking until Sonny can tolerate the silence no longer. He stands and straightens his clothes but then he sits down again.

"Now's the time to ask," Anna Huey says, "if there's anything else you need to know. After today I leave all this behind me."

"Just one more thing, Mrs. Huey. And it's not so much about them as it is about you."

"Say it, sugar."

"Why would you pretend to be a cleaning woman and live as Mi

Marcelle's servant when you were the one who owned this house? Why allow that indignity?"

"Indignity?" And she sits up in her chair. "I considered it an honor."

She leads him to the stairway and the portraits showing Juliet's forebears, the entire collection bathed now in light from cans in the ceiling. Sonny notes the Vaudechamp still hanging crooked, and the one of Johnny Beauvais at the top of the stairs. "My mother worked for that man there," Anna Huey says, pointing to a face. "And my grandmother for that fellow. And my great-grandmother for him. They were ladies, Sonny. As long as there's been a Beauvais in this house, so too has there been an Arceneaux. My people always knew this day was coming. The Bible promised it. 'The meek shall inherit the earth,' it says. Well, meek or not, it's our turn now."

Sonny nods to the portraits. "You gonna leave them up there, Mrs. Huey?"

"Hell no," she says, then laughs as tears grow large in her eyes. "Every last one of them sonsabitches is coming down."

Anna Huey walks Sonny all the way to the avenue and they embrace in the thin, early dark, the name BEAUVAIS visible through the clumps of morning glory on the gate. The wind stirs the magnolias and crape myrtles and Sonny smells their bright blossoms. Along the sidewalk lamps burn yellow, dropping pools on the black pavement.

"Even after all I've told you," Anna Huey says, "and all you already know—even after everything, if Juliet came to you and said she wanted you back . . . ?"

Anna Huey is unable to finish, and Sonny unable to answer.

"I never asked if it was you that killed her, did I, sugar?"

He shakes his head. "No, ma'am. You never did."

※

She hitches a ride to Bywater with a male white in a big car. The radio plays classical music of all things. Juliet decides to make conversation. "You don't have any jewelry you want to get rid of, do you? Any rings?"

"No."

"You got that one on your finger there. What about that one?"

The man seems uncomfortable all of a sudden. He is quiet as they thump over the railroad tracks between Faubourg Marigny and By-water and Juliet gets a better look at him. He's wearing black and his hair is short, his fingernails neat and trim. Something about him is just too clean, too soft, and in that instant her automatic priest detector goes off.

She leans forward and by the light of the instrument panel catches a glimpse of the white tab at his shirt collar. "I'll be damned. You are one."

"Yes. Yes, I am a priest. Father Michael from Saint Cecilia. Where are we going, miss?"

"Past Piety Street, but you can let me out wherever. Here, if you want."

He stops by the levee near Sonny's house and Juliet turns to face him. "Let me ask you a question, Padre. It's been on my mind lately." He nods and she says, "If someone were to come to you and confess a murder, would you be required to keep it a secret? Is there some kind of lawyer-client–type deal working between a priest and his people? Or would you give that person dispensation or whatever and call the cops?"

"Did you say dispensation?"

"I mean the thing you give that forgives him, that makes him clean again."

The priest keeps both hands on the steering wheel. "Would you like for me to hear your confession?" he says.

Tears show in Juliet's eyes and start to run but she's laughing when she says, "Got a few days?"

He reaches over the back of the seat and retrieves a box of Kleenex from the floor.

"Thank you," she says. "I hope I didn't scare you."

"No."

Juliet snorts into a blanket of tissues, making her nose even drier.

The priest looks at his watch then squirms in his seat pulling a business card from his wallet. "Here's my office number. I wish we could talk more but I'm already late for an appointment."

"Mama put barbed wire on the drainpipes," Juliet says, believing that will keep him. "She says it was to train her vines, but we both know better, don't we?"

"Well," the priest says, "it was nice meeting you."

Juliet glances at his card. "Father Michael Manny," she says. "You don't look like a Manny to me. When I see a Manny I see a hairy Italian behind a meat counter. I see a guy from the old country. He lives in a house full of screaming kids. His breath, even after he brushes, smells of pickled olives. Your name isn't Manny."

"Maybe not," he says. "Good-bye, dear."

Not two minutes after Juliet's left the car she realizes that she hitchhiked to the wrong neighborhood. It wasn't Sonny she meant to see. It was the other boy. Leonard.

She stands in weeds looking at the little houses, each a disaster on its own terms. She can't recall which of them belonged to Sonny. "It's me," she calls with hands around her mouth. "It's Julie."

Hammered by June bugs drawn to porch lights, she climbs front stoops and knocks to be let in, first one door, then another, now a third. "Oh," she says, finally finding a face past a frieze of black burglar bars, "I was looking for someone."

"You got the Labiche residence." The man, who must be eighty, points to the room behind him.

"Well, I wanted the LaMotts. You know where they are?"

"Cecil LaMott's in a home, but they live a ways up the street. The son, anyhow. The lady, I forget what they called her, a stroke killed her right in the yard."

Although it's a little more information than Juliet needs at the moment, at least there is someone to talk to. "You don't have any wedding rings you want to get rid of?"

"What?"

"Wedding rings?"

The man holds his hand up. "It's the only thing she left me. That and the hole in my heart."

"Let me be honest with you a second. Let me lay my cards out on the table. I've got this blistering cocaine hangover and only one thing will make it right."

"You said a hangover?" He leans in closer, his robe coming open, chest dark and hairless against the terry cloth. "You got a hangover try tomato juice. Something about the acid."

Finally she remembers the stairs. A pickup parked in the grass. ~ana plants and weeping mimosas. "Let me go," she tells the old man. ~ have a nice life."

238

"You, too," he says, and for once somebody really seems to mean it.

Juliet searches the street, her back to the levee. She doesn't find any trucks, but a flight of stairs, rickety and water-damaged and snapping beneath her weight, leads her to a door that feels right. She punches a lighted bell, and a woman, what looks like a woman, presents her face in the slot past a police chain. "Sonny LaMott live here?"

"Curly," the woman says to the room behind her, then disappears from view.

Now a fat man holding a can of beer, the lower third of his belly showing under his undershirt. "You still can't find him?"

"Find who?"

"Sonny. I told him you were looking for him."

Juliet looks past him at the small apartment, yellowed newspapers on the floor, a can of bug spray on the wagon-wheel coffee table. "Was I here earlier?"

The man takes a swallow from his can. He spends a long time look-ing at her. "Why don't you come inside and rest your feet. When Sonny gets back I'll walk you over." Stepping back he opens the door wide, and points to a mat on the floor where he seems to want her to wipe her feet. "Florence, we got any tuna surprise left?"

Florence, hugging her arms at her chest, stands in front of a TV set, framed by rabbit-ear antennae and illumined by a purplish glow. "That was last week," she says. "But maybe they got some left in the box."

Curly points to the kitchen. "Be polite and go get our company a plate." He glances back at Juliet and gives his head a shake. "Florence stepped into a door last night, in case you were wondering where them bruises came from. Florence, tell our company you stepped into a door."

"I stepped in a door."

"It was the bathroom door. Florence, which door was it?"

"Bathroom."

"I don't want any tuna surprise," Juliet says. "I'd take some tomato juice, though."

"We don't drink tomato juice in this house. But how about a V8?"

"You drank all the V.O.," Florence yells from the kitchen.

"It's okay," Juliet tells him. "I was just trying to find Sonny."

She steps back out on the landing and Curly joins her, pulling the door closed. It's a small space and they stand within inches of each other. She wonders if she spilled something on her shirt and it is a second before she understands what he's looking at.

"Well, I guess I'll be going back to the Lé Dale."

"That's a fine hotel." Curly could back off a little, there's room. But he seems to want to crowd her. "The Lé Dale, places like that. Give me a room where you don't feel self-conscious peeing in the shower, I always maintained that."

It isn't easy walking back down the stairs. Juliet keeps both hands on the railing, looking back over her shoulder every few steps. When she reaches the bottom she spins around and offers a wave. "Made it."

Curly clears his throat, preparing for a pronouncement. "I was digging around in the trash out back, this was a while ago. Guess what I found?" He takes a last sip before flattening his can underfoot. "I guess Sonny threw it out. You might not remember this but it was a movie and you were in there sucking off some boy." He kicks the can and it sails past her, landing in the grass without a sound. "Boy had a dick on him, now."

Juliet uses her hand to block his porch light, to try to see his face better. "The guy with the penis? That was my boyfriend."

"What about the girl, that one that licked you?" He laughs and his shirt pulls up higher. "She reminds me of Florence the way she's kind of scrappy."

Juliet starts walking toward the street, through the damp weeds, past an iron pole on the top of which rests a rotten birdhouse, its roof a ragged, open maw. "That was another life for me," she says. "I've straightened myself out since then."

"I'll give you fifty dollars you come let Florence lick you like you did that girl."

Juliet stops and spins around and looks back at the light.

"Florence," Curly shouts, flinging the door open wide. "Go wash your toot-toot, baby. Daddy's got a surprise and it ain't tuna."

Days later the detectives invite Sonny back to police headquarters. He sits in the same room and at the same table as before, Peroux and Lentini present, their shirtsleeves rolled up, jackets thrown over chairs.

The handwriting examiner, who identifies himself as William Ruben, a certified and court-qualified graphoanalyst, provides a pencil and sheets of plain white paper, each labeled on top with Sonny's name and a case number.

"Mr. LaMott, now your name please. Write it as you normally would."

"You want me as Cecil or as Sonny?"

Peroux says, "I was in the service with a guy from Toms River, New Jersey, name of Cecil. Cecil Bouchard."

"Either one," says the examiner. He points. "Here, if you would."

"At Okinawa he gets this letter. It's from his best buddy back home and the news isn't good. Turns out his girlfriend's been running around with a black dude."

"Uh oh," Lentini says, rubbing his face with his hands.

"So Cecil . . . Cecil has what I guess you could call a breakdown. He won't leave his bunk. A black guy walks by—me, for instance—he stares like he wants to kill the brother. 'What's the problem, Cecil?' And Cecil doesn't answer. At night you could hear him wailing, all over the barracks."

Sonny drums the pencil against the table.

"Now Cecil . . . now that boy wept."

"Jesus wept, too," Lentini says from the other side of the room.

"Yes, he did. Jesus is another one. Poor Jesus wept his ass off. You've wept, too, haven't you, podna? Make him write that, Mr. Ruben."

The examiner taps the paper with a finger. "Okay, Mr. LaMott. 'Jesus wept.'"

"Not 'Jesus wept,'" the detective says. "I didn't mean that. Have him write 'Sonny wept.'"

And so Sonny writes it, his hand shaking as it moves across the page.

The topless/bottomless is nicer than Juliet remembered, the owner more considerate and less heavily tattooed, the clientele not nearly as runty. The odor inside could use improving, however. Apparently somebody didn't make it to the bathroom. Well, okay, Juliet concedes that maybe half a dozen didn't make it. But overall the atmosphere is tolerable if not what she'd call homey. On the jukebox new songs have been added, most of them funk and disco classics. Although she can't well afford it, Juliet dunks coins in the machine and punches in selections by Donna Summer and the Ohio Players. The music comes up with a warble then rights itself after she bumps a hand against the glass display.

Donna doing "Bad Girl."

When Juliet returns to her stool another diet ginger ale is waiting.

"We all worried you'd run off with the schoolteacher," Lulu says, picking up where they'd left off. "I personally wasn't concerned myself but some of the girls had misgivings."

"No," says Juliet, "he was just needing a friend."

"I know what he was needing." Lulu sips her drink and forces her voice down an octave. "When you were done probably a shower."

Juliet lights a cigarette. She's wondering what tack to take when appealing for her job back. Should she mention the pain of losing the Beauvais? The death of her mother? Her desire to eat?

And then the unexpected. "I look forward to seeing you dance again," Lulu says. "That is if that's what you're here for."

Juliet's eyes puddle with tears. She could hold Lulu's face in her hands and kiss her dry, little mouth. Now here is a friend.

"You were good sliding down the pole. And your tits are above average."

Juliet places a hand on Lulu's. It's like touching something dead on the side of the road, or maybe a strip of tire rubber. "You're the mother I never had, Lulu."

"Thank you, doll. That means a lot coming from you."

The stage has two runways, each extending through the tables a distance of about ten feet. Juliet prefers to dance on the one with most of its footlights burned out. The bar today is empty but for Lulu and a big girl named Sandy, who might've been a guy not long before, or who might still be one now. Juliet is neither nervous nor self-conscious; this is old hat. Her three songs bleed together and become one and her ten minutes tick by like ten seconds.

She takes her break at the bar, alone with a cigarette and a tall glass of ice water. The air conditioner could be turned up but it's early yet to start demanding improvements. She wipes the sweat off her face with a handful of cocktail napkins then fans herself using a takeout menu.

She picks up the telephone by the waiters' station and calls Information. "Yes, do you have a lawyer listed name of Harvey? Nathan Harvey? Give me his office please."

She writes the number on the palm of her hand then punches it out on the dial pad using her drinking straw. "Maria, please," she tells the woman who answers.

"May I ask who's calling?"

"Tell her it's the client she owes a bunch of money to."

The phone rings again and Maria picks up.

"Where's my check?" Juliet says.

"Your check? Who is . . . ? *Miss Beauvais? Miss Beauvais, is that you?"

Immediately upon hanging up Juliet feels better; it's as if her load has been lightened. On stage again, she sends sweat flying on the little round-top tables crowding the runway. Lulu, shouting up from the footlights, is forced to move deeper into the room.

"Disco mama!" Sandy calls in a rich baritone.

As Juliet is sliding down the pole, sinew showing in her neck, bands of muscle in her arms tight against the skin, who but Sonny LaMott enters the lounge and takes a seat at a table by the door. Is she seeing things? Of all the strip clubs in the French Quarter how has he managed to find her at this one? It is an illusion, she tells herself. You are seeing things. But then Sandy, abandoning a fresh smoke, jumps to her feet and stalks toward him.

Juliet wheels into a tight spin, her momentum taking her down the runway, past a single hot bulb shooting upward. She could be in better shape, her lungs are about to burst. But somehow she completes the routine, finishing only a few beats before the song does.

A single hand of applause. A lone wolf whistle. And then her own moans, loud in the sudden humming quiet of the room.

Unable to stand any longer, Juliet slumps to the filthy runway floor. A groan leaves her body. She looks in Sonny's direction but his table is empty. At the bar Sandy sits where she sat before, her cigarette now half-smoked.

"Juliet? What's wrong, baby?" It is Lulu again. "God, you look like you saw a ghost."

Yes, she thinks, and now they don't even have to be dead.

※

Toward noon Sonny stops by the bank and closes his account. He takes the cash in small denominations, no bill larger than a twenty, and only two of those. There is much he never painted, this old building for instance, with its gilded façade, its canvas awnings faded and torn. The teller peeling off singles. The gleaming checkerboard tiles.

"You have a great face," he says to the uniformed guard at the door. The man smiles uneasily.

"It's epic. I should've painted you and that face."

Sonny drives along South Carrollton Avenue, columns of ancient royal palms ticking past, their upper fronds gold and desiccated, lower ones bright and green.

Why did he never paint these trees?

He stops at a gas station and parks next to a full-serve pump. "I'm treating myself," he says to the attendant through his open window.

"If you can afford to go full I say why not."

Sonny admires the man's humility. The care he gives to running his squeegee over the truck's bug-spattered windshield. "I'm going to be arrested," Sonny tells him.

"Ooh. Now that hurts." The man stops and looks at Sonny through the sudsy iridescent film on the glass. "You did something wrong or what?"

Sonny isn't sure how to answer. "I got hooked up with the wrong girl. You know the Beauvais over on Esplanade?"

The man stares at him a moment. "Women are the ruination of this country," he says, then goes back to work. "Now you wanna pop your hood?"

Sonny decides to take a last spin around the city, to search for images that he previously overlooked. He could've painted more churches, for example, and somehow he never got around to doing the mission downtown, the men standing in line for food and medical attention, the women crouched in the shadows. He never painted the tracks of defunct streetcar routes lying gray and broken in the asphalt, their years of service decades past. It might say something, a picture like that. "Boy, you're a deep sonofabitch," Sonny says, talking to himself.

The F&M Patio Bar on Saturday night. Sailboats on Lake Pontchartrain. The infant asylum on Magazine Street, with its exterior ironwork rusty brown from years of neglect. The oyster shuckers at Casamento's, their muscular forearms covered with chips and scales.

Fats Domino's funny-looking house as seen from the parking lot at Pugled's Super Market on Saint Claude Avenue, nor the Fat Man himself, nor any other musicians for that matter but Elvis and one of trumpeter Al Hirt for a tourist from Dublin, Ireland, who gave him a hundred-dollar bill and said, "To be right frank about it the jazz makes me willie hard."

The old German chapel in the Irish Channel where his mother worshiped when she was a girl. His mother in her mink stole that Christmas morning when his father surprised her with the last thing he could afford. The Arabi nursing home where his father lives, with Agnes standing out front. Sonny, driving there now, parks on Mehle Avenue, and walks in. He stands at the desk, waiting as she tries to ignore him. "Is he here, Agnes?"

"No. He just left for the library to study up on rocket science. Or maybe it was molecular physics he was interested in. Of course he's here, Sonny. God."

"I'd like to leave him a message, please."

"Why don't you just go down the hall and see him?"

"I don't want to see him. I want to tell him something."

"What do you want to tell him?"

"Would you mind writing it down? It's important to me."

She can't find any paper. No, someone has taken her pen.

"Tell him I'm sorry I never painted his picture," Sonny says.

More trees and streets after the rain, more Catahoula hounds sleeping on wood porches, more sightseeing mules wearing straw hats, more paddlewheelers coming around the bend, more winter sunsets on the levee when the river burns orange on the surface, more women other than Juliet Beauvais, and truly this time. Yes, he thinks, and *truly*.

Traveling now through Bywater and Faubourg Marigny, Sonny doubles then triples the speed limit. He downshifts as he crosses Esplanade Avenue and enters the French Quarter. So as not to disappoint, he floors the accelerator and uncorks a belch before braking and lowering the engine to a deep, dark rumble.

"Whatever happened to that piece-of-crap pickup?" he imagines them saying after he's gone.

Oh, for the horror of his gutted muffler! Oh, for the stench of his exhaust!

Why did he never paint the house he's passing now, with its shutters missing slats, and its warm, weathered patina, its garden overgrown with sourwood and wild azalea?

It comes to Sonny that most houses have better faces than the people who inhabit them. "Well, look at you," he says, passing another he never noticed before.

"And you," passing a third.

Many of his heroes in the field, those who came before him, for long periods could not see beyond that which obsessed them. Alberta Kinsey painted Vieux Carré courtyards, and Noel Rockmore the city's jazz musicians, and Boyd Cruise, he was the one, went years painting houses only. Houses were all he saw: the grand ones with names enjoined by hyphens, the lowly shotguns.

"And when you looked, what did you see?" Sonny says out loud.

"Juliet," he answers.

When he gets there she's sitting by herself at the bar, shouting encouragement to an enormous she-male lumbering around onstage. He waits in the lighted space of the open door until she turns and sees him, then he moves to his usual place, a table in the corner.

"Crown and water?" Lulu calls from her perch on a stool.

"Crown and water," Sonny says.

"Sonny, have you met Juliet? Juliet, that there is Sonny LaMott, world-famous French Quarter artist. Maybe you've heard of him."

"Juliet," Sonny says with a formal nod, offering the chair next to his.

It is easier than before, easier than the day several weeks ago when they sat consumed by silence at Café du Monde. It is warm in the lounge but not uncomfortable, and yet her face is damp with sweat, the golden hair on her forearms glistens.

"You gonna be okay?" he says.

"I guess I'm hot."

"I just thought of something," he says. He waits until she looks at him. "Put us each in a puka shell necklace and platform shoes and it'd be like old times."

She brings an unlit cigarette to her mouth. "What do you want, Sonny? Don't you think I've been humiliated enough?"

"I'm not here to humiliate you, Julie."

"Sonny, this isn't my life anymore. My life ended a long time ago."

"I'm not here to humiliate you," Sonny says again.

Lulu delivers his drink and he downs most of it before saying anything more. "Is it true in California they let the girls dance completely naked? I hear they don't even have to wear pasties."

"California has too much to worry about than whether you've got your nipples covered."

"What about something to cover your bottom?"

"California ain't worried about that either."

"You'd think New Orleans, with its low reputation, would allow for anything goes."

"Yes, you'd think that, wouldn't you? You'd think a lot of things about New Orleans. But you'd be wrong. You'd always be wrong."

She lights the cigarette and in the flame from her lighter Sonny can see that he never really got her right. Her mouth is less full than he painted it and her chin is actually more round than square. And why did he have to exaggerate the size of her breasts?

The way she wears her hair? He got that wrong, too.

"I've decided to go back home," she says.

"Home?" and he lifts an eyebrow.

"I mean to LA. I'm going to start over. It's not too late to change. I want to be a better person. Do you think that's possible, Sonny? Can a thirty-two-year old woman who's made every mistake there is start her life over again?"

He should've painted that small cluster of acne on her forehead. In his Juliets her forehead was always flawless. Also, her eyes are older than he made them, the bones of her face less prominent. Why did he make her features so perfectly formed?

"Maybe when I was a kid I fell off my bike and bumped my head," Sonny says. "There has to be an explanation."

"For what?"

"For why for so long I've been hung up on you."

"I was talking about California?" Juliet makes it sound like a question. "What I was saying before I was interrupted, and I hope you'll listen, I'm not staying in New Orleans much longer. I'm just working until I can save enough money to buy a plane ticket and pay off my bill at the hotel. That lawyer, that bastard Harvey? He still hasn't given me my check."

Sonny reaches into his pocket and removes the envelope holding the money from his bank account. He fans the cash out in a half-circle on the table. "It's not quite two hundred dollars. It's all I have left. I want you to have it, Julie." He stops himself. His voice has betrayed him, the nervous cheer giving way to desperation. "I was hoping I could be alone again with you, Julie."

She looks at the money and sadly shakes her head. Her mouth, as she brings the cigarette back to it, reveals what might be a nervous tic. "You have come to humiliate me," she says. "It's that fat slob neighbor of yours, isn't it? He told you."

"Let me go talk to Lulu, Julie."

"I must hate men. I know I hate you. Does it hurt to hear me say that, Sonny?"

"It's funny but hurt seems to feel like everything else lately."

"I hate almost everything about you," she says. "I hate how you need me. Sometimes I think it's my hate that you need because my hate is what confirms your opinion of yourself. It gives you a reason to get out of bed in the morning. Without it you could never go to that fence every day and hang your pictures. You could never accept the rejection. My hate—and I realize this might sound like a reach . . . but my hate defines you, Sonny LaMott. It defines you because it's all that stands between you and what's ordinary. The little ranch-style house in Saint Bernard Parish, bingo games every Wednesday night in the church recreation hall, the minivan, a barbecue kettle in the backyard. My hate has spared you that. Without it you join the rank and file. Just another working-class boy from the Bywater without a ticket Uptown. And certainly not an artist."

"Am I really an artist, Julie?"

"Oh, shut up, Sonny. You're an artist even in your sleep."

"They're going to arrest me," he says. "They've got motive and they've got opportunity. That's what they look for, you know? Motive and opportunity," he says again.

She points to the cash on the table. "I really, really need this." Cigarette clenched tight in her mouth, she folds the money and holds it in the palm of her hand, as if to weigh it. "We should have had us that baby, huh, Sonny?"

"Yes."

"Everything would be different."

"Everything. Everything in this world."

Outside the streetcar moves past with a roar and squeal, wheels grinding, electric line overhead reflecting the last of the afternoon light.

Juliet doesn't hear the car doors slam. She's in the middle of a dream. She's in her yellow Ford Mustang rental car but she's in California stuck in traffic on the I-5. Up ahead there's a wreck and no one is moving. People are getting out of their cars and trying to see. They block the sun with the flats of their hands. Horns are blowing *beep beep beep.* The jam extends for miles in a single direction, while on the other side of the interstate there isn't a car in sight. The lanes run forever, empty.

Maybe she doesn't hear the doors slam because in the dream people are slamming doors, too.

"We should try the other side," Juliet says in her sleep.

"I don't think I like it that way as much as just regular." Sounds like Sonny LaMott, but what is he doing in California?

"The other road," she says. "No one's there."

When they come through the door he rises to his feet and staggers to the middle of the room. He holds his hands out in front of him, as if at their mercy, ready to be cuffed. He is naked, his body washed yellow by the ceiling light.

Several seconds pass before it comes to her that he in fact is Sonny and she Juliet, that they are back in her room at the Lé Dale.

"And a happy good morning to you, podna," the male black says.

Behind him stand the male white and two uniforms. There is also a woman.

"Put your clothes on," the male black says.

Sonny reaches for his undershorts, his trousers. He places a hand on top of a chair and carefully steps into them.

"I didn't mean you," the male black says. And only now does she remember his name. Peroux. "I meant you, Miss Beauvais. Get out of bed. Let's go."

Juliet props herself on an elbow and pulls a sheet up over her chest.

The woman crosses the room and stands next to the bed.

"Juliet Beauvais, my name is Patricia Kimball. I am a prosecutor with the Orleans Parish District Attorney's Office, and you're under arrest for the murder of Marcelle Lavergne Beauvais."

"Get up," Peroux says again, stepping past Sonny. He grabs Juliet by the arm.

"Tell them it wasn't me," she says to Sonny. "Tell them." Sonny doesn't speak and she says, "You'll find the hourglass in his cart, Lieutenant. He hid it there, he told me."

"Is that true, LaMott?"

Sonny steps back from the detective and looks at her—he just looks at her.

"Only reason I ask, Leonard Barbier told me not two hours ago that a certain black boy from a certain housing project put it there, and that a certain Juliet Beauvais paid this certain boy to do it. Oh, and then we spoke to the kid." Peroux lowers a hand into the pocket of his jacket and fishes out her mother's wedding band. "This look familiar, Miss Beauvais? No? How 'bout this, then?"

One of the uniforms steps forward holding the hourglass in a plastic evidence bag.

"How long is forever, Sergeant Lentini?"

"Oh, it's a long time," Lentini says, "especially where she's going."

"Miss Beauvais," Patricia Kimball says, "you have the right to remain silent. Any statements you make can and will be used as evidence against you."

"Get dressed," Peroux says again.

"You have the right to the presence of your own counsel. If you can't afford your own counsel, the court will provide one for you prior to any questioning." The woman hands Juliet a sheet of paper. "Miss Beauvais, this document is for you to sign. It states that you have been apprised of your rights under the Miranda Rule. Do you have any questions, Miss Beauvais?"

"How long did you say forever was, Sergeant Lentini?" Peroux says. He has removed a dress from the closet, the same one Juliet wore on her trip in from California.

Juliet offers no resistance as the detective squeezes it past her head and pulls it down over her upper torso.

Lentini takes her shoes, the blocky ones, and checks them for contraband before placing them on the floor at her feet. "Forever?" he says, contemplating the possibilities. "Forever in Saint Gabriel? That's about as long as forever is in hell, I'd say."

"Know where Saint Gabriel is?" Peroux says to Juliet. "That's where we put our women prisoners in this state. And that's where you're going."

"Saint Gabriel," Juliet says in a whisper. "Gabriel was an archangel. Sonny, you were an altar boy. Wasn't Gabriel an archangel?"

From the pocket of his dress shirt Peroux removes Sonny's postcard of the Beauvais Mansion, the sepia one describing New Orleans as an unexpected paradise. "Mind if I give her this?"

Sonny shakes his head.

"We went by your place earlier, thinking she might be there. I hope you don't mind." He offers the card to Juliet and she holds it loosely in her open hands. "Something to look at in case you don't get a room with a view," he says.

They put her in cuffs and lead her past Sonny. She tries to get his attention but he keeps his head down. At the door Peroux stops and wheels back around, and Juliet waits with her back to the room. "I hung your picture in my bedroom," the detective says to Sonny. "But it's a funny thing, art. The longer you look at it the less you see what it shows."

"How do you mean, Lieutenant?"

"If you look long enough, and I mean give it some real quality time, it's the artist you see in the picture, not the person he painted."

"I think I understand, Lieutenant."

"I bet you do, podna. I bet you do."

They walk her down the stairs and past the lobby where Leroy waits in the doorway. "I hope you enjoyed your stay at the Lé Dale," he says, smiling red teeth. "If ever you're in our fair city again, please consider us as your destination of choice."

"Sonny," Juliet says, trying to break free of their hold.

"Easy now, Miss Beauvais," Lentini tells her.

"Sonny," she says again. "Sonny! Don't let them take me, Sonny!"

Outside on the sidewalk another streetcar rumbles past, its occupants watching as the two detectives usher her down the stairs and into the backseat of a Chevy sedan.

Juliet glances up at the building just as Sonny presses through the front door. As before in the room, he's wearing only trousers.

"What else did Leonard say?" she asks as they start on their way.

Peroux moves his head a little but doesn't answer.

"Did his father the fancy lawyer cut him a deal? I bet Leonard pled out probation and turned state's evidence. Tell me, Lieutenant. Did you give him immunity?"

"Leonard Barbier is a fine, upstanding young man with a promising future ahead of him."

"Leonard," she says quietly.

"Oh, it's true he might be confused about a few things at the present time but in my book he's made a hard turn toward straightening himself out. Give that boy ten years and he'll be Rex, king of Carnival, leading a parade down this very street."

"Well, I'll be damned," Lentini says, then taps a finger on the rearview mirror. "Sammy, you ain't gonna believe this."

Peroux turns in his seat and stares through the back glass, prompting Juliet to do the same. Sonny LaMott, still half-dressed and barefoot, is running after them down the middle of the street. His arms pump hard by his side, and he lifts his knees high like those of a sprinter with the finish line in sight. Through stop signs he runs, weaving around traffic, dodging occasional pedestrians. The wind bells out his cheeks and throws his hair back.

Lentini puts a spinning police light on the dash and begins to accelerate. He takes the car without braking through a couple of red lights and in seconds Sonny has faded to a black speck lost in a field of black specks. He disappears altogether after Lentini makes a few turns.

The city rushes past now. Entire blocks have gone by when it occurs to Juliet that they're headed in the wrong direction. "This isn't the best way," she complains, all the more dismayed when Lentini turns from Canal Street onto North Rampart Street. "Are you taking me to Esplanade?"

"We thought we'd let you have a last look," Peroux says.

"I don't want to see it."

"No?"

"Please, Lieutenant. Please don't take me there."

They drive on and she lifts her feet and kicks the back of the seat. "Don't do this to me, Lieutenant. Please. Lieutenant, please. Please don't do this to me. Please."

When they reach the Beauvais Peroux throws an arm over the seat and faces her with a smile. "Well, how's it look?"

*"Please . . ."*

"Oh, they're some busy around here today. Why, look at that."

Nerves send her bouncing in the seat, but she confronts it finally, and in that instant all the blood seems to drain from her heart.

People come and go through the open front door, none of them familiar. One pair carries her mother's wing chair out into the grass, a second a sofa, a third the desk from her father's library. Maids beat rugs with sawed-off broomsticks, sending clouds of dust floating in loose spirals. Gardeners, an army of them, trim the lawn with riding and push mowers, while others use electric clippers to prune the trees and shrubs. An ironworker is removing the name on the arc over the front gate, and the gate itself, propped open with a brick, is getting a fresh coat of paint. So too, Juliet notices now, is the house. Tiers of scaffolding stand on both the north and south sides. Crews of painters work in the fading light.

"Who's that?" Peroux says, pointing to the upper gallery.

Juliet's head snaps on a swivel. She strains to see and, yes, there really is someone standing at a window upstairs. She can see the silhouette, a shadow past lace curtains. What feels like an electric charge shakes her body and raises gooseflesh on her arms. "Oh, you," she says, watching now through the fan of fingers covering her face. "Oh, Mama!"

But a light comes on in the room, revealing the figure to be someone else entirely.

The detectives are quiet as they start for Central Lockup, quiet as upstairs Anna Huey sends them off with a wave.

# 7

HIS FATHER DIES IN JUNE 1988. AT THE
cemetery Agnes from the nursing home stands
beside Sonny and stares at the half-filled tomb.
"Do you have anyone else?" she says, reaching for
his hand.

"Oh, sure. Sure, I do."

"A man doesn't really become a man until
he loses his father. Remember that."

"I will. Thank you, Agnes."

She puts an arm around him and he is not
uncomfortable with the intimacy. She is wearing
a uniform from work and she smells of the
home, the boiled meals, the diapered adults.
"You'll still come visit us, won't you, Sonny?"
Her voice is warm and cheerful. "Can we count
on that?"

"Yes, I'll come. Of course I will."

But Sonny never visits the Maison Orleans

again. And on those occasions when he happens to drive near the place he tries not to dwell on those days when his father was a patient there. In memory Mr. LaMott is forever the top salesman at Paul Piazza & Son. He has life in his eyes. And eternally he sprawls in a field of grass, gaze turned upward, as purple martins turn circles in the near-evening air above his birdhouse.

That same year Louis Fortunato marries and moves back to Bywater. It is wholly unexpected, least of all because of his disabilities. "Tell you the truth I had a pump put in," he explains to Sonny. "All you gotta do is give me a little time and I'm as good as in the old days."

Sonny stands as best man at the wedding. The bride, Claire Lousteau, is a caterer for a French Quarter B-and-B. She and Louis plan to adopt as soon as possible, and so together they've been trying to find a home for Frank.

"Frank?" says Sonny.

"Frank my calico. Where's your head, bubba?"

"Okay. All right. *Frank!*"

At the reception the two friends stand in rented tuxedos in the formal parlor at Claire's B-and-B, spearing broccoli balls and fried crawfish with toothpicks crowned with swirls of colored celluloid, while a spirited jazz band performs "Do You Know What It Means to Miss New Orleans."

"So I call Coulon," Louis says. "I call his office and explain the situation. He agrees to try to help us out. Says he'll post a notice on the corkboard in his waiting room. Can you believe that?"

"What a guy."

"Yes, isn't he?"

Louis points to an old man in seersucker guzzling champagne. "Recognize him, Sonny? The one on his fifth glass already?"

Sonny does a double take.

"Think he was loaded when he killed my first one?"

Years later, it is April now, the tourist season is in full swing, Sonny and his comrades plant a tree in Jackson Square. It is a white dogwood, a sapling yet, and it enters the ground next to the magnolia across from the bakery.

A group of perhaps twenty attend, all of them fence artists but for the Vietnamese cashier from Café du Monde. Sonny, as chairman of the Jackson Square Artists Alliance, has organized the event. He's bought the tree, provided the spade, won permission from the city to dig the hole.

As it happens, he alone is aware of the tradition.

"Okay, maybe he made it up about the trees," Sonny says in his impromptu remarks. "But it's a good story and inspiring and it's helped me through some hard times. When you look at the flowers on this tree, and I hope you'll do that . . . I hope you'll remember him. They bloom for Roberts now and they'll bloom for him always. 'Am I worth it?' he used to say. He was talking about the people whose portraits we are commissioned to paint, but I always suspected he was talking about himself."

Sonny shovels a spade of dirt and carefully spreads it over the root ball. " 'Am I worth it?' " he repeats. "Yes, of course you are, Roberts."

Over time fewer artists make their living at the fence, as more and more tarot card readers successfully vie with them for space along the pedestrian mall, and tourists seem more inclined to pay to have their future foretold than to have their likeness preserved. Street musicians, jugglers and fire-eaters add to the rivalry for outside dollars, and Sonny realizes that the days of the Jackson Square artist truly are numbered when Japanese visitors begin rushing past portraitists to have their palms read.

In the beginning of Sonny's career some two hundred licensed artists practiced their craft at the fence but now there are fewer than fifty, some with families to raise, but most with no other idea of what to do with their lives. Sonny's cart fades to pink, the gold lettering chips and becomes unreadable. His claim to world fame vanishes along with his dream of being rich. And yet the dealers find him. They stand some distance away as he works at his easel and watch as if for a revelation. *So this is the boyfriend? And we passed on him, remember?*

They invite him for coffee at Café du Monde. Or would he prefer something stronger at the Old Absinthe House?

"Trying to cut back," Sonny says, shaking his head.

They leave business cards on his stool. Goldstein, the auctioneer. Elisabeth Someone from a gallery in the Warehouse District.

"It was a long time ago," he explains.

"But it was yesterday!"

"Sorry."

"No more Juliets?"

Sonny shakes his head. "No more Juliets."

He receives a letter with a postmark for the Hunt Correctional Center in Saint Gabriel, Louisiana. By now fourteen years have passed. The letter arrives in a manila envelope with Juliet's identification number and cellblock printed on the upper left side. As for the letter itself, the handwriting is a child's scrawl, though considerably easier to understand than the illegible snippets of "The Proof" that appeared in facsimile form in the *Times-Picayune* during Juliet's murder trial. In the margin she has drawn a picture of a stickman hanging from a noose.

> . . . she didn't fight but I wasn't surprised. They're like that, her people. I sat in my room and finished "The Proof" while Leonard wiped down the doors and stair rails. It's funny but as I wrote those last words I understood and forgave her finally.
>
> After we put "The Proof" where we put it I tried to take it out. I had one more thing to add. Forget the red plastic dinner plates and the Christmas tree icicles. Forget the spiders on the window and the rice on the floor. The worst thing she ever did was give birth to me.
>
> Here the preachers come for visits, and so do the nuns. One of them, Sister Perpetua, is about our age. I imagine she was a regular person once, with regular needs. I asked her the other day what she did for love. "I sleep with Jesus," she said.
>
> Sonny, I sleep with Jesus too but lately I feel I need more. I'm writing to say I can have visitors. Sonny, if I promise to be good this time—well, I do promise, because I will, I will be good.
>
> Please, darling, come to me . . .

And so, that same afternoon, Sonny leaves New Orleans headed west on I-10, Juliet's letter open on the seat next to him. Heavy fog grips the southern shore of Lake Pontchartrain and slows passage across the Bonnet Carré Spillway, and Sonny drives with his headlights on, wipers thwacking at the mist. Blackbirds and orchard orioles move in the cypress swamps and ibises fish the endless canals. Sonny exits at state highway 30 then again at state highway 74, which leads him at last to a large sign instructing visitors that vehicle searches are mandatory; body searches may be conducted as well. It is the entrance to the Louisiana Correctional Institute for Women.

The road twists through a landscape of such pastoral beauty that Sonny battles an impulse to pull over and paint it. Blooming flower

beds and pecan trees line the winding asphalt drive; in fields all around
Brahma graze with snowy egrets closely trailing. Rolls of hay, white
board fences, an ancient tractor baking in the sun. And then the seren-
ity of the scene ends as the prison comes into view. Sonny completes a
turn and there it stands: an orderly cluster of narrow yellow buildings
and guard towers contained by hurricane fencing topped with con-
certina wire.

Sonny has not yet reached the guardhouse at road's end, but nevertheless he pulls over and parks under the trees.

Down from the back acres inmates move in single file, flanked by
guards in black uniforms and wide-brimmed plantation hats. Sonny
steps outside and walks to the board fence. He is wearing a beret and
paint-stained clothing. His hair is longer than when Juliet last saw him,
and flecked with gray, but he should be easy to recognize. He is Sonny.

If her cell is in one of the dormitories on this side of the prison . . .

"Darling," Sonny says, nearly shouting. "Come out and stand with
me."

Nothing. Not a sound.

"Please," he says. "I need you now."

Her name is Katherine Rillieux. They met at Jackson Square when
she appeared at his kiosk and timidly asked for a portrait. A nurse at
Charity Hospital whom he somehow got exactly right. The mouth as
he painted it was Kathy's mouth, and so were the eyes. Her rich brown
hair stayed that way when he reproduced it on canvas. Sonny refused to
accept payment. "I think I'm the one who owes you," he said.

"Just stand next to me," he says now. "Just for a minute."

He hears the door open and close, her feet hesitant on the pavement. "I don't know," she says. "It's weird, Sonny. You can't possibly
think she's watching."

He puts an arm around her and kisses the side of her head, her face.

"Tell me it's over," he whispers in her ear.

"Sonny, this is spooky."

"Please. Kathy, please."

"Sonny, it's over. It had better be over."

Sonny looks out at the cellblocks and reaches up and removes his
beret. He is standing at his full height, chest thrust forward.

"Can we go back to New Orleans now?" Katherine says, then
leaves him standing there alone.

Minutes pass before Sonny grows embarrassed and surrenders the pose. He has made a fool of himself. "You sick, dumb fuck," he mutters under his breath. He shouts a laugh as he puts the beret back on and wipes a lather of tears from his face. In the field an enormous gray bull lifts its head and stares.

Returning to the truck, Sonny meets Katherine's gaze past the windshield stained with the lost forms of butterflies, mosquito hawks and other dead insects from the trip over. A picture comes to him as he wades through patches of sunlight on the tall gray weeds, and as always he is unable to resist. Juliet is seventeen, and the Mississippi River moves past them as together they sit on warm boards and kiss and talk and dream. "Just be my friend first," she told him that morning, clenching his hand in hers.

How do we survive the end of our dreams? Where does the courage come from? Sonny gets in the truck and closes the door. His hand shakes as he reaches for the ignition, and he is a long time before starting the engine.

"Is Juliet still yours, Sonny?" Katherine asks.

"I guess she never was," he answers, eyes carefully avoiding the rearview mirror as he starts for home.